# WASTELAND

# WASTELAND

*by*
# Kristin Keppler & Allisa Bahney

2021

**Credits**
Editor: Barbara Ann Wright
Production Design: Stacia Seaman
Cover Design by Jeanine Henning

# Acknowledgments

**Kristin:**

Brad, thank you for your constant support and encouragement. You are my favorite sounding board and my favorite person. You're definitely my better half and I love you. To my sons who don't care at all that Mom wrote a book: I love you all the time.

To my mom, my first editor and teacher, your patience is astounding. I love you more.

And to Kat and Weston, my biggest (and only) fans. Your support and optimism mean more than you know! Thank you for believing in me.

**Allisa:**

Courtney, your constant and unwavering support is unmatched. I could spend the rest of my life thanking you and it wouldn't be long enough. To Theo, who is too young to read this, I love you forever.

Thank you to my family for their interest in everything I do no matter how wild my dreams get.

To my "Girls Trip" friends—thank you for the laughs, the tears, the trips, and for being the best support system a girl could ask for. Thank you to Cat for being my biggest cheerleader through the years and to Breanna for always reading everything I send you.

We would both like to thank the BSB team for taking a chance on us. We couldn't have asked for a better home. A big thank you to Barbara Ann Wright for all of your hard work and for helping us become better writers.

To everyone else who has supported and believed in us over the years: thank you.

**Kristin:**

For Joe. I miss you every day. I know you'd be proud
to have our books side by side on the bookshelf.


**Allisa:**

For Courtney. Every day with you is the best day of my life.

## CHAPTER ONE: THE SCAVENGER

### *Dani*

The sun feels unusually hot today. The last few weeks have been cooler as the weather shifts from summer to autumn. The nights have been cold, often bringing frost in the morning. But today it's warm. As if summer refuses to fully leave without a fight.

I squint and cast my eyes upward. Not a cloud in the sky or a breeze on the horizon. Sweat trickles down the back of my neck and catches in the collar of my shirt. I pull the scarf around my neck a little higher across my face and glance down at my companion, Roscoe. He's panting happily as he looks back, waiting patiently.

I grab the sawed-off shotgun from the front seat of the busted-up Jeep and slip it into the empty holster strapped to my back. My brown leather duster is next, followed by a backpack that I fling over my shoulder. I shove the keys into my pants pocket and slam the door. Looking down the road, I don't see anyone in either direction.

I stare at the cracked highway. It's hard to imagine a time when cars traveled up and down this road frequently, coming and going without a thought along the paved black path. They didn't have a single worry about floods or sandstorms or the military halting their progress.

It was a different world then.

A short, clipped bark brings my attention to the herding dog still patiently staring up at me. His eagerness is contagious.

"You ready, Roscoe?"

He lets out another bark and stands, his entire back half wiggling in excitement. I shake my head, smiling. I push my thumb upward on my music player to crank the volume. I wait until the music fills my ears through the old earbuds, and I nod in the direction of the warehouse, knowing Roscoe will alert me of anything suspicious. He trots off ahead, knowing the drill despite not being invited to tag along in the first place.

I hold the strap of my bag in one hand and let the other fall to the pistol holstered on my thigh as I follow Roscoe to the old steel building. Abandoned trucks surround it, some half-buried beneath the earth, some with only the frame remaining, rusted and corroded from the floods and constant barrage of sand and debris. Their empty metal shells are a metaphor for what the United States has become.

Ignoring them, I head for the front entrance.

Dust floats in the air, highlighted by the streaks of sunlight pushing into the dark building. I remove my sunglasses and tuck them carefully into the V of my long-sleeved button-up. Pulling the faded red scarf from my face, I leave it loosely around my neck and look around.

Everything feels still, undisturbed since the last time I was here. It's quiet and peaceful. The shade and darkness are welcome reprieves from the heat outside, and I take a moment to enjoy the change in temperature.

I watch as Roscoe trots around the building for a moment before his black furry tail disappears deeper inside to explore.

I cast a glance at the debris scattered along the entrance, noting that nothing seems out of place.

Stepping over a fallen metal shelf, I watch the dust kick up from my boots as it lands back on the cement. There are fresh footprints. Boots not unlike my own. I crouch to examine them. It's not uncommon; this is an unofficial trading post. Scavengers like me come and go relatively often. It's even been known to shield a few raiders.

These particular prints don't feel quite right. There must be a couple dozen different ones. Way more than I've ever seen inside this warehouse.

I catch Roscoe sniffing something not too far away, and I leave him to his investigation as I tighten the hold on the butt of my pistol and move past the footprints. Roscoe doesn't seem alarmed. It's clear the twenty or so people who passed through are now gone, leaving the warehouse empty and silent.

Carefully, I step over fallen shelves and beams and nod in time with the music blaring in my ears. Making my way to the far end of the warehouse, I keep my eyes on my surroundings a bit more than usual and only stop once I reach an old metal desk against the wall. I push the rusted piece of furniture out of the way and squat so I can remove one of the lower cinder blocks. From behind it, I take several uncharged batteries and place them in my bag. I put freshly charged batteries in their place and insert the cinderblock back as though it was never removed. Pushing the desk back to the wall, I climb atop it.

Batteries are the best form of currency around here. Not many places have the capability to charge them except major cities. The military has such a tight control on old technology and electronics that if someone doesn't have access to batteries or a charging station, they probably can't afford to buy any. And out here in the wastelands, we have no other option than to trade. Thankfully, finding batteries and charging them has become my local claim to fame.

People will trade just about anything for a charged battery.

This back and forth started about four years ago. An accident, really. I ran into a scavenger desperate to get an old radio up and working. I promised I could help in exchange for some old car parts. Next thing I know, we're setting up a drop point in this warehouse. The town he scavenges for is known for things like herbs, medicine, and other perishable goods.

My town prospers in the tinkering business: cars, electronics, technology, explosives. The tradeoff didn't seem so bad. I agreed to leave charged batteries here every month in exchange for whatever his town could offer. He returns their dead batteries and trades for charged ones.

Since the beginning of the arrangement, we've never missed a drop-off. It's by far the most successful trading post I've been a part of, let alone seen.

I remove a different cinder block and grab a small bag from the hole in the wall. I stow it in my backpack and replace the block. I jump down, and as easy as that, my errand is finished.

Roscoe still has the white stripe on his snout to the ground, and his black tail is high in, unmoving as he works. I make a loop around the inside, looking for anything that might be out of place. Anything suspicious. I follow the sporadic boot prints until something glimmers nearby. It reflects the light that streams in from the large hole in the roof.

I rush to the object and crouch, running my thumb over the silver finish after I pick it up. It's small rectangular pin with three markings inside. It looks like something a military officer would wear on their jacket to signify rank. A Warrant Officer Third Class.

A heavy, sinking feeling comes over me as I stare at the pin. Anger builds in the pit of my stomach. I look around again.

The footprints aren't from fellow scavengers and traders or even raiders. They are military. My body tenses and my jaw tightens thinking of the military this far west.

A loud bark deepens my dread. I pocket the military pin and jog to what is left of a forklift currently being investigated by Roscoe. He watches me excitedly as he looks at his findings and back to me. I stare at the new piece of debris he proudly uncovered, willing it not to be there.

When it doesn't disappear, I pull the earbuds from my ears and squat. I take a deep breath and look beside me. "This can't be good." Roscoe whines in confirmation. I carefully pick up the provisions wrapper and inspect it. There are still remains stuck to the inside. It can't be more than a few days old, just like the button. I stand and shove the wrapper in my pocket to join the insignia. "We better head out if we want to get back before dark."

I glance around once more. It's open property. Scavengers and raiders come through here from time to time; that's to be expected. There's not much here, so any passersby usually just use it for short-term shelter. But military? That's new.

By the look of the footprints, they used this place to dodge the last sandstorm that rolled through a few days ago. The military isn't really known this far west. The closest established base is well over five hundred miles away. Their presence here has my mind racing. Not seeing them out today has me curious about their actual whereabouts.

One thing's for sure, I do not want to be caught out here alone with them wandering around.

Turning my music off, I tuck the earbuds inside my shirt and put my sunglasses on. I hurry to my Jeep and glance around for any signs of vehicle marks. I see none other than my own. No one really has many cars anymore, a luxury afforded by only the rich or lucky, and the fact that there are no tracks just adds to my confusion.

The military doesn't travel anywhere without their solar powered, well-appointed vehicles. Especially not this far from an outpost. None of this makes any sense.

I reach for the handle and look both ways once more. Still nothing. Everything remains perfectly still. Eerily still.

I open the door, let Roscoe in first, then slide in, not bothering to take off my jacket. I place my shotgun on the seat next to me and fire up the engine. It rumbles loudly, and I step on the gas, leaving much quicker than I came.

By the time I get back to town, the sun has set and the air is cooler. I slow the Jeep as I approach the main gates. I glance at Roscoe sitting happily in the passenger seat while I wait for the gates to open. Once they do, I pull into the front part of town slowly and turn into the garage.

Three other vehicles are parked inside the large space, all solar-powered and slow, pieced together from years of scavenging. They can't always handle the desert, not like my old Gladiator Rubicon. It takes a lot of maintenance to keep this old thing running, so I try to take her for a spin every couple of weeks to keep her greased up.

I pull into the spot reserved especially for her and exit, Roscoe hot on my heels. He sniffs the ground while I grab my bag, toss it over my shoulder, and head out.

Nodding at a few people, I approach the large watchtower close to the front gate. Glancing up, I catch sight of Jack. That would explain my quick entrance into town.

A bark grabs my attention, and Roscoe stares up at me as if waiting to be dismissed. I pat his fuzzy head and scale the ladder to the watchtower.

This particular guard post is the highest along the perimeter. A few dozen people make up guard duty, always rotating, always watching for trouble.

Once I get inside, Jack pushes the night goggles up on his head. "You know Rhiannon is gonna kill you, right?" he says with a satisfied smile.

"Did I miss dinner?" I ask innocently.

He snorts. "Probably. Who let you out the gate anyway?" He scratches his dark, tattooed arm.

"I did," I say, grabbing the pair of night vision binoculars. "When is your shift up?"

"In a few minutes. The old guy from up north has it next, and then Mike has it for the rest of the night." He leans against his rifle. "Your drop go okay?"

I hum, knowing he'll pick up that nothing too exciting happened. I know he's a little bitter I went out without him. He likes to get out from behind the town walls. But sometimes, the town gets too noisy, and I need to head out alone. If anyone understands that, it's Jack. Despite not being invited, he keeps his disappointment to himself.

Tightening my grip on the binoculars, I squint into them. There's no sign of anything. No fires, no wanderers, no wildlife. It's dead out there. Though my instinct tells me the worry I feel is warranted.

I briefly consider alerting the town council since they make all the big decisions. There will be a formal questioning if I go to them with a military pin and gut feeling. All questions and no answers until I can form a clearer picture of what we're potentially dealing with. For now, I'm chasing ghosts.

I toss the binoculars on the floor and decide against alerting the council just yet. "I need everyone hyperalert tonight, okay? Extra cautious. You see anything suspicious, I mean *anything*, you come get me. No alarm, just me. Tell the others, too."

"You expecting trouble?" He eyes me warily and straightens the too-small vest over his well-muscled chest. I find it so ridiculous that it makes me roll my eyes.

The humor doesn't last as I think of what might be approaching. The uneasy feeling returns, and I answer robotically with, "I don't know yet."

He grunts as if he wants to say more, but instead, he nods and slips the goggles back over his eyes. I leave him to it.

My stomach rumbles. I need to finish a few more errands, but I haven't eaten much today. Despite the tongue-lashing I'll get if I stop by the tavern, I walk in that direction. The possibility of grabbing dinner is just too great to pass up.

Nodding at a man exiting the tavern, I step inside. My stomach growls again at the smell of whatever Rhiannon has cooking in the back. I pull off my fingerless gloves and shove them in my back pocket. After dipping my hands into the fresh bowl of water by the door, I clean them as best I can.

I spot Rhiannon, her dark hair pulled tightly into a messy bun atop her head. She's behind the counter talking to a younger couple finishing up their meal. If she's out front, it means the rush in the back has dissipated, and she's already sent her help home for the evening. I haven't had anyone I could call a best friend before Rhiannon, and just the sight of her eases some of my tension.

"Hey, Rhi," I call as I head to the counter. I drop my bag on the empty stool beside me and place my forearms on the countertop. The lanterns are ablaze, and the dinner rush is long gone, leaving only a few stragglers.

Rhiannon looks up and tosses her towel over her shoulder. Grabbing the plates in front of her, she clears off the counter and puts the dishes in the bin behind her. She smiles again at the couple before giving me her full attention. Even in the poor lighting, I can see the scowl on her pale face.

"There you are," she drawls and stops directly in front of me. Her hands go to her hips, and I know I'm in for a scolding despite her even tone. "I was worried when you didn't show up for dinner."

"Yeah, sorry," I flinch. She stares back expectantly, her dark eyes burning with controlled anger. "You're mad."

"You went out by yourself. Again." This time, her voice holds a bit of an angry edge.

"I go out by myself all the time." The second it's out of my mouth, I know it is the absolute wrong thing to say.

She throws her hands in the air. "But you're not supposed to. It's dangerous. The sandstorms alone are enough to bury and suffocate you. Not to mention raiders."

"Nothing happened," I try, even though I know she's right. Those are the rules. Never leave the gates alone without a communication device. Hell, I am one of the people who created the rule. I missed dinner because I was out past the gates, and the only way to get something to eat this late is to play nice. "Besides," I try again, this time with a smile, "I wasn't alone. Roscoe was with me."

"Roscoe can't fire a gun."

I sigh. "Come on, don't be mad." She takes her hair out of the bun and redoes it, one of her tells that she's annoyed and anxious. I smile and clear my throat.

"No." She's giving me a pointed look. She seems to know what I am up to, but I can't resist teasing Rhiannon.

"Would someone go play E6 on the music box?" I call out.

"Dani," she warns.

No one in the room gets up. Undeterred, I open my mouth to sing the song myself.

"Please don't." She's begging already, reaching across the counter to clamp her hand over my mouth before I can get a word out.

I try and sing the best I can, but my words are muffled against her skin.

"I'll go get you something to eat if you please just stop singing." She waits until I stop and slowly removes her hand. I grin in response. With a groan, she goes to retrieve my food before I can respond. It's the lightest I've felt all day.

Yet that doesn't stop me from singing as loud as I can, "Rhiannon!"

I ignore the looks from the young couple loitering at the other side of the counter and smile to myself for the small victory. While I wait for her return, I rummage inside my backpack until I find the little black pouch.

Rhiannon quickly returns with a full plate of steaming food. It looks like bison with rice and greens and a generous slice of her homemade bread.

"I kept it warm for you," she says begrudgingly and places the plate in front of me.

"You're a goddess." I grab the piece of bread and tear off a bite. I push the small bag across the counter. "Here, these are for you."

Her eyes light up as she peeks into the bag before clutching it to her chest like it's sacred. "You're an amazing scavenger. Horrible singer but an amazing scavenger."

"Still mad?" I ask with a grin.

She pours me a glass of ale and eyes me carefully. "If I say yes, will you try to sing again?"

I open my mouth to give her an unobstructed verse, but her hand flies to cover my lips once more before I can squeak out a single note.

"Then no"—she gives me a pointed look—"I'm not mad." She takes her hand off my mouth and gives me a look of warning.

"This is really good, Rhi," I say as I shovel the food into my mouth faster than I can chew.

"With the spices you brought me, it's only going to get better." She places the bag in her apron pocket and watches me eat for a moment. "You better slow down, or you're going to choke."

I chuckle a little and do my best to take her advice, knowing that she only chastises because she cares.

"Today's heat was strange," she says as she stares across the tavern and out the front windows. "Think we'll have any warmer days before the cold settles in?"

"I hope so."

"It's been kind of quiet lately," she says almost cautiously. I don't miss the look she gives me from the corner of her eye as she starts to wipe the countertop. I know that look. She's digging for information.

"Well, you know how it is. The stormy season is here. No one wants to get caught up in those sandstorms. And you know how they kick up from out of nowhere."

"Yeah, like a few days ago, which is why you *shouldn't have left today*. But still," she says, "it's just unusually quiet."

"Why would you say that? That's the kiss of death." Jack plops onto the stool next to me.

Rhiannon rolls her eyes and tends to the large pot of stew warming on the fire behind the counter. "It's not a kiss of death. It's stating a fact," she says, her long frame turned away.

"I'll give you another kind of kiss later if you'd like," he says, leaning across the counter. I can hear the smirk in his voice.

Rhiannon's head snaps in his direction, her jaw clenched. "That's inappropriate."

"That's not what you said—"

"Jackson." Her tone is sharp.

I look between them. Rhiannon's face is red and angry. He looks guilty yet satisfied.

She glances at me, clearly embarrassed, and drops the bowl in front of Jack, stew spilling on the counter. The tension is palpable.

Everyone knows Jack and Rhiannon have been sleeping together for the past year or so. Still, she hates having their private life publicized, especially so crudely, so I try to change the direction of the conversation to save her some embarrassment. "Did I mention this is really good?"

She looks relieved. "Thank you."

Jack glances at his stew and then at my plate with a frown. "Why does Dani get a full meal, and I get some leftover stew?"

Rhiannon leans on the counter. "Because you're being rude, and I'm in charge."

I hate being the third wheel for their lovers' quarrels. "Transition go okay?" I ask Jack, changing the subject again.

He nods. "Guy from up north promises to be extra vigilant," Jack says as he takes a bite. "Promises to come get you if he sees anything weird. Jeez, this is hot."

"You really have to learn people's names." I point out one of Jack's more irritating habits.

"Why is the watch being extra vigilant?" Rhiannon asks, her eyes narrowing.

I sigh. She picks up on everything. "Just a precaution," I tell her, not ready to get into my suspicions just yet. "Who's that for?" I point to a second bowl of stew she's preparing.

"I'm making a bowl for Lucas. He didn't come in for dinner."

"He didn't come in to eat at all?" I frown, only mildly concerned that he has remained locked away inside the entire day. I wonder what has him so distracted that he forgot to eat. He doesn't usually skip meals.

Rhiannon shakes her head. "He was working on a project at Darby's house. I popped by at lunch with sandwiches."

"Thanks, Rhi."

"I'm worried about them," she says. "Lucas is—"

I give her a sharp look. She knows better than to say anything negative about my brother, but I warn her just the same.

"I think the more human interaction he gets, the better," she finally says through a sigh.

Here we go again. "He has plenty of human interaction. He's fine."

"Physically, yes," she says. "I just wish he'd take his nose out of those comic books from time to time. Maybe that would help."

Jack snorts. "Yeah, try prying them away from him."

"Look," I say, "Lucas is fine. He may not communicate the way we do, but it works for him. His brain is just wired differently, and those comics really help."

"Quoting Major Maelstrom instead of holding a normal

conversation is a little more than strange, though, don't you think?" Rhiannon asks gently.

"She's right. He can be a little hard to follow," Jack says. He mimics Lucas. "'Major Maelstrom reporting for duty!'"

"We can understand him just fine. So leave it alone," I say, forcefully enough for both Jack and Rhiannon to get the idea. They share a look but wisely decide not to press on. It's not the first time they've tried to have this conversation.

"Have you heard anything from the east?" Rhiannon asks instead.

I shake my head, glad to move the conversation in another direction. "No. Nothing new."

Rhiannon sighs and pushes off the counter. "Well, no news is good news, I suppose."

I nod but don't respond. I don't tell her just how wrong she is. I look at my dinner and listen as she and Jack begin to bicker about how quiet things are.

I hold the two bowls Rhiannon prepared as best I can despite their intense heat. Darby's house isn't too far from the tavern, so I get there quickly and scale the stairs to her porch.

A rumble of thunder catches me off guard as I bring my foot up and kick at the door several times. I glance at the rapidly darkening sky as the wind picks up, and I wonder how the clouds seem to roll in so quickly out of nowhere.

Darby answers the door in a long white coat, with bug-eyed plastic goggles over her eyes. Her crimpy blond hair is falling out of its tie and sticking out all over the place.

"You look ridiculous," I tell her. She has a few inches on me, but there is absolutely nothing intimidating about her lanky frame and rosy complexion. She pushes the goggles up and pulls the door open, not responding to my comment. "You've been holed up here for days. Don't you want some fresh air?"

"I'm so close, Dani. I can feel it," she calls over her shoulder as she walks away. Her house is a disaster with papers strewn about and books open on nearly every surface.

Lucas is flipping through one of his comic books on the couch off to the side. He's totally engrossed and doesn't look up. A sharp buzzing sound snaps my attention to the center of the room. A large metal tower shoots up from the floor, through the ceiling, and into the open air.

"Well, you sure are close to something," I mumble. "You might get lucky tonight. Looks like a storm is rolling in."

Lucas looks up, a large smile on his face. "A storm is coming through. A storm of the likes you've never seen. Are you prepared?" He smiles at Darby, quoting one of his comics. I feel a pang in my chest over what Rhiannon said earlier about him needing more human interaction.

"Issue number thirty-seven." She offers a smile.

"Thirty-six," I say. Not once has Darby ever gotten an issue right for one of Lucas's lines. I made it a point growing up to read every single issue over and over to communicate and understand him better. I can't memorize them as easily as Lucas. He's pretty special when it comes to that. But I try, and I think that's what matters. I guess that's what Darby's doing, too. Though it's not really necessary to shout out every single issue number every time my brother speaks.

The amused smile on Lucas's face shows he appreciates the effort.

Despite Darby's frustrated groan, I can't take my eyes off the new structure protruding through the ceiling. "If it rains, you're gonna get wet, you do realize that, right?"

She turns from jotting down her notes. "We have buckets," she says, as if it's the most obvious solution in the world. For an absolute genius, she sure is stupid.

With a sigh, I hold up the steaming bowls. "I brought you some stew before Jack ate it all." I place the bowls on the nearby table. After a moment, Lucas gently places the comic down and comes over to grab one. I give him a playful push. He catches his balance as his long, dark hair sways with him.

"Go on then." He points to my bag. "Let's see what the cat's dragged in."

I reach inside and hand the dead batteries to Darby.

"Anything good this time around?" she asks, tossing them in the pile to be charged.

"Not really. A few medical supplies. Some spices for Rhiannon.

A bottle of whiskey that, no, you may not have." I give her a pointed look.

She looks disappointed that no new technology was in the drop, but we all know it's hit or miss with these monthly runs.

I point at Lucas and give him a serious look, Rhiannon's words echoing in my head. "You better help me with that fence tomorrow, Lucas. Just 'cause Darby locks herself away like a weirdo doesn't mean you have to."

He stands up straight and gives me a sharp salute. "That's an affirmative!" He's so serious, I smile. He returns the look.

Darby looks hurt. "Really? Why do you always get the cool quotes, and I get quotes from issue thirty-seven?"

"Thirty-six." I lightly tap her face with the back of my hand. "Because you're the evil genius, and I'm the hero." She rolls her eyes, but I know she's not really upset. I secretly love that she's so smart she can barely function. It's why she and Lucas are best friends. Their brains see and respond to things differently than most of us. I give Lucas a wink and head for the door. A low rumble of thunder in the distance gives me pause. I turn around and give Darby a wary look. "Just…try not to fry the whole town, okay?"

I watch them for a moment longer as they prepare for their experiment. The wonder and excitement on their faces is contagious. The entire world may have turned on itself when the bombs dropped, but it brings me some kind of peace to know that not all creativity and kindness burned along with it.

The rain hits right as I reach my house. I barely have time to toss my jacket and things on the table before it starts. It's loud as it careens and crashes against the tin roof of my modest two-story, two-bedroom home. It's comforting despite the loud crack of thunder that breaks the otherwise calming sound of the rain.

I light a couple of lanterns and pour some of my newly acquired whiskey, then flop in the overstuffed chair in the front room and groan, happy to be in my personal sanctuary. Staring at the large map on the wall of what was once the United States, my eyes trace the state lines, all the major roads and cities. The intricately laid out and carefully planned borders exist solely as artwork now. There are few roads or cities to divide anymore. Not many lines truly exist, none of which are marked on a map like this.

Instead, the states are known by name only as a point to get around. Not that it matters. Every town, city, and area has its own rules. Unless of course, they're claimed by the NAF, then they fall under their rule. It happened back east, complete NAF domination. I wonder how long it'll be before we're claimed out here as well. It's been rumored since long before I was born that the NAF would control the wastelands, and yet the Resistance has so far kept it alive and out of militant hands.

I tip back another sip of whiskey and think about how my father used to talk about the fall of civilization. First came the floods. The climate shifted so rapidly that despite warnings for years, no one was really prepared. It started with heavy rains and heavy snow and ice that melted rapidly. Dams broke, livestock was stranded, crops were destroyed. It got worse year after year until eventually what was Florida and Louisiana sank. The entire East Coast was affected in some way, the borders slipping farther and farther into the sea.

The western states didn't fare much better. They lost most of their coastline and major cities. What the flooding didn't claim, the wildfires did. The west burned for years, until there was barely anything left that wasn't buried under water or ash.

All of the states in between the coasts washed out, too, the landscape eroding and sinking, trapped between two extremes. The wastelands.

Then came illness. A rapidly spreading virus killed millions. Airborne and deadly. Some didn't want to accept it and didn't take precautions because there was still a widely held belief that the government was using the virus as a hoax to control people. But it spread as fast as the wildfires in the west, and over a quarter of the population was lost. The stories of people dying in isolated hospital wards, alone and afraid, used to give me nightmares as a kid and still make my stomach churn when I really stop to consider it.

Last came the new leaders. The final linchpin in the rapidly disintegrating democracy. The country had fallen into the hands of a ruthless military president. He was a charismatic liar who made bold promises. He swore he'd get the nation through the hard times if they trusted him and continued to let him lead. The people believed him. They had to. There was no other hope. I don't blame the people of the past; they were scared and desperate.

The nation had locked itself off from the outside world, made enemies out of allies and allies out of enemies. He built walls, literally and figuratively. The country was on the brink of a world war for years, and before they had time to blink, they found themselves in the middle of the worst war the world had ever seen. The government fell at his feet for help.

When the bombs dropped, they obliterated much of the land. Millions lost their lives, and those that lived through the blast and radiation poisoning soon found themselves in the middle of a drastic new climate. After the firestorms, the temperature crashed, propelling the nation into a nuclear winter. Smoke filled the air, and particles drifted throughout the atmosphere. Colossal crop failure and famine soon followed and caused the next round of mass deaths. My mom used to describe it as the "end of days" while she lit a candle during a vigil for those who'd died and said a Lakota prayer about heaven and earth living in harmony.

By the time the ash settled, the nation found itself forgotten and alone. Without aid from other countries, people had no choice but to turn to the government who failed them. But what was once a democracy had crumbled with the bombs, and a new totalitarian regime had risen to power. It happened before anyone saw it coming: he replaced all government positions with military. No more representatives. No more balance of power.

The old country was gone. Unrecognizable. The state lines had been erased, and what was once the United States of America was now ruled by a single military entity. The National Armed Forces, the NAF.

Planes stopped flying after blockers were put into place. Jet fuel was dumped and burned along with every aerial piece they could find. All of it to prevent anyone from getting aircraft into the sky. Any access to remove these blockers, stash fuel, or keep plane parts was considered a serious offense. No one was allowed in, and no one was allowed out.

Any hope of returning to the way things were before the war was lost. Most technology was outlawed, except for the use of leadership. People were given a choice: fall in line or die.

Those who agreed to fall in line were the loyalists. The true patriots of the new land. They followed the new NAF laws and were rewarded with aid and supplies. And that's how it stands to this very day.

Currently, the NAF and its loyalists control all that's left of the East Coast and most of the South. Over the past twenty years, they've been building outposts at old military bases in the west and north to gain control over that, too. Slowly, they've been expanding, and it's only a matter of time before we're all completely under their thumb. It pisses me off that no matter how hard we try, we can't seem to stop it.

With the closed borders, no one is coming in to help, and no one is going to escape. At least, that's what we've been told. I'm sure people have tried to leave or enter, although I haven't heard of anyone succeeding. And those who are caught trying? The punishment is death.

Those who oppose the NAF are the Resistance. They're the ones fighting back just as hard because they don't recognize the new laws. They believe in the old ways, the old democracies and republics, and they have been battling for decades to overthrow the military and restore people-led government. They're the good guys, the ones fighting for us all.

I hold the glass in my hand just a little tighter as I think of the Resistance and wonder if they remember they're fighting for all the people and not just for themselves. Sipping my whiskey, I push down those thoughts. I shouldn't judge the movement based on my own selfish actions. My life in the Resistance is long gone.

I think about my life now. With all the struggle for power, there are always many who are stuck in between. The townsfolk, scavengers, wanderers…most of whom can be found out here in the north and in the west. That's me. That's this town. We just want to live our lives as peacefully as we can. We are good, honest people who just want to be left alone.

But unlike the innocents, there are always those who want to take advantage of the chaos. Those would be the raiders. Ruthless, violent people who only believe in thieving and killing. They have no interest in the way things were or the new law spreading across the country. They have no desire to contribute to a successful society or rebuilding. They just want to take, kill, and move on.

I don't know who I hate worse, the loyalists or the raiders.

I sigh and stand, putting my whiskey aside. Following an invisible path along the map in my mind, I head to the same spot I've been thinking about for most of my life. A spot untouched by the Third World War. Untouched by the bombings. Untouched by the massive floods.

Memories course through me: my father threading a worm onto the end of a fishhook. My mother drying clothes on the line. Laughing as I run aimlessly through a green field, and dipping my toes into the chilly stream waters.

I squeeze my eyes shut. It's only a matter of time before that spot, too, is under military control.

I wonder what my father would think of the life I've made for myself out here. Would he approve of me staying out of the war? Or would he believe that my decision to settle down is a coward's way out?

I miss him. Sometimes it hurts so much I think my heart might split. I've never been able to fill the void that losing him and my mother left. Some days, not even a good whiskey can dull the pain.

Falling back into my chair, I take a long pull straight from the bottle, forgetting the glass. I wince as it scorches my throat as I reach for the last letter I received from William, the current leader of the Resistance, several weeks ago. I've read it at least a hundred times since the courier delivered it, and I'll probably read it a hundred more before I reply.

*General Trent is dead. Judith Turner now has full control of the NAF. The eastern and southern cities have fallen. There is no more Resistance there. The loyalists are pushing greater numbers out north and west on General Turner's orders. More bases to come your way. I fear they are planning something big. I will be out there soon. Remain vigilant and stay safe. –W*

His warning is loud and clear: The NAF will soon dominate and have complete control over this broken nation, led by the ruthless General Turner. Her new rank makes me want to vomit. After what I found in that warehouse, it seems as if her plan to expand is in motion a hell of a lot faster than I expected. Pulling the shiny pin from my pocket, I stare at the ranking as I run my thumb over the sharp edges. The war I have been so adamant about abandoning is once again on my doorstep. I knew this day would come, and I knew the lure of being drawn back in would be strong.

The need for revenge has chipped away at me the same way the floods ate the land piece by piece by piece. I worked hard at restoring the part of myself that could control the rage, pushing down the need for revenge. I worked hard at becoming the peaceful, simple-living type that I am today, growing comfortable in my new life. I built up walls around myself, around that hatred and rage. Revenge for the death of my father has remained, but it's dormant, nothing but a quiet buzz in the back of my mind during quiet moments. There is no reason to revisit those feelings I worked so hard to repress. But with General Turner now in charge of the NAF, all those walls I carefully constructed are threatening to come crashing down.

The thought of fighting again, of seeking revenge for my father, sparks something inside me. I'm both uneasy and eager. The day I both dreaded and anticipated appears to be rapidly approaching. Soon, I will be faced with a decision: remain in my new life or jump back into the war.

I'm afraid with the new general moving west, soon within striking distance, I won't be able to resist the temptation of vengeance against Judith Turner, the woman who killed my father.

## CHAPTER TWO: THE TRAVELERS

### *Dani*

Mike pops his gum loudly. I grip the binoculars tighter to my face and count five of them.

He smacks his mouth again, and it grates on my nerves.

I watch as the handful of lightly armed people pick through the rusted cars about a couple hundred meters away. I smirk. They won't find anything there. Those cars were stripped down to nothing years ago. But they function perfectly as a lure. A distraction for travelers and the like, who are unable to resist taking a look for supplies while we take a look at them.

*Smack.*

I pull the binoculars from my eyes and glare at him.

He turns his head slowly from the scope of his rifle, a genuinely confused look on his face. "What?"

"Really? Gum?" I snap. I try to be patient when we're on lookout, but he's pushing it.

"It helps me focus," he says sheepishly.

I roll my eyes. "How many do you see?"

He brings the scope back up to his eye. "Five."

Scanning the small group again, I take note of the weapons they have. "Yeah, me, too."

"Raiders?"

Two rifles, a sword, a handgun, and a baseball bat. I shake my head. "Doubtful. Too much firepower. Traders maybe?" I lower the binoculars.

Mike arches a brow, casting a quick glance in my direction before his eye is back against the scope. "Wandering this far out in the stormy season?"

"Didn't say they were smart." I push up on my knees and nod at the group. "If they get too close, let me know. Otherwise, if they come to the gates, see what they're offering. You know the drill."

He nods sharply. "You got it. Sorry for the false alarm."

"No, no. You did just what I asked." I pat him on the shoulder and head down from the watchtower, anxious to finish the fence before getting caught in another storm. They tend to come every few days this time of year.

Heading to the back perimeter, I glance at the morning sun, squinting despite the sunglasses I never go without. Last night's rain has pushed away the heat and brought back the cooler weather. Despite the temperature drop, sweat builds up beneath my dark, long-sleeved shirt and pants.

Lucas is already there, hammering in a new plank over a gaping hole in the fence. The sandstorm really did a number on our perimeter, taking out a sizable portion. The fence needed repairing anyway; some parts haven't held up against the weather as much as others, and now with the hole, we have no choice. Repairs happen often, as we are on constant alert from raiders and other intruders. I watch as Lucas replaces some rotted, weathered wood barely hanging in place. His long, straight, black hair is pulled into a bun on the back of his head and off his neck.

His tongue sticks out slightly as he concentrates on driving the nails into the wood. He looks so much like our mother that sometimes it makes my stomach flip. She was born Lakota Sioux from out in the Black Hills. We both have her darker skin tone, but only Lucas has her dark, gentle eyes and kind, quiet demeanor.

Lucas finishes hammering the nail in the new piece of wood and wipes his hand on his worn-out shirt, careful to avoid the logo of the two slightly overlapping M's in the center of a swirling vortex. Major Maelstrom. His favorite superhero.

I sigh. There's a heaviness in my chest at what Rhiannon said the night before. As much as I'd never care to admit it, she was right. His entire world is centered around his comic books. A little more realistic interaction wouldn't hurt him.

"So how much water did you have to bucket out of Darby's house last night?" I ask, picking up and leaning on an ax propped against a nearby tree.

He turns, a sheepish look on his face and his dark eyes sparkling. "She's a little worse for wear, but she still stands proud and true."

I laugh. "That bad, huh?" He nods. "Well, I appreciate you helping with the fence. It's a lot of work considering you were up so late."

"Nothing pleases me more than completing the task at hand," he says, grinning. He nods at the ax. "You dare wield Major Maelstrom's battleax?"

I roll my eyes. Major Maelstrom's weapon of choice is an unnecessarily large battleax. Sometimes, the only way I can get Lucas to help chop wood is to present him with an ax of his own.

I hold it out. "You wanna chop? Feel free. I'd rather hammer anyway. I can pretend I'm Thor."

He wrinkles his nose. He hates when I blend comic universes together. Thor and Major Maelstrom would never, ever be caught in the same story arc.

He all but snatches the ax and hands over the hammer, and we go back to working on the fence. A long stretch of silence fills the air as we work. It's comfortable, normal. We both value a good day's work, especially since we moved into this town. Every little thing we can do to help makes us both happy, so we concentrate on getting the fence finished.

I'm not sure how long we've been working, but the front of my shirt is drenched with sweat when someone calls, "Hey, Dani."

I turn in the direction of the watchtower on the back gate fifty meters away and see a guard practically hanging off the side. He points to the front entrance. Turning my head, I search for whatever he's trying to show me.

"Front gate opening," I hear Mike yell from across the town.

It's not an emergency, but we don't normally announce locals dropping in. Curious if it's the travelers from earlier, I set the hammer down and jog to the front. When I see a familiar floppy hat on the head of an old man leading a horse, I slow my pace as relief sets in. George.

Lucas comes to a stop beside me and looks at George with anticipation. He pulls the bandana from his face and works to free some dirt from his white mustache and beard. I wipe my brow with the back of my hand and make my way over to say hello to our old friend.

He is looking pretty haggard these days. Continuous travel from town to town has worn on him even more than the last time I saw him. But he smiles that same wide, slow grin when he sees me coming, and that has me returning the gesture.

"Hey, George, good to see you again."

George nods as he pats his horse and brings the old mare to a stop. His face may be covered in dirt and dust through every wrinkle, but his bright blue eyes stand out amidst his deeply tanned, leathered complexion. "Hey there, kiddo."

I clasp his forearm. "How's the road?"

"Dusty," he says before clasping Lucas's forearm, too.

I can usually tell if he's coming or going by how worn his clothes look. Despite the rain the night before, George is covered head to toe in dried earth. His shoulders are slumped, and his body shows the weariness of a person who hasn't slept in days. He must be on his way home.

"Get caught up in the sandstorm a couple of days ago?"

He chuckles. "Nah, made it to shelter just in the nick of time. She was a doozy, though. Gave a lot of places problems from the sound of it. How'd you all fare?"

I motion to the back fence. "Our perimeter took a hell of a beating."

Jack approaches and wipes his hand on his pants. He clasps George's arm. "Hey, old man, how ya been?" he asks with a smile.

"Busy," George says, taking Jack's massive forearm in his grasp. "Me and Dani here were just discussing the storms. They seem to be coming later and later. Soon, we'll be getting those dust storms in the middle of damn winter."

Jack laughs. "We do. They're called blizzards."

George gives him a look and then chuckles as they release each other.

"Have you eaten?" I ask. "I'm sure Rhiannon can find you something."

George shakes his head quickly. "No, no, I can't stay. I'm trying to make it to the next town over before nightfall." It's quick, but I catch the hasty glance he gives over his shoulder, as if he's being followed.

It's not a mannerism he'd usually make. He's spooked by something, and it worries me more than I care to admit out loud.

"My horse could use some water, though."

I glance at Jack, and he nods. "I'm on it," he says and turns away.

"Then help us with the fence," I call after him. I receive a dismissive wave in response. I have to physically stop myself from firing off an insult. Jack acts like he won't help and like he's above the grunt work, but in reality, he'd bend over backward to protect this town. Even if that means a day of manual labor.

I motion at George's saddlebags. "Find anything interesting out there?"

Instantly, George's shoulders relax, and his demeanor changes from nervous to comfortable. He moves to one of the smaller bags and rummages inside. "Not too much," he says, lifting some items. "Just a couple of dead batteries and a few more of them trinkets Lucas loves."

Lucas perks up. He bounces on the balls of his feet and leans in for a better look. I gesture for him to wait and be patient.

George hands them to an overeager Lucas. It appears to be an old Major Maelstrom action figure, faded and worn and missing a foot, along with a weather-beaten comic. I glance at the issue number. Twelve. Pretty sure he has this one, but he won't mind. They don't mean much to me, but he'll be excited.

His smile is immediate and bright. It reminds me of when we were kids and our mother would call for him, asking if he wanted to read Major Maelstrom with her before dinner. Nothing brought Lucas more joy than being with Mom. That smile is rare and bittersweet.

George scratches the back of his neck and squints. "To tell you the truth, my memory ain't what it used to be. Not sure which ones you already have."

"It doesn't matter," I say. "He loves them all."

Lucas takes the action figure and grins widely. The second it's in his hands, he moves its arms and turns it over, examining every inch.

"Don't get too engrossed," I tell him. "That fence isn't gonna repair itself."

He looks at me with wide eyes. I know he's desperate to include the two items in his collection. "Only death's embrace can keep me from my mission."

I have no idea if he's referring to taking the new items to his house or the fence repair. He holds up the figure, getting his point across. Even if it is a tad on the dramatic side.

"Go on, take a break," I say, giving him a little shove. "I'll finish up with Jack. And give these batteries to Darby for a trade."

Lucas grabs the dead batteries from my hands before he rushes away. If Darby joins in his excitement, I won't see them again for the rest of the day.

"Major Maelstrom was unaccustomed to such kindness, but he was grateful for it all the same," Lucas calls excitedly over his shoulder, never looking back.

George shakes his head and chuckles. "Strange kid. I like him, but I can't understand a word he says."

"He loves them. Thank you." I cross my arms. "How's Jess?" I ask as casually as I can.

George's smile finally fades. It was only a matter of time before I asked about her. I always do. "She's good. Very good. Seeing a boy. Not too happy about that, but he seems to make her smile, so I guess I can't complain too much."

The updates on her life still manage to get to me. I'm happy that she's doing well, but I'm still grappling with my choice to leave, and messages like this bring me a mixture of joy and deep regret that I'm missing so much of her life. I'm grateful for the sunglasses covering my eyes, though they do little to mask the lump forming in my throat.

"Good," I say simply.

George sighs, and I tense, knowing what's coming next. "Why won't you let me tell her where you are? Or, hell, you know, go see her? I think it would do you both a lot of good. She asks me if I run into you out on the road. I hate having to lie to my own granddaughter."

I shake my head and uncross my arms, resting my hands on my hips instead. "No. I don't want her to know where I am. She's better off. We both know it."

"At least let me tell her you're doing well. She worries."

I point at him. "Not a goddamn word about me, George, you swore."

"Hi, George."

He looks past me at Rhiannon, who is approaching just as bubbly as ever, Jack and Roscoe following loyally. I'm grateful for the escape from the conversation.

George shoots me one last look that finishes his unspoken disagreement before turning. "Rhiannon! Now aren't you a sight for sore eyes." He spreads his arms wide to bring her into a bear hug. She always was his favorite. She's everybody's favorite, including mine.

"You're looking as handsome as ever." She leans in and kisses him on the cheek.

"And you are looking as radiant as ever, my dear." He beams at her.

After their friendly embrace, Rhiannon pulls away and hands him a bag. "I have some food for you."

He eyes the bag skeptically. "I don't know, I don't feel right taking so much food when I don't have much to trade today."

She brushes the comment aside and shoves the bag into his chest, forcing him to take it. "Nonsense. You're a friend. We feed our friends."

"You are quite the catch." George chuckles happily as he opens the bag to survey his score.

Rhiannon blushes and looks over at Jack, who clears his throat loudly. I smirk, glad I'm not the only one on the end of George's uncomfortable observations. Jack hands George a large thermos of water and places a bucket down for the horse to drink.

"Any news?" I ask.

George hesitates and glances at Rhiannon. He looks back at me, and I shrug. Knowing how she blows even the simplest things out of proportion, I appreciate his discretion. But she might as well hear whatever bad news he has to tell straight from him. She always manages to get it out of me anyhow.

George takes a large sip of water. "Was on my way back from Pierre. You know, a few days northeast of here? They heard news of Hot Springs from a standard courier. Word is, they were just attacked by the NAF."

Rhiannon looks between me and George, surprised. Makes me realize why George didn't want to speak so openly. I'm bound to get an earful of panic from her. "Hot Springs is two hundred miles west of here," she stammers. "The National Armed Forces attacking villages this far west?"

George nods regretfully. "Yes, ma'am. Burned the whole place down. Courier said he saw the smoke himself."

Jack crosses his arms, skeptical. "You sure it wasn't raiders? The NAF is usually more careful. Especially since their numbers aren't that great this far out. Raiders, on the other hand…"

"The folks up in Pierre swear by it. Passed a couple travelers on the way here who said they saw the NAF cruise on by a few days later. Described the gray uniforms down to every last detail. Complete with those solar-powered vehicles of theirs," George says. "They might have resisted their presence. I don't think the gray coats take too kindly to such things."

I tense at the nickname. I haven't heard it spoken in years, and it stirs a deep hate within.

"Shit," Rhiannon whispers.

"Do you know their numbers?" Jack asks.

George shakes his head. "Enough to attack and burn Hot Springs."

"Guess they resisted," Jack says dryly. I clench my teeth.

Rhiannon looks at me with wide eyes. I place my hand on her arm, trying to calm her. "Thanks for the heads-up," I say to George casually, so as not to raise any more alarm. I don't need Rhiannon to panic any more than she already is. "We'll keep an eye out."

George finishes his water and hands the empty thermos to Jack just as Darby comes back with fresh batteries, charged and ready to go. George shoves them in his bag. "Well, I guess I better be on my way if I want to make it home before nightfall. Don't want to be caught out at night."

Rhiannon takes his hand and squeezes tightly. "Take care of yourself, George. Please, be careful."

"Will do," he says with a smile and nod. Rhiannon gives him another breath-stealing hug, which he returns. He gives Jack a farewell nod and turns to me, beckoning me to follow.

He waves to Mike in the watchtower, and we step outside the town walls.

"You know," I say, "fire isn't their style. That's not how the NAF usually operates."

"No, but it ain't out of the realm of possibility."

"They'd blow that town into pieces with tanks long before they'd burn it to ashes."

"I'm just telling you what I heard." George mounts his horse, and I take hold of the reins, keeping it steady.

"I appreciate the heads-up. And I think you should take your own advice. When you get home, stay there for a while. This whole thing may blow over and turn out to be a one-shot deal, but if it's true, and the NAF forces are big enough out this way to start taking villages…"

"Then we're in for a whole lot of trouble," he finishes for me. "That's the other thing I wanted to talk to you about. Pierre ain't doing so good. They are running low on resources and have way too many mouths to feed. William hasn't responded to their messages. Says it'll take a bit of time before he can get out here."

"I'll see what I can do." I don't bother to tell him that leading the Resistance means William probably has a lot more on his mind than making sure every town and city has enough to get them through the upcoming winter.

He nods. "I know you want to stay out of Resistance affairs, but they're hurting. I don't want them doing anything desperate."

I know what he means. Vulnerable towns will turn to just about anyone to stay afloat. If the NAF manages to collect enough small towns across the wastelands, they might be able to gain enough ground to consider total control. "I'll try to figure something out. I'll even stop by myself." My jaw instinctively tightens at the thought of Pierre surrendering to the military. I know from my time in the war that the Resistance can't afford to lose any more ground.

"Thanks, Dani. It means a lot."

"Send word if you see or hear anything new."

"Same goes for you."

I let go of the reins and pat the horse as George gives it a little kick. "Keep these people safe. They're depending on you," he says as he rides away.

I rest my hand on the pistol strapped to my thigh. I glance behind me at Jack watching from within the walls. I have a feeling my happy, peaceful little world is about to be upended. I just hope I have enough fight left in me to get us all through the approaching storm.

❖

I push the intricate waves of wires into the curved metal casing and snap it closed, dropping it to the workbench and picking up the next one. The wires dangle loosely from within. I use my thumbs to press them within the shell and weave them along the curved metal compartment.

I knew this day would come. It had to. The NAF could only be content with controlling the east for so long before pushing more forces this way. It's been years since the gray coats have attacked this far west. We all have my father to thank for that. I know that, according to him, Lucas and I were his proudest achievements, but in my eyes, his greatest contribution was keeping the Resistance alive and the wastelands protected.

And now it seems pushing them out of the Badlands has been nothing but a temporary hold on their expansion. A damn adhesive bandage on a freaking bullet hole. General Turner's vision of a NAF-controlled nation is coming to fruition. It's only a matter of time before she's within striking distance of my home.

So now, it looks like I have a choice. I can stay and hope they pass our little town without incident and stand idly by as they torch noncompliant cities around us, or I can go out and meet up with the Resistance. Maybe try to keep them at bay a little longer, just like my father did.

The idea of picking up where he left off leaves a bitter taste in my mouth. I've been down that road, and it almost killed me. Not really looking to get back to that.

I toss the metal frame on the workbench and pick up the small circuit board. I lock it into place within one of the metal circular frames and connect two ends of the wires. Mindlessly, I work, attaching circuit boards to transmitters and connecting wires to batteries. My hands move without thought as I try to analyze the fight coming our way.

Meeting the NAF halfway is as good as useless if they really are coming out this way to take control. There are a handful of old bases and loyalist friendly cities the NAF could expand to, but without knowing for sure where they are headed, it's just a pointless guessing game. We don't have enough organized fighters out here in the wastelands to spread out and block every major city. Most people outside of White River aren't fully trained, at least not for all-out war.

The fighters these cities and towns have are better suited for a quick raider attack than long drawn-out war. And pulling anyone capable of firing a gun would just leave their homes exposed.

I run my hand through my hair and let out a long breath. Unless William brings men with him out west, the Resistance has virtually no presence here, and I really have no idea what he has planned.

Knowing that General Turner is closing in and ordering her troops to take down cities leaves an uneasy feeling in the pit of my stomach. I've made some pretty reckless choices in the past, choices that have hurt the ones I love. I need to be careful this time and not rush off into battle. I can't let Judith Turner coax me back in. Not when I plan to stick around long enough to make sure my friends stay safe.

That leaves me with only one choice: hope that they pass us by long enough to figure out just what the hell the Resistance has planned to stop them.

I really need to get a message to William.

The door to my shed opens, and light spills in, illuminating my overly cluttered workbench. I stay hunched over my project and pull the lantern on my desk closer so I can attach a particularly small shred of wire to the motherboard with my needle-nose pliers.

Rhiannon pulls up a stool and holds out a plate, warily eyeing my work. "I thought you might be hungry."

"Thanks." I take the plate, looking at the sandwich resting in the middle. She's cut it in half. I smile and push aside the scrap metal and wires so I can place it on the workbench.

She tenses. "Nothing is going to blow, is it?" I arch a brow in her direction. "Seriously, nothing is going to explode? It makes me so nervous how many explosives you tinker with just for fun."

"It's not for fun," I tell her, holding up my latest creation. Currently, it looks like half a metal doughnut with wires dangling from within. "These might come in handy sooner than you think."

She looks from the object to my eyes as if not convinced in the slightest. "There are no explosives in them yet," I tell her with a sigh. "You're fine."

"Are you okay?" she asks, seemingly coming to the conclusion that my shed will not explode.

I pick up half the sandwich and take a large bite. "Fantastic," I tell her when I'm finished chewing. She gives me a wary look, and I flash her a smile. "So what's going on between you and Jack? Things getting serious?"

She is so caught off guard that the shock on her face is almost comical. "What? No. Nothing is going on. Nothing serious."

"Sure doesn't seem like nothing." The blush on her face deepens, and she looks away. "Once you strip away the mohawk and the crude comments, he really is a pretty decent guy."

Rhiannon groans. "Dani…"

"And he's pretty good in the sack. From what I hear. Not that I know from experience," I quickly add. I shiver with disgust just thinking about it. He is absolutely not my type.

She turns to look at me, her face completely serious…and a little bit mortified. "Could you not?"

I put the plate beside me and sigh. "Everyone deserves a little intimacy."

"Please drop it."

"Okay, okay." I let her off the hook this time. Mainly because she brought me a sandwich. But the look on her face makes it clear she has no intention of telling me anything anyway. I take her hand, squeezing it lightly. "I think whatever it is between you and Jack is great. I just want you to be happy, you know."

Rhiannon squeezes back. "I am happy," she says, gazing at our hands. I've seen the look before, and I know she's wrestling with something. Her eyebrows get all bunched up, and she chews on her lip. Her tells are obvious. "Any news about Jess?"

Of course that's what she wants to know. I carefully remove my hand and reach for my sandwich. I did start it. I teased her about Jack. Payback is a bitch. "Just that she's interested in a boy."

Rhiannon waits for me to elaborate. Despite the careful planning she puts into it, it still pisses me off how she tiptoes around the issue all the time. I choose to stay silent. "Do you want to talk about it?"

I give her a sharp look. "Why the hell would I want to talk about it?"

I shove the rest of the halved sandwich in my mouth and pretend not to notice her staring. But hey, if she gets to shut down about Jack, I get to do the same about Jess. She gives me this sad look but sighs and wisely changes the subject. "Is the NAF really heading this way?"

"I don't think they're just headed this way," I say regretfully. "I think they're already here."

"What?"

I show her the button. "I found this in the warehouse yesterday. Along with a provisions wrapper."

Rhiannon stares at the shiny object for a long beat. "And you think they're going to come here? Is that why you're adamantly working on all this?" She motions to my workbench.

I know she's waiting to see how I respond before deciding for herself. She's a lot like a little kid in that way. As long as I'm calm, she's calm. And we could really use a calm Rhiannon right about now. The last thing this town needs is a rattled Rhiannon serving them food and going on about how the NAF is due to arrive and burn everything to the ground. But outright lying to her is next to impossible. She knows me too well.

I take another bite. "They might."

"Are you worried?"

I shrug. "Not yet."

She sits up straighter and lifts her chin proudly. "Then neither am I."

I finish my sandwich in silence, both of us just looking at the disassembled explosives scattered around my shed. Rhiannon is the best person in my life next to Lucas. If anything ever happened to her, I'd be lost. She filled a hole in my life that I didn't even realize existed. Almost like a younger mother figure. Almost. I glance at the small pistol strapped to her hip. I frown. If anything does happen over the next few days, she'll need a lot more than that dinky-assed thing. I reach beside me and rest my hand on the spare shotgun I keep within grabbing distance. You don't need to be a good shot to take someone out with this thing.

I casually slide the much bigger gun across the bench. She glances at it and then up at me curiously. "Just in case," I tell her.

I think about the message I need to get to William as quickly as possible. Last I heard, he was still back east, out near Knoxville. Our normal courier isn't due back for another several days. My only option now is to send the kid from the next town over. He's typically only good for short runs in emergency situations. I wonder if he can be bribed into going that far east.

"Hey, Rhi, will you put together a travel bag of food and water?"

❖

By the time the sun sets and everyone is getting ready to settle in for the night, I'm putting the finishing touches on my quickly plotted plan.

"What do you have in that safe anyway?"

I look up, curious as to where the hell that question came from. Jack stands in my doorway and points at my hand. I realize then that I've been idly playing with the key I wear around my neck. The key to my safe. I quickly drop it. "Nothing for you."

He snorts and goes back to examining my map of the old United States. "How could anyone follow this shit?"

"Well, most people have half a brain. That helps," I tell him as I finish my letter to William.

"Ha. Ha." He turns away from the map and sits in the chair on the other side of the table and grabs the bottle of whiskey resting there. He pours himself a glass but doesn't drink it right away. Instead, he picks up one of my books off the shelf behind him and thumbs through it.

"They really did a number on this place, didn't they?" he asks. "Our ancestors, I mean. With the bombs and climate change and all that shit."

"Yeah, they did."

It looks as though he wants to say more but instead goes back to flipping through my book.

I finish the letter to William, telling him the news from George. I don't sign my name. Don't need to; he'll know who it's from the second he gets it. I fold it and place it inside another piece of paper and paste the ends of it together, finally marking the corner with a W. I hold the envelope out to Jack, and he snatches it and sticks it into his front vest pocket.

"Remember, get there, give the kid the letter, and get back," I tell him again. "Don't take one of the horses. Take one of the buggies. I need you to get there fast."

He nods. "And remember to warn them about the NAF. I've got this."

I give him a pointed look. "Jack, William has to get this letter. Make sure that kid gets there as fast as he can. Do whatever you need to do to make that happen. Even if that means giving him your buggy. Your gun. Your fucking mohawk. Anything. You got it?"

"Buggy and gun I can do. But the mohawk stays with me," he says, running a hand through the dark strip of hair running along the length of his otherwise bald head.

I grab the bag Rhiannon packed earlier and toss it at him. He catches it easily and peeks inside. "Do you remember the directions I gave you?"

"Right up here," he says, tapping the side of his head and continues to rummage through the bag. Seemingly satisfied with the amount of food, he clasps the bag closed and drops it in his lap.

I look at him sitting in the chair and feel guilty for sending him out alone. But I can count the amount of people I fully trust on one hand. Jack's on that hand. Nonetheless, I ask again, "You sure you can handle the trip alone?"

He grabs his rifle and nods. "I'm sure. If it's true and the NAF are really that close, then no one else should leave. Besides," he says flexing his arm and kissing his oversized bicep, "no one messes with these babies."

Despite the blatant reminder of his brute strength, he's right. I know he is. We need all the help we can get watching the town gates, and one person is a hell of a lot more stealthy than multiple. That doesn't mean I have to like it.

"Get a radio from Darby. And if you're not back by tomorrow night…"

He takes the glass from the table and knocks it back in one large gulp. He licks his lips and slams the glass down and stands, swinging the bag over his shoulder and gripping his rifle tightly. "I'll be back before breakfast," he says seriously. "Now out of my way, Clark. I'm losing moonlight."

❖

Loud banging wakes me. I glance around my darkened room and try to get my bearings. It takes me a few seconds to remember where I am. Bringing the heel of my hand up to rub at my eyes, I try to push away the grogginess throughout my body. I must've fallen asleep sometime after Jack left.

Grabbing the radio, I wonder if that's what woke me. But it's silent.

The banging continues. I reach for the pistol under my pillow and yawn as I make my way to the door. Releasing the latch and lock, I pull it open. The light in my face makes me squint. It's Mike holding up a lantern.

"You need to come see this." His face is stony. Intense.

Now alarmed, I grab my jacket and shrug it on as I follow Mike past the hill, near the front gate, up to the crow's nest. Lucas is already there, holding still as he looks out. We climb up the nest as quickly and quietly as we can.

Lucas is looking intently into the distance with his binoculars. I put my hand on his shoulder. If he's surprised, he doesn't show it. Instead, he pulls the binoculars down, hands them to me, and gives me a wary look. "Major Maelstrom knew nothing good could come of this," he says and points southeast of the town.

It only takes me a second to see what all the fuss is about. Little blobs of light in the distance, evenly spaced apart. "When did the fires go up?" I ask through clenched teeth.

"About two minutes ago. I came to wake you as soon as we saw them," Mike says.

I count four separate fires. It looks like a cozy little camp. "Did you tell anyone else?"

"Not yet." Mike looks out at the camp fires through his scope. "Think it's the NAF?"

"Could be."

"I thought the nearest military post was a few hundred miles away," Mike says. "What do you think they're doing this far out?"

What do I think they're doing here? Expanding. That's what I think. But I don't say that. Not yet. Instead, I remain silent as I think of our next steps.

I think of Jack heading in the opposite direction, thankful he doesn't have to skirt around the camp. It's a good thing he went. At least we can let the people across town know that something is definitely out there. And that they're close.

Mike looks up from his rifle. "What do we do?"

I stare at the tiny specks of campfires through the binoculars and take a deep breath. "We wait."

# CHAPTER THREE: THE ATTACK

## *Dani*

The fires burned through the night. The embers and smoke trails spiral upward in the morning sky. Dark shapes slowly move in our direction, hazy silhouettes against the barren land. It isn't long before they emerge from the gray, and we see that they are, in fact, NAF. Their uniforms are as unmistakable as they are identifiable. I count twenty or so.

"There aren't a lot of them," Mike says. "Definitely not an attacking unit. What I don't understand is, why are they on foot? Why would infantry be this far from their base?" He discards his gum into a wrapper and opens a new piece to chew.

I groan internally at having to listen to his smacking again. "They wouldn't." George said the soldiers had buggies. These guys definitely do not. "I'm thinking the storm a few days ago got 'em. It took out some of their men, probably their vehicles, too. I think they're wandering around lost and trying to get back on track."

"They hoard all the tech in the country, and you mean to tell me they don't have *one* working compass?" Mike says. I don't blame him for the scoff that follows.

"We might never know what really happened," I say. It's a frustrating reality of a never-ending war. Some things always remain a mystery, for better or worse.

"It's been a while since we had to defend this place against anything other than the occasional raider. Do you think they'll try to attack?" His gum pops in his mouth.

"Doubtful, but twenty or so gray coats is enough to be a real pain in our ass. One thing's for sure," I tell him as my stomach drops with anticipation, "they're heading this way. We're the only lush piece of land this far from the river." I lower the binoculars and try to gauge their distance.

"You call this lush?" Mike looks around the great expanse of dirt in front of our little town and the sparse smattering of trees near the back.

"We have a water source, don't we?" I motion behind me to the small lake just beyond the fence. "The rest of the river flows miles from here. If they are hurting for water, they're going to look for green, and we're it."

He looks down at the townspeople. Many of them have pistols strapped to their waists or rifles on their backs. Always ready to defend the town and their families despite living in a pretty secluded area. He's no different from the rest of them. As our best sharpshooter, Mike offers a layer of comfort and always has a weapon ready to go.

"I don't think they'll attack," I say finally. There aren't enough of them. In my experience, the NAF don't usually start a fight they can't finish. "We'll probably have to feed and quarter them for a day or two. Worst-case until the next storm passes."

"Until the next storm passes? We don't know when the next one will hit," he says loudly. "Do we have to comply? Our people aren't going to want to see the NAF eating our food, drinking our water, and staying in our homes. No one here wants anything to do with them or their aid. We don't need it. We're self-sufficient and doing just fine."

Our eyes meet, and I tilt my head at him. He's arguing a point I already know. "It's their law, Mike. Something they enforce everywhere they go. It doesn't matter to them if we want them to or not. If we deny them, they can come back and blow our town out of existence. And they have the numbers to enforce it. Not in the group headed this way, but knowing the NAF, there are far more troops not far behind. If they communicate to anyone else that we didn't comply, we should go ahead and dig our own graves."

We may not follow their laws out here, but if they're knocking on our doors, it'd be stupid not to tread lightly.

"They wouldn't do that," Mike says weakly, as if asking me more than telling.

"Tell that to Hot Springs," I mumble. I don't tell him they'll probably be back regardless if we cater to their every whim. I've seen it happen. Now that they know where we are, they'll most definitely be back one way or another.

"What's to stop them from burning our town if we help them or not?"

"Nothing," I answer honestly. "Look, we can go that route if we want. Aid, no aid, ultimately, it's up to the council to vote on these kinds of decisions. But none of that will matter if they have already communicated their location and then end up dead." Mike seems to take this into consideration. "Go tell Rhiannon to make sure she has enough food and water for twenty men. And then go make sure Elise is ready in the clinic. It's a safe bet that someone is going to need medical attention." Lucas scans the opposite direction of the incoming NAF. "Lucas, stay here and keep watch. Sound the alarm if anything changes."

I barely have time to get the words before he turns frantically.

"The Tanker approaches, ready to fight," he shouts. He points. Just over the hill in the distance, a lone rider is galloping in our direction.

It takes me a minute to figure out who it is until I see the mohawk. Jack clearly traded the buggy to get the message to William faster, but by the way he's pushing the horse, something isn't right. Especially since he didn't radio any sort of warning.

"Open the gate," I yell to the guards below, leaving Lucas in the watchtower as I slide down the ladder.

Jack doesn't slow until he's within the walls, and even then, he's dismounting before coming to a stop. The gate slams shut as a precaution, and he tries desperately to catch his breath. "We've got problems," he says, wiping the sweat from his eyes. "I gave my buggy to the kid."

"I can see that. What happened to radioing?" I place my hand on his shoulder, trying to calm him.

"Gave him that, too." He puts his hands on his knees.

I give him a moment. "We know the NAF is headed this way. We counted about twenty."

"What?" He looks surprised and shakes his head. "No. Raiders."

I grab my pistol. Looks like there will be a fight today after all. "From where?"

He points in the direction he just came from. "I lured them away from the kid so he could take the buggy and get away with your letter.

He'll radio once it's delivered. Only problem is, now they're on their way here after me." He looks at me gravely. "And they're closing in fast. It's a big group."

"A new enemy arises," Lucas calls from the watchtower, confirming Jack's account.

Raiders coming from the west and the NAF coming from the east. My mind races to come up with some kind of plan. "Go get some water," I tell him calmly. "Catch your breath and get ready. I'm gonna need you out here."

He nods and looks around at the people gathering to see what the hell is going on. "Should I sound the alarm?"

"No. The NAF will hear it. It might put them on the defensive before they even reach us. I'm banking on them asking for food and quarter, so I don't want them coming in hot for a fight." I glance at the people starting to gather. Some are watching us curiously, while others are pacing anxiously. "After you get some water, make sure the kids are someplace safe and tell everyone loitering to be ready. Round up the fighters. I don't think the NAF will be trouble, but I don't want the little ones running around in case I'm wrong."

With a quick nod, Jack races off.

By the time Mike comes back to the watchtower, my mind is already playing out every scenario I can think of. Quickly, we climb back up.

"Elise is ready in medical," he says. He lifts his rifle and checks out the situation through his scope. "How are we holding?"

"Steady," I tell him.

"What are your orders, General? Maelstrom stands ready." Lucas looks at me expectantly.

My eyes dart frantically from one group to the next, and adrenaline courses through me as I carefully calculate the angle at which they are both approaching. I lick my lips. "We need to be prepared for a fight, but in the meantime, everyone stay put behind the walls."

We watch for a few moments while Jack rounds everyone up. Mike shifts anxiously while Lucas and I remain still, observing both groups. It's not our first time waiting out a situation and playing it by ear. It's been years since I've been on the outskirts of a fight of this magnitude, but my body remembers.

Patiently, I watch as anticipation flows through my veins. An old feeling overcomes me. The thrill for a fight that I've been suppressing for a long time.

It isn't long before the NAF is within firing range of the raiders. Even from this distance, I hear the pop of gunfire. There isn't much cover where both groups meet, only a lot of dirt and a few rusted cars. But even those seem out of reach. The NAF are smarter, trained, and much better equipped to fight from a distance. They try to pick off as many raiders as they can before it comes down to hand to hand.

"Do you see any radios?" I ask.

"No," Mike says looking through his rife.

Lucas shakes his head and hands me the binoculars.

"Our fighters are coming," Jack says, stepping up beside me. His sunglasses are on, and he's armed to the teeth. He has a rifle strapped around his chest, a pistol holstered snugly inside his shoulder harness, and a grenade belt filled with explosives. Impressive.

A slight breeze sweeps across, bringing with it the sounds of battle. Despite being pulled back and out of my face, my hair whips around me as I bring the binoculars up to my eyes.

The guns from the NAF continue to pop; the occasional spray of machine gun bursts fills the silence. Several raiders fall, unable to escape the smattering of bullets.

The NAF started this fight with the upper hand, but they are about to lose it as the raiders close in. They are skilled with brute force and primal weapons. They are fearless and ruthless, and it's wise not to engage them in hand to hand. But the NAF can't reach the only source of cover, so they have no other choice but to do the best they can with their ranged weapons.

It's terrifying how much these raiders are more animal than human. Somewhere along the way, their wires got crossed. They're mindless, merciless killers motivated only by shiny things and body counts. They sniff out vulnerability and use it for torture. There's no doubt in my mind that they'll come for us next, even if the odds are against them. Fighting, killing, and stealing is all they know.

I scan them for any kind of communication devices, but it's hard to tell with all their movement. The NAF shifts into the same smartly calculated patterns and small-band formations that I remember. But I can tell by the way they're spacing out their shots that they're low on ammo. And in the wasteland, where ammo is a premium, running out is a death sentence.

Roscoe barks below. I tear my binoculars away and look over the edge. He barks wildly at the tower as if lecturing me.

"So now what?" I turn to see Rhiannon standing on my other side, gripping the shotgun I gave her.

"Rhiannon, what the hell are you doing up here?"

She pries her eyes away from the battle and pins me with a scathing look. "Don't you dare tell me to get someplace safe, Danielle Clark. This is my town, my home, and I'll be damned if I'm going to hole up somewhere and prepare food while you are all out here fighting."

Roscoe continues to bark, and I motion to him as I try to control the irritation boiling inside me. Between his barking and Rhiannon wanting to play soldier, I am about at my tipping point. "You mind telling your dog it wasn't my idea for you to be up here?"

"Roscoe," Rhiannon yells. "Hush."

"Even he doesn't want you up here," I snap. All I get is a glare in response. "Fine, if you want something to do, round up the council. Get the elders together. If the NAF survive against the raiders, we're going to be their next target." She starts to protest, but I cover her mouth. "Not a word. Round up the council or I lock you in your tavern."

She rolls her eyes. "Fine," she says, despite my hand still over her mouth.

I place my hand back on the grip of my pistol and look at the battle. Both sides continue to drop at a rapid pace. That's the thing about combat. The buildup is huge; the actual fight is short and swift.

There is one soldier in particular that catches my attention, even from this distance. Grabbing the binoculars, I watch as the only woman remaining fires her pistol.

My grip tightens on the binoculars, and my heart starts racing. The ranking on her uniform catches my eye…it can't be this easy. I pull the lenses away and watch for a few seconds while my mind runs rampant. Not aiding an officer is worse than neglecting a common foot soldier. Is that what Hot Springs did before they were burned to the ground? Not to mention that a commanding officer of her rank would be privy to more than just standard need-to-know information. That much insider knowledge sitting on our doorstep is too good an opportunity to pass up.

"We're going out," I say, placing the binoculars on the ledge.

"What?" Rhiannon asks. "Why?"

"Because there's a commanding NAF officer out there. And I want her alive," I tell her simply. "And why are you still up here?"

"Have you lost your mind?" Rhiannon asks. The gunfire continues from the battlefield. "You're not going to let this take care of itself?"

The temptation to watch them kill one another is tempting. "Look," I say, itching to get down there. "If they live, and we stood by and did nothing to help, well, that doesn't look so good." She doesn't seem convinced. "Something big is happening, Rhi," I tell her honestly. "And I want to find out what it is. In order to do that, I need to try to extract some information from the source. And out there"—I point to the fight—"is a commanding officer. Do you know how big that is?"

"You want to question them," Jack says.

"An officer of that rank this far out can only mean one of a couple things. Primarily, setting up a new base. Don't you want to know where? Don't you want to know how close they are?"

"The Resistance would know. William would know." Jack says.

"The Resistance isn't here. And we can't wait for them to come." My tone is sharp, but I don't have time to convince them or to make them understand. "This fight is here and now."

Rhiannon shakes her head. "Dani, I don't think this is a good idea."

"Please, just get the council together. Tell them we need to meet," I beg, ignoring the protests and growing more impatient by the second. "And you." I grab the front of Mike's shirt so I know he's listening. "You're our eyes. Take care of the raiders. No NAF. Keep that blond officer alive. Got it?"

Mike looks startled as he clutches his sniper rifle. He doesn't take his eyes off mine as he nods.

"Raiders only. Keep the officer alive," I repeat.

"Keep the officer alive," he says back to me.

Satisfied, I turn to Lucas. "Stay inside the gates. Get some wrist ties ready for whoever we bring in. They aren't going to like our welcome, but there's no way the council will let them wander about without some restrictions." I point at the tattoo on his forearm. "And get that covered." I wait until he nods and slides down the ladder, Jack and I following.

There are thirty or so fighters gathered along the inside of the gate. Other townspeople rush for cover, and Rhiannon runs to gather the elders. Satisfied that things are going according to plan, I face the fighters.

I motion to half of them. "This group, stay inside the gates. We're going to need you here if things don't go according to plan. The rest of you, come with me. There's an officer out there, and I want to bring her in."

"It's raider killing time," Jack chimes in happily.

"Don't fire unless I tell you," I say, "but stay alert. There's no telling what could happen. The goal is to bring the NAF in alive. But *don't fire* unless I give the order. Everyone understand?"

I wait until everyone acknowledges, and I motion to head out. I fasten the buttons of my long-sleeved shirt at the wrists to cover my own tattoo as the gates open.

Carefully, we approach the dwindling battle, the remaining fighters in an even smaller group. In my periphery, I see my people raise their guns as we advance. Jack trips over some debris but quickly regains his balance and plays it off like nothing happened. I roll my eyes.

We're less than fifty meters from the remains of the fight. Neither the NAF nor the raiders seem to notice or care. Bodies lie everywhere. Over a dozen military and even more from the horde. The stench of death floats in the air. I pull my scarf over my face, and the others do the same.

Another breeze floats by, bringing the sharp scent of blood and the harsh smell of gunpowder. My body reacts as if awakened from a deep sleep. I grip my pistol, flexing my fingers through my gloves. The adrenaline I'd almost forgotten pumps through my veins as I watch another raider fall.

A few desperate gunshots ring through the air, and another soldier falls. There's a loud, guttural cry as his body crashes to the ground.

We step carefully, slowly, and I motion with my pistol in both directions to fan out. As we close in on the groups, something catches my eye.

Two towering raiders rush for the officer. She's much smaller than them. I watch with fascination as she fights them off. Sweat drips down her face, and she readjusts her grip on her combat dagger as she takes a moment to regroup before lunging. Her hand is crimson with blood. It's clear she's killed a few with the lone weapon, and she wields it expertly.

They're getting frustrated with how easily she dodges their attacks. The bigger of the two lunges with his own knife. She ducks effortlessly, almost lazily, to the side and drags her blade across the raider's throat. He drops to his knees. The second raider moves to tackle her while she's distracted. She shifts her weight to address his attack, but he's too fast, so she throws her arms out to try to keep him from toppling her.

A shot rings out. The raider falls. Mike. She barely glances around before steadying herself for the next bout.

The first attacker is still alive. Barely. He's lying on his back, one hand pressed tightly against his neck. With the other, he reaches for a pistol partially buried underneath one of the fallen raiders.

I frown. If he kills her, I'll never have a chance to question her. I square my shoulders and rush to step on his wrist, pinning it. I dig my heel into his skin. He releases the gun, wincing but unable to call out. I scoop up the pistol, continuing in the direction of the officer, and leave him to drown in his own blood.

Another fallen raider tries to scramble to his feet. I point the newly acquired pistol and pull the trigger. The raider falls back. Huh. Guess the gun wasn't empty after all. I motion for the rest of the group to close in, and within seconds, we have the survivors surrounded.

"Fire at will," I call.

In unison, my fighters take down the handful of remaining raiders, filling the air with gunfire and ending the fight within seconds. It takes one shot from my new pistol to pierce the skull of a raider closing in on the officer.

Without a moment's pause, she spins and faces me, the blade balanced between the ball of her thumb and forefinger. Ready to throw. But I have two pistols trained on her. She pauses.

Her hazel eyes meet mine, and for a moment, there is nothing but me and her. A showdown between guns and blades. The quiet takes over the battlefield, and I can sense everyone holding their breath as they wait to see how the standoff ends. My index fingers itch as I run them up and down the triggers.

I can tell she's debating who's the faster draw.

I can't help the small smirk tugging at my lips. "You might wanna drop that."

She glances over as her remaining comrades drop their weapons and seems to notice that they are surrounded, with more than a dozen guns aimed at them. Her eyes lock on me again. I can tell she's still considering throwing the knife anyway. I arch an eyebrow.

We both know bullets are faster than blades.

A moment passes.

A bird chirps overhead, and another breeze pushes through, kicking up the loose dirt. The surviving NAF are panting heavily, and Jack shifts from one foot to the other. Someone groans from the ground to my left.

Still, I wait for her to decide.

I can barely hear, "Fuck," as she drops the blade to the dirt.

"On your knees, princess," I say mockingly.

She snarls. There's no other word for it. I can tell she's not used to being in this position. The military is law, and I'm guessing she's not used to having someone else call the shots.

She glances at the remaining soldiers, all on their knees with their heads down and hands up. She clenches her teeth and slowly drops to her knees and wraps both hands behind her head, the blood on them staining her long blond hair orange.

"That's a good girl," I say with a condescending smile. I can tell she wants to say something by the way her eyes burn a hole through my head. "If they move, shoot 'em," I say calmly.

I don't take my eyes off hers as she's yanked to her feet. The name embroidered on the front of her gray uniform jacket makes my palms sweat and my heart race. Her eyes are unwavering and a little unnerving as she stares back at me.

I smile before I can stop myself. Your move, General Turner. I have your daughter.

# CHAPTER FOUR: THE OFFICER

## *Kate*

Without my sunglasses, the sun is utterly blinding. I have to squint to look up at our captors. At *her*. Even with the scarf, I can tell she's pleased.

My knees dig into the dirt, and my fingers are laced behind my neck. They are coated with blood and stick to my hair. The rest of my group is positioned the same way as these people figure out what to do with us.

I look away first, only to assess the situation.

There are only four of us on our knees.

My eyes meet my warrant officer's, and I release a breath. He's pretty banged up: a bloody nose, a black eye, blood dripping from his temple. He looks just as relieved to see me as his dark eyes quickly dart up and down my frame. I know without asking that he's looking for injuries.

I glance at the grisly scene around us. Most of my people are dead. But there are so many bodies, I can't be sure who's dead or who may be wounded and in need of help. I should be checking on the fallen. I should be tending to the wounded. I should be combing the dozens of bodies for survivors. But instead, I'm staring at the barrel of a pistol pointed directly at my face.

I should ask them to check. Demand that the wounded be taken to whatever passes for a town doctor here. But quite frankly, I'm not sure it matters much. From the gathering of sidearms and the hostile looks from the civilians, I'm not sure any of us are going to survive.

A barking dog pulls my attention. A scruffy-looking black and white thing sprints toward us, its ears upright but bent and flopping with each stride. It's surreal, really. Here we are, on our knees, surrounded by people who may have saved us just to kill us later, with the birds chirping overhead and a dog barking in the distance. I would laugh if I wasn't so irritated.

"Check for survivors," the woman with the red-tinted sunglasses says. She's completely unfazed by the dog. She doesn't take her eyes off me. "NAF only."

I glance at the civilians who check on my soldiers while completely bypassing the raiders and finishing off any who are still fighting death. The dog seems to join in, inspecting each and every person. I hold my breath as I watch them go from body to body.

I make sure my gaze doesn't stray from the woman in charge, showing that despite her pistol in my face, I'm not intimidated. I try to soak in as much information about her as possible. The way she carries herself. The orders she gives. The tone of her voice.

A long moment passes before the dog wags its tail happily over one of my soldiers. It then moves on, only to stop once more, barking wildly. At the end of the search, two, only two, of my soldiers get picked up and carried away. The dirt where they have been lying is soaked with red.

"Take what you can off the bodies," the woman says, barely turning her head to bark the order. "Then burn the dead."

She looks to me as if expecting a reaction. I merely lift my chin. I will not let her get a read on me.

"Take them in," she says.

A tank of a man with a short black mohawk lifts me to my feet. His dark skin is covered in tattoos. He shoves me forward, and it takes all the poise I have not to trip over my combat boots. My soldiers are also yanked to their feet. The woman in charge hangs back to have a few words with her people and then calls the dog as they all follow us inside.

Within the walls, it seems like the majority of the town has gathered, slowly exiting buildings, curiosity seeming to get the better of everyone. Soon, the townspeople stand close together, five or six rows deep.

They arrange us in a line, not quite shoulder to shoulder, and force us back down on our knees. For a moment, I think they are going to execute us right then and there, making a public display of it. My jaw tightens, and my shaky hands betray my attempt at blind bravery as fear consumes me. I don't know much about what's happening, but I do know that I'm not ready to die today.

I scan the area. It's pretty well-fortified, considering they're just about in the middle of a Brown Zone. The town isn't huge, but it isn't quaint either, most definitely a town and not a combat outpost despite the dozen or so guards. They aren't a full-fledged Resistance settlement, but their weapons are impressive. Their perimeter is secure, and they have two watchtowers, one by the front gate and another in the back. I look for the leader, there's always a leader, when my eyes fall on the woman who gave the orders outside.

Her arms are crossed, and she's talking to the meathead with the mohawk. They seem to be arguing in low tones, probably about what to do with us. Interesting. It appears she doesn't just control the guards but possibly the entire town. And even more interesting, it doesn't seem as if the decision to bring us in was discussed much prior to the action.

I take the opportunity to check my soldiers. My people are pretty beat up and dirty but otherwise appear to be fine. To my left is Ryan, my warrant officer. He motions with his head to the woman in charge, and I give a slight shrug. His eyes flick upward to the guard tower on our six. A sniper has a rifle on us. We've been together long enough for me to know what he's trying to say: play it safe, we're outnumbered. Agreeing, I nod past him at Simon Alexander, our corporal wildcard, and give Ryan a pointed look. We both know Simon is itching to make a move.

Ryan mumbles to Simon under his breath. Even from here, I can feel the anger radiating off Simon. I don't have to warn Miguel on my right. His head is lowered, and his eyes are closed. I can see his lips moving, and I know he's uttering a prayer.

When I turn, the dog is sitting in front of me, staring. I sit up a bit straighter, and it tilts its head as if intrigued. I'm usually a dog person, but the way this particular dog is looking at me, as if it can't make up its mind about what it wants to do with me, has me unnerved.

A minute later, Mohawk is back in front of us. He has plastic ties in his hands. Fantastic. I know where this is going.

He jerks my hands from atop my head and twists my arms behind my back, slapping the plastic restraints around my wrists and pulling them forcefully.

He leans in close. "Is that too tight?"

"A little," I admit.

I imagine him sneering. "Good."

He pulls the binds tighter, and I feel as if they are going to cut through my skin. He walks in front of me, and I lift my eyes. He's smirking.

"Thanks," I tell him through clenched teeth.

He does the same to the rest of my soldiers.

The silence that stretches across the town is deafening. I've changed my mind. The fear I felt before at the possibility of being murdered has all but evaporated, and now I'm ready to put up a fight.

Just as I'm about to push and pull for freedom, the shadow of my captor falls over me, blocking out the sun. I don't have to squint to see her now. She's wearing a tan, long-sleeved shirt tucked into fitted brown pants and heavy black boots that come up to mid-calf. Her brown hair is pulled back, and she has red-mirrored sunglasses over her eyes. The maroon scarf covering her face and neck is still in place, hiding the rest of her features. She has a darker complexion than me, closer to that of Miguel. Her pistols are holstered at her thighs, and a shotgun peeks out over her shoulder. She stands with confidence bordering on arrogance with her arms crossed, fingerless gloves covering her hands. She's intimidating, but there's something intriguing about her. A quiet assurance that seems to radiate from her being.

I wonder how many weapons she has stashed on her body.

Her arms stay crossed as she looks us over. All eyes are on her, making it pretty clear that she's calling the shots. No pun intended.

I wait for her to make a move before I decide how I want to handle this. It seems as though all my decisions of late haven't worked out in my favor. This time, I'm playing it safe. Everyone seems to be holding perfectly still, holding their breath as they wait for her to speak, to give some sort of instruction.

Only, she never does.

Instead, one of mine breaks the silence.

"Killing a member of the NAF is punishable by death," Corporal Simon Alexander spits out, shattering the quiet. "We radioed ahead.

Reinforcements are on their way." The utter definition of an oxygen thief, he never is one to keep his mouth shut. The only one who should be addressing these people is the brass, his ranking officer, and that would be me.

Instead of scolding him, I watch their leader carefully, curious about her response.

She and Mohawk share a disbelieving look. Then she turns to Simon and regards him carefully. "We didn't kill your colleagues. The raiders did," she finally says.

"Red on red, then," I say. She faces me and offers a little shrug.

"You left us there to die," Simon continues through clenched teeth. "That's the same as a death sentence."

I can't see her smile, but I can definitely hear it. "On the contrary. We saved you."

"Tying us up and holding us hostage—"

"Is not punishable by death," she says. "As long as we treat you humanely and give you food and quarter, there is nothing in your law that states we are to be punished." She's right, and I'm impressed. Not many people this far west know and obey the national law. Especially the loopholes within it. "As for the reinforcements, well, I don't think I believe that at all."

Simon singlehandedly overplayed our hand right from the start. It's only a matter of time before they realize there are no radios. I want to strangle him. I know he is seething, too. Nothing gets under his skin more than being outsmarted. And, unfortunately for us, it happens quite often.

"Not yet," he fires back. "But when the general hears about this, you will pay with your lives."

"Shut up, Simon." Ryan's closely shaved blond hair looks orange with all the blood smeared across his head. He sways slightly, unable to hold his upright position.

"Don't tell me to shut up."

Mohawk and their leader exchange amused glances. This is clearly going in their favor.

"They will find us, and they will kill you all," Simon continues. "Do you even realize who—"

"Corporal," I yell. "Silence. That's an order."

Their leader looks at me. With her eyes and face covered, it's hard to guess what she's thinking. But from the way her gaze stays on me, she must be processing the exchange.

"Separate them," she says. "Make sure our guests are comfortable. They're gonna be around for a while." A few of the guards make to grab us, and their leader motions to me. "Take this one to the main holding cell."

Mohawk grabs my arms and lifts. "On your feet."

We are all yanked upward, and I notice movement to my left. I turn just as Simon headbutts a guard in the face, making him cry out and stumble backward while reaching for his nose.

Ryan looks at me, and I shake my head. If Simon wants to get himself killed, then so be it, but I'm not making more trouble for us by interfering. Not yet. I want to see how this plays out.

Before Simon has a chance at another move, someone else steps forward and jams the barrel of a rifle against his stomach. Weapons are drawn, and several angry people, including the now bleeding civilian, surround Simon. With a growl, the dog rushes forward, positioning itself to pounce.

The leader hasn't moved except to uncross her arms and rest her hand on the grip of one of her holstered pistols.

The one with the rifle squints at Simon and shoves the barrel deeper into his stomach. "Sir, I am a genetically altered superhuman with over thirty years' military experience. What hope do you have by drawing on me first?"

"Pull the trigger, Captain Jack," Simon dares.

Ryan stumbles forward. He looks pale, and sweat drips down the side of his face. He looks as if he's struggling to keep his eyes open and sways drastically. The guard catches him and pulls him upright.

My stomach drops. No. No, not Ryan. Please, not Ryan, not like this. "Help him," I beg, hoping my desperation appeals to the leader.

Simon and the guard stop struggling as I attempt to twist out of Mohawk's tight grasp. Mohawk pulls me harder and traps me against his large chest. My eyes remain on the leader.

Her hand casually draped over her firearm, she studies me for a moment, unmoving. I would curse myself for such an emotional outburst if I wasn't so concerned for Ryan. I can't lose him. Not like this. Not after all we've been through.

"Get him to the medic," she finally says.

I release a shaky breath as Ryan is taken away by two men. I want to follow. I want to yell out orders to make sure he's the priority. Demand to know who will be caring for him and their medical standards. But I squelch the urge and grind my jaw tightly to keep from speaking. I've already shown too much emotion.

When I look back to the leader, she's still eyeing me. After a moment, she nods at Mohawk. He grabs my arms roughly and pushes me forward. I don't take my eyes off her, taking in all I can: the way she observes everything, her casual stance, the arrogance in her posture. I wonder who she is behind the sunglasses and scarf.

I'm marched down the street, vaguely aware of Simon and Miguel being led in opposite directions. I don't bother asking where they are being taken. I know I won't get an answer. Instead, I focus on my surroundings.

The buildings are in pretty decent shape, not what I expected way out here in the wastelands. The people who watch as I'm paraded down the street don't seem to be impoverished like we were led to believe. In fact, they look happy and healthy, if not incredibly indifferent.

I see yards with livestock, a large barn, and a warehouse-type building. There are rows of houses and even businesses: a blacksmith, a seamstress, a carpenter. Children are slowly coming out, curious. Dogs and cats wander the streets. It's a good-sized town, not nearly as large as the cities back east where I spent most of my life but nothing to easily dismiss either.

Many people carry weapons, but they don't appear to be Resistance. There are no uniforms, and no one is training. They don't seem to be infantry either. As for the tall wooden fence, there are no breaches as far as I can tell, though I'd like to check the edges for a point of weakness.

I predict that it will be easy to spot the guards within the watchtowers at the edges of town. I don't see any spotlights, which means an escape would be best during the night.

The dog from earlier trots happily beside me. This entire place catches me completely off guard. It's like a snapshot from the past. A fully functioning town with pets and businesses and no visible need for assistance.

We stop at an old building standing between what may be two large supply sheds. Mohawk unlocks the door and pushes it open, leading me inside. He shoves me into the single room and directs me to sit on a squeaky cot on the far wall. I sit as best as I can with my hands behind my back and hear him pulling on thick, metal chains.

Is this where the town drunkards go to sleep off inebriated and disruptive behavior? Or is where thieves or troublemakers are held for punishment?

Mohawk closes a metal band tightly around my ankle, chaining me to the ground. I give it a tug, testing. It may not be a jail cell per se, but I'm definitely locked up in this single room. It's not unlike the CCF's back home. I served in the Correctional Confinement Facility once due to a Field Grade Article Fifteen. It was stupid, really. I was out past curfew one too many times and as a result, got twenty days in what every soldier calls Charlie's Chicken Farm. Needless to say, my mother was not pleased, and it didn't happen again.

I tug on my restraints once more.

"Don't waste your energy," Mohawk says. "You're not going anywhere."

He cuts the ties on my wrists. I bring my hands in front of me and rub at the indents, soothing where the plastic cut into my skin.

"Enjoy your stay," he mocks and dangles the key in front of my face. He lights a single lantern across the room and leaves. I look at the pillow-less cot and groan. At least there's an extra blanket. Taking off my jacket uniform and tossing it on the cot, I untuck my shirt and use it to wipe my face. If I'm in the jail, where the hell are my soldiers?

I sit on the edge of the cot and stare at the single high window across the room. I'm worried about Ryan and how they're tending to him. I'm worried about Miguel and how he's handling the stress. I worry about the others undergoing medical treatment for wounds that could be fatal. I worry what Simon will do if left alone.

"Shit." I groan in frustration and run my still bloody hands through my hair, wincing as they snag.

How the hell am I going to handle this? Even extensive training only gets you so far. And when you're the one weaponless and being held prisoner, the first step is to wait for reinforcements. Well, I don't know if that's even a possibility at this point. Step two is to formulate a plan. What that plan may be, I have no idea. It was pretty clear even to our captors that Simon was lying about the radio.

How am I going to get us out of this?

It's vital that I speak with the leader. She's smart, well versed in the law, and not at all intimidated by the National Armed Forces being inside her gates. In fact, she may even be enjoying it. She has the upper hand, and she knows it.

I scratch my hands. The blood has dried, making me itch, and I do my best to wipe it off on my pants, but it's no use. I need to think, and I start to pace as much as the chain around my leg allows.

Recalling my officer training, I go through different scenarios. The town is definitely secluded without any neighboring towns within sight. It's well-guarded and appears to be efficiently run and maintained. But who are these people? What's their affiliation? I'm pretty confident it's not the NAF, but they don't seem overly hostile either. They wouldn't have tended to the wounded if they were.

It's too soon to formulate a plan of action. Not with three of my soldiers injured and little to no information on the environment and landscape. I also need a better feel for our captors. Sighing, I tug on the chain. We were vastly unprepared. I pull the chain again, harder this time. I'm pissed off, trapped, and seemingly without options until someone returns.

I turn and lie down. A bit of rest can't hurt anything at this point.

❖

When I wake up, it takes my eyes some time to adjust. Light no longer pours through the windows, and the lantern does little to illuminate the entire room.

Swinging my feet off the cot, I push to a sitting position. I rub the crick out of the back of my neck and groan; the joints in my fingers are still stiff from the blood and grime.

I give my leg a tug and find that my ankle, unsurprisingly, is still bound by the chain attached to the floor. With a sigh, I look around the room, and there are two very noticeable changes.

First, someone's put a table by the cot. There's a sandwich and a glass of water resting neatly on a tray next to the lantern that has been moved closer. The condensation on the cup tells me the ice is just about melted, but it hasn't been sitting there long. My stomach rumbles in response.

The second is that my jacket is not where I left it. I hear movement on the other side of the room, and the hair on the back of my neck prickles.

Someone else is here. "Shit."

I'm surprised to find it's not Mohawk perched on the desk near the entrance, shrouded in darkness, but the town leader herself.

As if waiting for this cue, she strikes a match and lights a second lantern resting beside her. "I was beginning to think you were going to sleep through the night."

"You've got a rather large room for just one person," I say as casually as I can, as if I wasn't just seriously startled. She doesn't answer. She doesn't even look at me. Instead, she begins to polish the barrel of the sawed-off shotgun across her lap.

She has one leg dangling off the side of the metal desk, and the other foot is propped up on the arm of the chair. Her weapon is resting on her thigh as she concentrates; a toothpick juts loosely between her teeth.

Her hair is down. It's brown and wavy. She's shed the long-sleeved top for something lighter, cleaner. The sleeves are still long, but the top two buttons are casually undone, and her sunglasses are dangling from the V of her shirt.

It's hard to make out her face in the dim lighting, but her expression is focused, intentional. I wonder if she's part of the Resistance. It would explain her arrogant demeanor and combat skills. She's clearly not dumb. Separating us was a good idea. So was not leaving us unattended. Maybe she's ex-military? That would explain her knowing NAF law. I look at the tray, at the sandwich and water. Food, aid, and quarters.

If she's Resistance, then that complicates things even further. I'm even more surprised she didn't kill us on the spot. Is she keeping us here to hand over? Is she going to use us for ransom?

"How long?" She casually lays her shotgun across her other thigh, pointing it straight at me. "Until the battalion gets here?"

She's testing me. Checking to see if we radioed for backup. I see no point in lying, so I shrug. "There is no battalion."

It's the sad truth. No one is coming. We were fifty strong when we deployed. We weren't meant to engage. Our orders were to go from one location to the next. Bring supplies and expect to interact, ensure a peaceful transition of power, and not fight. That's all. I'm pretty sure she knows that, too. Another clue that she's in with the Resistance.

She looks at me curiously. She's young, maybe early thirties. Her eyes are light, piercing, and in stark contrast to her tanned skin. Even from here, I can tell they are holding something back. It's almost an amused hatred. Like she's toying with me.

"A company, then," she says with a small smile.

I clench my teeth. I'm actually a little insulted she thinks so little of the NAF that she wouldn't expect more numbers even this far west. But I'm still exhausted. My assignment has failed, and I've let a lot of folks down. I have no energy for this kind of back and forth.

"You're a pretty skilled fighter. And your people seem to listen to you. Well, most of them anyway." She snickers. Clearly, she found Simon's outbursts amusing. Not that I can blame her. "And I got to thinking, what's an officer doing way out here?" My eyes stay locked on hers. "Then I see this piece." She holds up my jacket and looks at the gold oak leaf pinned on the breast. "That's quite the chest candy. Not just an officer but a major? This far west? Surely, something big is happening. I mean, why else would a major be wandering around, lost in the wasteland?" The sarcasm is dripping from her words.

I know where she's going with this. "You think this is a power projection. That we're outside our territory."

"Aren't you, though?" she counters. "But that's not what has me curious. Your family line interests me more than anything." She taps on the name embroidered on the chest of my jacket.

My mind goes back to ransom. I look her in the eyes and wait. But she doesn't continue her thought. Instead, she just stares, watching me thoughtfully.

I look at the shotgun in her lap and then back to her eyes. "Mind pointing that someplace else? I don't appreciate barrels aimed at my face in the middle of a conversation."

She looks at the boomstick as if she's surprised to see it pointing in my direction so casually. "Oh, this?" She picks it up and pulls back the action bar. "It's not loaded." She bends the barrels forward and shows me the empty chamber.

The hint of a smile on her lips is starting to annoy me. I want nothing more than to slap it off her face. She watches in amusement as I close the distance between us as far as my restraints will allow. There's a slight tug around my ankle preventing me from reaching her, but now, I'm only a few feet away.

She remains perched on the desk, unmoving and unfazed. I cross my arms. "You're part of the Resistance."

She shakes her head. "I'm not a part of anything."

"Which would explain why you let those raiders slaughter us."

She shrugs. "Wasn't really my fight."

The way she says it, so...blasé.

It infuriates me.

I take a forceful step, the chain keeping me from advancing any farther. "Then why not let them finish us?"

She arches an eyebrow. "You were the ones heading in this direction. Do you want to tell me how you ended up on my doorstep?"

I don't respond.

"Do you wanna know what I think?" she continues. "I think you were part of a convoy. The new general got impatient and pushed out west without doing her homework. I think she's setting up bases faster than she can handle. So fast, in fact, that she didn't even wait to update the technology to accommodate life out in the wastelands. You got swept up in the sandstorms, and you weren't prepared. You got turned around and lost most of your unit either in the storms or from attacks. Probably both. Then you saw our town and saw a chance to rest and invoke military privilege, and you were attacked on the way and were unprepared for that, too."

I still say nothing. She's frustratingly intuitive and predictably arrogant.

"But you're wrong about one thing. We didn't let the raiders slaughter you. We intercepted. And good thing, too." She runs her eyes up and down my body, and I shift uncomfortably. "Because by the looks of it, you would all have been picked off before nightfall. Where's the humanity in that?"

I laugh. It's bitter and humorless, and I barely recognize it as my own. "So you're really just saving our lives, is that it? Our saviors? We should be grateful to you? Thanking you?"

"Pretty much."

I clench my fists at my side. "Those people you let die? They weren't just my soldiers. They had families. Some of them were my friends."

She drops both feet on the floor and stands. "Maybe you should choose your friends more wisely," she whispers and walks to the door.

I throw my hands in the air, frustrated. "What the hell is your problem? We did nothing to you. We're not your enemy. We didn't attack you, and all we wanted was to regroup and be on our way."

She spins and takes five quick steps in my direction until she's almost pressed against me. I inhale sharply at her proximity. She's close enough that I can smell her clean, recently washed scent. Close enough that I can see the spark of hatred in her gray eyes. "Is that why you let that village burn? Is that why you let them die?"

I could reach out and strike her, but I don't. I don't even know what she's talking about. "We didn't let any village burn."

"Right." She drags her eyes down my body again before turning to leave, her shotgun resting easily across her shoulder. "And you're wrong. You *are* the enemy."

"Simon was right, you know," I say to her back. She reaches for the door handle but comes to a halt. "If we don't return, they'll come looking for us. And not a scouting party either. It'll be that battalion you were so worried about. When they find us, and they *will* find us, they'll burn your precious little town to the ground. Because that's the law for harboring the Resistance. Even if you *did* provide food and quarter."

Slowly, she turns, and her eyes bore into mine, unwavering. "Then you had better hope you're not still in it when it burns." Her expression is icy as she opens the door and leaves. It closes quietly behind her, and the lock clicks.

I run a hand through my hair out of habit, annoyed and exhausted. My theory that she's Resistance may have just been proven, but the small victory does nothing to quiet my anger. I want to rip the chain from my ankle and leave this godforsaken town and forget my marching orders. I want to go check on my best friend and the others in the medical facility. I want a shower and a fresh set of clothes. I want to clean my goddamn hands.

But most of all I want to know:

Who the hell is she?

## CHAPTER FIVE: THE VISITORS

### *Dani*

The tavern is empty except for the council. They sit across two large tables pressed together, all of them staring at me as I take a wistful look at my empty glass. What I wouldn't give for a double pour of whiskey to down as I face the firing squad.

A few of their gazes are skeptical after absorbing what I just told them. I can't blame them. It's the ones staring and trying to get a rise out of me that have me yearning for alcohol. I've been here before, and they do nothing to intimidate me. That doesn't stop them from trying, however. I guess that's a bonus of growing up in the middle of the war. I've been faced with much worse situations than a group of thirteen councilors, eight of them being thirty-plus years my senior—known as the elders—voting on whether or not the NAF can remain in town. Voting on whether they're with me or against me.

A handful of elders are displeased at the NAF already being here. Angry that I made that call without consulting them. Not that I had time. But that doesn't matter to them. In their eyes, I should've held out my hand to the unwanted guests outside of our gates with, "Please wait here while I assemble a group of middle-aged people to decide your fate. Thanks."

The chairperson, Bernard, stares at me through thick frames. He leans forward on his cane as he sits at the head of the table. His hair is thin and white, and I stare at the stray strands protruding from his nose. I stifle a shudder. The tavern is silent as they wait for him to speak.

"The military is here," he begins, repeating what I've spent the better part of an hour explaining. "And you want to know more about why."

"Extract information, yes."

"Why would we want information?" an older woman to his right asks. She leans toward me, and I know I have to talk loud in order for her to hear.

"Because we need to know where they are going," I repeat for what seems like the hundredth time. "What their plans are, how many are already out here." I tighten my jaw, and my words are clipped. My annoyance at the incessant questioning has to be obvious by now.

"We already know their plans," Jack adds, putting his hands behind his head and leaning back. "Complete control of this sovereign nation."

I do my best not to roll my eyes. "We need more information than just that they are expanding. Of course they're expanding. The wasteland needs to know when, why, and how so they can prepare. We're in a position to compel them to talk, and that could be vital to our way of life."

"That's not our job," Bernard says. "That's the job of the Resistance."

"What do you think she is?" Mabel shouts, pointing to me with her crooked finger. I somehow manage not to wince at the disgusted tone. She never did have a fondness for me.

"Aren't you getting notifications about all that from someone on the inside?" Bernard asks. He knows I am; they all know I am. William has been writing to me for as long as I have been living here. It's something they bring up every single time I stand before them.

Ignoring the jab like I always do, I press on. "If they are settling here, then we should know about it and tell the others."

Someone chimes in from the back. "Why would we care about the others? We only need to care about ourselves."

I clench my teeth, fighting the urge to tell them that's exactly the attitude that will get them all killed. It's exactly what the NAF wants, for nobody to take care of one another, to only depend on them. We're weaker apart, and I swear that my father and the Resistance are the only ones who had a true grasp of the concept of togetherness. I try a different tactic. "Well, then, don't you want to know what will happen here? To White River? What will happen to us?"

"Keep one of them alive and shoot the others," Darby suggests. I see a few of the elders with impressed expressions, not turned off by the idea.

"Despite the repercussions for murdering a member of the NAF," I remind them with a bit of bite, "they will never talk to us if we kill them all." Darby shrugs as if she didn't just suggest murder as a serious solution. She's not a sociopath or a mean-spirited person by any means. That's just what this constant war has turned us into.

"How do you plan on getting them to talk?" Mike asks genuinely. He's not normally on the council, but with his wife, Elise, busy with the injured, he's been asked to fill her seat.

"With my wit and charm," I deadpan. The others don't look impressed.

"What are you hoping to find that the Resistance won't find out eventually?" Bernard asks.

I don't tell them about having the general's daughter. I don't tell them that she's our best chance of learning personal information about the woman in charge. I want to keep that information, I want to keep *her*, to myself for now.

"Look," I try again, "the Resistance is great with getting tips and planning attacks, but it's rare that they have a chance to question an officer. We have that chance. Let me get a feel for them, and then I'll see if they're willing to talk or not. You'd be surprised how much someone can give up without even realizing it."

"Just turn them over to the Resistance. Let them take care of it," someone shouts.

I pinch the bridge of my nose. They are just not getting it. "The head of the Resistance is back east. It takes time to reach them. It takes time for them to travel."

"These soldiers are going to put a dent in our resources," another member says from the back.

"We've been over this." I sigh and run a hand through my hair. "We have more than enough for a few days. Aiding and quartering the NAF is the safest bet until we decide whether we're going to release them or hand them over to the Resistance." Speaking to the elders is like talking to a cement wall. They don't budge, and they don't change.

"I say ransom, trade them for some good booze," Jack offers with a wink.

"Or tech," Darby adds with excitement, her suggestion of murdering them changing based on what she can gain from the situation.

I glance at my empty glass. Then at the half-full bottle next to it. Would it really be so bad if I poured a double? I make a play for the bottle when a familiar voice stops me dead in my tracks.

"A time limit, then," Rhiannon says. All eyes shift to where she is standing at the counter, leaning casually. "We give Dani a week. If she can't extract information from them, we can vote on what to do with them. Release, ransom, contact the Resistance, whatever." Her eyes meet mine, and I nod, grateful for her input and grateful to have someone who can think critically enough to chime in on my behalf and compromise.

The others converse in low tones. I look to Bernard, who seems to be considering the option, and then to Mabel, who is scowling at me. After a quick deliberation, he slams the bottom of his cane on the floor to gain everyone's attention. "Let us vote," he says. "All in favor of giving Danielle Clark a week to extract information before reconvening, raise your hand." I watch as ten of thirteen hands go up. Bernard is not one of them and neither is Mabel. He does a quick count and sighs. "It seems as though the ayes have won. You will get your week." I release a slow breath. "They are your responsibility. If they harm anyone here or escape, you are to blame."

"Understood," I say simply, glad this meeting is finally coming to an end.

"Then we are adjourned until next week, when we will decide the fate of our guests." He spits the final word as if it's poisonous and then stands and waits until the others begin to file out of the tavern. He lingers to lean in close, glancing at the stolen officer's jacket lying next to my whiskey. "I have no idea what you think you're going to accomplish in a week, but the time is yours. Don't let us down."

He gives me a look that's less than friendly. I wait until he is out before falling into a chair at the table. I finally pour myself that double, roll up my sleeves, and take a long-awaited pull of whiskey. I relish the burn going down my throat.

I swirl the remainder in the bottom of my glass as I stare at the dark lines tattooed on my skin: an inverted triangle with a horizontal line splitting it just beyond halfway to the tip, and two diagonal lines, one shorter than the other, in a parallel line along the right edge. The sign of the Resistance. Despite the years it's marked my skin, the ink has yet to fade. In fact, it appears darker than ever before, a part of me.

I look down at the uniform jacket draped across the table. My eyes fall on the embroidered name. *K. Turner.*

Turner.

The name strikes rage and disgust within the Resistance. Within me. I'd almost convinced myself that I was out for good, that I wouldn't get involved. I saw the name, and now I'm not so sure. If there's anything that can drag me back into this war, well, it's this.

I run my fingers over the stitched letters. *K Turner.* I close my eyes and picture the way her wild blond hair whipped around her face as she maneuvered around those raiders. I'd been impressed. It was clear that she wasn't just a figurehead who sat on the backline giving orders. She was immersed in the fight along with her soldiers and for that, at least, she earned a little of my respect.

Unlike her mother, General Turner, who hid behind desks and barked orders. Already the two of them seemed different. It unsettles me to want to know if there any other differences between them.

All of the past generals have been pretty shitty human beings, but Judith? She's far and away the worst of them. She's vicious, conniving, deadly. And that was when she was a colonel. I can't imagine all the awful things she's done as a general. I'm certain my monthly correspondence with William isn't doing her justice. She's someone nobody wants to cross on a good day, let alone a bad one.

My mother believed that when someone dies, their journey continues, and they feel no pain as they walk on. We stay by the body until burial and grieve. We have ceremonies and prayer at the funeral and take turns paying our final respects. We have large feasts and help the dead into the spirit world.

Judith took that away from me. Took that away from my brother and our people. She left me with nothing but anguish. Judith took my father, his proper burial, and a piece of my soul.

Now her *daughter* is captive within my walls, and I want answers.

Rhiannon speaks softly to the stragglers as they filter out of the tavern. She lingers with Jack in the doorway, and I can feel their eyes on me. But I don't look up. Once Jack steps out, Rhiannon bolts the old door and disappears behind the counter. It only takes a moment before she's back and takes a seat next to me at my darkened corner table. She places a large glass of cold water in front of me. "Jack is checking on the prisoners." I wince at her use of the word *prisoners*. "Are you okay?"

I knock back the rest of my drink and reach for the bottle, ignoring the subtle hint to drink the water instead. "Never better."

She sighs. "Dani, what are you doing?"

"I'm pouring myself a drink." I thought that was obvious.

"That's not what I mean." I know it isn't, but I choose not to answer anyway. Not that that stops Rhiannon from pressing the issue. "I mean, why all this grandeur?"

I lean back and examine the full glass I've poured. "It's against the law to kill members of the National Armed Forces. You know that. I would hardly call this grandeur. More like procedure."

"Don't treat me like the council, Dani. I stood up for you." She leans back and mirrors my body language.

I close my eyes and take a deep breath. I know she did. She always does. The least I can do is treat her better than the elders. "I don't know, Rhi. I just want to get some answers."

"Answers for what?" She watches me carefully. "Does this have something to do with your father?"

"Rhi," I say, bringing my hand up to rub at my brow. I can already feel the headache coming on.

She holds up her hand and shakes her head. Clearly, she's not finished. "I know what you told the others. But I'm your friend. Let me help you. Whatever it is, please, let me help."

I take another long sip. "You can't help with this."

"They're burning towns, Dani. George said so just yesterday. People are going to be scared. And you owe us a better explanation than, you just want to talk to them to find out their plans. We know their plans. They're expanding. Everyone knows that. We also know the Resistance can handle this."

"Can they?" I snap.

"If they can't, you think you can?" Rhiannon leans on the table closer to me, her eyes dark, challenging, and focused. "I'm asking you, is this a personal vendetta?"

I look at her, careful to remain expressionless. I bring the glass to my lips and take a long pull. Rhiannon sets her jaw, but her expression softens as she studies my face, waiting. I grip the glass and take another sip. "I had my revenge."

Her eyes don't waver, challenging me. "Have you?"

"You have no idea what you're talking about."

Rhiannon leans away, clearly offended. "I know what you've told me."

I stare at the NAF jacket, at the name in black lettering. "I haven't told you anything." I bring my eyes back to Rhiannon and shake my head. "You have no idea what it's like out there. Or what's going on here and now. You have no idea what any of this means."

Rhiannon crosses her arms. Her eyes dare me. "Then why don't you stop being cryptic and tell me?"

"This isn't up for discussion," I tell her sharply. The betrayal in her eyes is like a slap to the face. "I appreciate your help, but from now on, you need to stay out of it. Please."

She shakes her head. "This is my home. You're putting all our lives at risk by keeping these soldiers here. The least you could do is tell us what the hell you're looking for."

"I don't know." I release a slow breath. "I don't know what I'm looking for. I just need a little bit of time to figure it all out."

"You have a week," she reminds me, her expression sad and disappointed.

I start to apologize, for what I'm not sure, snapping at her? Leaving her in the dark? Not trusting her? But I don't get a chance as the rear saloon door opens, and Jack strolls noisily back inside. He practically throws his rifle on the table and drops into the empty chair next to Rhiannon. Lucky for him, she is too busy staring me down to reprimand him for putting his weapon on a surface meant for eating and for forgetting to wash his hands upon entry.

"That guy will not shut up." Jack groans and reaches for the bottle in front of me. "'We'll burn down your village, we'll kill you all, do you know who I am? Do you know who you're messing with? We are the law!' Blah blah blah." He downs a considerable amount of liquor in one long gulp. "Couldn't he have stayed with Mike while I got pretty boy?"

Rhiannon continues to stare at me.

Not at all sensing the tension, Jack keeps going. "The others are staying quiet. Not sure about the one in the sick house."

The back door opens again, and Mike walks in. He washes his hands at the bowl beside the door and pulls his rifle strap off his shoulder. He props it gently against a wall beside the table and then proceeds to fall into the last empty seat next to me.

"How's Elise?" Rhiannon asks, finally turning her attention away from me. Can't say I'm not relieved.

"Tired but hanging in there. She's glad I was able to step in for her at the council meeting."

I push the whiskey in his direction. "What's the status?"

"The guy who almost passed out is fine. Name on his jacket says Matthews. He's a little banged up, lost some blood, pretty dehydrated, but fine." Mike grabs the bottle and holds it as if deciding whether he actually wants any.

"Has he been moved?" I ask.

"Yeah. Got moved during the meeting. All chained up and cozy in my shed."

"And the one who died?"

"He was put outside the wall with the others." Mike swirls the whiskey around in the bottle. "The other guy, Miller, is teetering on the edge. Elise doesn't know if he'll make it yet."

Jack leans back and places his hands behind his head. "When should we break the news that one of theirs croaked?"

"I'll take care of it," I tell them with a long sigh. "Were the bodies burned?"

Mike knocks back a shot straight from the bottle, making Rhiannon roll her eyes and get up from the table to get him a glass. "The raiders are all finished. They didn't have much on them, but we took what we could. We still need to burn the NAF. The guys needed a little break, so they're asking if they can continue tomorrow. It's been a long day, and burning bodies doesn't do much for the soul."

I hum in acknowledgment.

"Please tell me you washed up before coming back in here." Rhiannon sighs as she places a glass in front of Mike. Her nose is wrinkled in disgust as she sits back down and leans away from him.

"Of course I did."

Jack avoids her eyes, guilty. I'm too tired to call him out on it.

Mike still looks upset at the insinuation. "I just got status updates. I didn't do anything gross. I've been in here with you."

I bring the conversation back to the subject at hand. "Let them have their break. Tell them to go home. We'll resume tomorrow."

"Why?" Jack asks. "Let's just get it over and done with."

"Mike is right. It's been a long day. We'll finish it tomorrow," I say firmly. No one says anything further. Thankfully, I think most of us are too tired to continue this argument tonight. I reach for my glass and knock back the rest, my body finally starting to feel its warmth. "Get something to eat and then go home. I'll make sure of the guard rotation so our guests get taken care of."

I push back and stand, reaching for the jacket.

Rhiannon eyes me suspiciously. "What are you going to do?" she asks.

"I'm going to visit Elise and make sure she goes home for the night." I run my hand through my hair, exhausted. "And then I might get some sleep. I suggest you all do the same."

"You know we need to talk about this. About whatever you have planned," Jack says as I start to turn away.

I look to Rhiannon, who nods in agreement.

"Yeah, but not tonight," I say, and I'm pretty sure I look as tired as I feel.

I can see Rhiannon hold herself back from protesting. She's right. They all are. But right now, I'm not sure what to tell them. I need a few hours to think, and I can't do that with them asking questions I'm not sure I'm ready to answer.

Rhiannon gives me one final look before I turn and leave. I owe them an explanation, and I owe them one soon.

I make my way down the street under a cold blue wash of moonlight. While nodding at the one or two people I pass, I notice the tired expressions on their faces.

I stop to chat with the guards at the gate, let them know to round up the men outside the walls. That we'll finish in the morning. Then I make sure the rotations are all set for watching our guests.

Finally, I make my way to a small house in the middle of the town that's flanked by two other small buildings. To the right is a large shed guarded by a woman with a rifle. She gives me a nod, and I do the same; she's guarding one of the soldiers. I take the path to the left of the house, walk up to a tiny porch, and take both stairs in one step. There's a large white cross painted on a red door.

"Hey," I call quietly as I step inside our town's infirmary.

Elise smiles as I approach. "Hey."

The place is virtually empty. Only one bed appears to be occupied on the far side of the room. Elise is sitting behind a desk, working over a hotplate, busily mixing vials and sorting pill bottles and sterilizing whatever she used earlier in the day. The fireplace behind her is dark, but the one on the other side of the room is roaring, keeping the patient warm from the chill of the night.

The light of the lanterns dances off her dark skin. Briefly, my mind travels back to a conversation with my father when he told me that people of different colors and cultures used to hate and kill one another based solely on race. I can't imagine a world where Elise couldn't love Mike because of his Asian heritage or where Jack wasn't with Rhiannon because their skin isn't the same color. Even Lucas and Darby wouldn't have been best friends because of the tumultuous relationship between natives and white immigrants.

I wash my hands thoroughly and move closer to her, glancing at the injured soldier, Miller, if I recall. Regardless of race, we still hate and kill one another. Humans haven't really evolved at all.

"Mike said you've had a rough day," I say and sit in the chair across from her.

She doesn't answer for a long time. Her long dark dreadlocks fall in her face as she crushes something into a small bowl.

"It's just been a while since I couldn't save someone," she says. "Even if they were NAF."

I can't remember the last time Elise had to work on someone as critical as the men we brought in earlier. "Elise, it was a long shot, and you did your best."

"I just...maybe if I had the right supplies..."

"You did your best," I restate firmly. She glances at me and nods. I give her a small, reassuring smile "And the other one?" I ask. "The one with the blond hair? Matthews?"

Elise stops crushing the tablets and reaches for a glass with a small amount of water to pour over the powder in a pestle. "He's fine. Demanded to know where we were keeping Kate. I'm assuming that's the woman you took to jail?" Carefully, she pours her concoction from the pestle into a small, cast iron bowl that sits atop her burning hotplate.

"He threatened that if we touched one hair on her head, he was going to rip us apart with his bare hands. He said it real slow and serious, too. It was kind of creepy. Think there's something going on between them?"

"She's his superior officer."

"Does that matter? Either way, not thrilled that he's staying in my residence. Why can't we have a normal jail with multiple cells like every other town?"

"You don't want them together," I tell her seriously.

"Mike told me about the meeting. A week, huh?" Her eyes are kind, and I know that her council vote would have fallen in my favor because she always wants to believe in the good side of people.

"Yeah." I turn to look back at the soldier lying motionless on his cot. "And this guy?"

Elise looks over, then looks back at me with a solemn expression and a long sigh. "If he makes it through the night, he'll stand a fighting chance. The first few hours are critical."

"I'll stay and watch him," I offer. "Go home. Get cleaned up. Get some sleep."

She glances at the hotplate with a frown. "Dani, I don't think he's—"

"I'll stay with him. Please. I need you to rest. You and Mike both."

She sighs in resignation. "Okay. But I'll be back first thing in the morning," she whispers, wiping her hands on her pants.

"Deal."

Elise stands and motions toward her concoction. "Do you remember how to make this into liquid form?"

"Morphine?" I ask. She arches a brow, challenging me. I nod. "I remember."

She continues as though I hadn't answered. "Leave it over the heat until it boils, then strain it through—"

"I remember."

She smiles at me softly. "Of course you do." She walks over, and I pull her close, holding her tiny frame for a brief embrace. "You're an encyclopedia of knowledge," she mumbles against my shoulder.

I chuckle and squeeze her tightly. "You were a good teacher."

"You were in pain and desperate for relief. You would've listened to anything I told you," she counters.

"True."

Elise pulls away first and offers me a grateful smile. She looks over at the patient. "The elders would have my head if they knew I was keeping his pain down, but enemy or not, I can't stand to see suffering."

"That's what makes you such a good medic, El."

She hands me her medical journal. "Here are all of his stats and his recommended dosage. Please, be careful."

"I will."

She pats my shoulder and leaves me alone with the soldier.

I take her seat behind the workstation and look at the boiling liquid.

Reaching inside my back pocket, I pull out my music player. I unwind the cord wrapped tightly around the player and stick the earbuds in my ears. Turning it on, I press play, spinning the volume until all I hear is the simple melody and hypnotizing rhythm of the drums.

Slipping the slender player into my back pocket, I pull the liquid from the hotplate to cool. I glance at the lone patient and ready both sets of filters and double-check Elise's notes. I'm determined to keep him alive on my watch.

❖

The guard posted in front of the jail looks annoyed. It's still early, and Gwaltney, the newest recruit, stands on his toes atop a crate as he peers inside the cell. I stand beside him and listen to him grumble about guarding a boring prisoner.

"You finished spying?" I ask.

He startles to the point of falling off the crate. Slowly, he pulls himself up off the ground and wipes his hands on his shirt. "Didn't see ya there."

"Clearly." I wait until he's collected himself, and he stands a bit straighter despite the disappearance of his dignity. "Has she been out?"

He nods. "Yeah, but she didn't do much. Just stared at the sun and kicked a few rocks. Didn't say nothing, either."

"Did you give her clean water to bathe?"

He shrugs again. "Yeah, but she hasn't done that either, far as I can tell. Maybe just her face and hands."

"She's not going to bathe in front of you." I motion to the space around us. "Which is why you're supposed to be standing out here and not peeking in like a pervert. Give her a little bit of privacy."

"They're NAF. They don't need privacy."

He's tense. Can't say I blame him. It's the first time many of these people have had an encounter with the NAF. So far, I think they are handling it pretty well, considering the horror stories they grew up hearing and not having a clue as to why the NAF are being kept here. "You're still being a pervert. Stop peeking in on her and stand outside the door."

With a short, reluctant grumble, Gwaltney does as he's told. I give him another disapproving look and hold out my hand for the key. Once the door is unlocked, I shove the key in my pocket, bury the sudden burst of nerves in my gut, and step inside.

She's standing near the column next to her bed, leaning against it with her arms crossed casually, as if she has been waiting for me all along. I close the door, the sunlight disappearing and casting us both into the shadows. I push my sunglasses to the top of my head.

"Here to torture me?" she asks dryly.

I'm not surprised she thinks that. But I *am* surprised to hear her voice it so casually.

"Now, why would I do that?"

She shrugs. "I don't know. Because you're bored?"

I chuckle and shake my head. I walk farther into the room and hold up the bowl I've been carrying. "As tempting as that sounds, I'm just here to deliver breakfast."

She peers at the oatmeal and makes a disgusted face. "How do I know it's not poisoned?"

"Not my style," I tell her and continue to hold out the bowl. She just stares. I roll my eyes and take a bite. "See?" I say with my mouth full. "Not poison."

She takes it from my hands with a sigh. Her hazel eyes linger on mine.

We watch each other for a moment, both unsure.

Gwaltney is right. Her face is clean. So are her neck and hands. Her hair is damp, and it appears she tried to clean that, too. The water bin is now soiled with dirt, sand, and blood, the used washcloth draped over the side of the bowl. She looks younger now. Almost friendlier.

"I'll have someone bring you more clean water," I offer.

A hint of a smile tugs at the side of her mouth. "You know what I'd really like? A bar of soap and a bathtub. Or maybe that lake of yours. A small cloth and a bowl of cold water doesn't really do much to get someone clean, you know? And the prying eyes." She *tsks* disapprovingly and pushes her chin at the window. So much for friendly.

I take in her appearance, her stained white T-shirt. Her gray pants didn't fare much better, weathered and worn and stained from extensive travel. I know she must be aching for clean clothes. A hint of guilt creeps its way into my chest at her discomfort. It throws me off.

"The lake, huh?" I grin. "Plenty of prying eyes if you do that. Besides, you'd probably try to swim away."

She narrows her eyes. Apparently, she doesn't find this as amusing as I do. "Like your sniper would hesitate to put a hole in my head." She sits on the cot, frowning as she stares at the oatmeal.

I watch her closely, trying to figure her out. She's nothing like I imagined Judith Turner's daughter to be. "I'm curious about something."

She sighs. "Here we go."

I would be insulted if I wasn't so amused. I cross my arms and lean my shoulder against the column she just departed. "What's with that Simon guy?" She arches a brow. "Does he ever stop talking?"

She stirs the oatmeal, probably trying to figure out if she's hungry enough to attempt to eat it. "Not really."

"I figured."

She places the bowl on the cot and looks at me with an accusing stare. "My turn." She pauses and waits, and when I don't oppose, she says, "Are you in charge here?"

"No. We have a council who determines major decisions."

"How quaint," she says with a teasing smile, "an oligarchy."

"Eh, more like a representative democracy."

"Where do you fall, then?"

I shrug. "Just a regular townsperson."

She laughs. "I don't believe that for a second." Her eyes trail over my face. I don't shy away from her observations. I'm amused by this entire exchange, "No," she continues, "You're much bigger than that. In charge of the guards? Of the town militia?"

"Trying to get in my head, K?" The nickname gets her attention like I thought it might. Her eyebrows rise, and the surprise is evident. "It was on your jacket," I say, not yet letting her in on the fact that I know exactly who she is. "But it's Katelyn, right? Or Kate?" Her expression is priceless. It goes from shocked to nervous to indifferent so quickly that if I blinked, I would've missed it. It's clear she doesn't like me turning the tables on her.

"Am I ever going to get your name? It's only fair, seeing as though you know mine. Especially since you're my 'regular townsperson' hostess and all-around savior, right?"

"Dani." I wait for some sort of reaction, maybe similar to when I picked up on who she is. Instead, she appears to be taken back that I told her. A part of me is relieved she hasn't connected the dots. "All you had to do was ask, K," I tease.

Kate tilts her head to the side. "Why are you really keeping us here, Dani? I have a feeling that it isn't just to play nice and bring me breakfast."

I want to tell her that I know who she is. I want to tell her who I am just to see how she reacts. I want to tell her that I'm trying to figure her out, and the only way to do that is to keep coming back for idle chitchat. I want to tell her that I find her much too interesting to release. That I don't trust her not to come back and rain fire over us all. I want to tell her that I want answers. That her mother is the reason for my father's death, and someone has to answer for that.

But instead: "One of your men didn't make it."

Her expression changes once again. She looks upset and then pissed off.

"He died last night," I tell her, deciding the bigger conversation can wait. "There's another, Miller, who's barely hanging on."

She clenches her jaw and tugs a little at the chain around her ankle. She glances down, as if at the distance between us, and I know she's contemplating whether she wants to reach me. Her eyes lift. Her body is tense. I wonder what she would do if she could reach me. I half expect her to throw a punch any second. Part of me wants her to try.

"And the third?" she whispers angrily.

"The one who passed out, his jacket said Matthews." I can see she's trying not to seem too concerned, but she's doing a terrible job at masking it. "He's fine. Just needed some food and water. Dehydration is a bitch out here in the wasteland."

Kate stares for another moment before finally relaxing just enough to where I know she isn't going to attack.

"We have a burial pyre. We're going to burn your fallen later this morning. You should be there when we do," I say.

"Is this a joke?"

"No. You can have all their belongings, too, if you'd like, except for the weapons."

Her eyes narrow. "Why? Why would you do that?"

"They're your soldiers." I shrug. "Besides, everyone deserves a decent burial." I force the final words out as they burn in my chest. I'm giving her what her mother never gave me in regards to my father. I won't sink to that level. I'm better than that. Being Resistance means possessing a level of human decency.

We watch each other, unmoving. I know she's deciding whether I'm full of shit or being genuine. I can't say I blame her. I wouldn't trust me either. I sure as hell don't trust her.

A moment passes, and I realize there's nothing left to say. I push off the column and nod at the bowl. "Eat up. I'll come get you when we're ready."

She watches me leave without saying a word, and I feel like somehow, that's a victory.

## CHAPTER SIX: THE FUNERAL

### *Kate*

I'm not sure when Dani is supposed to come back. I'm not even sure how much time has passed. Time seems to stop when you're chained up with nothing but your thoughts. Seconds feel like minutes. Minutes seem like hours. I'm in a time vacuum. The only thing on my mind being how we're going to get out of this place and trying to figure out more about Dani. Who the hell is she? All I have are questions and not one single answer.

The light pours in from the single window, and it's slowly getting a little warmer in here. The best I can figure is that it has to be close to midday.

True to Dani's word, a fresh bowl of cold water is brought in not long after she leaves, with a clean cloth and a fresh long-sleeved blue shirt. I look at my dirt and bloodstained uniform, minus my jacket, and wonder if I can wring some of the grime out of my T-shirt at least. I glance at the window, and with no prying eyes peeking in, I take off the shirt and place it to the side. I wet the new washcloth and run it up and down my bare arms and across the back of my neck. The chill of the air and of the cold water makes me shiver. Once I feel at least semi-clean, I submerge the T-shirt and rub the fabric together until the dirt and grime are at a minimum.

After the shirt is as clean as it's going to get, I drape it across the back of the chair to dry. Reaching for the new shirt, I pull it over my head and sigh as I tuck it into my pants. It's a little snug, but at least it's more weather appropriate. Where did the shirt come from? Is it Dani's or someone else's? My curiosity quickly turns to guilt. Did my soldiers get clean clothes or just me? The thought is fleeting and replaced by more pertinent matters.

Flopping back onto the bed, I try to figure out the best course of action. I'm not in a position to make demands. And I'm certainly not in a position to make threats, not when I'm literally chained to the ground. Until we're back in NAF territory, there's only so much we can do.

There's no telling what the play is, not with a wildcard like Dani calling the shots. I don't believe for a second that she's just a "townsperson." She's a leader one way or another, and without more interaction or knowledge of her position, I'm not sure how to handle her.

She hasn't interrogated me yet, and I'm not sure she's interrogated my soldiers either. We're just here, trapped, with food and a wash bin. Completely toeing the lines of NAF law with their self-declared representative democracy. Not blatantly crossing our national laws but not exactly warm and welcoming to them either.

And now she's giving the rest of my soldiers a funeral? She's not engaging in psychological warfare. Instead, she's treating us with just a touch of humanity and following the law just enough where we don't feel threatened or lose morale. I glance at the food. Poisoning might not be her style, but the whole mind game thing certainly seems like it might be.

I think she knows she's screwed either way. Killing us is a death sentence. So is torturing us. Holding us for a long duration without intent or declaration of ransom is another no-no. This council of theirs might make the major decisions, but I'm damn sure she ushers them in the direction she wants them to vote.

I just can't figure out her long-term play, and it's driving me crazy.

This time, when the door opens, it's not Dani or the creepy guard stationed outside. It's Mohawk. I groan. He's even worse than the other two. Just the sight of him annoys me. I stand from the cot.

He strolls in and stops, dangling a key in front of my face. The door remains wide open behind him. "Sit," he says. I'm sure he's flexing more than necessary.

I glance behind him at the door and then back at the key and the restraint around my ankle. "I'd prefer to stand."

The arrogant smirk fades, and he leans in close. "I'd prefer if you weren't leaving this room at all or speaking to me. In fact, I wish you weren't even in my humble little town. But I need to switch your restraints. So sit the fuck down."

It would be so easy to drive my elbow into his nose, followed by a swift knee to the crotch, then strip the key off him while he's out of commission. I could grab the gun nestled in the holster by his side and make a run for it. Impossibly easy, really. I look him in the eyes and clench my fists, running as many scenarios and outcomes in my head as I can.

Several long seconds pass until I finally relax.

"Well, since you asked so nicely," I say.

Despite how easy and satisfying it would be to lay him out flat, at the end of the run, I'd never make it past a street or two. That sniper is guaranteed to be at his post, along with every other armed person along the way. Not to mention the walls, front gate, then the open expanse of vast nothingness if I make it past the perimeter.

"Hold out your hands." The demand comes the second my butt hits the cot. I reluctantly consent. "If you even think about making a run for it, I'll gladly put a hole in your head so fast, you won't even remember being alive."

I arch a brow. "I'd be dead. How would I remember anything?"

He snaps the restraints over my wrists and pulls tightly. "Exactly."

He really isn't the sharpest knife in the drawer. I wonder if he's on this so-called council. He tugs on the plastic wristbands and moves to unlock the ankle restraint. I laugh aloud when I catch him cautiously looking at me not once, not twice, but three times to be sure I'm not going to make a move.

I guess he's not that dumb, after all.

A second later, I am no longer chained to the ground.

Images of kneeing him in the face just for the hell of it flash inside my mind. But again, I refrain from temptation.

He backs away, and I stand, twisting my ankle in slow circles.

"Come on," Mohawk says and shoves me through the open door. I close my eyes. The afternoon light is intense. Bringing my hands up to shield my eyes, I squint and try to acclimate to the brightness.

It feels like an eternity, but eventually, I can make out basic shapes along the street. I finally spot Ryan, Simon, and Miguel coming from different directions all being led to the front gate. There are four different captors flanking them; one for Ryan, one for Miguel and two for Simon.

I feel a wave of relief despite Dani's assurances that they were alive and well.

Ryan raises his bound hands as if trying to get my attention. "Kate." He glances at his guard, the one who shoved his rifle in Simon's stomach, and picks up the pace over to me.

Surprisingly, the guard allows this but remains close behind, his pistol leveled at Ryan's back.

"Are you hurt?" I ask, lifting my hands to touch the bruise on his temple.

"No touching," Mohawk snaps, yanking me back.

Ryan shoots Mohawk a look and then turns back to me. "I'm okay. Are *you* okay? Did they hurt you? I swear to God, Kate, if they hurt you—"

Dani steps between us. I never noticed her approach. She glances from me to Ryan curiously. "You might need these," she says as she holds out sunglasses.

Ryan examines them, unsure. Dani appears to be studying me. It's hard to read her expression behind her mirrored glasses. I catch my reflection and wince; I look like hell.

I accept the sunglasses and slide them on without breaking eye contact. She turns to Ryan and extends the remaining pair in his direction. He takes his cautiously but seemingly as anxious to block out the light. Dani waits until he has them on and then, without another word, turns and walks away.

We both watch. "What was that all about?" Ryan asks, confused, his voice low.

"I think she's trying to figure us out," I tell him, watching her exit the town gate. Just what it is she's trying to figure out I still don't know.

"You ready, L?" Mohawk asks over my shoulder to Ryan's guard.

L smiles and nods. "The only way out is through. Blast the goddamn doors and finish this."

Ryan looks at me. I shrug. This place gets weirder and weirder.

"Move it, blondie." Mohawk shoves his rifle into my back and prods me to follow Dani.

I look back to see Miguel and Simon aren't far behind, wearing their own glasses, as we're led out of the gates, away from the town and far from the walls. It isn't too long before I see a large pyre with the bodies of my fallen comrades on top, wrapped tightly in white cloth, their uniforms over them. The area reeks of accelerant. I swallow roughly and force the lump in my throat back down.

There aren't any signs of the raiders from the day before, but there's a blackened, broken pyre not too far away. They must've burned them yesterday.

Gathered around the funeral site are Dani and several other town members, all armed to the teeth. One holds a lit torch. They look bored. The sight of them looking as though they'd rather be doing anything else makes me angry. It simmers deep inside me that they care so little about my fallen. Realistically, why would they? We have no affiliation with them, no connection, no relationship. We don't know them, and they don't know us. But seeing their expressionless faces, with no ounce of remorse, hits me like a punch to the stomach.

Dani turns her head and looks right at me. I turn away and look at the funeral pyre instead. I grind my teeth and swallow my emotions. I'm grateful to her for this, and I'm devastated to have failed my soldiers so horribly, but I'll be damned if I'll let any of them see me as anything but indifferent. Despite their covered eyes, I know they're watching.

I wonder if that's why we're here. Not because it's a decent thing to do, but so they can show us how much power they have. They want us to be emotional and weak. Vulnerable.

"Anyone want to say anything?" Mohawk asks. It's insincere and mocking. Everyone looks at me. I don't look away from the pyre as I shake my head. As much as it pains me not to speak, not to deliver a final send-off with words that probably wouldn't offer any comfort anyway, I remain silent. My words are not for our captors to hear. They are undeserving, and it feels much too raw to utter anything personal.

Miguel crosses himself, head bowed and eyes squeezed tight. His Spanish is so rapid, I can barely understand, but the words I catch make me believe he is offering up a prayer. I envy his belief and his ability to speak. I am unable to utter anything at all, knowing full well that if I tried, tears would follow.

"Find peace in your final place of rest and know you have served your land well."

My head snaps to look at Dani, who stares at the pyre as if she hadn't just recited the NAF final send-off, the words we say to all those who have fallen in battle. I'm too surprised to respond after hearing her speak them, wondering how she even knows about our traditions. Maybe she's ex-NAF after all.

"What the hell was that?" Mohawk says, confused and annoyed. It seems I'm not the only one.

Dani doesn't respond.

I can feel my soldiers also staring at her in disbelief.

Dani nods once and motions for the pyre to be lit. There isn't time for any other reaction as the fire catches quickly, burning high and strong, and my fallen comrades are engulfed by the flames.

I've had to bury fellow soldiers before. It isn't easy. And as their commanding officer, I feel like a total failure. I was supposed to keep them safe. I was supposed to keep them alive. The rational part of me knows there were things out of my control. But the officer part of me, the human part, knows I could've done more. I could've made different choices and been more prepared.

I swallow the lump in my throat as a cold breeze whips my hair into my face.

We stand in silence. The only sounds are the cracks and pops of the fire blazing in front of us. The smoke flows high into the sky, the wind pushing it away into the clouds. It's oddly peaceful. As if we are watching their souls being carried away to a better place.

It's all also surprisingly respectful.

Perhaps...perhaps this was just a funeral after all. Nothing more, nothing less. A funeral that we would've given ourselves under different circumstances.

I glance at Dani, who is staring straight ahead, at the flames, her hand resting casually on the grip of the pistol at her thigh. Her maroon scarf now covers her mouth and nose, masking her face.

Something about it all seems so...familiar. But I can't quite place why or how.

Before I can remember, an alarm blares from inside the town, startling us all. A crackling comes through on a radio at L's hip. He grabs it as we all look around frantically, wondering what the hell is going on.

After a brief exchange, L turns to Dani. "I fear the mission has been compromised."

When I turn, I am alarmed to see him crouch, his gun pointed away from Ryan and in the opposite direction. Out of the corner of my eye, I see Dani turn as well.

Despite trying to remain quiet, I gasp in surprise. Raiders. A lot of them. Not that far off and closing, sprinting our way. Some of them on horseback. Where the hell did they come from?

"Son of a bitch," I mutter.

"Are you fucking kidding me?" Mohawk shouts. "We've never had a back-to-back attack. Get back to town." He grabs my arm to jerk me back in that direction.

"No," Dani yells. "We'll never make it before they're on us." She pushes Miguel behind the pyre and then reaches for Simon. "Keep down and out of the way." She turns to her people. "Give them everything you got."

Mohawk steps around me and takes his own ready stance. He pushes me to the pyre halfheartedly. I stumble slightly and glance at the watchtower a hundred meters away. The sniper is already in position. I hope to hell he's a good shot; otherwise, we're in for a world of hurt. It terrifies me to leave my fate up to someone I don't know.

I spin. "Untie me," I say to Dani.

She glances at me as she pulls both pistols from holsters slung low on each hip. "Not gonna happen."

The raiders are closing fast. I count about twenty, a handful on horses.

I hear the loud blast of the rifle from the watchtower and see one of the raiders fall off his horse. Impressive. But even with the deadeye covering us, we're outnumbered. And that makes me nervous.

"These raiders have horses. Which means you've pissed off the wrong clan. You better hope they don't have guns, too," I warn. I've seen these guys up close and personal. They took out dozens of my men. I am not looking to go hand-to-hand with them again. "I'm not standing around to become goddamn target practice."

As if on cue, a gunshot rings out, and the dirt in front of us kicks up. I scan the raiders as I crouch, making myself a harder target. Dani does the same, cursing. She glances to the abandoned cars to our left. I know she's thinking about using them for cover. It's just a matter of racing there without getting shot.

"You just had to say something about guns," she says in my direction.

"Untie me," I try again.

"No," she snaps. "Get behind the pyre with the others."

I don't know these people. I'll be damned if I lose any more soldiers while I cower behind a burning burial pyre. "Untie me or give me a weapon."

"No way," she says again. She looks calm, collected, as if the advancement of these ruthless killers doesn't faze her in the least.

Another shot kicks up the dirt, this time dangerously close to Dani's feet. She remains undisturbed.

I, on the other hand, am not as cool and collected. "I'll die," I tell her through clenched teeth. I glance at my bound hands and then at Simon and Miguel anxiously watching from behind the pyre as they pull Ryan back with them. "You've already left us to die once. You can't just leave us defenseless."

She turns to look at me.

"I want these guys dead as much as you do," I tell her honestly.

She looks away from the raiders, who are nearly within striking distance and stares at me as if wrestling with thought.

"Just give me something," I yell frantically. "I can help you!"

After what feels like an eternity, Mohawk and the others begin to open fire. The raiders on horseback are here.

She shakes her head almost imperceptibly, lowers her hand to her belt, and pulls a dagger from a leather sheath. She gives me one last long look and then, so fast that I'm almost not prepared, tosses me the knife hilt-first. I snatch it greedily out of the air. I flip the blade edge around and begin to saw against the plastic binding my wrists.

It takes a minute, but I manage to sever the middle. My hands are free.

"Clark," Mohawk shouts in our direction. Dani turns, and they look at each other before advancing on the raiders, who are closing in on foot while the sniper takes care of those on horses.

Clark. Dani. The realization hits me like a harsh blow to my stomach, taking all the wind from my lungs. As if one of those bullets just struck my chest instead of the dirt at my feet. Everything slows.

Dani Clark. I feel the fight around me, and the horses circle the small battlefield, but all I can see through the kicked-up dirt is Dani walking confidently and firing both pistols at the raiders boxing us in.

Danielle Clark.

It all makes sense: her knowledge of NAF law, the arrogant attitude, the calm demeanor before a battle, her confidence while fighting, why she seems more than meets the eye and why she wanted to bring us in.

We're being held captive by a myth. By a legend. By the NAF's number one enemy: Jonathan Clark's daughter.

Danielle's reputation is equal to, if not surpassing, that of her father's. The number of NAF she's taken out single-handedly is in the hundreds. Many say could be in the thousands. Some believe her to be made up to scare us. Some believe her to be dead.

But here she is, alive and every bit as beautifully terrifying to watch in a fight as the rumors say. It's mesmerizing really. The way she spins, the way she takes out raider after raider with determined ease… it's as if she was born to fight.

I think maybe she was.

Almost forgetting I'm in the middle of the same fight, I realize I'm still exposed and in the open while the enemy pushes in closer.

Smelling him before I see him, I rip my attention away from Dani to the raider advancing on me. Flipping the handle of the dagger inward, I make a fist around the hilt.

He charges with an odd-looking pickaxe held high above his head, leaving his entire chest and stomach exposed. I grip the dagger and dig my heels into the dirt to brace for impact. This one should be easy. Especially with the newly acquired adrenaline pumping through my veins.

I let him come but crouch low. When he gets about an arm's length away, I shift to my left and leave the dagger high out to my side.

He doesn't have time to adjust. He impales himself on my blade, chest-first. As he dies, he brings his heavily muscled arms down in a death stroke but catches nothing but dirt with his weapon. When he falls to his knees, I put a boot to his shoulder and push. My knife comes free. He collapses backward in a heap.

Turning back, I look for Ryan. As predicted, he's right in the thick of things. He's not the hiding type. Weaponless and with his hands still bound, he still manages to tackle a raider and is bringing his bound fists down into the back of his attacker's head.

Miguel rushes to help out.

I sprint in their direction anyway, stabbing into the ear of the raider they have tackled. Rapidly, I pull out the knife and work on Ryan's restraints.

Ryan states the obvious. "We're outnumbered."

One of the townspeople goes down, blood coating the front of his shirt. The sniper from the watchtower takes out the raider on top of him, no doubt saving his life. A guardian angel.

"Grab their weapons and do what you can. We're not dying today," I order as I work on Miguel's restraints.

Once he's free, he rushes to the fallen townsperson and drags him out of danger while Ryan takes the hammer dropped by the fallen raider. We exchange weary glances before thrusting ourselves back in the fight.

I catch a quick glance of Mohawk. He's out of ammo and exchanging blows with a raider. He seems strangely in his element.

The loud booming of a shotgun rings out, and I turn to find Dani again. She's switched weapons. She brings the butt of the gun down with violent speed into the bridge of her attacker's nose. The raider staggers back in a daze and is promptly blown away when Dani flips the gun around and blasts him with the business end.

What she doesn't see is the raider coming at her from behind.

I take a step forward and raise my knife with the blade between my thumb and forefinger, ready to let loose.

But then I stop.

Danielle Clark.

The bounty on her head is a small fortune. Bringing her in, even dead, would mean fame and reputation. A higher rank and anything I ever want or need for the rest of my life. It would prove that I deserve my current rank. That I belong in the NAF.

It might make the loss of my soldiers and the failure of my task hurt a little less. It would make losing them worth it.

If she dies, my life would change astronomically.

Dani turns her wrist, pointing the shotgun behind her and away from her body. Without so much as a look over her shoulder, she pulls the trigger again. The blast surprises me and catches the raider full-on, lifting her off her feet and sending her flying. I assume she was surprised, too.

I guess Dani did see her after all.

Another raider twice her size seems to materialize from nowhere on her right. With almost no time to react, she has to bring the shotgun up with both hands and use it as a shield to hold back his advance.

I glance around quickly and see that, amazingly, these civilians have managed to bring the raiders' numbers down to just a few. Thanks largely in part to Dani. But the rest of her group is too busy finishing off and chasing the last of them to notice her struggle.

Pushing the sunglasses on top of my head, I watch as she struggles with the raider twice her size. He has her back pinned to his chest and snarls with delight as he keeps her trapped within his large arms.

My, how the tables have turned.

I think about how she left us out here to die. How she casually strolled up after several of my soldiers were plucked off by these beasts. I think about all the soldiers still burning on the funeral pyre beside me, and how their families will never see them again. It all could've been avoided.

Danielle Clark is directly responsible for more NAF deaths than anyone in our history. Many of those men and women were mentors of mine. Good people.

But then there's the funeral she tried to give my comrades. The respect she showed them when she didn't have to. Allowing us to be a part of it all. She recited our words when I didn't, making sure my soldiers got their proper send-off. Despite how much shit her people must have given her for bringing us within her town walls, she did it anyway. She could have just killed us and been done with it.

She didn't. I want to know why, but I also know I probably won't have the chance to take her down again.

Knowing now who she is, I'm not sure why she untied me. I look at the knife in my hand. What a stupid move on her part.

She tries to wrench free from the giant raider who now has a single, massive arm around her throat in a deadly headlock. Her other arm beats relentlessly but uselessly against his thick neck, her shotgun at their feet.

He pulls tighter as she claws at his arm. Her legs kick in the air as she is lifted off the ground, and she tries desperately to gain some kind of momentum to break loose.

I think about what she has planned for us. Death? Ransom? Torture? I think about the food she brought me and the water and the brief but complex conversations. Danielle Clark. The NAF's number one enemy even after all these years. All those people she's killed. *My* people.

And without even realizing, I bring my hand back, my decision made. I whip the blade with practiced ease. The dagger flies end over end, whistling as it hurdles at deadly speed directly at Dani's exposed front.

As the knife hits its mark, the tension in my body seems to ease. In a strange way, I feel like I can breathe again.

# CHAPTER SEVEN: THE THROW

## *Dani*

I bring my feet up and try to shift the momentum in my favor while pulling desperately at the massive arm around my neck, anything to gain some sort of advantage. My shotgun lies uselessly on the ground, but if I could just reach one of my pistols, I can whip my way out of his grasp.

Just as my fingers brush the butt of my gun, his arm goes slack, and I can breathe again. The weight constricting me falls away, and my feet hit the ground. I fall to my knees. While I pull in a deep breath, I yank my gun from its holster and spin to face my attacker. I see the hilt of a knife protruding from his forehead as he sinks to the ground, eyes still wide in shock.

What the hell? I whip my head back the other way to try to figure out where the knife might have come from. My eyes meet Kate's. She's staring, her sunglasses pushed atop her head. There's an intense expression on her face that I don't really understand. Her chest heaves as she pulls in deep breaths.

She looks as shocked as I feel.

I rub my neck and look at the dead raider. Blood trickles down the sides of his face as he lies in a crumpled heap.

It dawns on me then. Was that knife meant for me?

Careful not to take my eyes off Kate for long, I pull myself to my feet. Bodies of raiders lie scattered across the ground. Riderless horses gallop around us as if unsure where to go. Fortunately, most of my people are up and fighting, with Jack leading the charge at the last of the raiders.

Kate's still watching me as the fight dwindles. There's something about her expression…

It hits me like a ton of bricks. She didn't miss. Katelyn Turner saved my life. And from the look of it, she's struggling with the weight of her decision.

A yell pulls my attention to the right. Jack finishes the last raider, snapping her neck and screaming in satisfaction. When the body falls to the ground, he pulls the bandana from his face with a large grin.

When I turn back, Kate's still staring at me, tense and cautious.

Before I can open my mouth to…what? Show some sort of gratitude? Ask why she saved me? Jack jogs over.

"Where the hell did they come from? I've never seen this many raiders in such a short time," he asks, stepping up beside me. "A couple of them had guns, too. Where'd they get those? Terrible shots, though." He's out of breath, but he's grinning ear to ear. He always likes a good fight. Me, I've had enough fighting for one lifetime.

"I don't know," I answer, pulling my scarf down. I tear my eyes away from Kate as her companions wander over to her, dazed but surprisingly alive.

Jack and few others point guns in their direction, halting their movement. Everyone but Simon has been freed of their restraints, and after being held at gunpoint, they drop their newly acquired weapons and stand with their hands in the air.

Leaning down, I pull the knife from the raider's forehead and stand, rotating my shoulders and stretching. As I step over the body, I wipe the blade clean on his pants and stick it back in its sheath on my belt, my breathing finally evening out.

Jack lets out a long whistle, clearly impressed. "Right between the eyes," he says, looking at the gaping hole in the raider's head. "You do that?"

I look over at Kate. "Nope."

He looks between me, Kate, and the dead raider. "Hell of a throw."

I nod. "Yes, it was."

I can practically hear the gears turning as he puts the pieces together. I hand him my shotgun, equally stunned.

"What the fuck was that?" Simon yells. "Bringing us here to have the raiders finish us off? Use this little burial as a setup? Was that your master plan? Use us as bait?"

"Listen here, you little shit," Jack says, advancing, shotgun pointed at Simon's face.

Before he gets far, I grab him by the bicep. I don't want any more dead. All I have to do is shake my head. "Sweep 'em," I say. It gives him something to do other than pummel Simon and cause more trouble. "And get the wounded to Elise."

Jack darts toward Simon, causing him to flinch and stumble back. Jack laughs and turns to follow my orders, and Simon takes a step after him.

The soldier with the blond hair, Ryan, steps in front and puts his hands on Simon's chest, stopping him. "They wouldn't be out here with us if we were bait," Ryan tells him. "No one leaves themselves exposed for an expected ambush."

Simon's lip curls. "This is in violation of Article Three, NAF Code Two Section 15b, that firmly states, 'Any act that is directly done in furtherance of an intent to kill—'"

"Shut up, corporal," Kate snaps. "That's an order."

It looks as though Simon wants to say more, but he looks away angrily.

Lucas steps up beside me, winded and disheveled, his long dark hair half out of the tie atop his head. I pull him in close and give him a once-over from head to toe; his glasses are clipped to his shirt, and his eyes are wide. Blood's spattered across his face, but I determine it's not his fairly quickly.

"Are you hurt?" I ask, terrified that my decision to hold a public burial could've gotten him killed.

He shakes his head, and I wipe some of the blood away with my thumb, relieved he's uninjured. "Major Maelstrom was concerned for his men."

"I'm good," I assure him. He grabs my shoulder and gives it a squeeze.

"You will all be charged with conspiracy to harm or kill ranking officers of the National Armed Forces," Simon tries again.

"Lucas," I say, ignoring him, "get Mike out here and have him help take the injured to see Elise. Jack?" I call as he frees a pistol from a downed raider. "Get those bodies on the pyre. Just get rid of them."

Kate watches me, her hands resting by her side.

Lucas calls Mike over the radio. My eyes remain locked on Kate's as I hear the gates already opening behind me. Lucas clips the radio to his belt and pushes his long hair out of his face just as a large gust of wind sweeps in. I can feel the familiar tingle in my bones as I look to the sky, then at the dirt as it seems to rustle to life in the breeze. A surge of impatience consumes me. We need to hurry this up.

"Make sure these four get back to their rooms in one piece." I point to our guests, who are now standing in a close-knit clump, watching us, waiting.

Lucas approaches them, and I tug an extra pair of restraints from his back pocket. My eyes fall on Kate once more, and she continues to stare back, not making a move. I close the distance between us and hold out the restraints. She glances at them and then at the knife strapped to my belt.

I wait. I've never felt more scrutinized than in this moment.

Another breeze comes in. It's picking up. I glance at the pyre as Jack begins to drag a body over. The flames are pulling sideways, riding the wind.

Roscoe barks frantically, sprinting in our direction through the gates as if warning us. Mike jogs behind him with two other people. When I look back to Kate, she holds out her hands, a small, knowing smile on her lips. She's just evened things up between us with that deadeye throw. She knows it.

What's worse? Judging by that smirk on her face, I'm pretty damn sure she's figured out who I am.

I slip the loops over her hands and pull the ends hard, tightening the plastic against her skin. I give her one last impassive look and step away so Lucas can lead them off. I watch them go, my eyes glued to Kate's back. I wonder why she didn't take any of us out given the chance. Maybe she knew it'd be a death sentence. Maybe she's trying to level the playing field by putting us in her debt. Perhaps she's just playing games. Or better yet, maybe she's now looking for answers from me.

"You're bleeding."

"What?"

Mike comes to stop beside me. He nods at my arm, and I look down, startled to find blood seeping through my shirt.

When did that happen? "I'm fine. Come on." Roscoe tries to wrangle the horses, herding them away from the battlefield. "We need to get these horses inside. And we need to be quick. A sandstorm is coming."

Mike looks to the sky as a cloud passes over the sun. He quickly joins Roscoe to help collect the horses while others tend the wounded. I walk through the tangled limbs and look for anything useful while Jack hauls another body to the pyre. Pulling my scarf back over my face, I move through the dozen or so bodies as quickly as I can before helping Jack get them to the flames.

When the last body hits the pyre, I order everyone back inside. Roscoe barks wildly as I mount one of the horses and take the reins of another to get them within the gates.

Jack does the same, riding one horse and leading another while Mike brings up the rear, guiding the last horse, Roscoe hot on their heels.

"Raiders and a storm in one day. What'd we do to get so lucky?" Jack's tone holds no hint of amusement.

Rhiannon runs to greet us the moment we step through, the gate slamming shut behind us. "What the hell happened?" she asks, breathless.

"We got jumped by raiders," Jack answers dryly as he dismounts.

"What? More of them?" Darby asks, stepping into the conversation.

Erica drops a crate filled with confiscated items at my feet. "A storm is coming," I tell her and dismount. "Sound the alarm and make sure people are indoors."

She appears to be exhausted, and she's sporting a swollen eye. She looks annoyed but nods anyway and does as she is asked. We aren't always fortunate enough to know when a sandstorm is about to hit. But when we do, we make sure our people and livestock are hunkered down to weather the wind.

"Now what are we going to do?" Rhiannon asks, staring at the dark clouds.

"I'll tell you what you and Darby can do." I pull the scarf from my face and push my glasses up on my head. "Take that stuff to my shed. Then get these horses to the stable. The alarm is bound to spook them, so do it fast. And get inside before the sand comes."

"And the prisoners?" Darby asks as she reaches down to grab the crate.

I wipe my brow with the back of my hand and look at the closed gate behind us. I think about Kate's wide eyes, the surprise and anger in them as she stared at me. Just several inches lower, and that blade of hers—of mine—would have been in my head. I could be on that pyre right now with the rest of the dead.

Why did I give her that knife? And why didn't she kill me? As hard as I try, I can't shake those questions. What was I thinking? What was *she* thinking? The questions repeat over and over in my head. And I am keenly aware that I'm not going to be able to answer either of them out here with curious eyes staring at me. I need to be alone to process why she saved my life.

First things first: the prisoners.

"Jack, make sure the NAF aren't hurt," I decide. "And bring them some water. Make sure they're safe to ride out the storm. And maybe bring them something to eat. Who knows how long this storm will last?"

"Should I offer them a hot bath? Or maybe a massage?" he asks sarcastically.

"Just do it," I snap, not in the mood.

He shares a quick look with Rhiannon, hands her his reins, then shakes his head and sets off.

"Mike, make sure our wounded are taken care of." I take the reins of his horse. "Great shooting today."

He nods and gives one of the horses a loving pat.

Rhiannon steps close, her eyes narrowed and knowing, her voice low. "What are you thinking? I know that look. You're plotting."

She isn't wrong. "Come on, we need to get these horses to the stable." I try to take three sets of reins as best I can. Then I look to Darby. "Tell Lucas I need to talk to him. I'll meet you at my shed."

"I hope you know what you're doing, Dani," Rhiannon says, wrapping the reins tight around her hands as the warning alarm again blares through the town.

❖

I've been in this shed all day. The wind howls outside, kicking sand and debris against the walls and roof. I'm sore and exhausted. And damn if my arm doesn't hurt. The room is hot from three of us crammed inside, and the air is stale. I could really use some fresh air and a stiff drink, but I have no idea how much longer this storm will last.

Fortunately, we're almost finished with the new restraints. Just another hour or two. If only this damn sandstorm would slow down.

"Are you sure this is a good idea?" Darby asks as she leans against the counter. She glances at the mess Lucas and I have successfully accumulated in my otherwise spotless work shed.

"You have a better one?" I ask as I chew my toothpick, focused on my work.

"Several, actually," Darby says arrogantly. She picks up a rusting piece of pipe and grimaces before moving it away. "We could shoot them."

"We're not going to shoot them."

Darby sighs. I turn my attention to Lucas seated across from me. He's stuffing clay into the interior of the hollow metal band. "How is it looking?"

He glances up with a smile. "Explosions are messy things, but sometimes, messy is necessary to get the job done."

"Don't joke," Darby says, running her hand through her untamed blond hair. "I hate when you two play with explosives. It makes me uneasy. Especially when we're locked in a tiny shed."

"Which is why you're in charge of the fence," I remind her. "And why I'm wondering why you decided to lock yourself in here with us instead of your own place where you could be working on said fence. We need to install those transmitters along the perimeter the second this storm lets up."

Her mouth opens with what I can only guess to be a witty response when the door flies open, crashing against the wall. Darby jumps as sand, dirt, and earth blows inside, scattering items atop my workbench. I reach out to keep whatever I can from swirling in the gust of wind.

"Dammit, Rhiannon," Darby shrieks, holding her hand against her heart. "Don't you know how to knock?"

Rhiannon slams the door shut, pulls an old gas mask off, and tosses her hood off her head. She marches right for me, her face set with determined anger. "Are you insane?"

I ignore the seething look and pull the lantern closer so I can see what I'm doing. "Apparently." I don't have a clue what she's talking

WASTELAND

about. When it comes to Rhiannon, it could be anything. "But I'm not the one wandering around outside in a Cat Five sandstorm."

"Giving her a weapon?" she shouts.

Oh yeah. That.

"She could've killed you."

"Word travels fast, huh?" I ask, glancing at Lucas. He shrugs. Jack must've finally voiced his observations on what happened out there. Traitor. I should've known they'd be locked up together.

I hold out my hand, and Lucas gives me the metal band now stuffed with clay.

Rhiannon steps closer. "Danielle. She threw a knife. At your head."

"She threw a knife at a *raider's* head," I mumble, still internally debating why she went for the raider instead of me.

Rhiannon huffs and crosses her arms. "Maybe she missed."

I shake my head and look at the short, twisted wires. Gently, I press the pointed ends of each into the soft clay Lucas has molded into the metal ring. "She didn't miss."

Lucas looks from me to Rhiannon, wringing his hands. "Gentlemen, these absurd disputes will advance us no further."

I glance at Darby, who has no doubt noticed his anxiety. She pushes herself off the counter and places her hand on his shoulder. "Come on. Let's leave the lovers to quarrel. I'd rather brave this weather than a pissed-off Rhiannon. Besides," she adds with a roll of her eyes, "I have transmitters to finish."

I keep my eyes on my work, ignoring the heated stare from Rhiannon. Lucas and Darby slide into their long coats and cover their faces with two gas masks hanging by the door. I notice the way Darby makes sure Lucas's hood is securely over his head. He does the same for her. They'd be cute if they weren't so annoying.

"That was issue sixteen, wasn't it?" Darby asks.

I shake my head while Lucas laughs. "Eighteen," I say.

Darby mutters through her mask and opens the door. The wind flies in, bringing pieces of earth. I reach for the small, lightweight items that have been shifted in the large gust and place them back where they belong.

The door closes, leaving us alone.

"Seriously, what were you thinking?" Rhiannon asks.

I let out a heavy sigh and put my tools down, resigned to the conflict. I shrug derisively. "I don't know. That no one should be unarmed in a fight?"

"From what I hear, you didn't free the other three."

"Yeah, well, they ran and hid behind the pyre," I mutter in annoyance. "Two of them freed themselves."

"Oh, only two of the others managed to free themselves?" she says sarcastically. Her eyes fall to the pile of scrap metal and wires in front of me. "What are you doing?" Her eyes flick back to mine. She points at the restraints, now almost complete since the last time she saw them. "Dani, what are those?"

"An upgrade," I tell her casually. I pick up my pliers, determined to get these finished.

"Wearable bombs? You've been in here all day building *wearable bombs*?" she screeches. "You are insane. You're going to blow up the entire town."

"I'm not going to blow up—"

"Are these for the prisoners?"

"They aren't really prisoners."

"Well, then, what are they?" she asks. I shrug. I'm not sure how to honestly answer that. It's not as simple as locking up an enemy. No, having them here, having *her* here, is much deeper, more personal. Guests sounds too casual. Prisoners sounds too formal. "Danielle!"

Wincing at the volume, I throw my tools back on the bench and lean back in my chair, exasperated. "Rhi, look. I'm exhausted, okay? I haven't slept in days, we were just ambushed by raiders, my damn arm won't stop bleeding, I had to listen to Darby prattle on for three hours, and now I'm being screamed at. So could you please, *please*, just sit down and hand me that screwdriver?"

Her expression changes as her eyes fall to my arm and the hint of blood seeping through my sleeve. She frowns. "You're hurt?"

I sigh.

She hurries to the cabinets on the other side of the room. "Why didn't you go see Elise?" she asks over her shoulder as she rummages.

"She was busy. I'm fine. It's just a scratch."

"That won't stop bleeding." She sets aside some items before turning to wash her hands the best she can with my small jug of water.

When I eventually turn, she's standing next to me with a wet washcloth and an armful of bandages, iodine, and various other medical supplies. "Roll up your sleeve."

When I make no effort to move, she stamps her foot and sets her jaw.

"Dani, it's going to get infected."

Relenting, I roll up my sleeve. I wince as the fabric sticks to the wound, which is trying to scab over. Slowly, I peel back the fabric and bite my lip, wondering if I've just ripped off a layer of skin. I bite the toothpick and snap it in half. Spitting the splintered wood from my mouth, I kick myself for not doing this the second I got to shelter.

Waiting with what little patience I have left while she examines my arm, I reach for my small box of cigarettes and frown when I only see a few left. Removing one, I place it between my lips and grab my lighter.

Rhiannon coughs dramatically and waves her hand as the smoke exits my lips. "Are you sure you should be doing that in here? Won't that like…detonate them?"

"No," I say with a snort. I take another long drag and blow the smoke away from her, relaxing back into my seat. "There isn't a fuse."

Her eyes narrow. "Well, could you please put it out anyway? You'll smell like a furnace, and so will I."

We stare at each other for a long moment, Rhiannon waiting, and me wondering if she's actually being serious. "Rhiannon," I start slowly, realizing that she is, in fact, serious. "Do you know how hard these things are to come by?" Not that it matters. I've seen the look before; she's got her mind made up. Which means she's going to get her way. There aren't many people that I'd honor that sort of deal with, but Rhiannon happens to be one of them.

She stares me down, unblinking, and taps her foot while she waits. Giving in, I take one more drag before snuffing it on the table.

Rhiannon presses the cold wet cloth to the wound on my arm. I suck in a breath at the sudden sharp pain as she dabs at the fresh blood around the opening that I probably made worse when I peeled my shirt away.

When I look down, I see she's cleaned up the scratch quite a bit. I also am somewhat interested to note that the "scratch" isn't so much a scratch as it is a gash. She gives me a new "I told you this was bad" look and sets to work on removing the black-red blood that has already dried.

"You're going to need stitches," she says.

"There's a needle and fishing line over there." I motion at the medical shelf, not at all looking forward to what's to come. I hate stitches. She gives me a look. "Wouldn't be the first time you've stitched me up."

"And I told you last time, I wouldn't do it again," she reminds me.

"That's fine." I shrug. "I'll do it myself." I stand, and Rhiannon groans and pushes me back down.

"I've seen what happens when you stitch yourself." She motions to my thigh. "You end up looking like a jigsaw puzzle."

I frown at my pant-covered legs. "I don't look like a jigsaw puzzle," I say with a slight pout, suddenly self-conscious about my scars. "Do I?"

She gives me a look and sighs dramatically. "Let me finish cleaning it first. Lord knows you can't even manage to do that."

I watch her clean with a frown. Now I'm even more irritated that I had to put out my cigarette. I'm also annoyed that I let a bunch of raiders get the jump on us while we were exposed. Two stupid decisions in the same day.

Glancing at the mishmash of plastic, metal, and kinky white wire on my workbench, I wonder if I am going insane. I used to live for this sort of thing. Fighting, explosives, manipulation, revenge…

Now all I want is to be left alone. At least, I thought I did.

But I can't stop thinking about Kate. Or the look in her eyes after she threw that knife or what she was thinking. I can't stop thinking about my dad and the last time I saw him. I think about how Lucas was there to hold me tight as the scream tore through my throat when he died. A piece of me died with him that day.

I don't know why, but I replay both memories, one new, one old, over and over and over.

"Are you okay?" Rhiannon asks softly as she gently dries my arm.

"There's a bounty on my head, you know," I say quietly.

"I know."

"A big one."

Rhiannon pulls fishing line and a needle from the medical kit and drags a lantern closer so she can begin a vigorous routine of disinfecting. "I know."

"And you're right. She could've killed me," I say.

She watches me, her eyes sympathetic and understanding.

"Why didn't she?" I ask. "That's what I keep thinking. Why didn't she?"

She lowers the needle she is washing with soap and water and offers a small shrug. "Maybe for the same reason you didn't kill her."

I slump a little. The wind knocks violently against the shed and rattles the roof.

Rhiannon's words circulate in my mind. My head pounds as I try to focus on them. I close my eyes and rub at my temples, wishing the ache away.

I'm exhausted. I lived for the fight, for the hunt, for the chance to take out as many NAF officers as I could manage. For most of my life, the one I wanted, the *only* one I wanted was Judith Turner. I would've settled for anyone close to her. I would've done anything and everything to hurt her. A couple years ago, if I had run across her daughter, I wouldn't have hesitated to drag out her death, slow and painful. A message to Judith for what she did to my father.

But now? All I want are answers. I swore I would never let Judith Turner hurt anyone the way she hurt my father. But then she rose in rank. She stopped leading charges and surrounded herself with more security than any other general of the NAF. She became untouchable. Calling the shots as she hid in the shadows.

And I called it quits. It was too much. I had lost too much. My grudge with Judith affected the ones I loved, hurt the ones I loved, and I just couldn't do it anymore.

But all those old feelings? The ones I thought I successfully pushed down? Well, they came rushing back the second I realized we had not only a commanding officer on our doorstep but Judith Turner's daughter. My single thought once again became retribution for every person she took from me. From the Resistance. From my people.

But is this really what I want? To go back to the way things were? After I worked so goddamn hard to leave that life behind?

It took me a very, very long time to get away from my past. And now, here I am, right back in the thick of it. Is it true what they say?

That you can't run from your true self? Maybe I should accept it and embrace it and go back to what I know: violence and destruction.

Part of me actually wishes that Kate had thrown the knife at me. That I would've been able to understand. I mean, that's what's supposed to happen, isn't it? NAF and Resistance don't take turns saving each other. And I don't fear death. It would've been easier.

As if sensing my inner turmoil, Rhiannon carefully places the needle back into the medical box and pulls me against her until my head is resting against her chest. She wraps her arms around me and runs her fingers through my hair. I close my eyes and choose to take the comfort she offers. I am so grateful to have someone who cares about my well-being enough to be angry with me when I get reckless but who also knows when I need comforting. I close my eyes as I try, and fail, to stop the pounding in my head and the aching in my chest.

# CHAPTER EIGHT: THE CHAIN

## *Kate*

Despite the rattling, the storm shutters have done their job and kept the sand and dirt outside of the surprisingly sturdy little shack. I am surprised someone took the time to close the shutters on the one window. I'm not sure if it would've broken or if anything would've gotten inside, but I'm grateful I didn't have to find out.

These sandstorms are much worse than I've ever experienced back east, and after being caught in the last one, I'm just glad to have shelter to ride out this one.

I'm hungry. I haven't eaten in hours. The storm kept me up most of the night, and the single lantern burned out over an hour or so ago. Thankfully, it's morning. I can tell by the sliver of sunlight trickling in from the cracks in the shutters. I wonder when we will become enough of a priority to get something to eat.

I can hear talking, which means the town is awake and starting their day. They're probably getting a jump-start on cleaning up after the storm. How much damage did it cause?

The door swings open violently, causing me to jump and interrupting my musings. Mohawk steps through, bringing a flood of sunshine as if the sandstorm never even occurred.

I squint against the harsh light and bring my hand up to shield my eyes.

He stops, staring at me through his oversized sunglasses and unnecessarily flexes his muscles as he checks me over.

A witty quip is teasing my lips, begging to come out, but the slight smirk on his face stops it. Something is happening. I can tell by his smug expression. He's not usually this excited to see me.

"Dani wants you all out in the yard," he finally says.

I remain motionless on the cot. We stare at each other for a long moment before I extend my leg and give it a shake to remind him that I'm still confined.

His smirk stretches into a smile as he finally steps into my space. He pulls out wrist restraints and holds them out, waiting for me to slip them on. Once my wrists are bound, he lowers to unchain my leg and takes a step back.

He makes a sweeping gesture as if saying "after you." I grab my sunglasses on the way to the door. Mohawk pushes me roughly on the back, shoving me outside. I guess I'm not moving quickly enough for his liking.

We wind our way to the center of town, and I take stock of the damage. Debris is caught on the edges of buildings, a few planks are missing from roofs, and there are piles of dirt and sand trapped against houses where the wind couldn't push it any farther. All in all, it looks as though the town has fared rather well. Much better than we did out in the Badlands.

As my eyes adjust to the light, I look anxiously to the center of the town where the remains of my group are already waiting. A sense of relief washes over me. Despite looking uneasy and confused, they seem to be all right. Four civilians with rifles flank the group. A few townspeople have gathered, watching curiously. Maybe I'm being marched to a firing squad. Perhaps Danielle Clark has had a change of heart now that she's been exposed and realizes killing is the best option. Not that I blame her. It does little to calm my rapid thoughts.

Mohawk pushes me to stand with my soldiers, and I scan the crowd, looking for Dani. I know she's here. She has to be.

"What's happening?" Ryan whispers as I step up beside him.

"I have no idea." I continue to search. And then I see her.

She stands a short distance away, watching us with her arms crossed. Per usual, large sunglasses cover her eyes, making it hard to read her expression. Her brother, Lucas, is next to her, holding something. There's a girl with long dark hair standing just behind her, watching uncomfortably from the doorway of a larger building.

This kind of audience adds to my fear.

"Is it true? Danielle Clark?" Miguel asks.

"It is," I say, almost regretfully. Being held captive by our greatest enemy means the stakes have gone up. It definitely makes our stay here more interesting. However long that stay is.

"I fucking knew it," Simon roars. He glares at Dani. "When I get my hands on you—"

"Did you bring us out here for lynching?" I interrupt, in no mood for Simon's outbursts.

"Even better," Mohawk answers with a smile. "All of you, line up. Side by side."

Dani continues to stare with little interest as we fall in line. Well, more like pushed into line. Mohawk has no problem positioning us as he sees fit. He holds up a knife and grins. "Who wants to go first?"

No one says anything as he looks down the line. If he thinks we're going to volunteer to be sliced open, he's sorely mistaken. Not that dying today is something I want to face at all, but I'd take lynching over being slowly gutted.

I stare at Dani. The entire town falls silent. Miguel shifts uncomfortably beside me. Even with her glasses on, I can tell Dani is watching me. Her eyebrows rise slightly from behind her frames.

"I will," I say, accepting her subtle challenge.

"Kate—"

I shoot Ryan a look, silencing him, and step forward, standing directly in front of Mohawk. I lift my chin higher, standing tall as he sizes me up. I'll be dammed if I let him see any fear from me.

"Should've known." He reaches out with the blade and looks me in the eyes. I stare back. Whatever he's going to do, he needs to just do it. "See up there in the nest?" he asks, nodding to the watchtower.

My eyes flick up to the sniper, his long-range rifle aimed at me. I bring my eyes back to Mohawk's.

"If you run, he'll shoot you." He leans in close to my ear. "Please run."

The feel of his breath on my face causes me to shudder. I don't bother answering. There's no point. He reminds me of this every time I see him. Run and we get shot. Though, depending on how this plays out, running might actually be the best option. Not that there's anywhere in this godforsaken town to actually run *to*.

He slips the knife forward, below my sightline. I don't even look.

Instead, I keep my eyes on Dani and brace for impact. It takes me a moment to notice, but my wrists start to shake. Surprise gets the better of me, and I look down and see Mohawk sawing through my restraints. I look back up at Dani in confusion, but she just stares back, emotionless.

Mohawk smiles and steps back. My hands are unbound.

Well, this I was not expecting. What do they want me to do? Run? Fight? I contemplate both. Instead, I rub my wrists and wait. It isn't long before Lucas approaches and smiles almost kindly. He lifts his glasses onto his head, and I'm startled to see gentleness in his dark brown eyes. It throws me off balance slightly. I'm about to give up and ask what the hell is going on when I notice the circular metal band he's holding in his right hand, out and away from his body. He gets an arm's length away and kneels at my feet. Realization begins to flood in as he pushes up my pants leg and snaps the contraption right above my boot. The weight isn't much, but the fit is fairly snug.

Mohawk moves to Ryan next. And then Miguel. Lucas gives each of them their new piece of mystery jewelry.

"What the hell is this?" Simon asks.

Lucas bends, closing the last of the new metal bands around Simon's ankle. Once it's secure, he stands and smiles, leaning in close. "The future of the world hangs in the balance. The entire population holds its breath and waits. But with one swift command, the order is given: Drop the bombs."

Simon narrows his eyes. "What the fuck are you talking about?"

Lucas arches his eyebrows and slides his sunglasses over his eyes.

"Are you screwed up in the head?"

Mohawk takes a threatening step. "What the fuck did you just say?"

"Enough," Dani says, suddenly very close. She puts a gentle hand on Mohawk's shoulder, keeping him from advancing, though he seems to have already let go of the idea.

Miguel pokes at his anklet. "What does he mean?" he asks. It's hard not to notice the fear dawning in his eyes. "Drop the bombs?"

"I wouldn't do that if I were you," Mohawk cautions, his smirk back in place.

Lucas's weird phrase begins to repeat in my head. Drop the bombs...drop the bombs...

Well, isn't this just great. "It means these new restraints are wired to explode," I say, much more calmly than I feel. "Right?"

Dani doesn't respond.

Miguel drops his finger from the metal band and stands, the color draining from his face. "You're turning us into human bombs?" he all but squeaks.

Of course we're strapped to bombs. That's where Danielle Clark excels: explosives and wreaking havoc.

I see the dark-haired girl turning to walk back in the tavern. Judging by the clear look of disgust on her face, I'd say the four of us aren't the only ones upset about this new development.

"Who has the detonator?" I ask, growing steadily more pissed at the notion of a homemade bomb strapped to my ankle.

"There is no detonator," Mohawk says with amusement.

"What, are they on a timer?" Ryan asks, looking back and forth between the restraint and Mohawk. He knows the history of Danielle Clark very well. We all do. Perhaps this is her play: talk in a certain amount of time or you blow. She's more twisted than I was taught.

Mohawk glances at Dani, who gives a nod, apparently giving him permission to proceed. "You have parameters. You can't go more than fifty meters from the fence, or else the explosives will be triggered, and half your body will be blown to bloody bits. If you try to take it off without the proper key, it will explode. If you poke at it too much, it will explode."

"Who has the key?" Ryan asks. No one responds.

Simon crosses his arms and narrows his eyes. "How do we know they work?"

"We strapped one on a cow and led it away from the gates," Mohawk says seriously.

"Then what happened?" Miguel asks.

"We had ground beef for weeks." Mohawk cracks up, along with several members of the town who are still surrounding us.

"You're lying."

"They work," Dani confirms, silencing us.

"I think you're full of shit," Simon barks.

She arches a brow. "Am I?"

And just like that, she turns and walks away. The rest of the townspeople follow her lead, no longer interested. Mohawk is the last to go, giving us one last wicked grin before he does.

"So we're free to wander around?" Ryan calls. Mohawk makes a dismissive gesture over his shoulder. And that's the last of that.

I glance at the sniper and see he's turned to look out over the gates. "I guess so," I mumble as I watch them all disappear into their daily routines. Within seconds, we are left standing alone in the middle of the town. Their sudden disinterest is a bit disconcerting.

"I think they're bluffing." Simon leans over and tugs at the band around his ankle.

"I wouldn't mess with that too much," Miguel says, watching Simon uncomfortably. "You heard what they said."

Simon gives the anklet one final tug and stands, clearly annoyed. "It's not going to blow up. I'm telling you, they're full of shit. That's what the Resistance does. They play mind games. Tested it on a cow? Give me a break."

"I don't know. I think we've been strapped to explosives," Ryan says as he eyes his restraint.

Simon glares.

"Ryan's right," I say. "Jonathan Clark was an explosives expert. So was…*is* Danielle. Remember how many NAF buildings she wired to explode after her father died? Do you remember the landmines?" I point at the band. "She's more than capable of this." It angers me to be part of Danielle Clark's party tricks.

Simon scoffs. "Those stories are exaggerated. She's a myth created by the Resistance. She was pissed that her daddy got blown up, so she threw some grenades and killed some people and then went and hid with her tail between her legs."

"A myth?" Ryan says. He gestures to where Dani was. "That myth is right here. In this town in the flesh." He points to the anklet around the top of his boot. "This is a goddamn bomb that *myth* just strapped to my leg."

"You took the classes. She's exaggerated," Simon says dismissively.

"Is she?" Miguel says. "We saw her fight. We know our officers are scared of her." He casts a nervous look in my direction. "And we know she hates us."

"They're built to lie," Simon says. "And I think she's lying."

I make a sweeping gesture in the direction of the front gate, challenging him. "Then by all means, Simon, please prove us wrong."

His nostrils flare, and his jaw sets firmly in place. "Fine. I will."

He marches forward with purpose. I look around. No one seems to be paying attention to us.

Simple fact is, I don't trust Dani. Especially since she knows who I am. Who my mother is. What's worse, I can't quite figure her out. So while I'm pretty confident that proximity explosives easily fit within her skill set, I'm also equally sure that she's intent on messing with our heads.

I hold my breath as to which route she has chosen.

Simon starts to slow as he approaches the gate. A couple of townspeople are chatting by the entrance. They spare him only a brief glance before turning back to their conversation. The door behind them appears to have only a single horizontal bar as a lock.

I cross my arms and wait.

I hear Miguel suck in a deep breath as Simon reaches out to lift the latch.

And then pulls his hand back to run it through his hair. He casually turns and walks back to us as if nothing had ever happened.

I'm not going to lie, a part of me is a little disappointed he didn't go for it.

Miguel wanders in search of the tavern for some food. Simon sulks in the shadows doing God knows what. After a brief exchange, Ryan and I decide to visit the medical ward. He remembers the general direction, and after a few minutes of wandering, spots it tucked between two houses.

I knock hesitantly on the door. A young woman pushes it open and stands in the entryway with one hand on her hip. A cloth headband keeps her long dark dreadlocks from falling in her face. She examines us for a moment, as if weighing her options about letting us enter. She's small in stature, but her dark eyes are focused, and it's easy to tell that when it comes to her place of medicine, she doesn't mess around. She pushes the door farther and steps aside to let us in.

"Wash your hands," she says as she tends to something on a table across the room.

I notice the wash bin and soap next to the inside doorway and do as instructed, scrubbing the dirt and grime from my hands as I look around the space.

The inside is larger than I thought it would be, with two doors in the back. It appears to be only one level, with a half dozen beds scattered across the floor. Two fireplaces flank either end, but no fires are going. All of the windows are open, letting in the fresh air and sunlight, brightening the room.

She steps forward and indicates Ryan's head. "How are you feeling?"

"Much better, thank you," he says. It catches me off-guard to hear her care enough to ask.

She continues to examine him with her eyes and finally nods with a satisfied hum. She returns to her desk, and I resume looking around. The place is spotless, even considering the medical supplies scattered about a large table in the corner. It appears as though the medic is taking inventory. She pokes around her supplies and jots down notes on a piece of paper attached to a clipboard.

"You can pull up a chair if you'd like," she says and points to the one occupied bed.

I glance at Ryan, who washes his hands diligently, and I slowly approach the cot against the back wall. My stomach drops at seeing Private Miller's bruised face.

"How is he?" I ask, clearing my throat.

The medic looks at my soldier lying motionless. "Stable. He came to for a few minutes in the middle of the storm. Being here really freaked him out. Poor guy didn't even know which way was up. A stranger trying to calm him down didn't help. I had to sedate him to keep from injuring himself any further."

She goes back to her inventory, and I pull up a chair next to the cot wishing I had been there for him when he woke. The small table beside him has both a glass and a bowl of water resting on top. There are several washcloths and a book, *Gone with the Wind*. It's tattered and worn. Someone else has been sitting with him. The thought of him not being alone brings some comfort.

"Do you think that he'll make it?" I ask, looking down at Miller.

"I think he has a pretty decent chance. The first few days are always the worst," she says, placing the clipboard on the table. "It's a good sign that he came to. Once the sedative wears off and he wakes up again, we should know more."

"When will that be?" Ryan asks.

"A few hours, maybe more, maybe less." The medic shrugs. "You're welcome to stay. There's water in the pitcher over in the ice chest, and I'm running to the tavern for some lunch. I'll see what I can bring you to eat."

"Thank you," I say sincerely. She has definitely been the kindest person we've encountered since our arrival. The medic offers me a nod and slips out the door.

I look back down at Miller and sigh. I take in the bandage covering his ear and the wrap around one of his hands. His brown hair has been pushed back over his face, and the black and blue around his jaw and eye stands out in stark contrast to his pale skin.

"He looks so young."

"He is," Ryan says.

I know he is. Private Anthony Miller, nineteen, only child, explosives and counter explosives expert. I glance at the band around my leg and am acutely aware that he would've been very useful right about now.

"How am I going to tell their families?" I whisper. My jaw tightens as I fight against the tears threatening to spill over.

"You tell them the same way you've always told them," Ryan says as he pulls a chair next to mine.

"It doesn't get any easier," I say sadly through a shaky breath. "I don't know why I thought it would."

His expression softens. "I know."

"How did this happen?" I swipe at my eyes to grab the few tears that managed to escape. Ryan opens his mouth to answer, and I hold up my hand to stop him. "That was rhetorical. I don't need a recap." I clear my throat and adjust my shoulders to transform back into Major Turner once again.

He smiles and sighs. Leadership comes at a price. Losing soldiers. Losing friends. Telling families their loved ones aren't coming home. This is where I struggle the most. Watching my comrades die. Watching kids die.

"What are we doing here, Kate?" he asks after a long beat of silence.

I'm not entirely sure which *here* he's referring to, so I don't answer. Instead, I watch Anthony's chest rise and fall in steady rhythm.

"How did we end up prisoners of the Resistance? Prisoners of Danielle Clark?" he asks. I close my eyes. Oh. *That* here. "How are we the ones in chains, strapped to explosives? Why aren't we the ones taking in the rebels? How did we lose control?"

"It's not that simple."

"Yes, Kate, it is," he says, his voice getting louder. "We control this land."

"Clearly, we do not. The wastelands have never followed our rule."

"It is our job to instill rules, to bring order to these people."

"You sound like Simon."

"What are we doing here?" he repeats.

"I don't know," I say loudly. "We are vastly outnumbered, outgunned, and clearly lost. Our maps were wrong, and our equipment was shoddy. That's how we got here. We have a man hanging on to his life, and the rest of our forces have no idea where we are, our legs have bombs wrapped around them, and our greatest enemy is calling all the shots. None of which I saw coming. So if you have any suggestions on how to get the hell out of here, I'm all ears."

I give him a scathing look, way too hungry and way too tired to be questioned right now. It's his job, I know it's his job. He's good with strategy, and he specializes in advising in difficult missions. But right now, pressing me about everything that has gone wrong isn't helping.

He stares back, his brown eyes softening as he absorbs my outburst. He runs his hands through his cropped hair and looks at Anthony.

"Why didn't you kill her, Kate?"

This time, I know what he means. Why didn't I kill Dani when I had the chance? And boy, did I have the chance. I was hoping no one else would notice my moment of confliction.

"Why didn't she kill me?"

"Ransom? Information?" he guesses. Both of which I've already thought of.

"Revenge?" There's no need to elaborate. We both know my

mom hunted her father for years and was there when he was killed. Something the Resistance has pinned solely on her.

He doesn't offer any other theories. Instead, we sit in silence. I'm done with arguing. Especially when one of our own lies in front of us, fighting for survival.

"Danielle Clark," he says with a humorless chuckle.

"Yeah," I agree and slouch in my chair.

"She's got to hate you so much."

"Yeah."

After a moment, Ryan takes my hand. He runs a thumb over my knuckles, and like an old memory surfacing from hibernation, my body relaxes. I squeeze his hand tightly. He squeezes mine back, and I know, no matter what, he's with me.

The rapidly cooling air and orange tint that seeps into the room tells me it'll be evening soon. I lie on my cot and stare at the ceiling as I try to figure out our next steps. I need a plan of action, one that doesn't involve getting us all killed.

The sound of boots on the hardwood floor has me turning my head to the door I left ajar. I see her boots and skintight pants first before trailing upward. Her arms are resting casually by her sides, and even in the low light, I can tell she's here for a reason.

"You're free to wander anywhere in the town, yet here you are, back in your cage," she says. The corners of her lips are slanted upward, amused.

I look back at the ceiling. "And here I was thinking you were avoiding me."

Dani steps farther in the room and tosses something at me. "I wanted to return this," she says as my missing jacket lands on my chest.

"My jacket and a lovely new accessory." I lift my leg, revealing the metal band around my ankle. I look at her with a smile. "Whatever shall I do with all this kindness?"

"When did it click?" She crosses her arms as she looks at me. "Figuring out who I was?"

My eyes land on her covered arms. "I'm betting there's a tattoo on your inner forearm. Am I right?" She says nothing. I take her silence as confirmation. "Nice touch keeping it covered." I swing my legs over the side of the cot and sit up, running a hand through my hair. "When Mohawk called you Clark…kind of a huge slipup."

The sides of her mouth turn upward "Mohawk?" She shakes her head and laughs. "Oh, he's gonna love that."

"I gotta say," I continue as I openly examine her, "I like the new look." She tilts her head. "The only time most of us have seen you was when you were sporting the black sunglasses and bandana. It was very menacing. The red glasses and scarf are much nicer."

"I've matured."

"Are you worried? That I know what you look like now?"

Slowly, she smiles. "Are you worried that I know what *you* look like?"

"Plenty of people know what I look like." I shrug. "I'm sure there are an abundance of photographs around the Resistance."

"Maybe. But now I know your face. Where you are. How you fight."

I don't say anything. We just stare at each other. She's probably soaking in my appearance the way I am with hers. After all the stories I've heard, she is not at all how I pictured her. The NAF made her out to be a god, but standing here in front of me, she is merely a woman. She doesn't strike fear in me like I assumed she would. Instead, I am intrigued.

"A lot of people think you're dead. But you're really hiding," I say, the fact still hard to grasp. Not once did I ever think Danielle Clark would hide. I thought she'd be dead long before hiding. Regrouping? Definitely. But hiding?

"I'm not hiding. I'm just trying to move on."

Now that surprises me. "From killing the NAF?"

She looks away. "Something like that."

I lean back on my elbows. I thought I knew her. I thought I knew how she operated. Years of hearing about her, studying her…I thought I'd be better prepared for this meeting if it ever happened. That we'd fight until only one of us was left alive. I guess there's a high probability of that still happening. Yet she has done nothing but surprise me since I've been here. It's throwing me off balance.

"What about you?" I ask. "When did you figure out who I was?"

Her arrogant smirk is back in place. "The fact that you're an officer is a pretty huge red flag there, K. We stepped in when I realized you weren't just a random officer but mommy's little major."

I narrow my eyes at her insult. "I earned my rank."

"I'm sure you did," she agrees sarcastically.

"So you want a ransom."

"No."

"Then what do you want?"

"The pleasure of your company?"

I scoff. She's frustrating. "I'm sure that's not true at all. If it's information you want, I'm not giving you any."

"I figured."

I sigh. "So now what?"

She shrugs.

Gone is the shotgun strapped to her back, and she's only carrying one pistol on her thigh. Her posture is almost relaxed, but I don't underestimate her at all.

My gaze roams upward to the key attached to the chain around her neck. I wonder if that's the key to my freedom. If they are rotating who keeps it. Mohawk, Dani, Lucas, the sniper…all of them probably guard it at some point. "You've given us free rein over your town. How do you know we won't try to kill you in your sleep?"

"We don't. But you're vastly outnumbered. And if you try, we'll march you out the gates." She makes an exploding sound, complete with hand gestures.

"You're not doing anyone any good by keeping us here, you know."

She nods. "You're right. I mean, we could kill you, banking on the fact that you didn't get a communique off about your whereabouts. Which I strongly believe is the case. And when your search party finally comes, which I know they will, we could play innocent. Act as if we've never seen you. Maybe they'll believe us, maybe they won't. But either way, they wouldn't know you were ever here."

She's right. She's absolutely right. A search party will come. And odds are, not one single person here would give up the fact that we'd been brought in. The NAF would look until they felt that finding us wasn't worth their resources, then give up. The thought is slightly disconcerting.

"I could let you go, but then you'd come back with your tanks and your army and blow us all out of existence."

She's not exactly wrong. Especially now that we know these people have been harboring two of the NAF's most wanted.

"So right now, I'm waiting until your man is healthy, and then we'll see if a release happens. Take you to a Resistance outpost and let them figure out what to do with you. In the meantime, you're stuck here. With your new piece of jewelry. And who knows, I might get lucky, and you'll tell me everything I want to know."

"And you're telling me all of this because..." Not that I'm not entertained by her somewhat vague thought processes, but there must be a reason why she's being so forthcoming.

"You asked," she says simply. "And you? Any plans of escape?"

"Not currently," I tell her honestly. If she can be forthcoming, I can, too. To a certain extent.

We watch each other for another moment before I look at my foot. I turn my ankle, feeling the slight weight wrapped around it. "You didn't really strap one of these on a cow, did you?"

"Nah," she says, shaking her head. "It was a pig." But I can tell she's lying.

I look away, examining the anklet once more.

"Why didn't you do it?"

The softness in her voice pulls my attention back to her. She's watching me curiously, the playfulness all but gone from her face.

I know exactly what she's asking. It's the same question that has been plaguing me since it happened. Why didn't I do it? I can't answer. I have no idea why. It was the perfect opportunity. Probably my one and only shot of getting the better of her. And instead of bringing down the enemy I was born to hate...

I saved her life.

I shrug, hoping I appear more casual on the outside than I feel on the inside. "Why didn't you?"

She regards me carefully. I never realized until this very moment how amazingly telling her eyes are. Her face shows indifference, but her eyes...show confusion, hurt, curiosity.

And understanding. Maybe this is why she always wears sunglasses? Her eyes give her away. They didn't teach us that back at the academy. Danielle Clark is quickly humanizing herself for me, and I'm not sure how I feel about it.

Neither of us seem willing, or able, to tell the other why we did what we did. But I'm beginning to wonder if it's because she isn't what or who I thought she was. And perhaps I'm not how she envisioned either.

Dani pulls something out of her back pocket. She tosses it to me so quickly that I'm barely able to catch it. It's a bar of soap.

Surprised, I look over at her, but she's walking out the door. "Can I have my knife back, too?"

"After seeing what you can do with it? I don't think so." She laughs without turning around. Oh well, it was worth a shot.

# CHAPTER NINE: THE BATH

## *Dani*

I run my eyes over the dozens of thick paper journals tucked away in the safe in my front room. My father had one for everything: locations, weaponry, tactics, battles...the list goes on. There are multiple volumes of each, dated and riddled with notes. But today, only one set of journals holds my interest. My father's personnel files: officers and ranking members.

Taking my time, I go through the organized stack occupying one corner of the safe until I find the volume I am looking for. With a glass of whiskey in one hand and the tattered, leather-bound chronicle in the other, I slide easily into my worn armchair and pull the lantern closer.

I push through the pages, skimming the neatly scrawled words. The list of names seems endless. Judging by the dates and the intel I get from William, I know many are still current, but there are also plenty listed who are no longer active. Just a simple list of names and ranks, and yet this meticulous collection is one of the most valuable strategic pieces the Resistance owns.

This was the journal that helped me pick and choose which NAF buildings and camps to target after he died. The higher the rank, the more damage I could do to the NAF by taking them out.

It was vital to me then, and it's suddenly important to me again.

I scan the names until I land on the one I'm looking for: Judith Turner. At the time her name was added, she was a lieutenant stationed in the old Commonwealth of Virginia. I was a baby, and she was already decorated.

Over the years, however, most of the names surrounding hers on the page have been crossed out, either KIA or MIA. Only a handful have survived and been promoted, but none higher than Judith Turner.

Under her name are a few personal notes written by my father: Deadly. Arrogant. Focused. Main objective: expansion. Willing to do anything to become general. Husband Theodore, engineer, smart, consistent, designed new NAF communication devices.

Deceased.

I pause at the word. I added it myself several years ago when I heard of his passing. A bombing set up by William. It was gratifying, then, when I added the word. A piece of payback for what his wife did to my family. Now I just feel sad. I know what it's like to lose a father. And I know what it's like to have nothing left to bury.

Underneath, written in print so small that it almost seems an afterthought, are the two words that came back to me the instant I read the embroidered name on her NAF jacket: Daughter Katelyn.

I stare at Kate's name and the date she was born. It's an approximation but useful nonetheless. We're not that far off in age. I'm curious about her childhood and what her upbringing was like. It was probably similar to my own, thrust into a war with no other choice but to fight.

I'm reminded of a conversation I once had with my father. We had been skirting around the perimeter of a military base, scoping it out. My mother didn't want me to go, but I had insisted my father take me with him. I had to have been about eight or nine. I was confused when I saw children playing in the streets. My father must've noticed my expression because he pulled me close.

"These are the children of gray coats," he said. "They are not innocent. They are born into this war, and are being raised to kill you. Because you are my daughter, they will grow to spite you and will stop at nothing to see you dead."

I close my eyes as my father's lecture runs through my memory. I swirl the liquid in my glass and take a deep breath. Kate isn't the first officer I've met face-to-face. But she is the first officer I haven't killed when given the chance. Is it because I turned a new leaf? I shake my head, not ready to answer that question.

Maybe a part of me hopes she'll give me something, any reason, to keep her around and not face the fate of the council.

I'm not naive enough to think she'll open up and tell me everything

I want to know. *Where is your mother?* isn't going to work. But maybe if I play this right, a crumb of information here, a sliver of it there, and I can paint the pieces into a big enough picture to understand what their plan is out west. How many men are they investing in the expansion? A single piece of intel can go a long way. Maybe then, the council won't want her dead.

In the meantime, here we are, two people on different sides of the war, the daughter of an infamous NAF general and me, the daughter of the Resistance's greatest warrior. It's pretty funny when I think about it because truthfully, it's a helluva gift. Taking out Kate would cause such a spectacle and remind her mother that I am still to be feared. That I still remember what she did. I could make a show of her death. An eye for an eye. That sort of thing. Prove that I haven't gone into hiding.

I snort into my glass. I'm definitely not hiding.

But as much damage as I could do to the NAF by killing her, I can't bring myself to think about it. Is it because she's the NAF's version of me? Is it because she doesn't seem much like her mother at all? Or is it because ridding the world of someone so attractive would be sinful?

I groan. Her looks should have absolutely nothing to do with my decision, but she does distract me.

I'm squinting at the names in front of me and notice that it's getting dark out. I close the journal and take a deep breath. In that moment, I know, without a doubt, that I won't kill Kate. I don't care if she is as deadly and hateful as my father warned me about. If it comes to defending myself and this town, then so be it, but I won't be making the first move.

The weight of this little revelation is broken when someone walks by my window. I'm not even surprised to see it's none other than the general's daughter herself. I spot something in her left hand and move to the window to get a closer look. It's a bar of soap.

Huh. I guess she really was serious about taking that bath.

Intrigued, I give one last plaintive look at my father's journals and inherent warnings before shoving them back into the safe and slamming it closed. I rush through my front door.

"You were serious about taking a swim in the lake, huh?" I call to her retreating form.

She slows and turns. "So this is where the infamous Danielle

Clark lives," she says easily as she makes a show of eyeing my humble abode.

"She's sturdier than she looks." I pat the door frame. "I'd avoid bathing in the lake."

She hesitates for a moment. "Are there flesh-eating parasites?"

I laugh. "No. But it's probably barely above freezing this time of year."

Her brows are drawn down as she frowns. "Do you have something against me getting clean?"

I grin. "Not at all. I just don't want to have to explain to Elise why you're hypothermic."

Kate's frown fades and is replaced with a glare. "If only someone had let us bathe earlier."

"Come on." I push myself from the doorway. "I can offer warm water, no prying eyes, and a set of clean clothes."

I can see her hesitation from here. "In exchange for what?"

There are so many things I could say. In exchange for information about your mother. In exchange for a map of where you were headed and why. In exchange for the number of soldiers being directed out west, a current list of active officers and personnel. "Article Four, Code One, Section Five states: 'Provided nevertheless, and it is hereby enacted, that the officers and soldiers so quartered and billeted as aforesaid shall be received and furnished with diet and drink and given water for cleansing—'"

"I got it." She stares before seemingly deciding my offer is better than a cold lake, curious townsfolk, and the possibility of flesh-eating parasites.

By the time she steps into my house, I wonder if this is such a good idea. I can tell she's wondering the same thing by the way she carefully examines her surroundings. I watch as she scans my books, nodding here and there. She stops at the large map on my wall and studies it for a moment, her head tilted curiously to the side.

"Not many people are interested in the old country," she murmurs as she drags her finger along the Midwest. She glances over her shoulder with a small smile. "Care to share where we are exactly?"

"Care to tell me where you were headed?" Her finger stops moving. Yeah, I didn't think so. I show her to the staircase. "The tub is up this way."

She gives the main room one final look before following me up the staircase.

We pass my bedroom, and I stop in front of the door. "Bathroom's in there. Let me just go turn on the generator. It'll heat the water."

She studies my eyes for the briefest of moments and then heads in the bathroom.

It doesn't take long to get the generator going and to grab some linens. By the time I enter the bathroom, Kate has the water running.

"Is it safe to go in water with this thing?" she asks, glancing at the metal band wrapped high around on her ankle.

"Sure," I tell her with a shrug.

Her eyes narrow. "That's not very reassuring."

"You'll be fine." I welded that thing shut so well that not even air could get through it, but I'm not about to get into schematics with her.

She inspects the anklet a moment longer before reaching to the hem of her shirt. She tugs briefly upward, showing only the slightest amount of skin. I suck in a sharp breath. She stops and catches me staring at her midriff before I can look away.

"I brought you some clean clothes. And a towel," I say, holding out the things I took from my dresser. "Feel free to wash your uniform. I have a drying rack over there you can use. I will bring it back to you once it's good and dry." She eyes the clothes before slowly taking them, as if she's scared it's some sort of trap.

I keep my face impassive as she studies me for another moment. Finally, she takes the clothes and towel and inspects them carefully, holding them away from her as much as she possibly can. "Are these yours?"

I fake offense. "They're clean, if that's what you're implying."

"Are there explosives hidden in these, too?"

"Trust me, you don't need any more. That ankle band of yours is more than enough. If that thing blows, it'll take half your body off." I shake my head and turn away, walking into the hallway to give her some privacy, amused at the stunned look on her face.

"I'm still not sure I believe there are explosives in this thing," she calls after me.

"Oh no?" I ask, popping my head in. "Then why don't you take a jog outside the gates? See what happens."

She rolls her eyes. "What are your friends going to say when they find out you let me bathe in your home?"

"What are your soldiers going to say?" I'm bordering on flirting. I can't seem to help it. Still, my growing attraction for her is incredibly inconvenient. I clear my throat and pivot away from going down that rabbit hole. "I'll be downstairs if you need me. Take your time, but the water won't stay warm forever."

I want to give her a little more time to fill the tub before I turn off the generator. I only use it to get hot water, just like most of us around here. Electricity we can do without. But hot water for bathing? That's a hard luxury to pass up.

I stand at the bottom of the stairs for a moment, wondering if Kate will take this time to go through my things. Not that she'll find anything up there. All my valuables are locked in my safe, and my stockpile of weapons is locked in the trunk of my room.

When it's safe to say she's chosen cleanliness over information, I shut off the generator just as Lucas appears on my doorstep.

He smiles. "But first the day's grit and grime must be washed away."

I shake my head and motion for him to follow. "It's not my grit and grime. Major Katelyn Turner is currently in my tub upstairs, getting herself clean."

Lucas grins. "Isn't this a precarious situation?"

I don't appreciate what he's implying. "Get in the house, Lucas."

He rushes inside with a smile and makes himself at home in my favorite chair. I allow it because I haven't seen much of him these past few days. Building explosives in a tiny shed doesn't count as quality time, even if it is somewhat bonding.

I'm anxious to get his take on the situation. His opinions and thoughts mean more to me than anyone else's. He's one of the smartest people I've ever known. He can't be that opposed to my decisions—he would've vocalized discomfort straight from the start—but that doesn't mean everyone else feels the same. He reads people extremely well and has an empathy for others unlike anything I've ever seen.

While we wait for Kate to finish bathing, I ask, "How pissed are the others?" while falling into the worn leather sofa.

He thinks for a moment, probably racking his brain for a quote he wants to use. I don't mind waiting. He has a hard enough time communicating that a little patience on my end doesn't bother me.

"While the Third World War threatens our very existence, the nation stands torn, split down the middle."

I stretch out on the sofa and tuck one arm under my head as I look at the ceiling. "Yeah. I get that." Nobody wants the NAF on their doorstep, and here I am, inviting them in and providing them with food and shelter. "William says the NAF are pushing this way. The major and her soldiers are proof of that. I'm assuming they came from Minneapolis. Maybe Grand Forks. That's the closest base I remember William telling me about. Where do you think they're heading? Cheyenne? Maybe Omaha. Denver's too far, right?"

Lucas grabs an apple I was saving for later and takes a large bite. "Leave him alone with me. Skull Splicer will get him to talk."

I shoot him a look. For both the theft of my apple and for bringing up Major Maelstrom's weapon of choice: a giant double-sided battle-ax. "I hate that name. They couldn't think of anything less murdery? And I know for a fact there are at least two more quotes about interrogation you could've used."

He laughs. "I do not take kindly to un-useful suggestions."

"She's too stubborn to interrogate. I'm learning that real quick." I rub my hands over my face, suddenly very tired.

"Marines never back down." He takes another large bite. "It never hurts to ask."

I scowl at him for another moment before looking back at the ceiling and trying desperately to shake the thought of a naked Kate from my mind. "I tried asking. She didn't elaborate."

For a long, drawn out moment, the only sound that fills the room is his crunching. "Tell it to me straight. How bad is it?"

I sigh. It's heavy and deep. But the weight carried behind it doesn't fall away with my breath. I want answers. I want to know where Judith is. I want to end this war. I want to fight, but at the same time, I want to be done with it all. I want to not have old emotions stir in the pit of my belly when I see the NAF. I want to know why I still feel this way after all this time.

Instead, all I can say is, "I miss Mom and Dad."

The crunching slows, and I know he's waiting for me to continue.

I want to look at him, but it's hard sometimes. I miss Dad. I miss Mom. And Lucas looks so much like her that it breaks my heart to catch his eyes because it feels like she's staring at me through him.

The weight of missing them gets to be too much some days. Talking about it with Lucas helps to distribute that weight, so I'm not alone in carrying it. He understands this and does the same with me. It keeps us from being buried.

"Do you remember that day? When Dad died?" It's a dumb question. He was fourteen, only three years younger me, so of course he remembers.

His voice is a whisper. "The rain fell, flooding the land and expanding the oceans."

I nod. "Yeah, it was raining pretty hard. The damn detonator was busted. We worked on that thing for days, and it was still busted. He stood there, slamming the button with his palm. But he wasn't panicking. Remember? Even as they closed in." I swallow the lump in my throat. I can see him vividly, the rain pouring, making it hard to hear. We were soaked all the way through in that muddy field. Water must've gotten into the casing, or the wires weren't good, I don't know. I could see the NAF advancing, hear their artillery. We were behind the one wall that remained standing on an old brick building. We needed them to come, to advance, and to walk into our trap.

I remember Dad turning to me, getting on one knee and grabbing my shoulders, forcing me to look him in the eye. I remember thinking Mom would've killed him for taking us out into battle if she was still alive. We were just kids.

I shake my head, unable to finish the memory, and clear my throat. "Kate's mom got off the shot as he ran. Left him to die in his own explosion," is all I can manage to say. "I owe her a bullet."

"Revenge has left a bitter taste in my mouth," Lucas says softly.

"One that I welcome," I say. "Isn't that the rest of the line?" I remember that issue well. It stuck with me the most after Dad was killed. At least Lucas has the decency to look a little sheepish at leaving out the entirety of the sentence.

He tries again. "I need answers. And I need them now."

"She's different. There's something about her, Lucas. She's just different."

"Atomic Anomaly, you are a rare breed. You could do a lot of good," he says after a moment. "So now you must choose what it is you want."

Ah, the use of the name Atomic Anomaly. From the three-story team-up arc where Major Maelstrom fights alongside several other anti-fascist superheroes. At least Atomic Anomaly is cute in the comic. Even if she does have white hair and glowing eyes.

I meet his curious gaze. I don't know if I have the words to tell him what I'm feeling. Thankfully, I don't have to because the sound of boots on the stairs has me sitting up and running a nervous hand through my hair.

When Kate comes into view, I stand, followed by Lucas. My mouth opens slightly at the sight of her, clean and wearing my clothes. The black shirt is a little tight around her chest, but the tan pants seem to fit her rather well. She pushes the wet hair from her face and shifts her weight awkwardly from foot to foot. "Am I interrupting?"

I realize I'm staring and shake my head, snapping out of my daze and mentally collecting myself. I wonder how long she's been listening. "No, not interrupting. This is my brother."

"Lucas," she says knowingly. "Trust me, I know all about you two. Though I never envisioned I'd be standing in a room engaging in small talk with the two of you while wearing Danielle Clark's clothes and strapped to a bomb." She sucks in a long, winded breath.

"Well, when you put it like that…" I know what she means. I've never pictured this scenario either. It's rather unsettling.

Lucas bows slightly. "Maelstrom's pulse quickened. He was unaccustomed to such beauty in this world."

"Lucas, you dumbass." I mutter as my hand flies to my forehead.

Kate blushes slightly and offers me only a quick glance. "Lucas Clark is charming. That's quite disarming, honestly." The compliment makes him smile.

"Okay, Casanova," I say, pushing my brother out the front door. "You need to go, and I need to eat. So, everybody, get the hell out of my house."

Kate smiles but nods and casts one last look in my direction as she pushes past me and my embarrassing brother. I shoot Lucas an annoyed look, and he beams in my direction before following Kate. I stand in the middle of the room and take a deep breath. It's been a weird day: my enemy wearing my clothes and my brother trying to awkwardly flirt. I'm not sure which one disarms me more.

❖

The tavern isn't crowded. Most people have decided to stay in tonight, I suppose. Guess I don't blame them with the NAF wandering around. But there's still a decent number of people scattered around the tables. I scan the room as I wash my hands at the door and spot Elise and Jack eating at the bar.

I sit on an empty stool on the other side of Elise and inhale. Whatever Rhiannon is cooking smells amazing. "How are the injured?"

"Our people are okay," Elise says between bites. "Marty has a pretty nasty stab wound to the side but is demanding to go home. I'll check on him later to make sure he's resting. Maria was cleared to go home a few hours ago with minor injuries. The soldier is stable. Still unconscious, but I think he'll pull through."

"That's a shame," Jack mutters around his plate of food.

"Rumor is, you got sliced up pretty good." Elise reaches for my arm and pushes up my sleeve. I wince when she peels back the bandage. "Heard Rhiannon stitched you up, too. She did a good job. She's better at it than you are."

I look at her, offended. "Why does everyone keep saying that?"

Elise smiles and examines my wound. It still hurts, but I'm not mentioning that. "Looks good. No sign of infection. You got lucky." She leaves out the "again" and places the bandage back.

Rhiannon brings over a hearty plate of food. Fresh fish and vegetables. She says nothing as she drops the plate in front of me. I'm about to ask what I could've possibly done to piss her off this time when she looks past me.

There, stepping inside, are Kate and two of her men.

"Well, look at that. Here comes trouble," Jack says, looking over his shoulder.

To call them hesitant would be an understatement. They're practically creeping in on tiptoes, ready to bolt at the first sign of alarm. I don't blame them. It must feel like stepping into the lion's den.

They take turns washing their hands. At least we all have that in common.

One of our people at the table closest to the door stands and glares at them. I ready myself to step in, but it never gets that far. The man's wife drags him back to his seat. He doesn't look happy about it, but thankfully goes back to picking at his plate. At least Simon isn't here. It could have been a lot worse with that loudmouth.

I catch Kate's eye and arch a brow, curious at how this is going to go.

"You must really be hungry to drag yourselves in here," Jack yells.

"What, are you denying us food now?" Ryan asks.

"Do you want us to?" Jack snaps.

"Easy there, Mohawk," I say, reaching around Elise to pat him on the shoulder. He gives me a strange look at the new nickname. "Rhiannon, can you please bring our guests some food?"

She sets her jaw and looks the trio over with unabashed curiosity. She lifts her head a little higher and wipes her hands on her apron with a nod. "Sure," she says nonchalantly, as if she doesn't care.

Her eyes land on mine, and I smile, letting her know I appreciate her tolerating them in her tavern. I lean over the counter to pull out a few glasses. "Beer okay? Or would you rather have water?"

"You have beer?" Ryan asks in stark surprise. Suddenly, the staring contest with Jack doesn't seem so important to him. Slowly, the trio make their way to the bar.

"Jack brews it himself," Elise says proudly. "And moonshine."

Kate glances at the other two and nods. "Beer would be great."

I head behind the counter to grab a growler from the ice chest and place it on the bar in front of Kate. She pours three glasses, and I rest my palms flat on the countertop as I watch her bring the glass to her lips. "Careful, it's strong," I warn.

Kate takes a long pull, her eyes never leaving mine. Jack lets out an impressed whistle while I smirk. The girl really does love a challenge. It's a trait I can appreciate.

"Three plates," Rhiannon announces, balancing them as she steps from the back and lowers the food to the counter.

The second man, the one I don't know anything about, helps her place them on the countertop. "Thank you," he says with an insane amount of affection.

"No problem, Miguel," she says. Her voice sounds tired but not unkind. It appears these two have already become acquainted. Well, that's interesting.

I notice Jack look between them both. Rhiannon shoos me out from behind the counter before I can say anything to embarrass her.

Jack leans back in his chair and faces Ryan with a sneer. "Where's your little friend? The one who won't shut his mouth," he asks, topping off his own beer.

Kate taps her ankle restraint on the leg of Jack's barstool. Everyone in the vicinity winces at the contact. "Trying to find a way around these restraints, more than likely."

Jack slaps the countertop as if amused. "We might get lucky and hear an explosion tonight."

Kate glances at me. I take a long pull from my own drink. She looks around and nods at the other two. "Come on," she says, taking her plate off the counter. "Let's eat over there." She leads them to a table near the fireplace. She's probably cold without her uniform jacket. I should have lent her one of mine while her clothes dry.

Miguel hesitates, his eyes never leaving Rhiannon. "I think I'll stay."

"No, you won't." Ryan grabs the back of his collar and pulls him along. "We're eating over here," he says and begins to drag him away.

Miguel barely has time to grab his plate. "It looks and smells amazing," he calls to Rhiannon as Ryan drags him across the tavern.

Rhiannon looks surprised. She hesitates. "Thank you," she responds. Miguel smiles and finally allows himself to be led.

I am immensely intrigued and amused as Rhiannon's cheeks turn red as she tucks a strand of hair behind her ear and stifles a small smile. I look at Elise, who has an equally amused, if not shocked, look on her face.

"What the hell was that?" Jack asks looking from Rhiannon to Miguel once more.

"What was what?" Rhiannon asks innocently.

"That *was* kind of weird, Rhi," Elise agrees.

"'Thanks, this looks delicious,'" Jack imitates in a high-pitched voice that sounds nothing like Miguel. "Really?"

Rhiannon straightens her shoulders. "At least someone around here has manners."

"Wait a minute, I have manners," Elise protests.

Rhiannon turns abruptly and storms off. I chuckle, not quite sure what just happened. I glance at Kate. Seems I'm not the only one having mixed and confusing feelings about our guests. I continue to eat my dinner, but Jack leans forward and looks straight at me.

"And what's going on with you and blondie?" he asks, nodding to Kate. "Inviting her over to eat with us and bathing with her at your house and shit."

"Wait, what?" Elise asks.

The sip of beer I'm swallowing practically shoots out of my nose. "I didn't bathe with her. And how the hell do you even know about that?"

"She smells like you." He chugs the rest of his beer.

"Again, I say, *what*?" Elise repeats.

"You know how I smell?" Now it's my turn to shoot him a disgusted look. "What's the matter with you? Why are you so cranky and creepy?"

"I'm not cranky," he snaps.

"You're kind of cranky," Elise says.

"Whatever."

I turn back to my plate and pick at the remainder my food. Jack's mood is infectious, and now I'm cranky right along with him. Elise seems to feel the tension. She sits without saying a word and casts curious glances in our directions.

I hear laughter from the back of the tavern and look over my shoulder. Kate has her head back and laughs as though she isn't being held prisoner by a town that hates her. I can't turn away. Once again, I realize that she is absolutely nothing like I thought she'd be. There is nothing worse than finding humanity in my enemies because it muddles decisions and causes hesitation. There needs to be a definitive line between us. It's the only way to survive anymore.

Rhiannon leans on the counter and watches them anxiously. "You're lucky I let them stay. You know how I feel about bombs."

I glance over at the trio and then back to Rhiannon. "The fish is good. What did you use to season it?"

"Lemon," she says curtly.

I sigh and turn back to my meal, knowing that my time in Rhiannon's good graces is rapidly coming to an end. Now, it appears, we are all cranky. We sit in silence and listen to the laughter behind us.

Eventually, Ryan and Miguel bring their plates to the counter. Miguel proceeds to make no mystery of the fact that he's trying to catch Rhiannon's eye for a refill. Jack glares daggers at him the whole time. I hear the tavern door open and close, but I don't turn. I know she just left.

My instinct is to follow her, but my better judgment tells me to stay where I am. I kiss Elise on the cheek, tell her good night with the promise of stopping by the clinic first thing in the morning, and proceed to follow Kate. So much for that line.

As I open the door, I find her standing not far from the stairs and staring at the cool night sky. "Do you think whoever is on rotation in the clinic will let me sit with my soldier for a while?" She folds her arms to fight the cold.

"Yeah," I say sidling up to her. My gaze drifts to the sky, and I feel an odd sense of comfort. Whether it's from the folklore my mother used to tell me about the constellations or something else, I'm not sure. "Elise says he's stable."

She nods as if she already knows. "And your people?"

"They'll pull through. Do you want my coat?"

She shakes her head. "I'm okay."

"I'll bring your uniform back in the morning." A comfortable silence falls over us.

"Your brother seems sweet," she says after a moment. "It's hard to believe you are both capable of killing as easily as you do."

I tilt my head, curious as to where that statement came from. Maybe she's seeing the humanity in us, too. "Yeah." I scoff, feeling the need to remind us both that we're supposed to hate each other. "Because you're so innocent."

She shrugs. "I never said I was. That's what we were born to do, isn't it? Kill each other?"

I start to respond, but the sound of the tavern door and a voice cuts through the heavy silence. "You ready?"

Kate straightens and looks past me at Ryan, who comes down the steps to stand beside her. "Yeah," she says, smiling. She offers me a quick glance before turning to walk away with him.

I shove my hands in my pockets to warm my fingers and watch them walk into the darkness, wondering what just happened and why I feel so jealous.

# CHAPTER TEN: THE GAME

## *Kate*

"Is it just me, or is this place abnormally creepy?" Ryan asks as we walk up the several concrete steps to the front door.

I glance up at the housing unit and squint against the rising sun. "I think it's the tenant," I tell him with a sideways smile. I suppress a shiver as the wind whips at us and pull my jacket tighter. I was surprised this morning to find my uniform folded nicely on my temporary doorstep. Dani had kept her promise and returned it, but she hadn't said a word to me. I'm not sure why it disappoints me so much, but I can't seem to shake it.

As we reach the top step, the front door flies open, and Simon pops his head out. He looks up and down the street and motions for us to speed up. "Hurry before the meathead comes back."

"Is this a secret meeting?" Ryan asks.

Simon pushes the door open enough for us to slip through, giving one last look down the street. "I don't like these people watching me."

"Whoa," Ryan says, coming to a halt inside the small, near-pitch-black building. He reaches out to keep the door from closing. "Maybe you should pull back those curtains. Unless you can see in the dark."

I snort and draw back the dark curtains to let in the light, ignoring the sounds of protest from Simon. I inspect the dilapidated room. The second floor collapsed at some point, leaving a staircase to nowhere and a ceiling with dark marks from water damage. But it isn't the state of the house that catches my attention—I've grown accustomed to war-torn buildings abandoned without repair—it's the pile of random items off to the side that gives me pause.

Beside a clump of clothes in the corner is a decent accumulation of fruit, vegetables, and bread. The bed on the far side of the room appears not to have been used. Same with the large bowl of water on the table beside the bed. That explains the smell. I doubt Simon has so much as washed his face. And he definitely hasn't changed or cleaned his clothes.

Ryan looks at me, the surprise evident on his face.

Simon casually walks to the piles and tosses a blanket over them but not before snatching a roll from the stack of food.

I'm stunned. "You're stealing from them?"

"Is that what you've been doing creeping around?" Ryan asks with a surprising amount of disapproval.

"I'm taking what's mine." Simon snarls and scarfs the roll in a bite or two. "They think they're so smart, strapping us with these 'bombs' so we won't leave. No one pays any mind to the walking explosives. Most of them don't even lock their doors. They make for easy targets."

"Simon, you shouldn't steal," I say, rubbing my forehead and closing my eyes. We haven't been here for five minutes, and he's already giving me a headache. "Especially when they're offering it to us to begin with."

"Like hell I shouldn't," he says angrily. "They stole my things. And according to NAF Law, Article Six, Section Four, those of non-military affiliation—"

"Give it a rest," Ryan says. Simon must really be getting bad if Ryan is telling him to knock it off.

"It's insulting," Simon spits back venomously. "They owe us. We should get whatever we want."

He is unbelievable. I shake my head. "That's not how it works."

"They owe—"

"We're prisoners of war," Ryan says. "They don't *owe us* anything. I'm surprised they haven't locked us in a basement and starved us to death, honestly. You've lost your mind, brother."

"Sorry, I'm here," Miguel announces as he walks into the room. He stops as if he runs into an invisible barrier. "What is that smell?" He closes his eyes and covers his mouth and nose.

No one says a word, but Ryan and I both glance at Simon.

Miguel leans away from him. "Is that you? Have you not bathed?"

"I haven't had time," is all Simon says as he hurries to close the door.

"No, I'm sure you haven't, not with all the pillaging," Ryan snaps.

Simon advances on him. I step between then and hold my hand out, stopping Simon from doing something dumb. "Just tell us why we're here. What's this plan of yours?"

After a long beat, Simon looks at me. "I've gotten a good look around their garage. They have two sand buggies and an old motorized jeep. Can you believe that? A town of this size has that much in way of transportation? What we do is, we slip—"

"It won't work," I say, cutting him short.

There's that exasperated look again. "Why not?" he asks, part whine.

I cross my arms and extend my leg forward, a reminder that we are still very much confined to the town.

He nods and starts to pace. "Okay, you still think these are armed. That's fine. We'll get these damn things off first. I'm still not convinced these are rigged to explode, but these people are terrorists, so I suppose we should play it safe."

"How do we get them off?" Miguel asks, still covering his nose. "They said if we messed with them too much, they'd detonate."

"You're right." Simon lowers his voice conspiratorially. "But they also said there's a key. And I'm pretty sure that key is around Clark's neck." He licks his lips and rubs his hands together and looks proud, as if this is the most brilliant thing anyone has ever said about anything.

I stiffen at the mere mention of her name. It's a bad idea if his brilliant plan is to make a play on Dani. "There was a key around Mohawk's neck when they put them on."

"Clearly, that was just for show. She has the key, I'm sure of it. I've seen the necklace she wears," Simon says as if it's the most obvious thing in the world. "All we need to do—"

"No," I say sharply. Even Ryan turns to me, surprised. Whatever he's going to say, I don't want to hear it.

He steps forward. "Maybe Simon has a point. We get these things off our ankles, bomb or not, and we've got a lot more options. And hell, you've been able to get some one-on-one time with her, so it's not completely out of the question."

Simon seems positively giddy about the backup. "If we can make some sort of poison or something to make her pass out, maybe we have a shot at getting that key."

"*So*," I start slowly, "You want to drug her when she's alone and slip the key off her neck?"

"Not drug, poison. Finish her off here and now," Simon says. "I'm sure there are some herbs in that kitchen that could do it. Hey, private, you took a class on that, right?"

Miguel seems panicked as we all look at him. "I took an herbology course at the academy, yes."

"And you've been sweet on that tavern owner. Have her give you a tour. Swipe what you need and bring it to the major. She slips it in Clark's drink, steals the key, frees us, one of us takes out the guards in the watchtower, another steals the buggies, and we get the hell out of this dump." He looks proud. As far as plans go, this one wouldn't be too bad if our target was someone other than Danielle Clark.

Ryan must be thinking the same thing. "It's risky, but it might be worth talking about."

Simon has this smug look on his face. I hate it. And I hate that he actually came up with a decent, yet highly flawed, plan.

"Do you really think there are deadly herbs in the kitchen?" I ask Miguel. I don't let him answer. "Highly doubtful. Rat poison on the floor, maybe, but nothing stronger. And what if the key around her neck doesn't go to the ankle bands?" I do my best to keep my tone level and not let my frustration show. "It could be to the food pantry for all we know. Not to mention, we'd have to take out a half dozen men before we could even attempt to steal the buggies. Which are also guarded. You should know that since you got a 'good look' at the garage. But let's say for the sake of argument that we did manage to get gates open and a buggy stolen, the noise would alert the town, and more guards would come. Almost everyone in town owns a gun. It just takes one of them to shoot us. We'd never make it."

"Then we break into their armory. We fight back," Simon says as if it's the most obvious thing in the world. "One goes for the key, one for the weapons, another for the guards to get the gate open, and the last to secure the buggy."

I sigh. Simon was never one for subtlety. Or thinking things all the way through, for that matter. Before he landed under my command, he was every bit a bully who abused what little power he had. He strived for a higher rank, to command his own unit, but recklessness and poor planning were his downfall. He never made it any higher than corporal. I know it infuriates him to have to answer to me, someone he despises, instead of my mother, who he idolizes. He's made that more than clear in the weeks he's been under my command.

I sigh and shake my head. "Your plan is dangerous and risky. What about Private Miller, you know, our man fighting for his life in the infirmary? How does your plan involve him?"

"He's a liability at this point."

I clench my teeth in anger. "That liability is your brother-in-arms. Your comrade. We are not leaving a man behind. Is that understood?"

Simon does a double take. It's clear that isn't the answer he was hoping for.

"I asked you a question, Corporal."

"Understood, *ma'am*." The venom drips off his voice, thick with hatred.

"We can try to get our hands on a radio," I say. It's the best I've been able to come up with. "I don't know where they're kept or how far the transmission will reach, but it's worth a shot."

"Radioing for help." Ryan nods. "I think that could work."

There's no point in finalizing any other kind of plan until I can sort through everything in my head. I'm not about to let Simon run loose, especially against Dani. She'll kill him if he so much as blinks funny around her, and even though I can't stand the guy, he's still one of my men. And one of my jobs is to protect them. Especially from asinine and deadly escape attempts. Swiping a radio might be our only solution. At least poisoning Dani is off the table. Even if it could work, the idea of killing her doesn't sit well with me.

Simon shakes his head and gives me the most disgusted look of pure hatred I have ever seen. "Look for a radio instead of fighting back? That's it? That's your plan? Your mother would disown you if she knew you were just lying down and taking it."

That gets Ryan moving again. "What did you just say?" He takes another step closer to Simon. His fists are balled up tight at his sides.

Simon doesn't seem to notice. His attention is solely on me. "You don't deserve to be a major. You don't deserve to command anyone, let alone the Midwestern army. You can't even get us out of this shit-for-nothing town. Most of our unit is dead, and you're too much of a coward to do anything other than twiddle your thumbs and let these rebel-lovers order you around."

"You're out of line," Ryan says.

He glances at Ryan. "Somebody has to do something before we all die."

Ryan starts forward, but I step up to Simon, my face in his, taking up all of his personal space as I stare up at him. "Remember your rank. I didn't want you on this mission. I didn't want you to be part of the Midwestern unit at all. You were assigned to me for your marksmanship, and that is the *only* reason you are here. Keep your little opinions to yourself. Your job, your *only* job, is to follow my orders. Is that understood?"

He straightens and looks away. I can tell he's fighting hard not to snap. To his credit, he doesn't. "Yes, ma'am," he mumbles.

I can see his jaw clenching as I remain standing in his space. "I've put up with your attitude and your insubordination for too long. If you step out of line again, I'll push you out of the gate myself and watch you explode. Is *that* understood?"

"Yes, ma'am."

I stare at him for another beat and wait for him to blink. Once he does, I grab the front of his shirt and pull him close, pressing his nose to mine. "Stop stealing and take a goddamn bath." I push him away and walk out of the house, leaving the door open. It's too bad I don't have my gun. I could really shoot something right now.

Ryan is hot on my heels, and Miguel takes off in the opposite direction. Can't say I blame him. "Simon has a point, you know."

I whirl around so fast Ryan has to pull up short to avoid running smack into me. "Excuse me?"

"You've always had this weird fascination with the Resistance. I don't know why you always defend them."

His accusation hits me square in the chest. "I have not, and I don't."

"You have. You always have," he says with a pointed look.

"We've been told stories about the soldiers of the Resistance, Ryan. We've fought them back east. We've killed more than I can count. We hate them, they hate us." I extend my arms to the buildings that surround us and to the handful of people wandering the streets or doing chores. "But what about the regular people? What about the people who are caught in the middle? We've never seen the war from their point of view. We just swoop in with supplies like goddamn heroes."

"That's our job, Kate. They ask for our help." Ryan says.

"I know, and to be able to help is amazing. But those who don't want it? Those who don't comply or want our leadership when we come marching through? They're traitors. And we treat them as such. Why is that?"

Ryan looks away, uncomfortable. I allow him to pull me behind a building so no one can see us argue.

I keep going regardless of where we're standing. "Because we're told to. We listen to what our commanding officers tell us, what our parents and friends tell us. What we're taught. But we're never really given a choice on how we see the world. We never get a chance to form our own opinions or understand theirs."

"They've been out there a lot longer than we have. Fighting harder than any of us."

"You're right," I nod. "But that just makes me question them even more. What drives the Resistance to hate us? I mean, what really started this war? Is it how we were taught or something else? Something more? That's what I want to know." I drop some of the heat in my tone. I don't want to fight with Ryan. "So, yes, I might be 'fascinated,' but it's only because I want to know both sides and make a decision for myself."

"You're a major, Kate. You're going to be promoted and leading a new army soon," he reminds me. "You gave up your choice and your own decisions a long time ago. You've been in towns before. Why is this one any different?"

"It just is." I rub my temples. "Every time we go to a citizen-run area, they fall over themselves to cater to us. We stay a night, maybe two, replenish or strike a deal, and we're on our way. Why do they welcome us? Our guns? Our position? Because they need us or because they're scared?"

"Because they believe in the cause?" He lifts his arms and then drops them. "Because they believe what we stand for and know that without us, they'd have nothing? Because they need our supplies to keep them stable? Because we can protect them?"

"Protect them." I sigh. This argument isn't helping my rapidly approaching headache.

"Without the NAF, this nation would've gone to shit a long time ago. We are the only reason it still stands, and we are the source of the reconstruction. The people know that. Most of them know that."

Realizing Ryan's in an arguing mood and that I'm too tired to argue back, I refrain from questioning him any further. "It's just not how I expected it to be out here."

"And how did you expect it to be?" he asks more gently.

I glance around the town and motion to the houses. "Everyone here, they're just so…normal. They aren't unlike us. They just want to live their lives without interference."

"Kate." He puts a hand on my shoulder. "They're harboring rebels. Not just any rebels but Danielle and Lucas Clark. They should've turned them in years ago, but they didn't. There has to be repercussions for that."

"I know." I shrug his hand off, run my hand through my hair, and try not to sound defeated. "I'll come up with a way out of here. Something that doesn't involve a surefire way to get us killed. But in the meantime, I wasn't kidding when I said I wasn't leaving a man behind."

"I know."

"Go sit with Anthony. I'll take a shift later this afternoon." He starts to protest, but the shake of my head stops him. I need to be alone. "I want to think for a little bit." I don't give him a chance to object. I'm already walking away before he has a chance to stop me.

Sitting on a cinderblock just outside of the door of my temporary living quarters, I watch the townspeople meander about, finishing their chores and making sure their community stays strong and functioning. The afternoon sun is warm, and the wind has all but stopped. I'm surprised when I feel sweat on my face. I'm going to miss the small pockets of heat once the cold season completely settles in. I watch fondly as a father carries his son on his shoulders, the toddler laughing happily. It creates a knot in my stomach I can't fully explain.

The sun warms my face as I cast my gaze upward. I close my eyes and think of my mother. She loved teaching me about law-abiding people and about the Resistance that threatened us. From as early as I can remember, she made sure I absorbed every last detail about them. She would test me and study my reactions to their strategies and critique how I interpreted their lawless actions. It was part of my "training," and she was deeply passionate about it. She said I was her little girl aspiring to become the next general of the National Armed Forces.

And that was the extent of our relationship.

It's not so much that she doesn't care about me. My mom loves me very much. Growing up, I wanted for nothing. I was spoiled, sure. It took me a long while and some serious, unpleasant soul-searching to come to the sad realization that Judith Turner wasn't bringing up her darling little girl like other mothers were with their daughters; she was raising a commanding officer to replace her. I was meant to finish everything she started and continue the family line. To think like her, share the same beliefs, the same goals. It's not a realization I arrived at easily, and it still hurts to even think about, but it is what it is.

At an early age, I started to rebel against her in my own way. No snacks after dinner? I'd smuggle an apple from the kitchen. Placed in a nice desk job for strategies and planning? I enlisted for the front lines. Told to specialize in long-range weaponry? I opted for the daggers. Just little things to remind my mother that even though she was an officer at the time, she couldn't control me or my opinions. I had my own wants and needs.

Even as I attempted to think for myself, I always believed in what the NAF stood for. I didn't always agree with all their methods for achieving it, but I understood the bigger picture. I saw firsthand how we helped and created a stabilized society. It didn't make any sense to me why anyone would cause an uprising against that, against us. We were the good guys.

If you had told me then about townspeople who harbored the Resistance, who aided these murderous traitors? Well, they were as bad as the Resistance themselves. But as I watch a teenage boy present a girl with a flower, somewhat awkwardly, I can't seem to understand why they should be punished for existing. It doesn't seem as though anyone here is causing any sort of stand against the NAF. It doesn't seem like they are harboring anyone I consider an enemy, regardless of the fact that they are. They aren't taking a stand against us; they're just...living. They didn't welcome us, but they don't seem to be against us, either. If they were, I doubt we would be alive.

No, they seem like normal, regular people, like the ones living around our military bases. Raising their children, doing their chores, catching a meal or a beer here and there at their tavern. Just regular people doing regular things. It's beginning to really sink in that people like this have the most to lose. The war rages, and they're the ones caught in the middle.

A small commotion and barking by the front gates catches my attention. I stand and wipe my hands on my pants. I head to the gates to see what the fuss is about. Dani and Mike are greeting someone. It's the first time I've seen her all day, and it leaves me unsettled to think she may be avoiding me.

The new arrival is a teenage boy, with worn clothes and a satchel held tightly across his chest. A courier? Mike hands him a canteen, and I see the boy talking but I can't hear what he is saying. The dog circles the courier, sniffing him happily and vying for attention.

Rhiannon is standing nearby, and I decide to press my luck with her. "Morning."

She glances at me and straightens. I know she doesn't like me. But she doesn't walk away either. "Morning," she says curtly.

"What's going on?" I play dumb.

"Courier is here," she says like it's the most obvious thing in the world.

Dani takes a letter from the boy. She opens it up while Mike continues to make small talk. After a moment, Dani's shoulders appear to tense, her mouth forming into a small, straight line.

When she's finished, she folds the letter and sticks it in her back pocket. She looks at the boy and tells him something before ruffling his hair. She says good-bye, gives Mike a quick glance, and turns to walk away. I'm not sure what's going on, but it can't be good. Not with the way she tensed. I look at Rhiannon, who appears to be worried.

Dani passes by with her head down, clearly lost in thought.

Rhiannon places a hand on her arm, gently stopping her. "What did it say?"

Dani does a double take as if just now noticing Rhiannon's presence. Her lips are still tight, and she forces out the words. "Jess just turned sixteen."

Rhiannon gives her forearm a light squeeze. Dani nods, her frown deepening, and she continues, passing us both.

I'm completely confused. Why is she so tense over a birthday? "Who's Jess?"

Rhiannon says nothing as she watches Dani walk out of sight, the barking dog following. She re-ties her apron and casts a dismissive look in my direction. "A very special girl who just came of age to join the Resistance."

I stand dumbstruck as Rhiannon goes back into her tavern. I am beginning to realize I know nothing of the outside world or of my enemies. I don't know what startles me more, the idea of Dani being so vastly different than I imagined or the realization that perhaps I don't know nearly as much as I thought I did about the whole of humanity.

❖

By the time I leave the clinic after my shift with Anthony, it's pretty late. He's still in and out of consciousness, and despite Elise assuring us that he's on the mend, I still worry about his condition. Miguel was nice enough to relieve me so I can get some food and sleep. I doubt Simon has ever taken a moment to sit with him, but that doesn't surprise me.

If we don't figure a way out of here, I fear Simon will snap. More so than he already has. That's not only dangerous for these people but for us as well. I'm not sure he'll listen to anything I have to say, especially words of comfort. Perhaps Ryan can get him to settle. At least enough to give us a few days to figure something out.

The sun has set long ago, and the moon is high. Which is why I'm surprised to see the lights are still on in the tavern. My curiosity carries me in the direction of the lights and the muffled sound of music. I open the tavern door cautiously, revealing a surprisingly busy room. A dozen people hang around the music box in the corner. The song isn't one I've heard before. Rhiannon looks at me in the doorway, frowns, and goes back to wiping down the counter.

I scan the crowd until I notice a lone figure in a darkened corner. I see the tall glass in front of her, untouched. She's leaning on her forearms, staring at the table top, seemingly lost in thought. Interesting. I clean my hands and walk over to her. The dog lies beside her feet, and his head pops up when I approach, but he doesn't make a move other than to watch me.

"I find it a little disconcerting that big bad Danielle Clark is sulking in a dark corner alone."

She looks at me with wide eyes. "I'm not sulking," she says defensively.

"I could see your lower lip poking out even in the dark. You're pouting."

"Go to hell, Turner."

I laugh. "I think I might already be there."

She regards me with narrowed eyes, and for a minute, I'm sure she's going to tell me to get lost. Instead, she lifts her foot to the edge of the chair next to her and pushes. The chair slides out, a clear gesture inviting me to join her.

I take a seat, and she leans back, watching me curiously. "Cute dog." I glance the black and white herding dog, who is no longer interested in my intentions.

"Roscoe. He's Rhiannon's. He's probably only out here because she isn't giving him any more scraps."

Leaning back, I take stock of her. The note this morning really seems to have messed with her head. It bothers me that I want to know why. "How often does that courier come by?"

"Why? Planning on sneaking him an SOS?" Her tone is short and dripping with sarcasm.

"Me? No." I chuckle. "Simon, however…"

Dani nods, a small smile appearing on her lips. "Well, by the time the next one comes, the NAF will be closing in on us anyway. You can just hitch a ride with them."

Her eyes meet mine as if looking for confirmation. She knows they're coming with or without our release. Of course she does. She's the Daughter of the Resistance. She knows much more than she lets on. The timing of their arrival, however, is unknown, even to me. It's especially disconcerting because I have no idea where "here" even is.

My suspicions about her only keeping us for information grows more and more apparent each time we converse. I wonder if I can use that to my advantage. If she wants information, I can give her just enough. However, nothing is for free. And if I want a way out of here, I'm going to need information from her as well.

"Let's play a game," I suggest.

Her eyebrows rise slowly. "A game?"

"Honesty hour." I reach for her untouched beer and take a big swig. "For a certain amount of time, we have to tell each other the truth. Complete honesty."

She squints, looking both suspicious and intrigued. "How will we know it's the truth?"

"I guess we'll just have to trust each other." I have a feeling she's as stubborn as I am and won't back down from my challenge.

"And you're just going to offer up information about anything?"

I shrug. Her eyes look darker than their usual shade of gray in this low light. "As long as you do the same."

Her eyes don't leave mine as she considers my proposal. Finally, she pulls her beer back. "How about a question limit? Three each."

I knew she couldn't pass up a challenge. "Complete honesty?"

"Complete honesty."

We shake on it. "Okay. You go first."

She runs a hand through her long brown hair, pushing it away from her neck and sweeping it to the side. Her brows knit together as she thinks. A small smile finally forms on her lips, and she takes a long pull from her beer and leans forward. Her eyes sparkle in the light of the lantern resting between us. Judging by her look, this game isn't going to go the way I thought it would. "What do your people say about me?"

I roll my eyes. Of course she'd ask that. She could ask about my mother, our positions, battle plans, or locations. She could even ask about our next stations or bases, security, or classified equipment questions. Instead, she wants to know about her reputation. How very quaint. Leaning back, I sigh at her arrogance and cross my arms, settling in to answer honestly.

"If by 'people,' you mean the NAF, they say all sorts of things. When I was in the academy, they taught us about your father and some of the other Resistance leaders like William Russell. When they talked about you, they said you are the product of terrorists. How dangerous you are. You used to be one of their biggest threats." She looks impressed with herself. "Those who saw you fight and lived to tell think that you're death incarnate. You fight with determined precision, and everything is well thought out. We learned that you're smart and calculated. In officer training, we studied your patterns. Your techniques. Those who don't think you're dead swear you're planning something big. That you're biding your time. They're scared of you."

"Go on," she tells me with a wide grin.

"I don't think your ego needs any more inflating." Even if I do find it oddly charming.

"I don't know what makes you think I have an ego." Her smirk is reason enough.

I pull the beer closer. "My turn," I say, taking a sip. There are so many questions I want to ask. So many things I want to know but today has made me curious about her as a person. I used to think Dani had no weaknesses besides her family, and after her father died, she acted as if she had nothing to lose. But seeing her now, in this town, and the way she responded to the news brought by the courier, well, it appears that the great Danielle Clark has more reasons to live than I previously thought. "Who's Jess?"

Just like that, the arrogant smile drops from Dani's lips. She is a completely different person, quiet and withdrawn. There's an obvious look of sadness on her face that makes me realize I asked a pretty significant question on my first go.

The pause stretches on. I stare at her, carefully observing every twitch, every breath. She leans back, no longer playful. The laughter from the tavern reminds me we're not alone, but I refuse to look away from the shaken woman across from me. As each second passes without her speaking, I come to the realization that this game could be over before it ever really began.

"She's a girl who means a lot to me." Her eyes drift to the beer, and she reaches for it, pulling it back. "I haven't seen her in a long time."

I watch as she takes several long sips. "Is she related to you?"

She watches me for a stretch, a pained and thoughtful expression on her face, as if she's weighing her answer very carefully. "No," she says finally. "But that doesn't mean she isn't family," she adds with a thoughtful look. "What's going on with you and your warrant officer?"

Now it's my turn to be surprised. Is she asking me something personal because I asked her something personal? "Jealous?"

"No, just curious."

"He's my warrant officer. I value his advice." She doesn't look convinced. "We were in a relationship a few years ago. My mother wanted me to marry him, but I was never in love. I thought I was a long time ago, but…" I shrug. "I trust him more than anyone else." There isn't much else to say on the matter.

"But he still has feelings for you." She's picked up on more than I realized, and it excites me that she's interested enough to pay attention.

"He hasn't given up hope that I'll change my mind."

She scans my face. My eyes stay on hers. My body thrums under her gaze. It's becoming incredibly clear that Danielle Clark might be my undoing.

Finally, she tilts her head. "Do you like your mother?"

I expected "What's your mother planning?" To say the real question throws me a little would be an understatement. "She's my mother. Of course I love her."

"That's not what I asked," she points out gently.

I look away, careful not to show how much I'm struggling with the question. I love her, yes, but do I like her? My entire life, I've been judged by who my mother is. Certain behavior has been expected of me since I was a child. I've never really questioned it. I've just gone along with it. But when it comes down to it, when it comes down to my relationship with my mother and how I really feel about her, I've always bottled it up inside. I've never let my true feelings show. I've never really allowed myself to think about not liking her or agreeing with her. Not liking my mother would make me a terrible daughter. Wouldn't it?

She's watching me with a curious expression. There's no judgment, no accusation, just…genuine curiosity and maybe a little bit of sympathy. If there's anyone who might understand my complicated relationship with my mother, it's her.

"No. I don't like my mother," I admit softly. Her expression changes, and somehow, I feel exposed and vulnerable. It makes me uncomfortable so I reach for the beer. "Okay, my turn."

"You already asked your three," she says, pushing the glass to me.

I look at her, confused. "I did not."

"You did. Who is Jess, is she related to you, and you asked me if I was jealous of your warrant officer," she says, ticking the questions off on her fingers.

"That last one does not count. It was an extension of the responses you gave."

"It sounded like it had a question mark on the end to me," she says with a shrug. "You made the rules. I'm just following them."

Despite my small protest, I know she's right. She's beaten me at my own game. Somehow, I knew this would happen, and I was still ill prepared. I bring the glass to my mouth and try to hide the blush I feel making its way up my cheeks. "You are such a conceited ass."

"So I've been told," she says proudly.

I put the glass down, and I know I'm pouting. It's childish and ridiculous, but I can't help it. I rarely lose. At anything. And I am seldom caught in a situation that makes me look foolish. I'm not used to it, and I'm not sure how to proceed. I'm disappointed I didn't get to ask her anything of substance. I had one chance to ask her something meaningful, and I screwed it up.

She sighs heavily and leans back, her hands in the air like she's surrendering. "Okay, okay. I'll give you one more," she relents and smiles at me. "Even though the pout is kind of cute."

I narrow my eyes and take another drink to hide my smile.

I vaguely entertain the idea of not asking her anything else, just to prove a point, but the temptation is too great. I want to make this one count. I shuffle through the infinite number of questions bouncing back and forth in my head. Finally, I settle on the one I have wondered about since discovering her name: "You used to be the deadliest woman on the planet. Everyone feared you. You were this force to be reckoned with, and now you're here, hiding in this town. Why?"

I can tell by the sad look in her eyes that I've asked the right question and that she's not going to hold back with me, either. "Sometimes, you find that what you've spent your whole life fighting for isn't worth *giving* your life for." Her eyes meet mine briefly, and I understand exactly what she means. "When my father died, my entire world died with him. I was a kid, left alone, angry, hurt and confused. So I ran. I vowed to kill every single gray coat I came across to avenge my father's death. Your mother being number one on my list." She pauses as if to gauge my reaction. I don't take the bait and keep my face neutral.

When it's evident I'm not going to give her any sort of reaction, she continues. "I locked out the world and threw myself into that hatred. I killed...hundreds of people before I was even eighteen. I just went on a rampage. William tried to rationalize with me, get me to settle down and get my head right. If not for me, then for Lucas's sake. He needed his sister and I...I didn't want to listen. I wasn't ready. I pushed him away and ran, Lucas right there beside me."

I nod along with her explanation. When my father died, I channeled my rage. It was put into my work and my studies, and I busted my ass to get promoted. I understand her anger; mine was just quieter. It catches me off guard that Dani and I aren't really that different.

"I went from town to town, soaking in the praise and worship. I was taking out the NAF. I was their champion. But the whole time, I felt empty inside. Hollow. And then one day, I woke up, and I just didn't have any fight left in me. Years of nothing but bloodshed and I didn't want to do it anymore. I didn't know where to go. I couldn't go home, not after what I had done. I was a disgrace."

It hurts to hear her voice crack. She pauses and takes a shaky breath as if steadying herself to continue.

"I went to this town, one my dad would take me and Lucas to when we were kids. I didn't know where else to go. An old friend of my dad's, George, he kind of took us both in and convinced everyone to let us stay, gave me a place to get my head on straight. Lucas was great. Patient. Understanding. He never left my side. I tried my best to push the war out from inside me. He deserved a place to settle. And for a while, I was happy. Really fucking happy. But even then, I couldn't stay out of the fight. One day there was...an accident. It was my fault. I tried to stay and make up for it, but I couldn't face them. I hurt people that I loved. So I ran from that, too."

Dani pauses and chews the inside of her cheek as she stares at a spot on the table. I don't say a word. I just wait, silently and patiently, to see if she continues.

"I didn't get far before I saw a bunch of raiders attacking this place. The townspeople were doing a pretty good job defending their walls, but I knew if I didn't help, the raiders would make it past the gates and take over the town. I was so tired but still so angry. Angry at the war. Angry at my dad for leaving me. Angry at the world. Angry at myself. I did what I do best: I fought. I threw myself at the raiders."

The more she talks, the more I see her. The *real* Danielle Clark, beyond the reputation and stories.

"Jack told me later it looked like I had a death wish." She chuckles sadly. "Maybe I did. I told Lucas to get inside, defend the people while I held off the raiders. Took a bit of convincing, but he did. I almost died. At least, that's what Elise tells me. I got banged up pretty bad. Broken arm, fractured leg, more stitches than I could count, a pretty bad blow to the head, my wrist was all fucked-up…"

I frown at the mental image of Dani lying beaten and broken.

"Once they were in the clear and the raiders were taken care of, they took me in. Elise helped set me straight and Rhiannon"—she lifts her eyes to look past me at Rhiannon talking to some people at the bar—"Rhiannon helped stitch me up and never left my side. Not once." Her eyes meet mine. "When I was well enough to start wandering around on my own, I wanted to repay them for saving my life. I helped with Rhiannon's garden, with the livestock, repairs, anything to earn my keep. They gave me a house and said Lucas and I were welcome to live there for as long as we wanted as long as we stayed out of the war. But we earned a place with them; we saved their lives. But if it hadn't been for these people, for this place…" She leans back in her chair with a sigh. "I have a normal life here. I have friends, I have a family. It's not just another shot at a new life but probably my last shot. People like me don't get many more chances than this. I can't waste it."

I've never considered wanting a life like Dani's in a town like this, but the way she speaks so lovingly and passionately about this town and these people…I envy her.

Her eyes meet mine again. "I'm just trying to move on from being the woman I was expected to be and start being the woman I want to be."

I am utterly stunned. I never expected her to be so open, so honest. Especially not with me, someone who is part of the group she hates so deeply. Not with the daughter of the one person she hates more than anyone in this world. I slowly pass the glass across the table.

She brings the beer to her lips. "Bet your professors didn't teach you any of that."

I try to respond, but I can't seem to find the words. I was taught so many awful things about her: her ruthlessness, her murderous intent, her disregard for human life, her lack of a conscience, but never that she was so vulnerable. So complicated. So broken. Her eyes meet mine, and I can see her apprehension, her hesitation and sadness. It twists my stomach into knots.

And just like that, her vulnerability is gone. Back is her look of indifference. It throws me completely at how fast she can turn it on again.

She downs the remainder of the beer and takes a deep breath. "I don't know about you, but I'm wiped. I'm going to go get some sleep." She pushes herself from the table and stands. She waves briefly to Rhiannon, pats Roscoe on the head, and turns to leave.

I watch, still dumbstruck by her honesty. Dani steps through the door, and I scramble to get out of my chair to rush after her. She can't just leave it all in the open like that and then walk away.

When I finally catch up, it takes several steps in the opposite direction of her house before I realize that we're walking in the direction of my room. I glance at her, wondering how she knew I'd follow her. I want to ask, but I can't seem to find my voice. Her eyes are focused straight ahead, her hands shoved deep in her pockets.

We walk the entire way in silence. How is it that after all she's told me, I still want more?

As we approach the front door, I realize that I still haven't processed how I'm feeling. What was supposed to be a simple game turned into something much more serious, much more than just prime enemy intel.

It was deeper, more personal. Dani confided something very few people would ever share with anyone, let alone their enemy. And I'm not sure why she did it. Does this mean she trusts me? Is this something she wanted shared? Or is she toying with me? Is this what Ryan was warning me about? Am I letting my guard down? Is what she told me real?

We come to a stop in front of the house and face each other. "Thanks for the beer," I blurt out awkwardly, still not knowing what else to say.

"No problem." She looks at the sky.

My eyes fall to her necklace. It's tucked underneath her button-down shirt. Even with the top button undone I still can't make out what's attached. My stomach drops. Maybe Simon was right, and she's the one with the key. There aren't many people milling about, all of them in for the night. It would be one-on-one if I were to make a grab for it. I glance at the single pistol at her thigh and then to the knife clipped to her belt. It's easy enough to access.

With a sigh, I reach for the doorhandle. "Thank you for being so honest with me," I tell her, pushing down my desire to invite her in and ask her more. "And please don't say it was only because I asked."

She laughs lightly. It makes me smile.

I take a deep breath and push open the door. I step inside, but something pulls at me and I spin to face her, confused. "Why didn't you ask me about my mother's plans? Or what she has set in motion? Why didn't you ask me anything of substance? I would've answered."

"You said it yourself, Kate. It was a game." The reminder stirs something in me.

"So everything you just said back there about being sick of the war and wanting to be a better person about almost dying, you just, what? Made that up?" I ask, more confused than ever.

"No." She takes a step closer. "No, it was all the truth." I must look as exasperated as I'm feeling because she smiles softly. "But sometimes, even the truth can be taken out of context. Things omitted and glossed over. If I asked you where your mother was and you said a thousand miles east of here and gave me the name of the town, I'd be so focused on that that I wouldn't notice the troops marching in from the north. Even though it was a fun game, it wouldn't have been the whole story." She takes another step. "Just like what they taught you in school about me isn't the whole story. Besides…" She stops when she's directly in front of me and reaches out. For a moment, I think she's going to lean against the side of the building and trap me against it, getting in my personal space. The warmth of her body is not unwelcome as I stop myself from reaching for her.

Instead, she grabs the lantern over my shoulder. I hear the click of a lighter, and a moment later, an orange glow surrounds us, lighting up the space. She removes the lantern from the hook and hands it to me. I deflate in disappointment, but I'm not sure why. Did I want her to kiss me?

Our eyes meet. "I learned a lot more about you as a person tonight than I ever could've by asking where your mother is currently located." Dani lifts her hand once more, this time to push the hair from my face and gently tuck it behind my ear. "Good night, Kate."

It's something about the way she says my name. So softly, like she knows that if she utters it any louder, this moment will be over and forgotten. She drops her hand to her side, shoves them both into her pockets, and turns to walk away into the darkness.

It isn't until she's out of sight that I release my breath. I absolutely wanted her to kiss me.

## CHAPTER ELEVEN: THE MESSAGE

### *Dani*

I take a slow sip of tea, the steam warming my face. I can't stop thinking about Kate. I almost kissed her. I wanted to kiss her. Her eyes closed when I leaned in close...did she want me to?

Not only that but how easily I answered her questions is occupying every corner of my mind. Why did I do that? I divulged so much of my past and was so vulnerable. I rarely even show that side to Lucas.

I don't want to think about what it means or why I wanted to show her a side of me I usually keep hidden. I don't want to think about how I wanted to press her against the side of the building and kiss her senseless. I don't want to think about how if she had invited me in, I definitely would've gone.

Instead of dwelling on *those* issues, I think about how she answered my questions. Half the NAF thinks I'm dead. The other half suspects I'm hiding. William told me a few years ago that there were units out there looking for me. Asking questions, seeking revenge, trying to cash in on the reward. A pretty sizable reward, if I remember correctly. I wonder if the bounty has increased or decreased since it was first issued. Either way, it's been a while since anyone has come looking for me. But that doesn't mean I'll ever be safe.

I've been poring over my father's notes for most the day, reading about Judith Turner's troop movements and most frequented locations. About her strategies, mindset, and most importantly, about her ambitions and the key statements she's made about how she wants the NAF operated. I can't seem to stop digging and hoping I'll find new information that might trigger something. What that something is, I'm not quite sure. This entire thing feels like an itch I'm unable to scratch.

General Turner's movements are calculated, but she was always two steps behind my father. Almost as if she had been studying him as much as he studied her, waiting for him to make the first move then targeting a response.

All the notes I started after my father died also point to the possibility that the general has been following me as well. Kate's comments from yesterday confirm that to be the case. And worse than that is the fact that she's been way too quiet in the years since I've been hiding.

Not hiding. Retired.

I set down my tea and stand to pace. The sudden drop in activity would make sense if they believed I was dead. With me out of the game, Turner could focus her attention elsewhere. Based on her latest movements and William's updates, it appears that her sole focus is on expanding the NAF and pushing her resources farther west, toward complete domination over the country. But that's not a surprise. That's what they've always wanted. I just didn't think it would happen so soon.

I run my fingers through my hair and over my face. Think. I need to think. Just because some things make sense doesn't mean I understand or can piece all the information together. Some of the content doesn't add up. It sure as hell looked like General Turner was keeping herself geographically close to my father before he was even truly a threat to the NAF. Back before I was even born. But why would she do that? How would someone like Judith Turner even know about Jonathan Clark? I stop pacing and drop my hands to the table in frustration. I don't get it. And there's nothing in my father's notes to explain.

My father never went after Judith Turner until a year or so before I was born. He took up with the Resistance when he was sixteen, like most members do, but he only ran valuable messages for a few years. Judith was only a private then, so neither was a major threat to either side. It wasn't until Judith became a lieutenant and my father graduated to running strikes against small NAF camps that the notes in his journal began to take a very strong slant toward all things Judith Turner.

But there's no reason why. There didn't seem to be any major face-to-face encounters. And it appears they were never really in the same location at the same time. And General Turner was never the one in charge. Not completely. General Trent still held the highest military rank in the NAF.

So what had provoked this fascination? How did Judith even know who he was? Did my father do something to one of her units early on and elect not to log it? Or was it something else? I'm missing a large piece of this puzzle, and I can't believe it took me this long to notice that it's missing.

Light knocking on my door snaps me out of my frantic thoughts. With a sigh, I put the journal back in the safe and reach for the shotgun propped against the wall by the entrance. I look out the peephole. I frown, not sure I'm ready for round two after exposing so much last night.

Shotgun in hand, I unlock the door and swing it open. Sure enough, Kate is standing alone on my front porch, her hands in the air.

"You've been avoiding me."

Of course I have. Not that I want to showcase that. I go for indifference and shrug.

She glances at the gun. Her brow arches slightly. "Mind if I come in?"

I look at her for a moment and wonder if that's such a good idea. My mind is a mess. Aside from trying to piece together our parents' enigmatic history, there's also the fact that I have two more days before we vote on her fate, and I don't have a clue about what we should do with her.

Not to mention the nagging attraction and the fact that I still so very much want to kiss her. She utterly fascinates me. I get the feeling that letting her in my home again will blur a lot of lines, which is why, as she so clearly noticed, I have been avoiding her today.

Despite my better judgment, I step aside to let her in.

"I couldn't sleep. I had a lot on my mind."

I grab the jug of water by my door and pour some into the empty bowl. "I know how that is." I snag a clean towel from the other room and hand it to her after she washes up. What else brought her to my doorstep? "Why did you come here?"

She regards me carefully for a moment. "Simon's been stealing from everyone," she finally says. Her eyes widen. I wonder if she meant to say that.

I chuckle and put my shotgun back against the wall. "I know. I saw him swipe some bread on my way back from the infirmary this morning. And I saw him poking around in Rhiannon's garden a couple of days ago. She's pissed that someone took her corn."

Kate nods as if not at all surprised by my reaction. "He also wants to poison you and get that key around your neck." Her eyes fall to the chain leading under my shirt.

I reveal the key dangling from the end of it. "This? Why?"

She shrugs. "To unlock the ankle bands and make a run for it."

Her lack of regard for secrecy makes me want to laugh. Is she telling me this because she's already come up with a counter plan, or is she trying to play some sort of mind game with me? I carefully tuck the chain back in. "This doesn't unlock the bands on your ankles. It unlocks my safe. The key to your freedom is with Jack."

Kate looks at the safe on the far wall, then at me. She tips her head back and laughs. The sound twists something inside me. "I knew it. Simon's an idiot."

I clear my throat and look away. "So how does he plan on poisoning me?"

Before I even finish my question, she's wandering through my house, scanning everything as if she's looking for something in particular. "He wants me to get close to you. Kind of like we are now."

While she's turned away, I take the opportunity to study her. She has her uniform jacket back on for warmth, but she's still wearing one of my shirts. I like the way it looks on her. I don't think I'll ask for it back. Her hair is down, slightly wavy from the inconsistent weather. Her skin is sun-kissed from the days wandering in the wastelands with her soldiers. She also has on the fitted brown cargo pants I gave her the other day. The bottoms are tucked in her ankle-high black boots. On one of her legs, there's a slight bulge just above her boot-line where the explosive is attached. I try to ignore the guilt of putting it there. She stops to study the old state map on the wall and doesn't elaborate any further on Simon's plan. "Here to slip something into my tea, Turner?"

She shakes her head and chuckles. "Hardly." She glances over her shoulder and catches me staring. "Not my style."

I lean against the door frame as she makes a slow circle in the main room. She runs her fingertips along the spines of the books. This is the second time she's been in my home and the second time she's been drawn to my books. "You have quite the collection."

"I like books."

"As do I." She turns to explore again. Whenever she finds something that piques her interest, she cocks her head and examines it. Of course, I'm aware that she's making a bit of a show of demonstrating how comfortable she is just waltzing through my home. But I'm somehow okay with it.

"I just left the infirmary. Ryan said your guy has been given the all clear. He also heard from Elise that you've been visiting your guy at home every day while he was on bedrest." There's a hint of curiosity in her voice.

"His name is Jamie, and it's my fault he got stabbed. The least I can do is bring him food and keep him company."

"You know, you're nothing like I imagined." It's said suddenly, as if she has been holding it in for quite some time.

"You imagined me?" I tease, amused and flattered.

She rolls her eyes. "Envisioned you. Pictured you."

I want to taunt her more, tell her how I envision her sitting alone somewhere and daydreaming about me, but my curiosity about how she thought I looked outweighs my teasing. "And how did you imagine me?"

"Grotesque." She laughs when I frown. "I fit your looks with your actions. Monstrous and unattractive." Her laugh returns. Only this time, it's shy, nervous. "Guess I was wrong about a lot of things." She turns away with a slight blush instead of elaborating further.

She continues to look at the items in my house as if she didn't just lay one hell of a flirtatious line. It's clear to me that this attraction isn't one-sided. I briefly consider that kiss again and then just as quickly dismiss it. We're enemies. Enemies don't kiss.

To my surprise, and relief, she ignores the safe nestled in the corner, wide open, the contents exposed. It isn't until she spots something on the table that she comes to a complete stop. She points. "What is this?"

"A music player."

She picks up the small device and runs her fingers over it. "I've never seen one like this before." She practically falls backward when it lights up in her hands. Her eyes go wide with wonder. "It works?"

"It does," I say with an amused smile.

"My mother said the NAF doesn't have time for these. We have more important things to focus on," she says sadly. "Can you show me how it works?"

I push off the wall and cross the distance between us. She watches with obvious excitement as I grab the ear buds. I put one in my ear and hold the other to her. "Put that in your ear." I wait as she mimics my actions. It's unnecessary to place my hand over hers as she holds the player, but I can't resist the urge to touch her. I take her thumb and place it on the wheel. I guide it in a circular motion, acutely aware of my body pressed against her side. "What do you want to listen to?"

"Something soothing." She watches everything I do with a curious intensity and makes no move to pull away. I inhale deeply, taking in the slight scent of soap. "Then what?" she asks, lifting her eyes.

"You find what you want and press play," I press her thumb against the button, my eyes never leaving hers.

I take my earbud out and place it gently in her other ear. I take a step back as the music starts. It's nothing fancy, just a simple melody, something slow and soothing like she asked for. But as the music begins, her entire face changes. Her eyes grow wide, and her jaw drops slightly as she cups her ears. She stares at me with such wonderment and awe that I can't stop my smile.

I briefly wonder if I looked the same way the first time I listened to a music player.

Maybe she's never heard music like this before. It's different from the musicians who stand around town or in the pubs and taverns, plucking guitars and banging homemade drums. It's even different from the music box we have in the tavern.

This is entirely more personal.

Her mouth works, but she can't seem to form the words. I gently remove the earbuds from her ears. "I want to show you something else," I tell her, excited.

I toss the earbuds back on the table and move to the large speaker on a shelf against the far wall. I set the music player down in the recessed groove and press play again. The speaker comes to life, and the same song drifts throughout the room.

I'm amused to find Kate somehow even more amazed than she

was a moment ago. "Pretty great, huh? Darby made this work for me a couple years ago. She might be strange, but she's a genius."

She stares at the speaker. "What's his name? The man who's singing."

"Frank Sinatra," I say as I drop into my favorite old recliner.

"It's relaxing. It's perfect," she says with a sigh.

"That's the idea." I look at her curiously. "You really don't really listen to music in the NAF?"

"We have music. We just don't listen to it much. My dad used to tinker with music devices. He would get them working, and when my mom wasn't around, we'd dance around the house." She smiles fondly. "I would stand on his feet, and he'd twirl me around."

I try and picture her as a child dancing on her father's feet. It's such a stark contrast to the disciplined and rigid childhood I envisioned for her. "That sounds nice."

She stares at the music player, her smile fading with the memory. "When he died, the music just kind of died with him." I'm not sure what to say so I stay silent. Her eyes snap to mine. "Do you dance?"

"No. I definitely do *not* dance." My answer is quick and definitive.

She arches a brow. "Why not? What good is music if not for dancing?"

The way she says it, the way she's swaying slightly makes me remember the story of how my parents met. I haven't thought about it in a long time. "That's how my father met my mother." Kate stops swaying and looks at me curiously. "He was lying low in this little town near the reservation where she was born. He had just stolen a horse from the NAF and decided to hide out in said town until they stopped looking. He went into their tavern to eat, and a few of the locals were playing music. She was in the middle of the room dancing. He said he took one look at her and fell madly in love."

"Is that why you won't dance with me? Afraid you'll fall madly in love?" Her smile is soft, and her eyes are shining. I may not be afraid of falling madly in love, but I *am* afraid of doing or saying something I would most definitely regret.

"Something like that," I say with a smile. If she only knew how badly I want to be reckless in this moment. Never in my wildest dreams did I imagine I would be so drawn to Katelyn Turner, and here I am, about to give in and dance with her.

She steps in front of me, grabbing my hands and pulling me to my feet. "Come on. Don't be such a baby."

I narrow my eyes. "Do you want me to stand on your feet, or…"

She rolls her eyes dramatically as I fall back into the recliner. I wasn't kidding; I don't typically dance and I really need to avoid being so close to her. She's making my body and my mind contradict one another. She sighs, giving up and glancing again around the room. She tilts her head to peer inside the safe, finally noticing. "What are those books?"

"My father's old war journals."

Kate stiffens, and I bet she's going through a range of emotions. I watch her carefully, intrigued by her reaction but bracing for the worst. She's curious. I know she is. She looks at them again and hesitates.

"Go on," I tell her, taking a sip of tea. We might as well get this over with.

Slowly, she reaches for the journal on top of the stack. It's the one I was just reading. The one that focuses on her mother. It dates back from before we were both born. I take another sip of lukewarm tea as Kate carefully thumbs through the pages, her eyes widening, and her mouth parting in surprise.

"This is about my mother," she whispers. I say nothing. "This is everything my mother has ever done." She doesn't look at me as she turns the pages, and curiosity transforms to surprise. "This is everything all the way up until…" All the color drains from her face. Her eyes meet mine, and it looks as though she's about to be sick.

She stares at me for a moment. She closes her mouth and clenches her jaw as realization dawns on her. I finish the last of my tea and gently place the cup on the table beside me, my eyes never leaving Kate's. I watch as she goes from confused to understanding and finally settling on anger.

This is about what I expected her reaction to be. Maybe if I had danced with her, she wouldn't have noticed the safe. But then maybe this is what we need to finally stop theoretically dancing around whatever is developing between us.

After a moment, she closes the journal and stands a bit straighter. "Who else have you been tracking?" Her voice is low and measured. As if she already knows the answer.

*Everyone.*

I say nothing. She takes my silence as confirmation to what she already knows and nods. She looks back at the stacks of journals neatly placed along multiple shelves within the safe. "All that you said last night about wanting to be done, about wanting to be out of the war, that was what, all one big lie? To see how I would react? To mess with my head?"

"It wasn't a lie," I tell her simply. And it wasn't.

"You're following the NAF. You're keeping up with everyone and everything. You act as if you don't know what's going on out there, but that's not true, is it? It's all right here." She holds the journal up, then tosses it unceremoniously back into the safe with the others.

"I didn't lie. I've contributed nothing to either side."

"No," she scoffs, "you've just been sitting here collecting information and updating your journals because you have absolutely no interest in the war."

The sarcasm drips from her lips. I sigh.

"Let me guess, it's William, isn't it? He's the one feeding you information. In the hope that you'll...what?"

"In the hope that I'll stay out of it."

Kate lets out a bitter laugh. "Oh, yeah, that's right. He's keeping you informed, and you're jotting it down so you can stay out of it. Does he know I'm here? Did you tell him?"

Her question feels like a betrayal. "If I told him, you'd already be dead."

"Tell me the truth." She looks upset. I don't blame her, but it seems unlike her to actually show it. "Are you still in the war?"

I lean forward and rest my forearms on my knees. "Kate, it's not that simple."

"You're either in or out."

Carefully, I thread my fingers together and pin her with a serious glare. "You mean to tell me that if you wanted out of this war, I mean, if you really didn't want to be in the middle of the fighting and the killing and all the bullshit that comes with it, and you decided you were going to stay right here and be done with it, you could do it? Just walk away and not look back? That you wouldn't care if William was still coming for you? Or coming for your family? Or if there's someone new to worry about out in the middle of it, murdering your friends? You wouldn't want to know if everything you worked for your entire life was in jeopardy of being ripped away? If your mom was okay? If Ryan was alive and safe?"

That last one seems to really nail my point home. Kate looks away, her jaw still clenched, her hands in fists by her side, but not arguing.

I can tell she wants to say something but I don't give her the chance. "It's not that easy to just turn your back on everything."

Her eyes meet mine, and maybe it's the light from the lanterns scattered across the room, but from here, they look a little bit misty. Maybe it's the anger. Maybe it's defeat. Maybe it's something else. Betrayal? Again, I push away the guilt.

I relax my shoulders a little and take a deep breath. "I'm not setting things in motion. I'm not going after anyone. I'm not even making suggestions on what the Resistance should be doing. I'm just existing. Here. Farming, building a fence, scavenging what I can out there in the wasteland."

"Strapping bombs to the enemy," she says bitterly. So the shine in her eyes is anger.

I lean back. "Just because I'm not fighting you doesn't mean you aren't the enemy. You'll always be the enemy. I'm just choosing not to pull the trigger."

Kate makes a point of looking at her ankle. "Funny way of not pulling the trigger." Okay, so she has me there. "What do your journals say about me?" I'm surprised to see hurt and betrayal in her expression. "What are you writing about me?"

"I haven't written anything."

"But that's why you kept us alive. For information. All of our conversations…" She doesn't finish. She doesn't have to. She's just realized she's been used this entire time.

Except that's not necessarily true. Not after last night when I realized the lines I tried to draw between us were utterly useless. "To start, yes."

We stare for a long moment, Frank Sinatra long over, and a new, equally calming song fills the silence. But it does nothing to ease the tension. I can tell Kate is struggling to make a decision. So I wait.

I liked it better when we were flirting.

It seems like several minutes stretch out as Billie Holiday sings until Kate finally decides what she wants to say. "I think you should—"

But whatever the hell it is will have to wait because loud knocking interrupts the moment. I'm both relieved and pissed. Kate startles as I stare at the door, thinking of not answering. The next knock is louder. I once again grab the shotgun and fling the door open.

Mike stands there with his rifle and a lantern. "There's a kid here to…is that Billie Holiday?" When his mouth drops open and his eyes go wide, I know he's just noticed Kate.

"Mike," I say, snapping his attention back to me.

"Uh." He looks from Kate back to me. "Um, oh, yeah, there's a kid here to see you."

"A kid?" I glance at Kate. Her frown tells me she's as baffled as I am. I step around her and slam my safe shut. Whatever hostility Kate is feeling shifts to business, and she falls in step with me as we leave the house. I glance at her and am taken aback by her completely neutral expression, as if we hadn't just shared an insanely tense moment. The three of us walk down the street.

I have no idea why anyone is here this late looking for me, let alone a kid. But I have a sinking suspicion it can't be good news. Kate finally shoots me a look that lets me know that regardless of our heated exchange, she's a bit unsettled as well.

We round the corner, and I can finally see the front gates. Standing next to two of the night guards holding up lanterns is a teenage boy, maybe sixteen, wringing the reins of his horse nervously. His hair is curly and wild, and his face is flushed.

Kate leans in closer. "I thought you said there weren't any more couriers due to stop by." Her tone tells me everything. Another lie she thinks I told.

"There weren't." I didn't lie to her about the courier. This one isn't mine. The boy straightens when I get closer, and his horse shifts. "He's not a standard courier."

Mike nods at the two guards, and they leave us to return to their posts. I rest my hand on the butt of one of my pistols and wait for him to settle his horse. "What's your name?"

He lifts his chin. "Max."

"What brings you here so late, Max?" His nervous shifting makes me uneasy.

"I was told to give you this," he says and hands me a sealed letter, glancing briefly at Mike and then Kate. "For your eyes only."

I scan the outside quickly. No markings. "Are you hungry?" I ask without looking at him.

He shakes his head and bounces on the balls of his feet. "No, I had some dried fruit not too long ago."

"Thirsty?"

"I'm okay." He pats his horse. "But my horse could use some water."

"We'll get you both some." I motion one of the guards back over, and Max hands the reins to the guard and waits.

I break the seal. As I read the message, I can feel the others staring, waiting for a reaction. I get down to the bottom, see the single letter scrawled there, and know exactly why Max came so late. It's the first time in seven years I've been asked to meet with the Resistance.

I turn to Max and nod. He relaxes now, his job finished. There's no need to give a reply. I rest my hand on his shoulder. "Thank you, Max." He straightens and smiles. I pull the guard in close. "Please make sure both Max and his horse get food and water. He's come a long way. Make sure he has a comfortable place to stay and anything else he might need."

The guard nods. "Come on," he grunts to the boy.

I look back down at the letter and read it again, clenching my jaw. "It's from William," I say, my eyes still on the message. "He's close."

"What does he want?" Mike asks.

"A meeting." Whatever's going on must be pretty big. William wouldn't have sent for me like this otherwise. When I look up at Kate, I see she's staring. I can't decide if I wish we were alone or if she weren't here for this exchange at all.

"What are you going to do?" Mike asks.

I look away from Kate and focus on him. "Go get Rhiannon. Tell her we need her to open the tavern. Then go get the elders. The council needs to meet immediately."

Mike glances at Kate but to his credit, doesn't say a word. Instead, he jogs back up the road like I asked.

I fold the letter, sticking it in my back pocket. "Your mother is close. She's assembling a search party to look for you."

I walk away before I can gauge her reaction.

❖

"Baba O'Riley" echoes quietly through the tavern. The music is supposed to create a more relaxed atmosphere but somehow makes the mood even more ominous. I'm sure Jack's choice of song was more for my benefit than to relax the others. The town elders along with Jack, Mike, Elise, Rhiannon, Darby, Lucas, and Max the messenger are spread across three of the back tables. The dozen or so people stare at me as I face them while leaning against the side of the table with my arms crossed.

The large fireplace blazes behind them. Roscoe sleeps unperturbed on the small rug in front of the fireplace, unaware of or just uncaring about the thick feeling of tension radiating from person to person.

"I don't understand," Darby says, rubbing at her eyes. "How did the courier get to William so fast? There's no way William could've gotten to Rapid City that quickly."

"Because the courier never went all the way to the East Coast," I explain for the second time since gathering them all at the tavern. "All of my letters to William go through the Resistance base Freedom, not through Rapid City. We agreed that sending a non-Resistance courier to the east was too dangerous. But every courier stops by the major towns and bases anyway, so it just made sense to send them to the base and have a Resistance-marked courier take it the rest of the way, depending on wherever William happens to be."

"I would've gone to Freedom myself, but Dani and I agreed it would be better if I got back right away. Instead, I went to the next town over, and Max took the letter," Jack says between chugs of beer. "Where the hell is the radio I gave you? And where's my buggy?"

Max, still slightly disheveled, ignores him. "When I got to Freedom, William was already there. He gave me the letter and told me to come straight here with his response."

Now Elise looks confused. "But that's just a three-day ride from here. I thought William was on the East Coast."

"Because the war has landed this far west," I tell them regrettably. "William was already here because he knew the NAF was coming this way. He warned me not too long ago, and George confirmed it when he last stopped by."

"And this letter you just got," Elise says slowly, "is from William, and it says the general is close and is preparing to send out a search party for the missing soldiers."

"But why?" Mabel calls out. "Why is this a big deal? Didn't we know this was a possibility?"

I shift ever so slightly and try to remain stoic and undeterred. "It matters because one of the NAF members here, Major Katelyn Turner, is the general's daughter."

"Seriously?" Darby says, putting her head in her hands with wide eyes. She's not the only one muttering in disbelief. Everyone save for Lucas and Jack looks utterly floored.

Rhiannon leans forward. "The general's daughter? Are you *insane*?" It isn't her words that hit me like a punch to the gut but the look of utter betrayal etched across her face. I've had so many opportunities to tell her, to tell all of them, what was really going on, and I didn't. "Is that why you hid her jacket? So we wouldn't piece it together?"

"I didn't even know the general had a daughter," one of the elders says. Of course they didn't. Out here where we aren't affected by NAF rule, people don't tend to keep up with them. Not in the way the Resistance does. Not in the way that I do.

I let them voice their outrage, all of them barking questions, murmuring to themselves, and yelling in my direction what they think we should do about it. I wait until things start to die down, and I run my hand through my hair, bracing to try to explain.

"Why didn't you tell us sooner?" Rhiannon asks. I can read her tone perfectly: *Why didn't you tell me sooner?*

Lucas places his hands flat on the table as he leans forward. "You're on a need-to-know basis, and you most certainly did not need to know. If you did, it'd create a panic and spread like wildfire."

"Okay, so you didn't want us to freak out, but the general's daughter? Of course they're coming here after us," Rhiannon says.

"We're all as good as dead," Mabel shouts dramatically. "And will someone please turn off that god-awful racket!"

Rhiannon casts me one last disappointed look before slowly getting up and unplugging the jukebox.

"You should've told us," Mike repeats quietly.

"She didn't tell us because she wanted to do things her way and didn't want us to have a say. She claims to want to stay out of the war, but the way I see it, she never really left it, and this is her ticket back in." Bernard meets my eyes. "Isn't that right?"

"It's not like that."

"Yes, it is," Bernard says. "You put this whole damn town in danger because you found out one of those soldiers is the daughter of the woman who killed your father, and you've been itching for revenge."

I clench my jaw but continue to stare back at Bernard, neither of us backing down. He's not wrong, or at least, he wasn't. But revenge is definitely not the reason I'm keeping Kate in this town. Curiosity, maybe.

I straighten my shoulders and tip my chin in the air. Bernard is the chairperson, and when he speaks, everyone listens. But that doesn't mean I have to sit here and take it.

Jack beats me to a response. "Who cares who she is? None of you have ever been face-to-face with a gray coat before this, so get off your high horses and try not to land on your ass when you hit the ground."

"Young man, that is wildly inappropriate," Bernard says.

In typical Jack fashion, he doesn't seem to care. "Calling it like I see it. Was Dani stupid and selfish for wanting to keep the prisoners here? Yes. Are the rest of you cowards who like to hide behind meetings to avoid making hard decisions and getting your own hands dirty? Also, yes."

Rhiannon sits beside him and places a gentle hand on his forearm. "Jack, stop."

His insulting outburst will only rile everyone up even more, and I'm tempted to let him have at it. Maybe he will say what I can't.

Darby leans back and crosses her arms. "I still say we kill them."

A few of the elders nod and mutter in agreement. I chew on my lip and nod as though I'm considering the option. After a moment, I unholster my pistol and take a few strides to close the distance between me and Darby. She looks confused as I turn the grip to her. She glances at the gun and then back at me. I give it a little shake. "Go on, then, take it." She doesn't. "If you want them dead so bad, then take the gun and do it. Right now."

Darby sits up straighter, and all eyes are on her. Her arm twitches as though she's going to take the pistol, but she deflates and looks away.

I hold the gun out to the elders. They, too, all look away. Jack was right about them hiding in their meetings.

"You're all so eager for those soldiers to die, but you refuse to be the ones to do it. You want me to. The murderer can murder on your behalf, am I right? You trust me when it comes to providing this town with resources and supplies. You trust me to take down the raiders. To keep you safe. You trust me to be your weapon when it suits you. But when it comes to my choice to keep someone you hate alive, you don't care what I have to say?"

Jack goes to stand. "I'll do it." Rhiannon grabs his arm and yanks him back in his chair.

No one else says anything for a long time. In fact, most seem to be at least slightly embarrassed for their chants of death.

I holster my pistol. "You have a right to be angry. I was wrong for not coming to you sooner. About not being fully transparent. But it's complicated, and I was hoping to get more information from them before presenting you with options."

"And what are those options?" Jack asks. He may have my back, but I can tell he's angry. That I didn't confide in him. That I didn't trust him enough to come up with a plan. I don't blame him. I'd be angry, too. "Look, I don't care that you brought them in. I mean, do I wish we had let them die out there with the raiders? Absolutely. But you wanted information, and you can't get that from a dead guy. I get it. I think we all get that. What we don't get is why they are still here? Why didn't you tell us about the general's daughter? Why not just hand them over to William?"

"Because William would've killed them."

"Who cares?" someone yells.

"That officer is our only chance at knowing what to expect, and we won't know that if William kills her."

"We just want to know what's going on," Rhiannon says quietly. The rest of the crowd agrees.

I grab a chair and turn it so when I sit, I'm facing the lot of them as if I'm on trial. I struggle to put into words all the things I haven't wanted to admit to myself, let alone a room full of people I genuinely care for.

"You're all right. I haven't fully let go of the war. I've stayed true to my promise, and I haven't brought Resistance fighters here. I haven't pushed to make this a safe haven for them. I haven't gone looking for trouble. But I've been following the war. Tracking movements."

Mike raises his hand. "No one is accusing you of breaking your promise. We don't care that you want to stay informed."

"When William told me the NAF were coming west, I knew the NAF expansion was going to happen sooner rather than later. Especially with General Turner in charge. And when George confirmed that they were close, it was only a matter of time before they found us. If we had killed those soldiers, more would have come in their place. Either way, it was only a matter of time before the NAF came for this town. Our home. Judith Turner only cares about pushing west and taking over the rest of what's left of the country. She's pushed more men out west in the past month than General Trent did his entire career. She won't stop until everything is under her control or burned to the ground." I allow the urgency of the situation to sink in. "It may not be tomorrow, but the NAF is coming."

I think of White River and of all our neighboring towns burning or being taken over by NAF. They don't have soldiers to fight back, and there aren't enough Resistance members to help. None of us stand a chance if the NAF continue to push out west. It hurts more than I ever imagined to think of this place, these people, and the wastelands being destroyed.

I steady my breath and try to convey just how serious I am. "They are coming to claim the wasteland, and we can't fight back. Resistance is not an option."

No one says anything. Perhaps I am finally getting through to them.

I soften my tone, "You all let me in when no one else would. You saved me and Lucas, and I will forever be indebted to you. In exchange, the Resistance used their resources to have your town wiped off NAF maps. I believe that no matter what we do, it's inevitable that we'll be found out. Especially now that the NAF are so close." I look down and brace myself for what I'm about to say. I raise my eyes and steady my voice. "I know it's hard to hear, but with the NAF moving in, you need to leave town. All of you. And soon."

The outrage starts strong, with everyone calling out their disbelief, their anger, their refusal. People shoot from their seats and point fingers at me. No one wants to leave, and who can blame them?

"This is our home," a voice near the bar calls out.

"You," Mabel says, pointing her cane right at me. "You did this. You put our lives at risk."

I shake my head. "The NAF did this."

"You didn't help," someone shouts.

The murmurs and accusations intensify. Breaking through the chaos comes a single, strong voice. "Everyone, stop!" It's Rhiannon. She's the youngest councilmember but also one of the most respected. "Stop," she repeats, softer.

The talking trails off, and everyone allows her to speak. "Listen. We always knew this was a risk. When we took Dani and Lucas in, we knew this was a possibility. We voted to let them stay. We agreed they deserved a second chance, and we agreed that they needed us as much as we needed them." She scans the crowd and stands tall at the bar. Her shoulders are back and her head high, but she's avoiding my eyes. "The NAF would be coming this way whether we were in this situation or not. Dani knows this war better than any of us. She knows their tactics, and she knows how they think. And if she says it isn't safe, it isn't safe. This town has seen its fair share of danger over the years, and Dani has always seen us through. The least we can do is hear her out."

"Then what's your plan?" Jack says, his voice tense with annoyance.

I swallow hard. "We're going to release the soldiers." Silence swallows the room. "First thing tomorrow morning." I find the key players. "Elise, make sure their injured man is ready for travel. Mike and Jack, separate the soldiers into two groups so you can take them back to their base. Both of you pick someone to go with you." Despite being gutted and angry, all three of them solemnly nod, so I continue. "I'm going to leave tonight, before the sun rises, to get ahead of this and try to get help for White River from William and the Resistance. I'm taking Lucas with me."

"You're just gonna leave us?" Darby asks.

"Yes. We're more danger to everyone if the NAF finds us here."

Just as I think the silence in the room may crush me, Mabel speaks up. "How do you know we won't kill them the second you leave?"

I let out a breath, grateful, for once, that she's spoken up, "Because getting them safely back to base is your best chance for survival."

"But then they'll know where we are," Elise says.

"Yes." My voice barely cuts through the murmuring. "But it'll at least buy you some time."

"If we kill them instead, that would buy us more time to prepare to fight," Bernard says. "It could take months for the search party to get here."

"You can't win against them, Bernard. Whether it's tomorrow or two months from now." I plead with everything I can muster. "Pack up and leave. The sooner the better."

"Where will we go?" an elderly woman asks.

I give her a sympathetic look. "I have a place in mind several hours south of here. But you have to leave within two days."

Another voice, steady and angry, comes from the back. "And if we don't? You said it yourself, we aren't on their maps. Maybe they won't find us."

They're scared. Hurt. At this moment, they don't trust anything I am telling them. "Then fortify the fence, arm the bombs out front, and pray that the NAF doesn't come. They found this place without maps before, and they'll do it again. This time, they'll be looking." Several of them begin to murmur. "I'm going to do my best to get help. I swear on everything, I will try, but you need to leave in case I can't find it in time."

Rhiannon lets out a long breath. She's still avoiding my eyes. "Well, then. I guess it's time we vote. Release the prisoners or kill them."

The vote is narrowly in my favor. Thanks to Lucas, Elise, Rhiannon, Jack, and begrudgingly, Darby. The only thing everyone does agree on is that the only choice is to protect what they can, however they can. And I don't believe they'll kill Kate or her soldiers. These aren't murderous people.

"This is ludicrous," Bernard says, no doubt mad the vote didn't go in his favor again. "We will wait until the prisoners have been released, and then we will give the people the option of leave or stay. We cannot force people to flee their homes."

I wonder how many will actually go. Probably very few. This place is established and well-functioning. The resources and trading are remarkable. Why would anyone want to leave? Even if they are threatened with being burned to the ground.

With nothing left to do until morning, people mutter amongst themselves as they flood out the door. I try to ignore the sting when nobody speaks to me.

The final few people trickle out. Jack stops to hand me the key to the devices and give me a small nod, then leaves me with my brother and Rhiannon. Lucas reads my body language better than anyone. He probably recognizes my inner turmoil, but it still surprises me when he swoops down to hug me. It's brief but tight. I pat his chest as he pulls away. "You don't have to come with me, Lucas. You can stay. You can leave with Darby. Help get these people to safety and start all over."

"I'd follow you into any battle," he says with a smile and punches me lightly in the arm.

I want to argue. Tell him he doesn't deserve this, and he should be happy and safe and settled. But I know it'd be of no use. He won't leave me just like I won't leave him. I push the hair from my face and nod. "Better go pack, then. And fill up the Jeep. We're leaving before the sun comes up."

Once Lucas leaves, I glance at where Rhiannon is pretending to be busy over by the counter. She's picking at something, a splinter from the countertop, and I walk over to sit on the stool beside her.

She doesn't speak, and I'm not sure exactly what to say either. I fold my hands in front of me on the countertop and play with my fingers, reminding myself that this is the only way to keep her safe. She looks tired. Defeated.

"I don't know what I'm supposed to do," she finally says, her voice soft and filled with sadness. "This is my home."

"Rhi—"

"I don't even know how to live out there," she cuts me off, louder than before. "Beyond the walls. This is all I know, the only home I've ever had, Dani." A tear rolls down her cheek, and she doesn't even bother to try to wipe it away. A pang of guilt stabs through my chest.

It's the way she says my name. So full of hurt. So...betrayed. Between her voice, Lucas's hug, and knowing I may never see Kate again—something I'm not quite sure how to process—my intolerance for feelings is at an all-time high. "Rhi..."

"My grandma owned this tavern. My mother named me from a song on that very music box. My great-grandma helped build this place with her bare hands. This is my entire world."

"I'm sorry."

"I know you are. But it still doesn't make the hurt go away."

"You're my best friend, Rhiannon. You're hurting because of me." There's a lump in my throat that doesn't seem to go away no matter how hard I try to swallow it. "If I thought staying here and fighting them would help, I would do it. I would take them all on by myself. But it would only make things worse. Make them more vindictive."

She doesn't say anything.

"If I could take you with me, if I could take all of you with me, I would." I shake my head knowing that would only put her further in harm's way. "It was only a matter of time before the war caught up with me. And that's no place for you. You deserve better than that. You deserve to be safe and away from it all."

"I don't have a choice, do I? You said the NAF was coming no matter what."

I stare, her defeated and disheartened expression twisting like a knife in my gut. Needing a distraction, I stand and rummage behind the counter. She watches but doesn't stop me. I finally find something to write with, and I grab a piece of wrapping for the meat and jot down a set of coordinates I know by heart.

"Promise me you'll leave. As awful as this is, promise you will pack what you can and get the hell out." I hand her the paper. She glances at the contents and then tilts her head to the side. "You'll be safe here."

Rhiannon stares at me for what feels like an eternity. I want to beg her to go now, but in her state of mind, that would only make things worse. She needs time to grieve and accept the situation.

"Would it have ended differently? If we had killed them instead of taking them in?" Her voice is quiet. Guilt ridden at having been the one to allow them to stay and swaying the others into agreement. All for me. She's asking if she made the wrong choice.

"A search party would still be coming. Whether they are dead or alive. Whether we knew Kate was the general's daughter or not." I am sure of it.

"And if the soldiers had never showed up?" She looks at me. "Would we have to leave here?"

I shake my head. "I don't know. But I think, if this hadn't happened, the NAF would still come, eventually. They were already closing in." It's the most honest answer I can give her.

"Where will you go?"

"North. To see William first. See if I can get some help. It's a long shot, but I have to try." I think about what will happen after that. "Then probably back home." It tastes wrong in my mouth, calling someplace that isn't here home. "But if the Resistance can't stop them, then there will be nowhere left to go."

I stand and wait for some sort of acknowledgment that she understands what I'm trying to say. Finally, she nods once and throws her arms around my neck. She buries her face in my shoulder, and I hold her tightly. "Will I ever see you again?"

I squeeze her a little tighter. "Of course. When all of this blows over." This time, she's the one who tightens her hold.

## CHAPTER TWELVE: THE RELEASE

### *Kate*

*Your mother is close. She's assembling a search party to look for you.*

Dani's words roll over and over in my head as I rush to find Ryan. My heart is racing. A search party. I round the corner and all but run to where he's being quartered. I don't even bother to knock but burst through the door.

"Ryan! Ryan!"

I hear a soft thud from above and race up the staircase just in time to see him appear at the top of the steps, disheveled, rubbing at his eyes, and holding a lantern. "Kate? What's wrong? What happened?"

"Get down here." My words are rushed. "The general is close. She's assembling a search party to look for us."

"What?" he loudly whispers as he shuffles down the steps. He rushes past me into the sitting room where he lights a second lantern. The room fills with a soft glow. He turns to me with wide eyes. "When are they coming?"

"I have no idea." I search for the emotion I know I'm supposed to have in this moment. The thrill of my mother actually caring enough to look for me.

"Then how—"

"A letter came for Dani." Ryan stares at me, expressionless. We stand as if stalled in this tiny room, each waiting for the other to crack and give some sort of a response. I'm anxious to see his, to both the news of the search party and the implication of what it might mean for our fate.

Slowly, I watch the light come to his eyes, and a small smile forms on his lips. He's more focused on the rescue, it seems.

"Kate, this is huge." He starts moving first. His hands on top of his head, then the sides of his face, down to his chest. He lets out a grunt of relief.

"Yeah, it's huge." My response of excitement is forced. I know I should be happy. I know this is a very good and very big thing. I'm just not sure it's a positive thing for us.

Ryan bounces as he steps nearer, then stops short, frowning. "Why do you look so put out by the idea of being rescued?"

I move away. Uncertainty floods every inch of me as I pace. "Because now we might really be as good as dead."

His frown deepens and his shoulders tense as if finally coming to the same realization. "You think the townsfolk are going to kill us so we aren't found?"

I slump. "It would make the most sense. And given the history between Dani and my mother, I can't predict what she'll do."

"The general is smart, smarter than General Trent ever was. She'll have a plan that no one will see coming." I can hear the hopefulness in his voice, even if it's obvious neither of us really believes that.

"Danielle Clark has been tracking my mother since childhood." I step away, thinking about the journals locked away in Dani's safe. The anger I felt when finding them comes flooding back. "And she's still tracking her. Right now."

"What?"

"Apparently, Jonathan Clark kept war journals. Lots of them. They have information about everything from combat techniques to personnel numbers. Intel that is damn near impossible for the Resistance to know without being on the inside. Dani has been keeping the journals current. With special attention to the movements and actions of my mother." I think about the maps and coordinates off in the margins.

"How do you know that?"

His doubt fuels the fire I feel inside. "I saw the journals," I snap. "I saw the notes from both Jonathan and Dani."

"When?"

"Just now," I yell and resume my pacing. "Before the letter was delivered. She keeps them in a safe in her house and has done a pretty damn good job keeping them up-to-date."

Ryan looks taken aback. "You were in her house reading her father's journals? How did you manage that?"

"She showed them to me." I say it like it's the most obvious thing in the world, but after the words are left to linger in the space between us, I realize just how absurd it is.

"She just handed you her intel? Why would she do that?"

I don't dare tell him about her confessions to me at the tavern or that she might've almost kissed me. I don't tell him about the music or my request for her to dance with me. It's abundantly clear that I'm crossing a line with Dani, and she's crossing a line with me. There's no other way to explain why she let me read her journals.

But there's no way in hell I'm saying any of that to Ryan.

Instead, I shift the conversation back to us. "Will you focus?" I push his chest as I stride past, loop around a chair, and walk back again. "More troops are headed this way. The town can't withstand the NAF's firepower, which means they don't have long to act." I'm speaking more to myself than to him. I need to sort this out.

"Good, then maybe we stand a chance of getting out of this shithole." He rubs at his chest like my push actually hurt.

"You're not understanding. Dani knows my mother, and she knows troops are coming." I stop pacing and sigh heavily. "Whatever the town's going to do with us, whether it's hand us over to the Resistance or kill us, they're going to do it fast."

"Do you think we'll stand a chance if we get handed over to the Resistance?" he asks.

"I think we're as good as dead either way." I try to keep the dread out of my voice but based on Ryan's expression, I do a pretty crappy job of it.

"What do we do?" he asks softly. This isn't just about awaiting orders. He truly does care about me. About my opinion. My feelings. He has always cared for me in a way that I've never been able to reciprocate. Even when he questions my interactions with Dani, I know it stems, at least a little bit, from jealousy. He'll never *not* support me. I know he's ready to follow me into any storm I lead us into.

"What *can* we do?" I run my hand through my hair, having no idea how to get out of this situation. I can only hope that whatever spark has ignited between Dani and me is enough to keep us alive.

"Do the others know?"

I give him a look. "Of course not."

I can see the gears turning in his head. "Where is Dani now?"

"She's meeting with the council to decide our fate." It brings me no comfort when Ryan's face pales.

He runs his hand over his short hair and nods. "We should be together when it's decided. And we shouldn't rule out taking as many rebels with us as we can."

"You sound like Simon," I say. He's serious, though, and I know what he's saying. If we're going die, we should make our deaths count. I feel as though all the air has been sucked from my lungs. My stomach twists in knots, and I will myself not to cry. But he's right. We shouldn't go down without some sort of fight. I really hope Dani won't let it come to that. "Don't tell the others anything, yet. Just be prepared for the worst."

"And what are you going to do?"

I release a long, shaky breath. "I'm going to try to figure out which fate we're about to face."

Before I can go, Ryan pulls me in for a long embrace. I break away first, and he watches me leave from the doorway.

Everything is eerily quiet here tonight. Windows are dark, and the moon is the only thing giving decent light. Even the air is calm, albeit a little cold. I move quickly and quietly along the path. I'm heading to Dani's house, and I'm not sure what to expect when I get there. I'm still angry, still scared, but if she's there, I have to try. Even if that means pleading for my life and the lives of my soldiers. I'm not even sure that will work. I truly don't know where her head is now that my mother, the woman she simultaneously hates and is obsessed with, is so close and sending troops.

Dani seems to thrive on strategy. Maybe she's come up with another plan. Maybe she'll use me as leverage so my mother won't invade. Leave the town alone or she'll kill me. That sort of thing. Unfortunately for me, I'm not sure that would be good enough for my mother. I don't know if her love for me outweighs her hate for Dani.

Her windows are dark when I arrive. She's probably not back yet. I reach for the knob regardless. Unlocked. I hesitate for a moment. I want to see more of those journals, but there's no way that Danielle Clark didn't lock them up. The temptation to check is too intense to not at least try.

I push the door open and step inside. She's left a low lantern near the safe and I see that the journals are, indeed, safely locked away. I'm disappointed but not surprised.

There's a book sitting on a display table near the safe. I noticed it before but didn't comment. I scoop up her lantern, get closer, and see that it's a photography book about Native Americans. It's prewar and in immaculate condition. I've seen pictures of Native Americans in the past, but before Dani and Lucas, I had never met anyone of Native heritage. Is this all of Dani's past life that she kept, or is there more? I drag my fingers softly over the cover. It's beautiful.

For a moment, I wish we could go backward, Dani and me. All of us. Back to a time before the wars. Before the climate shift and disease. Would we be leading different lives? Maybe ones where we could exist together. How far back would we need to go in order to achieve that, or was this nation always meant to be divided? I slide my fingers up the edge of the book, tempted to flip through its pages.

I snap out of my daze realizing that wishes are empty. I extinguish the lantern before leaving, closing the door behind me.

The lights from the tavern draw me in. They are still meeting and deciding our fates. Deciding their own, as well. I know my mother searching for me throws a wrench into their plans, even if they did know it was a possibility. I move in closer. It's a clutter of voices, and I can't distinguish a single one or what is being said. I move around the building and look for a cracked window. None.

Disappointed, I realize this is useless. I just have to hope I'm right and that Dani will fight to keep us alive. Until it's decided, I will have to wait until she comes to find me. Plus, I'd rather not run into Mohawk or any of the others. They wouldn't be as understanding about my snooping.

I briefly consider going back to her house to wait, but instead, I head for the lake. The guards, clearly unaware of the new development, allow me to pass without question.

The moon is bright enough to light my path and reflects off the still water. It's calm here. Tranquil. I sit for a moment before arching my back, stretching my arms, and slowly sinking back into the earth. I try to get my body to relax.

General Judith Turner is sending a search party. I honestly didn't think she cared enough. Familial bonds tell me I should be excited.

Thrilled that she loves me enough to send troops out looking for me. My gut says otherwise. She's probably more interested in the equipment and supplies we lost along the way.

I run my fingers through my hair, holding my head, and close my eyes. I don't know what I'm doing anymore. A cool breeze buffets me and the tall grass I lie in along the lake bank. Maybe I should just swim out past the bomb's perimeter and end it? Maybe if I'm gone, my soldiers can be released, and their problem with holding the general's daughter would be decided. I doubt anyone would comb the lake for body parts.

It's a morbid thought and one I don't give much time to entertaining. Besides, the town would eventually be discovered anyway, and I'm not sure the others hold much value for ransom. Another grisly thought.

I close my eyes and lie on my back to try to clear my mind. How the hell did I end up in this situation?

"You're in my spot."

I open my eyes to see Dani staring down at me.

My stomach flips. I'm not sure if it's because that means my fate has been decided or if the mere sight of her stirs something deep inside me.

"We can't share?" I ask innocently.

"I don't know, there's not a lot of room," she says, looking around the lake and the shore. I sit up. "You looked lost in thought."

I hum in response.

"What were you thinking about?"

"Blowing myself up." I keep my voice even.

She whistles dramatically. "Do you want me to leave you alone or…"

I laugh and give in to her charm. "I was just thinking about my mom," I answer honestly.

"Ah." She sits beside me and looks at the lake. Picking up a flat stone, she runs her fingers along the smooth surface and tosses it toward the water. It skips several times along before sinking.

"How did the meeting go?"

"It had its highs and lows," she says dismissively. "You talk with your people?"

"Just Ryan." Silence falls between us, and all I can hear is the gentle lapping of the water and the chirp of crickets. "Do you know what this means? The search party?" I catch her staring at the moon. "Of course you do. You have journals on everything."

"I wasn't trying to betray you, Kate," she says it softly, as though it's a secret not meant for anyone but me. "With the journals."

"Why wouldn't you, though? We're enemies." I say it to convince myself.

She turns to look at me curiously, as if she's trying to figure this out just as I am. "Are we?"

"You're Resistance." I motion to where her tattoo is hidden beneath her sleeve. "I'm NAF. You hate my mother."

"You're not your mother." Even in the poor lighting, I can see the sincerity in her gaze. I can't trust her. I shouldn't trust her. She would say and do anything to protect herself and to protect these people. Rationally, I know she's not my friend or my ally. But dammit if my body isn't screaming at me to give in to her, to trust her.

"My mother is coming, Dani." I don't think I can stress this hard enough. "And she's bringing the whole NAF with her. She's been plotting and planning and putting things into place to overtake the west. Now she has more of a reason. This search party, it's just a ruse." I'm revealing too much about my mother. It's nothing Dani doesn't already know but borderline treasonous all the same. "Killing us or not, she'll destroy your town if she finds out you're here."

She stands and wipes her hands on her pants. "I'm letting you go."

"What?" I am so confused that it takes me a minute to realize she's serious. I make a move to stand next to her, but she holds out her hand, motioning me to stay put.

"You and the others. First thing in the morning." Her words and clipped and matter-of-fact, like this is the most obvious solution in the world.

"Did you hear what I said?" I don't think she understands. My mother will kill them. She will kill *her*. I start to panic.

"I heard you."

"Then why—"

"Do you *want* me to execute you?" Her expression softens, and she squats beside me. "Look, Kate, we may not be on the same side, but I don't think of you as an enemy. Not anymore. And as far as I can tell, we need more people like you in the NAF to prevent outrageously bad things from happening. And that can't happen if you're dead. So I'm letting you go."

"They'll burn your town. We'll have to report that these people have harbored you and your brother." It's a reminder I know she doesn't need to hear. "Even if I don't say anything, Ryan will. God, Simon will for sure."

She groans. "Dammit, Kate, you're practically begging me to kill all of you. Do you want to die?"

"No." I shake my head. "No, I just…you need to know what will happen."

"I know what will happen."

I'm confused and taken aback. Dani stares, her face so close I can see the pain of her decision within her eyes. I glance at my ankle. "It's going to be rather difficult to leave, considering we're physically confined to your town."

"Yeah, that is a problem." She slowly leans in.

The shift in my emotions happens so fast, I barely register it. I can feel her warm breath on my cheek. I tilt my head back just slightly, waiting and bracing myself. Is she finally going to kiss me?

But the pressure of her lips never comes.

Instead, I hear a soft click, and the weight around my ankle is gone. I look at my leg, confused. Dani holds the metal band in one hand and the key in the other.

I exhale, my cheeks warming in embarrassment. I hope like hell she can't sense the rapid beating of my heart. "Just like that?"

She snaps the band closed. "Just like that."

"Why didn't you tell William we were here?" I ask.

She doesn't answer for a long time. But when she does, her voice is soft and sincere. "You're nothing like I imagined, either."

The air is thick with her confession. In just a short amount of time, Dani has completely thrown everything I thought I knew about her into a tailspin. I have so many questions, and I want to know everything about her. I want to know what she was like as a child or if she has nightmares about the things that she's done. I want to know what makes her happy or how she envisions her future. Does she like being settled down? Does she want to get married? Has she ever been in love?

I have a strong urge to take her hand. To tell her we're more alike than I ever envisioned. I want to lean into her and ask her what happens next. What happens with us. If there *is* an us. Instead, I look at the cylinder that she removed from my leg.

"She's going to come for you when she finds out you're alive."

Her shoulders fall. This isn't news to her. And if I'm being honest, I'm not sure why I'm saying it.

"I know."

"And I don't think I can stop her." This time, I've said something unexpected. "You shouldn't be here when they come. It'll only make it worse. Maybe if you and Lucas are gone, this place will stand a chance. I'll do what I can but—"

Dani takes my hand. "Thank you." Her thumb brushes over my knuckles. I look down as she slowly caresses my skin. I wonder how I can be so angry with her one moment and rendered speechless by her the next.

When I lift my eyes, Dani is staring at my lips. I lick them in the hope that she'll lean in. This is the second time I've wished for her to kiss me since we've been out here.

But for the second time, she doesn't.

She pulls her hand back and clears her throat, turning her attention to the water. The fact that I'm so disappointed startles me. Perhaps I'm misreading this entire situation. Maybe this attraction is one-sided, and I'm making a fool of myself.

I motion to the band still in her hand, desperate to cut some of this tension and ignore what my body is screaming. "Simon was right. They're fake, aren't they? They were never rigged to explode."

Dani's eyebrows rise, and she laughs. "Oh no, they're real."

I'm not convinced. "I don't believe you."

She looks at me for a moment, that arrogant smirk still on her lips. I'm about to grab the band when she brings her arm back and throws the device at the lake as if she's skipping stones. It spins far out across the water, and I'm about to say something arrogant when the boom hits.

The explosion is loud and lights up the night sky like celebratory fireworks. I jump so hard that I actually come up off the ground. "Holy shit!"

She looks at me with yet another satisfied expression.

I hadn't expected that at all. "You...you honestly strapped bombs to us?" A part of me is absolutely furious. And another part of me is incredibly impressed. All in all, I'm downright stunned.

She throws her head back and laughs. "You honestly thought I didn't?" I'm utterly speechless. Despite the new revelation, it does help ease the tension around our release.

Many heavy footsteps come from the gate. I'm surprised to see Mohawk with a dozen armed townspeople and Ryan, Miguel, and Simon all running in our direction.

Mohawk gets to us first. "What happened?" he asks, pointing a rifle at me.

Dani stands and shrugs. "Just a demonstration," she says casually. She hands one of her people the key, her expression serious. "You'll leave first thing in the morning under guard. All that's left of your supplies will be returned once you arrive at your destination. Get with Elise in medical to make sure your injured comrade is comfortable for travel." She turns to Mohawk. "Get everyone back inside. There's nothing to see here, and it's cold."

He smiles snidely at me as I stand and wipe the dirt from my pants. "Too bad that band wasn't still attached to you, blondie." He cups his fingers and then thrusts them outward like they're exploding. "Boom."

Ryan advances, but I hold my hand out to stop him. No time for that.

Mohawk turns and yells to the small crowd to head back inside. Everyone retreats, leaving my soldiers with Dani and me. The guard with the key waits by the gate.

"Wait." Simon's head swivels from me to Dani and back. "We're leaving? We're getting out?"

"My God." Miguel reaches for his rosary.

"Chief Matthews." The authority in my voice has all three men snapping to attention. I've barely addressed them by rank and title since we've been here, but I need to get Dani alone for another moment. "Take Corporal Alexander and Private Silva to medical. Meet with Elise and find out what we need to get Private Miller ready for travel."

"Yes, ma'am," he says. "Major Turner?"

"Yes, Matthews?" I chance a glance at Dani and see that she's watching this exchange with rapt attention.

"How do we expect Private Miller to walk in his condition?" His question is more for Dani than for me.

My eyes shift between Ryan and Dani. He's right, Anthony would never make it out there on foot.

Dani looks at Ryan for a moment. There's a fire behind her eyes. "You'll be driven," she explains calmly. "I suggest you get some sleep. It'll be a long day tomorrow." She starts to walk away.

I take a few quick steps to catch up and be out of earshot of my soldiers. I motion for them to stay put. "What about you? Will you be escorting us?"

She stops, looking at me almost sadly. "I'm leaving tonight," she explains. "Like you said, it's best for everyone if I'm not here."

I frown and chance a step closer. I know my soldiers are watching, waiting for my dismissal. I lean forward and whisper, "This is it? Just like that? I won't ever see you again?" I can't stop the obvious disappointment in my voice.

"I hope it all works out for you." Her voice is different, as if she's trying so hard to hide herself that she's exposing everything.

My hand twitches, itching to take hers, to intwine our fingers for even the briefest of seconds. I need to touch her, to be reassured this isn't the end, to ask if there's something between us besides being on opposite sides of the war.

Her look lingers for a moment as if she's fighting the same urge. "Good-bye, Kate." I clench my fist as I watch her turn and walk away from me.

My throat itches to call out to her. I should be elated. She's releasing us. We're surviving this. Instead, the dread of never seeing her again washes over me.

I collect myself quickly, swallow hard, and turn back to my soldiers. "Let's go," I bark as I grab Ryan and pull him closer. "I thought I told you to sit with Anthony."

"He's sleeping, and I got worried. I was on my way to find you. Miguel was trying to go to the tavern, and Simon was sneaking around the gardens. Then we heard the explosion. Are you all right?" Ryan looks equal parts annoyed and worried.

"I'm fine." I keep walking, picking up the pace.

"They're really releasing us?" Miguel asks.

"First thing in the morning." I'm irritated. But not with them.

"It's not a trap?" he presses.

"I don't think so."

"Does he have the key to these bombs?" Simon motions to the guard waiting for us.

"He does." I keep striding forward. I can't see Dani in front of us anymore. Either she knows another way into town, or she's literally running away from me.

"Then what are you waiting for?" Simon stops walking and lifts his leg. "Take them off."

❖

By the time Anthony knows what's going on, there's nothing else to do to prepare for the morning. Simon argues again about trying to steal and use the bombs to blow up parts of the town or try and strap them to Dani. Thankfully, it's Miguel and Ryan who tell him to shut up so I don't have to.

After lecturing Simon about vowing revenge before we are safely back with the NAF for the hundredth time, I think he finally understands. The last thing we need is for the town to hear him shooting his mouth off and change their minds.

I tell my soldiers to stick together for the night and get some sleep. I'm sure we'll be leaving bright and early. I'm desperate to steal one last moment with Dani, and I'm running out of time.

"What about you?" Ryan asks. "Are you planning on sleeping?"

"I'll get some sleep. I promise." Offering a weak smile does little to remedy his apprehension, I know.

Dismissing them again, I watch them walk away. They're exhausted. Nervous. Excited. I'm still a little uneasy about it all. Where are they planning on taking us? Our escort service could drive to the middle of nowhere and execute us. And with Dani not among them, I don't have a lot of trust in this process.

That is precisely the reason I need to talk to her. At least, that's what I tell myself. I try to ignore the desperate feeling of unfinished business stirring in the pit of my stomach.

By the time I reach her residence, it's still dark. When I try the door, I find it unlocked, and once again, I let myself inside. This time, by the light of the moon flooding through the windows, I see that her safe is open and empty.

The book on the table is gone, along with several maps from the wall. A chest is open in the corner of the room. Her half-empty bottle of whiskey is still on the table with an empty glass beside it. Jogging up the stairs, I bypass the bathroom and head straight to the bedroom. I'm not sure what I'm looking for exactly, but I know that whatever it is, it isn't here.

Her dresser drawers are open, and when I peer inside, it looks as though she's cleaned out most of her clothes. A slight panic sets in. She's really leaving. She may already be gone. I feel desperation start to set in. I'm too late.

The distant sound of an old car shakes me out of it.

Dani.

I sprint down the stairs and out of the house.

When I reach the front gate, I stop a short distance away and watch the small group that has gathered. Dani and Lucas toss a few large duffels into the back of an old Jeep while Roscoe circles anxiously. Elise hands Dani a small bag, and they share a hug. Lucas stops to chat with Darby, and I'm pretty sure Darby gives him something as well. Lucas claps Mohawk's forearm and then Mike's, and Dani does the same.

Lucas hurries to take something else from Rhiannon, who approaches the group almost hesitantly. He pulls her into a somewhat awkward hug. She must say something to him because he nods before pulling away, taking whatever she brought. Rhiannon bursts into tears and pulls Dani into her. They embrace tightly. I clench my jaw and try not to feel jealous.

Dani cups Rhiannon's cheeks and says something that makes her smile. Roscoe barks, and Dani reaches down to scratch behind his ears. It's then that she notices me.

I don't even know exactly what I want to say but I'm desperate for just a few more minutes alone with her. A heavy feeling settles in my chest; we have an unfinished conversation lingering between us. Yet neither of us makes a move to rectify it.

For a brief moment, we're suspended in time. It's just me and her, alone. I see it more clearly now than I ever have before. Any anger I felt over the journals no longer matters as an overwhelming feeling of sadness sweeps over me. I'm not ready to say good-bye. I don't really get *why*.

She nods once. Maybe she understands.

Dani hops in the Jeep. And just like that, the moment ends.

Lucas kisses Darby on the cheek and enters the passenger side. The gates open, and before I can call out for Dani to wait one more moment, the Jeep slowly drives out of town and disappears into darkness.

Lately, it seems all I do is watch Danielle Clark walk away from me, and it leaves me with an emptiness that I can't explain.

I fasten the remaining button on my uniform jacket and run my hands through my hair. I try to make my appearance as presentable as possible. It's the NAF way. I adjust the collar of my jacket, having forgotten how much it scratches my neck when it's worn properly.

I sigh and swipe at the front of my jacket. I am freshly washed and dressed in my semi-clean uniform. I have no other belongings except the clothes that Dani let me borrow. I most definitely can't take those with me. Instead, I fold them and place them in a neat pile at the foot of the cot. After one more glance around my prison cell, I make my way to the front of town.

The sun has just started to rise, but it does nothing to warm the cool morning air. I find that I am both anxious and ready to be gone, despite the ease of falling into small-town life. I'm not meant for the quiet, regardless of finding it so easy to let go of my duties and responsibilities for a brief time. I am a major in the NAF. I need to get back into that headspace.

The others are already there, Elise and Mike walking with Anthony as he staggers to the center of town. I eye the two solar-powered sand buggies warily. They aren't unlike the NAF models and are the reason we were caught in that sandstorm. They offer little protection against the elements, and the flashbacks of narrowly escaping them and of being buried in sand, barely able to breathe, comes rushing back.

Upon closer inspection, I see that these buggies are solid and more fortified. They're made to withstand the sand, but I'm still unsure if they'll withstand the wind. I glance at the sky. There's not a cloud in sight, absolutely no indication that a storm is on the horizon. Then again, there were no indicators the day the sandstorm of the century wiped out my unit either.

The next several minutes happen in a blur. Mohawk and Mike argue about how to divide us into the buggies, only stopping when Elise tells them to shut up and orders me, Anthony, and Simon to go with

Mohawk and her and Ryan and Miguel to go with Mike and Darby. Mohawk makes a snide comment about why she has to go at all, and Elise shuts him down with some medical lingo and a dramatic motion in Anthony's direction.

It comforts me to know she will be coming with us to make sure Private Miller makes the trip okay.

Then the gates are opening, and Rhiannon is watching worriedly from her tavern, crouched with her arm around Roscoe. I glance at the gathered townspeople; some are shouting at us and others frowning. I find it odd that so many people have come to witness our departure when I notice they are all headed for the tavern. Breakfast? Another meeting?

I want to try to figure out what's going on, but Mohawk orders us to stay still as he holds pieces of cloth in one hand and binds for our wrists in the other. Simon starts to argue, catching on before I do, and next thing I know, we're all being blindfolded, our hands bound behind us, before being shoved into the buggies with Mohawk announcing, "Let's get moving. We're wasting daylight."

Before I can fully get a grip on the situation, we are whisked out of the town I was growing used to and away from the people who never wanted us there in the first place.

❖

It feels as though we've been squished in the buggy for hours, but I know it hasn't been more than thirty minutes. No one has said anything except for Elise making sure Anthony is comfortable in the front seat next to Mohawk where he would have the most room. I'm not sure I envy him being that close to Mohawk, however.

I can feel the air through the cracked windows. I press closer to the door, soaking up the cool breeze and away from Elise seated beside me.

We hit a large bump in the road and make a sharp turn. "Where are you taking us?" I finally ask. "We have a right to know." I am met with silence.

"You don't have a right to anything," Mohawk snaps from the driver's seat.

"They're probably taking us to the middle of nowhere to die," Simon practically snarls from the other side of the back seat.

"We're not leaving you to die," Elise assures us.

"Shut it, Elise," Mohawk barks. "You can at least make them squirm." I smile to myself. Elise seems like a genuinely good person.

"Then where are we going?" Simon asks loudly.

Mohawk grumbles. "You'll see soon enough."

These buggies run on solar power. Wherever they're taking us has to be less than twelve hours away in any given direction. We're either going south to the base we originally departed from or to a northern base much farther away. My guess is we're going back north.

Either way, I'm sure Dani knows exactly what she's doing. Especially since she's been receiving updates on NAF movements.

Once the sun sits higher in the sky, I might be able to decipher which way we're headed. We jerk roughly to the left, and I lean at the sudden motion.

Anthony groans.

"Are you okay, Private Miller?" I ask.

"Jesus, Jack, could you not do that? He's injured," Elise calls in annoyance.

"I'm okay," Miller grunts when Mohawk doesn't respond.

"I have to piss," Simon announces.

"Hold it or piss yourself. We ain't stopping for a long time," Mohawk says. Elise groans, and I can't say I blame her.

I rest my head on the seat and sigh. We're hot, crammed, blindfolded, and we have no idea where we are going. Today is turning out to be utterly fantastic.

❖

Finally, *finally*, the buggy slows to a halt. I think if we were stuck in this back seat any longer, Simon really would have pissed himself just to spite us all. The driver's side door opens and closes, and I wonder if we've reached our destination.

Elise goes against Mohawks orders of staying quiet. "We're stopping to eat and stretch a little bit. Plus, I want to check on Anthony to make sure he's hanging in there," she says in my ear.

I try taking advantage of her generous mood. "Where are we exactly?"

"We're about halfway," is all she gives me.

"Can we take these stupid things off our eyes?" Simon complains. I can feel him jerking about on the other side of Elise.

"That's Jack's call, but we'll unbind your hands for a little bit so you can stretch." She sympathetically pats my leg.

My door jerks open, and I practically fall out. Elise grabs my arm to steady me only to have Jack yank on my other arm to haul me out. To my surprise, my blindfold is ripped from my head, and I wince at the hair pulled right along with it. I squint into the harsh daylight as Mohawk releases my wrist ties.

"There," he grunts. "Quit bitching."

I gingerly rub my wrists and roll my shoulders, happy to be unbound and able to stretch. My eyes take a long time to adjust, and by the time I am able to look around, Simon is unbound, and Elise is gently easing Anthony from the buggy.

The other buggy pulls up behind us, and Mike and Darby help Ryan and Miguel from within and unceremoniously shove them in our direction.

Mohawk makes a show of having a gun on us at all times.

"All right," he says, "Mike, Darby, take them one at a time to relieve themselves. Elise, you got him?" He gestures his pistol at Anthony while Elise is easing off his blindfold and sitting him down. She nods and offers Anthony a small smile once his eyes adjust to the light. I notice his hands weren't bound behind him, and I'm thankful for that. "We eat, and we go. No chitchat and no wasting time. If you run, we'll shoot you." He smiles on that final note, like a silent hope that one of us will actually run so he can, in fact, get to shoot us. It's nothing we haven't heard from him a thousand times before.

Ignoring him, I take in our surroundings. Trees. Lots of trees with yellow and dying leaves. It's hard to see beyond the forest to determine what the landscape looks like. I'm sure this was on purpose. Mike and Darby disappear into the woods with Simon. I can faintly hear his complaints at having two people watch him urinate.

Mohawk pulls some sandwiches from the back of the second buggy. Rhiannon must have made them for us this morning. Just another example of the townspeople catering to our needs and being generous where they could be selfish.

I catch Ryan's eye. He's looking around, seemingly trying to gauge our location the same as me. I stretch my arms and roll my head side to side. Then I let my head fall backward and glance at the sky. I can see the sun peeking through the trees. It's not quite midday because the sun is still slightly to the east. I put my arms over my head and stretch my back as I drop my chin and glance at the tire tracks as far back as I can see them. We came from the west, slightly south. We're going north. Farther away from our base. I push a breath through my nose and stifle a humorless laugh.

I finish my stretching routine and look back to Ryan. He shrugs. There's no way of knowing where we are exactly, so I shrug back. I mouth the word "North," and he nods. It's all we can manage at this point.

Mohawk comes back with the sandwiches as Mike and Darby come to retrieve Miguel for a bathroom break. He seats us far enough apart that we can't speak and hands me a sandwich and a small canteen.

"No talking to your little boyfriend, sweetheart."

I don't give him the satisfaction of a response. I eat in silence and wait my turn to be taken into the trees.

Everyone eats and rotates into the wooded area quickly. Before I know it, they're loading Anthony back into the buggy. I push my luck and approach them as they reach the passenger door. Mohawk jumps in my path. "Nope. Turn around." He points past my head.

"Can I speak to my injured, please? I'm his commanding officer, and I'd like to check on my soldier." His disregard for anything other than himself is infuriating.

"Jack, just let her talk to him. It won't do any harm," Elise offers. "I'll listen in if it makes you feel better."

Mohawk spits out a laugh. "Y'all are soft." He steps out of my way and bumps me with his chest as I move past. "Thirty seconds."

I reach Anthony with quick strides. Elise has just finished buckling him into the seat. "Miller, how are you doing?"

He gives a grateful, somewhat shy smile to Elise and then turns to me. "I'm doing just fine, thanks to her."

She smiles back and dips her head.

I whisper dramatically, "I think she's involved with their sharpshooter, Miller. You better be careful."

Elise chuckles and backs away to give us some semblance of

privacy. It pains me to think she could die after all she's done is show us kindness.

He lowers his voice. "We're going north, Major."

"I know, Private, thank you. I just wanted to check on you and let you know that as soon as we're back, you're going to be given proper time to rest up and get healthy. Just hang in there a little longer." He nods, and I give his hand a reassuring squeeze and close the door.

Elise holds up a fresh set of bindings, and with a sigh, I turn so I can be restrained. At least she doesn't pull them so tight I lose feeling in my hands.

I go back to my seat without having to be told. I'm sure Mohawk is disappointed that he won't get to bark at me about it.

Our blindfolds are back on, and within minutes, we're driving again.

The rest of the ride is quiet. I can tell by the lack of warmth on my face that the sun has shifted completely, and it's closing in on evening.

When we stop again, I know it's for the last time. Once again, Mohawk yanks me from the buggy and pulls off the blindfold. The sun is low in the sky. We don't have much daylight left. It's much cooler out now. This time, I can see old abandoned buildings in the distance, proof of past settlements. I doubt anyone is around. Mohawk wouldn't have gotten so close if there was.

"You're going to head that way," he says, motioning for the town.

"And what's that way?" I ask.

"You'll know soon enough."

I stare at the town skeptically. I know the area, but that doesn't mean there aren't threats hidden within. "Our weapons?"

"We'll drop them off a few hundred yards in front of you," Mike offers gently. "But your guns won't be loaded."

"And we're supposed to trust this isn't a trap?" Simon says and then scoffs.

"We're a few dozen miles outside of Grand Forks," I say. I'd been through this area when I was stationed here before.

"Why the fuck are we at Grand Forks?" Simon asks.

That pretty much confirms my suspicions. Dani has taken us much farther than where we came from. I can barely contain an amused laugh. Instead, I make my way to Anthony. "You gonna be okay to walk?"

"I think so," he says with a less than encouraging smile.

"He'll need help. Go slow and no sudden movements. He'll rip his stitches," Elise says. She carefully slips her arm from around his side and backs away.

"Thank you," I say and mean it. Elise has been more than kind. I take a step closer. "Please leave town," I whisper. The thought of her burning when the NAF comes makes me sick.

She narrows her eyes, confused.

"Are you going to untie us?" Ryan asks. He does his best to allow Miller to drape his arm over his shoulders and help steady him, but it's hard with his hands still tied behind his back.

Mohawk laughs. Simon yells about protocol, and I take the opportunity to lean closer to Elise. "You have to leave town. Before the NAF finds you." She straightens, finally understanding. "Did Dani really leave?"

"Yes," she replies quietly.

I glance at the others to ensure that nobody else is listening. "Where did she go?"

Her body seems to slump a little, and she puts a hand on my shoulder and whispers, "I don't know. Even if I did—"

I shake out of her touch and nod to cut her off. I hate that she recognizes that I care more than I should. And if she sees it...so do others. "You need to leave, too."

Finally, she nods.

Hopeful that she'll heed my warning, I clear my throat and push my emotional investment in her safety aside. "That's enough," I yell to Simon. "We better get going. It'll be dark soon."

The four townsfolk get back in their buggies and drive off, only slowing a few hundred yards away to toss the rest of our gear out the windows.

Simon yells profanities at their taillights, and Ryan and I share a look. I square my shoulders, slipping quickly back into my leadership role.

"Let's get moving."

## CHAPTER THIRTEEN: THE REUNION

### *Dani*

Music blares through the speakers of the old Jeep. The song is dark with a low, deep bass. The top is on the old Gladiator Rubicon, but the doors are off. I have one foot propped against the frame and one hand on the steering wheel, the other resting on the gearshift. I glance at Lucas in the passenger seat, the wind blowing his dark hair loose from where he tied it back. For a moment, I see our mother in him, and a vivid memory of her hair blowing in the wind floods my mind.

I'm envious. Even in the most stressful of circumstances, he still manages to appear weightless. He smiles at me as we pass through Sioux Falls, memories of my time there and my past life haunting me. I've never been the honorable type. Lucas was, by far, the easier child to raise. Regardless, she loved us both endlessly and never showed favoritism. I think about my dad, and it hurts, but when I think about my mom...it absolutely guts me. Especially when I think about Lucas living without her.

We don't encounter any problems along the way. It's not a hard trip if you know the spots to avoid. It just seems to drone on and on, with us taking extra precautions as visibility isn't the best. Stopping only to eat and refuel, we speed through the broken roads, the vast emptiness illuminated only by my high beams. Occasionally, we pass dilapidated buildings where civilization once stood, but we don't encounter anyone else in the openness.

My mind wanders to Kate and the others as the sun begins to peek over the horizon. They will be leaving soon, about four hours behind us. A short message from the old transmitter radio Darby fixed up comes through, and Lucas looks at it instantly. His nods, letting me know the others have left.

I slow the Jeep only when we approach the city limits. The road takes us through the shell of a town that once thrived. Now it lies in ruins, destroyed by the war and weather, bombs and disintegration, abandoned homes and stores left to decay. Lucas turns the music down. I bring my foot back in the Jeep and put both hands on the wheel as we approach the cement and brick walls, what's left of Fargo.

I stop a safe distance from the large gate. "You sure you want to do this?" I know what his answer will be. There's no real point in asking, but I owe it to him to ask one last time.

"To hell and back, my friend," he says with a gentle smile.

I try to smile back, turning off the motor just as a side door in the city wall opens. Three large men I've never seen before step out and approach us slowly, their rifles aimed at our heads.

I raise my hands, and Lucas does the same as we wait for them to order us out of the car. "Get out. Nice and slow, and keep your hands where we can see them."

Lucas and I do as they say, my hands on top of my head, my sunglasses still on. A large man stares back, his rifle close to my face. Lucas is facing the same on the opposite side of the Jeep. The third guard begins poking and prodding through our belongings.

"You've got a lot of shit in here. State your business," he orders once he's done.

Keeping my hands on my head, I rotate my arm so that my tattoo is peeking out from my sleeves. "We're here to see William Russell. He sent for us. Many Horses one-eight-six-four."

It's been so long since I've used my code that I wonder if it still holds clearance. I used to know all the guards by name, but this guy isn't familiar. He's built like Jack with his oversized muscles stretching his much too-tight T-shirt, something only the overtly muscular wear during the transition to the cold season. He glances at the tattoo. We stare at each other for a long, drawn-out moment. It's annoying how long he makes me wait.

The side door opens again, and finally, a familiar face comes jogging out, his rifle smacking against his back as he runs. "Hey, I got this one," Teddy says. "She's legit." Muscles and his men don't back down. "Did she know the code?"

I'm starting to become angry. What the hell are we doing standing around arguing about clearances when I was sent for?

"She could've intercepted intelligence and stolen the code," Muscles challenges.

"Seriously, man, she used to live here. Don't you know who this is?" His question is met with silence. Teddy lowers the rifle pointed at my face. "It's Danielle and Lucas Clark. Show some respect."

Muscles grunts and motions for the others to lower their rifles. "If things go south, Teddy, you're to blame," he warns before motioning to the guards up top to let us in. "Even if she does know the code."

"Does he not know how the code system works?" I ask.

Teddy laughs. "He's a work in progress."

"Little Teddy Bear, you've grown up." I give him a once-over and let out a low whistle. When I stayed here, back when I was about nineteen, he was a twelve-year-old kid following me around, trying to learn the ways of the Resistance. I let him tag along here and there around town. He was a nice enough kid but not really Resistance material. Looking at him now, I guess I was wrong. He's shed the baby weight and has grown into his oversized feet. Now he's six feet of scrawny muscle with a clean-shaven head.

"No one's called me that in years," he grumbles. "I thought you were dead."

"Not yet." I slip back in the driver's side, Lucas in the passenger's, while Teddy hops in the back, pushing our bags to make room. "By the way, 'used to live here' is a bit of a stretch." I start the car and slowly make my way through the gates, not even bothering to glance at the guards as we pass.

"What did you want me to say? You frequented for booze and sex on the regular?" he counters.

"You've beefed up security," I say, ignoring his question as we make our way through town. It's been years, but the place hasn't changed much at all. People are already awake and spilling into the streets to go about their day. I know my way around the city as though I never left.

"We've had to." Teddy leans over the console. "The NAF has been pushing this way at a pretty steady pace, especially since General Trent croaked and the new one took over. People are getting nervous. More and more NAF are being stationed out here, mostly up in Grand Forks.

There aren't enough Resistance out this way to stop them. Some think it's only a matter of time before we're taken over."

I take a slow left turn. "How are you on weapons?"

"We could always use more. Bring anything with you?" He lifts one of the bags.

"Nah. Not here for that."

"Pleasure, then?" Teddy waggles his eyebrows at me through the rearview mirror.

"Not here for that either." I pass a spot I used to take my dates and picture Kate pressed between me and the brick wall of the familiar alley beside it. I'm glad I didn't meet Kate back then. I was stupid and hurt people. Though thinking about how I left White River, I'm not sure I'm much better now. "Here to see William."

Teddy nods. "He's been here a few days. Hasn't left the gates but he's sent some of his guys out here and there."

I nod occasionally to let him know I'm listening, but in all honesty, I don't care. I don't plan on being here long. I just need to ask William for a favor, and then I'll be on my way.

By the time we get to the main lodgings, Teddy hops out with a smile. "You missed the breakfast rush, but everyone should be awake." We start to unload, and I toss a few bags Teddy's way. "Seriously?" he asks.

I give him a smile, one that hopefully reminds him that I remember a ton of embarrassing stories about him, and he huffs as he pulls two duffels over his shoulder and makes his way inside. I stand outside the lodging with a sinking feeling in my gut. The last time I was here, I was destructive, reckless. I had just lost my father and would've killed anyone wearing a uniform without batting an eye. Now all I can think about is Kate and Rhiannon and Jack and everyone else I've put in harm's way.

"Are you ready for another bout?" Lucas asks as he steps up beside me and stares straight ahead.

Smiling slightly, I want to tell him no.

I don't answer for a long time, though, wondering the same damn thing. It feels as though walking through those doors will erase the new me who I've tried so hard to maintain since leaving this place. I know I'm not that reckless person anymore, but the way I left White River in danger is mutilating me internally.

Taking a deep breath, I grab the remaining duffels and sling them over my shoulders. No use dwelling on it. Not when I need to try to get my people reinforcements. It's time to get down to business. Turning to Lucas, I point my chin at the door. "Let's go."

I don't even bother looking around—the less I see of this place, the better—and debate whether to leave my sunglasses on. Pushing them on top of my head, I try to find our host. There's a woman I don't recognize at the counter chatting happily with Teddy. I sigh in relief at the sight of her. The last girl to work that job, Julia, spent her free time in my bed. I didn't treat her well with the way I left, so I'm glad I don't have to spend my first few minutes here apologizing.

Teddy catches my eye and motions us over. When we get close enough, he smiles and holds out two keys. "Two suites."

"You've got more pull around here than I remember, Teddy Bear," I say, taking the keys.

"Teddy Bear?" The woman laughs. He shoots me a look. "He married the mayor's daughter," the woman whispers.

"How the hell did you manage that?" I ask, not even trying to hide my surprise. Teddy looks offended and rightfully so.

The woman behind the counter snorts and motions for us to put our bags down. "I'll get someone to carry your things."

"The downside to being on the top floor," I mutter. I keep one of my bags over my shoulder, not wanting to let it go, and let a teenage boy carry the other. Two more kids appear out of nowhere and scoop up the other bags with a grumble. Guess they hate the top floors, too.

"I'll get your Jeep refueled. Planning on staying long?" Teddy asks casually.

"God, I hope not." I hand over the key to the Jeep, knowing she'll be parked in a guarded location. Vehicles are a precious commodity around here, and I'm sure I'll get a few good offers for her. Not that I'm selling.

We grip each other's forearms. "Thanks, Teddy. I appreciate your help."

"Of course." He gives my arm a friendly squeeze. "I gotta get back. I'll leave the keys here at the desk for you." He continues to stare, and I arch a brow impatiently. "I'm not sure if your presence here should have us concerned or not, but a lot of folks are gonna be pissed to see you. Like Julia." I nod, not knowing what to say. Teddy grins wickedly and turns to leave but calls over his shoulder, "I'll make sure to let her know you're here."

Lucas gives me a knowing look, and I ignore him, choosing instead to smile at the woman behind the counter. "Could you please tell William Russell that Dani and Lucas are here. We'll meet him at the bar."

"Sure thing, sweetheart," the woman says with a wink.

I sigh, hoist the bag up a little higher, and climb the stairs to our assigned rooms. A little winded and a lot annoyed, I stop in front of my room where the kids have dropped our bags and left. "Jerks," I mutter. Lucas stops at the suite beside mine, and we both open our doors. I keep mine open with my foot. "I'm going to take a long hot shower," I say. "Make sure everything is locked up if you leave. Take anything valuable with you. If Julia comes looking and she's still angry…" I shudder. "Meet you at the bar in an hour?"

Lucas gives me a quick salute and a smile and then starts to drag his four bags into his room. Most of it is crap from Darby, only one duffel holds his clothes and personal items. I do the same with my two bags, and the door shuts with a slam behind me, making me jump.

I blindly fumble through the dark to open the curtain, allowing the light to spill in. I look around with a grimace. This is the suite? A bed, single dresser, a beat-up looking table with two chairs, a nightstand, a closet, and a bathroom? I close the curtains again, leaving enough light to function.

In the bathroom, I light a lantern on the counter and test the water. At least that seems clean. I get the shower going, hoping it'll warm up, grab a towel from one of my duffels, and lock all the bolts on the door. I test the water again. Still cold. Awesome. Short, cold shower it is.

❖

Lucas is already at the bar when I get there twenty minutes early. His hair is down and dry. I pull up a chair beside him, drop my bag, and finger the ends of his hair. "No shower?"

"Maelstrom hated the cold. It sunk way down deep within his bones and settled there, unrelenting." Lucas shivers for effect.

I laugh and pull the drink he ordered for me close. "Yeah, this place is a real shithole." I look him over as he ties his hair back into a low ponytail. Mine is up in a messy bun atop my head. I can't stand the feeling of wet hair against my shirt, and I didn't have time to let it dry as much as I would've liked. I take a long pull from the homemade beer and cough a little before spitting it back in my glass.

Lucas laughs as he pats my back. "I'd rather drink cyanide."

"That"—I push the glass away—"is not beer." I throw my hand in the air. "Hey! Whiskey neat over here."

The barkeep grunts and stomps over with a scowl. "The beer is on the house. The whiskey is gonna cost you."

"You can put it on my tab," a voice calls from behind us. The barkeep grunts again, slides a bottle of whiskey in my direction, and pulls a couple of glasses from under the counter.

By the time I turn, Lucas has already jumped out of his seat and thrown his arms around William's neck, an action not taken lightly by those on the receiving end. William laughs happily and gently returns the embrace until Lucas has had enough and pulls back, breaking all physical contact.

I stand and extend my arm, smiling. William swats my arm away and pulls me into a hug as well.

Sinking into his embrace and turning my face into his neck, I take a deep breath. He smells exactly the same: mint leaves, sand, and gunpowder. I grab the back of his shirt just a little tighter than I mean to and swallow the lump in my throat.

When William pulls back, it's only to grab me by the shoulders and examine me carefully. "Let me look at you," he says with a smile. His eyes are watering, and I know he's missed us just as much as I've missed him.

He checks me over, and I do the same. He's not as tall as I remember. Only a few inches taller than me. His normally sandy hair is a lot grayer than the last time I saw him, but his shining blue eyes are exactly as I remember, open and bright. His face is a little paler than before, with a few more lines. There's a new scar over his left brow. His nose is still slightly crooked from when he broke it when I was a kid, but his smile is just as wide. He's wearing dark pants with big boots and a fitted, long-sleeved gray shirt. His pistol is holstered against his ribs, and I know he has a knife or two tucked in his boot.

"Wow," he says happily. "Look at you." His eyes shift to Lucas, and he releases me, inspecting him the same way. "And Lucas! You two have grown so much." He cups Lucas's face. "Soft eyes and deep dimples. Just like Kaya."

The comment knocks the wind from my chest. I haven't heard my mother's name in years. I clear my throat and playfully push his chest in an attempt to steer the conversation away from shit that makes me cry. "Get a grip, William. We're not teenagers."

"Almost thirty-three and twenty-nine, right?" He laughs, puts his hands on his hips, and looks at us again. "Wow." I share a look with Lucas and sit on the stool to grab the bottle of whiskey. Upon a quick sniff, it seems legit enough to drink, and I pour some in the three glasses laid out for us. I hand one to William, who looks more amused than anything else. "Are you gonna take it or what?"

"Isn't it a little early to be drinking?"

I pull the glass back and down it in one gulp, not in the mood for a lecture. I take it and the bottle to a table and sit. William laughs, and he and Lucas take a glass and follow me.

"I am so glad to see you two. How have you been?"

I debate giving him shit about being a sentimental sap, but he looks so happy to see us that I don't have it in me to tease him. Besides, it's really nice to see him, too. "We're good. It was a long drive."

His face falls slightly. "I'm sorry to make you come all this way, but I didn't think it was safe to come to you. Not with all the movement lately."

Lucas is watching me carefully. I refill my glass in an embarrassingly long pour and take a swig, wincing as it goes down. I'm not quite ready to get into the real reason I'm here.

"Old friend, it's good to see you. How have you been?" Lucas asks William with a smile.

"Oh, you know, same old, same old," William says, taking Lucas's quote in stride like he always has. "Still alive to fight another day."

I look at my glass, not having heard that expression in so long. It was something William and my dad would say to one another. Then when I joined the cause, I'd say it as well. It became my mantra, bitter and angry. Alive and fighting while my dad...

I knew this would happen. Old memories surfacing is one of the reasons I ran from places like this. From William. I couldn't bear to face them. The memories. Taking another swig, I try to anchor myself in something other than thoughts of my dad.

William seems to catch on; he clears his throat and lowers his voice. "I don't mean to drag you back into this, Dani. Not when you've gotten your life together."

"So," I start, changing the subject. "General Turner."

William purses his lips and nods. He glances at the barkeep and the few patrons scattered around the dark and dingy bar. He stands abruptly and downs the contents of his glass. "Grab the whiskey and come with me."

Following him to someplace less public can only mean one thing: confidential information. Lucas takes the bottle and flashes me a devilish grin.

I grab my bag and follow William up one flight of stairs to his room. It's much, much nicer than mine. "What the hell?" I ask, dropping the bag and looking around at all the amenities: extra lanterns, a pristine table with fresh fruit, a large plush couch, extra linens, a wash bin with a pitcher of fresh water and a generator for hot water in the bathroom. "How much do they hate me around here?"

William gives me a sympathetic look. "Do you really want me to answer that?"

"I armed their town. I helped them fight off NAF and raiders." After all I've done for them, I feel betrayed.

"You slept with their daughters and drank like a fish," William reminds me flatly. "Not to mention that little incident in the tavern with the—"

"Okay." I hold up my hand to stop him. "I get it."

Lucas pats my shoulder sympathetically. "It's the uniform. Women love a man in uniform."

I groan. He's directed that one at me before. Rolling my eyes, I shrug his hand off. "Not helping, Lucas." He and William share a chuckle, and I turn away from them with a scowl.

William unlocks a chest under the bed and pulls out some papers and maps, placing them on the table. He leaves them folded and motions for us to take a seat. We pour another drink, but I place mine to the side, knowing that if I drink much more, my head will start to get fuzzy. He pulls out an old pair of small rectangular glasses, places them over his eyes, and pushes them up his nose as he checks over the maps.

"What the hell are those?" I ask, pointing to his face.

William looks up, confused. "What are what?"

I point at his face again. "Glasses?"

"I'm getting old, Dani. I don't see as well as I used to," he mutters in annoyance. Whether it's directed at me for calling him out or his old age, I can't tell. "Anyway, I'm surprised you came. I wasn't sure you would."

I lean back with a shrug, procrastinating my real reasons until I hear what he has to say. "You haven't sent for me in seven years. I figured you must either be desperate or scared."

"Both, actually." He swirls the amber liquid and watches as it moves in slow circles. "We've always known General Turner was dangerous. But she set taking the wasteland into motion long before she became the general of NAF. She has more loyalists than we thought, and most of them have been put into place months, maybe even years, ago."

"Biding her time for when old General Trent finally dropped?"

"Something like that." He sighs. I wonder if there's something he's not telling me. "Like I told you in my latest correspondence, the NAF isn't just moving west. They're already here. In large numbers. And they're planning on expanding quickly. And now with the issue of her daughter missing, it adds a whole other layer for concern."

I guess my time is up. "What do you know about that? Her missing daughter?"

William holds up his finger and reaches for a rolled-up piece of paper. He unravels a map, one he's been working on for quite some time by the looks of it. There are bases circled and squared and arrows and lines and all sorts of markings. "This is where most of the troops are coming in, here at the old Air Force base near Grand Forks. We got some good intel a few months ago that the general's daughter would be taking control of the Midwest."

Lucas flicks a quick glance in my direction, but I hold my expression steady, giving nothing away. I follow his fingers on the map, and he taps on the city of Omaha. I had a feeling that was where Kate might be going.

"Once she's taken control here, another unit will mobilize farther west, near Helena and then Denver." William looks at me over his map. "Several days ago, two convoys departed for two different locations. One from Grand Forks to Omaha and the other from Omaha to Pierre."

"Wait," I say. "The NAF were on their way to Pierre?"

William sighs dramatically. "Pierre has been having problems with resources, and their population is expanding faster than they can handle. Word of their desperation is no secret. From what we can gather, the NAF has been targeting vulnerable cities to offer supplies in exchange for their loyalty."

George told me several days ago that Pierre needed help, but I had no idea the NAF were already targeting them.

"Major Katelyn Turner was the commanding officer leading the small convoy to Pierre with supplies and terms to secure their transition into loyalists. Only her convoy never made it. It looks like they were shut down by a sandstorm."

"And the other convoy?" I ask.

"They made it to Omaha." William pulls out more papers, and I look to Lucas. "The remains of Katelyn's convoy have been found by scavengers. It looks as though they were jumped by raiders not long after the storm passed. They were found around here." He points to a place dangerously close to White River. But we already knew that.

"We've managed to hide the location so far, but now we've received word that General Turner demands her daughter be found dead or alive. The general should be arriving in Grand Forks within the day, and then she'll move to Omaha with the scheduled supply run to oversee the search party." William looks at me with sad eyes. "I'm not sure we'll be able to stop the search. And with the NAF that close to White River, it's only a matter of time before the town is discovered. I thought it best if you were out of there when they arrived."

I hold my hands on top of my head and pace away from the table. William's words spin in my mind, and I try my best to decipher everything he's told me. All of this new information comes like a punch to the gut. Kate wasn't going *to* Omaha; she was coming *from* Omaha. And she was on her way to claim control over Pierre. That was why she was so close to White River. I had it all wrong.

"Katelyn Turner is on her way to Grand Forks." I feel so dumb. I delivered the prisoners right to the general.

William looks up from his map. "What?"

"Katelyn Turner is on her way to Grand Forks."

"What? How is that—"

"Because we just dropped her off." My pace quickens, and I rub the back of my neck. I need to think. How could this have happened? How could I have not known?

William straightens. "Dani, what's going on?"

"You didn't tell me any of this." I round on him. Maybe if he had told me what was going on with Kate to begin with instead of focusing his entire attention on Judith… "Why didn't you tell me they were coming after Pierre? Why didn't you tell me they were already out there flipping cities?"

"Dani," his voice is low, as if he's trying to not startle a crazed animal. "I told you they were here and that more bases were being established. I didn't tell you about Pierre because you specifically asked me not to involve you in those types of matters." He watches me pace. "What aren't you telling me?"

"Katelyn Turner landed on our doorstep five days ago. We kept her prisoner in the hope of getting information. After we got your note about the search party, we released her outside the base in Grand Forks because I *thought* that was where she came from." I stop pacing and release a long breath. I put my hands on my hips and stare at the opposite wall and wonder what else I don't know.

"Dani." His tone drips disappointment, and I feel like a kid being scolded for a poor decision. "Why didn't you tell me?"

"I didn't want you swooping in there, making the whole situation worse."

"Unfortunately, your town is now going to be attacked. You know that, right? They're going to turn right around and crush the whole place. Maybe even send units in from Omaha to finish you off." William's voice gets louder with every word. "If you had just handed them over to me—"

I take a dangerous step toward him. "You would've shot them on the spot."

"No, I wouldn't."

"And the NAF would still be coming. Search party or not, Katelyn or not, they're here. You said so yourself." I have to clench my hands into fists to keep from doing something stupid.

Lucas steps between us and holds out his hands. "What's done is done. We must not dwell and instead look to fight another day."

William and I stare at each other. I feel angry and betrayed. I feel guilty that I let it get this bad and that I put so many people in danger. But most of all, I feel out of place. This used to be my forte, my strength: planning and strategizing. But how can I do that without all the pieces to the damn puzzle?

William looks away first and hangs his head while he leans over the table. "Goddamnit, Dani."

I want to defend myself, defend my actions. But Lucas is right. It's done. We need to look forward. "I need people," I say, finally asking for my favor. "I need them in White River to help get everyone out."

"I don't have any to give you." He looks up. "We're stretched too thin."

"So you're just going to let them die?"

"I don't want anyone to die." He shakes his head, and I can see in that moment just how tired he is. "I can contact some of my inside guys. Try to see if anyone will retaliate and when. Maybe buy you some time, but that's all I can do. I'm sorry."

He looks dejected, betrayed. All I seem to be doing these days is hurting the ones I care about. And now I can't even save my home. I knew it was a long shot. I knew this probably wouldn't work, but hearing the confirmation that there's nothing else I can do, well, it sucks the energy from my body. The only thing left to do is beg everyone to leave their home before they crumble with it.

I unzip the duffel, reaching inside and tossing one of my dad's old journals on the table. "I thought you could use this."

William stares at the black journal as if it's the most sacred and precious thing in the world. "Is that…" I don't answer. Instead, I watch as he slowly takes the journal. He stares at the cover, running his hands across the worn material with a feather light touch. "I thought these were lost. You told me they were lost."

I fall into a nearby chair, cough, and avoid looking at him. "I said a lot of things."

Carefully, he thumbs through the pages, his gaze wide, tears once again pooling in his eyes. "Your father and I started writing these when we were just boys. We thought every single piece of information we overheard or pieced together would help us to make the Resistance stronger. That with our information, we could take down the corrupt military and be heroes."

"You're not wrong," I say lightly.

"The older we got and the more involved we became, the more we knew these journals were important. They helped guide us and keep us on the path of the Resistance. They were…everything to us." A few tears trickle down his face, and he doesn't bother to wipe them away.

I feel exceedingly guilty. All this time, I let William believe they were gone, that I destroyed them, because I was angry with him. All these years when he got in touch, and when he went out of his way to keep the NAF as far away from me as possible, I still didn't tell him I had them.

They have been around all of my life and most of his. These journals are something revered, treasured by us both. I remember my dad and William huddled beneath the light of a lantern, hastily writing information they received from couriers and flipping through them to plan attacks.

I want to apologize, but I don't know how. Taking them now seems like the ultimate betrayal. We fought, and I blamed him for so many things. I'm still blaming him. I was greedy and selfish and wanted this piece of my father for myself. I didn't want to share. It was all I had left. And now, watching William carefully look through one of the many volumes he helped create, I hate myself a little. It was all he had left of my father as well.

He gets to the end and looks up in shock. "You kept them updated."

"Clearly not all the way." At least he has the decency to look admonished. "They're nowhere near as accurate or in-depth as they would be if you had kept them."

"No, this is…Dani, this…" He places the journal down and covers it with his hands. "This is everything. Thank you."

I nod, still not knowing quite what to say, and motion to the bag. "I brought all of them. It's about time I gave them back."

"They're yours, Dani." His words surprise me. My face must reflect as much because he smiles and pushes the journal across the table. "Your father would want you to have them."

"No, he'd want you to have them," I counter. "To help with what you two started." I look to Lucas for help.

"If you would just take the damn injection," he says, agreeing with me.

William sighs and gently flips through it again. "We'll argue about this later," he insists. "We've done enough arguing for the day."

"Well, until then…" I rummage until I find the journal pertaining to Judith Turner. "You might want to update the section on her daughter. But for the record, she's nothing at all like her mother."

He looks at the journal for a long moment. "Why did you let her go?" His voice is quiet, and when he looks at me, he tilts his head with curiosity.

For some strange reason all I can think about is how I wish I had danced with Kate when she asked me to.

I shake my head and reach for the whiskey. "Like I said, she's not like her mother."

William watches as I pour another glass. I guess he finds no reason to press me any further, at least not now, because he changes the subject. "I promise, Dani, I'll do everything I can to stop the retaliation."

There's a knock on the door, and Lucas and I reach for our pistols. William stands and motions at us to calm down before opening the door. "Speaking of, these are my two of my best. My intel specialist, Hugo Wiley." A scrawny guy with long, disheveled black hair pulled back away from his extremely pale face and baggy clothes that barely fit his lithe frame offers a wave and steps inside. The other guy, larger and with a little more muscle, black hair, and a precise haircut walks in behind him. His complexion is slightly darker than mine, and he has dark eyes and an arrogant smile. "And Ericson Rogers. Boys, meet Danielle and Lucas Clark."

The bigger one stops in front of me and stands at full height as if sizing me up. He's a good head taller, and his smile widens as he looks me over. "Ericson Rogers," he says again. "Explosives expert. Everyone calls me Boom."

"Boom?" I scoff. "Yeah, I'm not calling you that."

William closes the door behind them. "How did it go out there? Is everything in place?"

Ericson grabs the bottle of whiskey and takes a long pull straight from the bottle. Guess I'm done drinking that. "Ready and steady." He wipes his mouth with the back of his hand. His eyes are still on me.

I examine both Hugo and Ericson openly. They don't seem like the sort I would ever consider "the best" of anything.

"We have a bit of a situation," William says. "New intel suggests that Katelyn Turner is alive and on her way to Grand Forks."

"Seriously?" Ericson looks to Hugo. "Did you know about this?"

Hugo grabs a banana from the fruit bowl and peels it as he plops on the plush sofa. "Nope." He takes a large bite and doesn't wait to swallow before elaborating. "Guess the search party due to leave in the morning will be canceled."

"Or adjusted to attack," I say.

"Are they still planning to continue with the second convoy to Omaha?" William asks. "Will the general be on it?"

"With the return of her daughter, not likely." Hugo thinks for a moment while he snacks. "But supplies are still needed in Omaha, and General Turner likes to keep a tight schedule. She'll still deploy in the morning if she's able. I just don't see any need for her to go."

William sighs, and his shoulders slouch. He appears to be disappointed. "Hugo, I need you to confirm that's the case once Major Turner makes it to the base. We'll still proceed with or without the general moving. Do all our people know the plan?"

"Waiting on our mark." When Hugo talks, bits of banana spit from his mouth. Seriously? This is who William recruited to replace Lucas and me? This is the best the Resistance has to offer?

William adjusts his glasses again and gives me a look before turning to his maps. "If they leave tomorrow morning and go slow, they'll arrive at Sioux Falls in approximately eight hours. The bulk of the attack will take place in Sioux Falls, about ninety miles north of Sioux City, where the NAF were planning to stop and resupply. We will have a second unit there to intercept if anyone makes it through."

Listening to them talk and plan, it hits me. They're planning an ambush. "This is why you can't spare men? Because you're using all your resources to stop a convoy?"

"A convoy that could be carrying General Turner," William says.

"If we're lucky, maybe her daughter will be on it, too." Ericson takes another swig of whiskey. I suppress the urge to cold-cock him.

"We don't know who will be on it now that the plans have changed." William looks at me. My little stunt of returning Kate to Grand Forks appears to have messed up everyone's plans. "Regardless, we will take out the convoy."

I try to keep the panic I feel at bay. I know the general, and I know she's going to attack White River, convoy or not. I have to choose. Go after the general or save my friends. The choice is surprisingly easy.

"If the general knows I was there, or thinks I could still be there, she will have to go after White River. She won't wait." I look to Hugo for any sort of backup.

He shrugs. "They could change tactics, but I doubt it. They'll probably go after White River from Omaha directly and keep the supply run to Omaha on schedule."

I openly groan. Some help he is.

"It's a large convoy," William says in agreement. "I doubt she would reroute this late."

Ericson chuckles. "Guess you've been out of the game too long to remember how this works."

I take a step into his space, and he straightens, ready for a fight. I'd love to give him one. "You don't know anything. She'll do both if she can help it."

Ericson leans into me, and William throws his hands up. "Knock it off, both of you."

Lucas gently pulls on the back of my shirt, and slowly, I take a step back. But I swear on everything, if Ericson so much as looks at me funny again, I'll knock his teeth out.

I take several deep breaths and try to steady myself. Finally, I grab William's battle plan off the table and scan over the notes.

"You're planning for no survivors," I say, easily recognizing this type of plan. We used to do it all the time back east but for shorter trips with less NAF traveling. We'd intercept their supply runs and cut off weapons and aid from one town to the next. Usually, I'd plant explosives to divert their attention while a bunch of us would come in and take them by surprise. I have a feeling this is not quite the plan this time. Especially when I see how many people William plans to use. "We've taken down convoys with a fraction of this number."

William nods. "We expected the general to be on it. We're pulling all our resources."

"You're going to let innocent people die so you can attack a convoy with more people than necessary" I can't keep the disgust from my tone. "Even if no one of importance will be on it."

"We don't know that yet," William argues.

"What the hell is she talking about?" Ericson asks.

William's voice is pleading. "Dani, if you can see another way, please tell me. But pulling people on such short notice to guard towns is only going to distract from our cause."

I shake my head. "I thought that was the cause of the Resistance. To help people who need it and to protect them from the NAF."

"And we can't do that while the NAF still expands. We have to stop the expansion so we're able to help the people." William sighs. "We've been planning this ambush for weeks, even before the possibility of the general being a part of it. We all have our assignments and unfortunately, it's too late to change anything. But if we are successful in stopping this convoy, I'll do all I can to get some people to White River. That's the best I can do."

"By then, they'll all be dead." I cast one more look at the man who helped raise me, then leave the room, ignoring his calls for me to come back. If William's too busy and too invested in his asinine plan to help me, I'll just have to take care of it myself.

## CHAPTER FOURTEEN: THE GENERAL

### *Kate*

It's an absolute cluster once the perimeter patrol realizes who we are, who *I am*, and that I am not, in fact, dead, after we finally make it to the gates of the base. They are frantically trying to get messages to the medics, to the soldiers' families, and to my mother. Everyone is to be alerted that we've been found. Blankets are draped over our shoulders as we are shoved into officer vehicles and whisked away to the medical unit.

Doctors and nurses clear space so we can all be examined right away. They give us water and shout a thousand questions in our direction. My head is pounding, and I push a nurse away as she tries to look in my ear, but she steps right back up to me.

The chaos and poking and prodding does little to settle my nerves. I thought I would be relieved to be back. Instead, I feel overwhelmed and exhausted.

Ryan keeps directing them to Miller while Simon screams about our mistreatment and malnourishment and Danielle Clark. It all becomes too much, a sensory overload. It feels like I'm suffocating. "Enough," I yell, and everyone freezes in place. It would be comical if I wasn't so damn annoyed. "Give us some space to breathe, *please*."

The nurse checking my ear slowly backs away, and the others follow. Once they are a fair distance away, I take a deep breath.

A small voice comes from somewhere beside me. "I'm sorry, Major, we're just following protocol." At least the nurse has the decency to look apologetic.

I loosen my uniform collar and dismiss her comment with a wave. "I understand. We've just had a very long journey, and right now, all we want is something to eat, a bath, and some rest."

The doctor steps forward and nods, but whatever he is about to say is cut off with a firm, sharp voice in the doorway. "And you shall have all of those things." Everyone snaps to attention at the sight of my mother, surrounded by four soldiers, watching us from the doorway. I jump to my feet and do the same, looking straight ahead. "Leave them with me."

Once everyone has cleared the room, my mother slowly crosses to me, her eyes focused and sharp. Her new rank is on her uniform, a fifth star now, and all of them connected in a circle. Her graying blond hair is pulled into a tight bun at the base of her neck. It's the first time I've seen her since her promotion ceremony several weeks ago.

"It's good to see you home, Major," she says as my commanding officer.

I ignore the use of the word *home*. This will never be my home. "It's good to be back, ma'am," I say, still standing at attention.

She stares at me for another moment and finally relaxes her shoulders. "At ease." Just as I start to loosen my stance, my mother pulls me into a very tight hug. I stand there, my arms outstretched in surprise as she holds me close. "I was so worried about you. I was just about to send a search party."

It sounds sincere, and I cast a glance at Ryan, who offers me a small smile. Awkwardly, I hug her back. I'm not used to any sort of physical contact from my mother, and the embrace feels devoid of any warmth, like it's more for show.

When she finally pulls away, she holds me by the shoulders and drags her eyes along my body. "Let me get a good look at you," she states obviously. "When I heard you went missing, I feared you were dead."

My jaw clenches. Most of us are dead. I glance at my remaining soldiers, four of them, and lower my eyes in shame. I failed everyone.

My mother releases me and turns her attention to the others. She awkwardly pats their shoulders and tells them how happy she is to see them. "There were reports of a horrendous sandstorm. We believed you all had perished."

"Nearly half," I confirm. "Our buggies couldn't handle it, and we were caught in the open. Afterward, our equipment stopped working, and we were traveling blind. The rest of us were picked off by several raider attacks. They must've seen we were vulnerable."

Simon, of course, doesn't dare keep his mouth shut. "Not to mention being strapped to bo—"

"That's enough, Corporal." I shoot him a look.

My mother's eyes go from me to Simon and back to me, watching us curiously.

"Well," she says with a small smile, "I want to hear all about it. But first, the doctors need to check you over. Then we'll get you cleaned up and fed. We'll debrief after that." It's an order, not an option.

I stand at attention and salute, message received.

The rest of my soldiers follow suit. My mother nods once, satisfied for now, but I can tell she's anxious to hear exactly what went wrong and what Simon was about to say. She stops in the doorway and turns. "Welcome back, soldiers," she says simply before leaving us as quickly as she came in.

And just like that, I feel suffocated all over again.

It's strange being back in my three-bedroom unit from months ago. There's a clean uniform hanging on a peg by the door. I ignore it and step farther inside, locking the door behind me and looking to the flickering glow to my right, the main living quarters. My head spins at being back here.

I feel disconnected. Nothing about this place feels like home. It's all familiar in a way that doesn't seem real.

There aren't any personal items within the house—all of my belongings are back in Omaha—but it appears clean, as if someone routinely came in to tidy, knowing I'd want it kept that way. I was here for a few weeks before being sent to Omaha, but the place still remains foreign to me. The last time I was here feels like a dream that never really happened.

I sigh as I look around. The bookshelf by the fireplace is still filled with books I've never read, and there are a few trinkets here and there serving as decorations. The large plush sofa near the front bay window has a scattering of matching pillows and an end table with nothing on it.

Two armchairs sit on opposite side of a large coffee table in the center of the room, facing the darkened fireplace. There's no warmth here. It's just an empty shell. No children are running around outside, and there's no happy chitchat throughout the streets. This is a job, not a home.

I glance at the lanterns on the mantel. There's a hot meal steaming beside them with a pitcher of cold water. I unbutton my jacket and stare at the plate, wondering if it'll still be warm by the time I finish getting clean.

Someone knocks on my door, and I suppress a groan as I stride to answer it. The soldier on the other side salutes when she sees me. "What is it?" I ask, exhausted. I just want to rest and eat before facing off with my mother.

"I've come to see if you have everything you need, ma'am," the soldier says without looking at me.

"I'm fine, thank you." She goes to salute again when a thought hits me. "Actually, can you bring me maps? Specifically, one of the routes to Omaha and another focusing on the Badlands? Mine were lost in the storms."

The soldier salutes. "Yes, ma'am."

"Just let yourself in and leave them on the table," I instruct before she nods and turns to leave. I pinch the bridge of my nose and wonder what my turnaround time will be before I head back down to Omaha. I catch a whiff of something and crinkle my nose. It doesn't take long to realize it's me, and I cringe at how dirty I feel.

Glancing at the food, I grab the uniform. My meal will have to wait. I need a shower.

By the time I get clean, eat my lukewarm food, and go over the set of maps left by the solider, it's time to meet with the general. I was expecting a grandiose display of her new powers, like guards and other personnel, lavish food, drink, and battle plans surrounding her office, and full-on general attire. Instead, she's conversing casually with Simon at her enormous desk.

I stand at attention in the doorway until the general points at the unoccupied chair for me to join them. The smug look on Simon's face doesn't go unnoticed.

"Corporal Alexander has been telling me about what went wrong once you set out," my mother explains, sipping from a glass of water.

"Would you care for a beverage?" she asks, showing off her selection on a golden cart against the wall.

"No, thank you," I say politely, looking once more at Simon and wondering what the hell he told her.

There's a knock on the door, and Ryan and Miguel enter, both stopping to salute. My mom stands to invite us all to the sitting area near the fireplace. "Please, let's take this discussion to a more comfortable setting. I know you're all tired and want to rest. The sooner we can debrief, the better." I cast a look at Ryan as I stand, and he offers a shrug. Normal debriefs don't go like this. And they certainly wouldn't involve all of us. It makes me nervous that mother is going against protocol. "Private Miller will remain in the medical unit for observation overnight, so we will proceed without him."

She sits in a grand leather armchair close to the fire while I sit in the chair closest to her. Ryan, the next highest officer, sits in the matching armchair, while Simon and Miguel occupy the sofa across from us. The general sits back and waits.

"The first four hours were fine," I begin.

My mother listens intently as I tell her about the huge sandstorm that caught us by surprise and clogged our vehicles and took out dozens of soldiers as we frantically tried to find shelter in the middle of nowhere. How our communications were wiped out, and we lost all signal. How we were turned around and walked north in the direction of Pierre, how we tried to follow the river but were ambushed and forced to retreat. Raiders seemed to pick us off at every turn, and we were running low on supplies, lost in the wasteland. It's more difficult to get through the debrief than I expected. As I recap our story, I can feel the grittiness of the sand in my mouth and hear the screams of the fallen. We left the dead behind without a decent burial. I didn't realize how much that hurt me until now. As I finish summarizing our journey, my mother's face goes from intense to curious.

"That's when you reached the town," she says, her eyes never leaving mine. I hold her gaze. Simon must've told her more than I thought. I realize now why my mother called us all in here. For intel, not our well-being. I should've known. "The rebel town."

I debate telling her about the last raiders and how Dani fought them off and kept them from killing us. "I'm not sure they are officially a Resistance-backed town." I know instantly that it is the wrong thing to say.

"They house Danielle and Lucas Clark, do they not?" She sits up, spitting their names like venom. I look to Simon, whose smile grows. "And did they or did they not put bombs on you?"

My stomach lurches. I knew she would find out, of course we had to tell her, but I was expecting it to come from me and not Simon. Hearing her say their names with such disdain rubs me the wrong way. My mind is telling me to admit everything, but my gut is screaming to play my cards close. I need to settle down and ignore Simon. I'm the town's only chance at survival at this point so I have to choose my words carefully.

"That sounds like a Resistance-backed town to me," Simon chimes in.

"They took us in, fed us, quartered us, and took care of our injuries." I think of Elise and Rhiannon and all the others who don't deserve to die. "They may have been living with the Clark siblings, but the town itself obeyed the law."

"Except for threatening you," my mother says with a smile. "Except for harboring known rebels. That alone is punishable by death."

"Danielle and Lucas Clark aren't even there anymore," I say with a sigh. "They left before we were released."

"And how did you manage to get released?" she asks, leaning forward.

She knows I'm not divulging every single detail, but I'm not about to say that I was released because Danielle Clark has a soft spot for me. I'm assuming that's true based on my own softness for her. I hate to admit being weakened in any way by any person, but I certainly freaked out when I saw her journals, then was devastated to discover we'd be separated that same night. Possibly forever.

"I believe they found out you were close, ma'am, and wanted to plead for leniency," Ryan says. "By letting us go, they hoped you might let them live."

I don't allow any outward reaction to his words, but internally, I thank him. I hold the composure of a major, but my emotions aren't in check. I need some space to think.

My mother stands, and we all follow suit, standing at attention while she paces. "And where exactly is this town?"

"Somewhere southwest of here and northwest of Omaha. My guess is it's within a hundred miles south of Pierre," Ryan continues. "They blindfolded us and took us on one hell of a confusing path up to Grand Forks."

My mother stops at a large map on the wall. "Show me."

I dutifully approach and do my best to retrace our steps. I can feel her watching as I study the main routes. "We lost communications around here," I say, pointing north of Omaha. "My guess is we got turned around here and ended up somewhere around this location, based off when we were intercepted."

"By the rebels," my mother says, coming to stand where I'm circling.

"By the town, yes," I gently correct.

If she's mad about my correction, she doesn't say. Instead, she looks at the map as if confused. "The town of Mission? That place has been abandoned since the bombs."

Ryan and Simon also come to look at the map. Miguel continues to stand far away, looking uneasy.

"We weren't that far south," Simon says.

"We had to be," Ryan argues. "There's nothing else on the map in the area. We update them excessively."

"I know for a fact we were not that far south," Simon counters.

"They must've rebuilt." Ryan points to the map. "See, there's a body of water and everything. The town had a lake. It had to be Mission."

My mother holds up her hands for silence, and we all stand straight and stop arguing. "We'll get with Archie about the maps later. The most important takeaway from this, besides you all being alive, is that Danielle Clark is not dead like we hoped." She turns and faces us again. "She is out there and knows exactly where we are stationed." She pours herself a drink, then takes a small sip of the amber liquid. "How involved is she, and why has she hidden for so long?"

The journals. She's very involved. I need to give the general something, but I'm not quite ready to give her that. Not until I decide what it all means. "She's been getting messages from William Russell."

"William Russell?"

I nod once. "He's close. And he's the one you should worry about, not Dani. She doesn't seem interested in the war."

As soon as the nickname leaves my mouth, I know it's a mistake. My mother stares at me, her lips thin and her eyes narrowed. I can tell she wants to say something, but she looks at the others. "Thank you all for your input. I will call if I have any further questions. Please return to your quarters and rest. Again, I am glad you're well." We all salute and turn to leave when my mother calls, "Katelyn, a word with you, please."

The use of my first name and quick dismissal doesn't go unnoticed. I stop, and Ryan offers me a small nod before leaving the room.

Once the door clicks shut, my mother sits back down and stares at the fire. "The second convoy is leaving for Omaha in the morning as scheduled."

Tomorrow. Okay, that doesn't give me a lot of time to regroup, but I'm sure I can pull together all I need and still manage to get a couple hours' rest before setting out. "I'll be ready," I assure her.

"You won't be going."

Her words are a slap in the face. "If this is about not securing Pierre, I can still guarantee their commitment. I did my best to repair the communications array. The sandstorm was one of the worst we've seen in years, and we were unprepared, but I can handle—"

"This isn't because of what happened. I know what it's like to lose most of your command. And to lose them on a diplomatic assignment of goodwill is even harder. I know you did all you could. No one blames you."

I shake my head and fall back into the armchair, running my hand through my hair. I blame myself.

"You will still be commanding officer of Omaha. You will still oversee outreach to Pierre and other vulnerable outposts. But right now, I need you and the remainder of your unit here. With Danielle Clark so close, we need to prepare."

"Prepare for what?" I ask, my judgment lacking in my tired and confused state. "She's out of the war. She told me herself."

"And you believe her?" My mother scoffs. "Katelyn, she attached a bomb to you. I would say that's an aggressive act by someone very much still involved in the war."

I run my hands over my face, nowhere near ready to have this conversation, even with myself.

"You also said William Russell has been feeding her information. Does that sound like someone who's out of the war?"

"I don't know. I don't really know what's going on in her head."
I wish I did.

"Exactly." She takes another sip.

"I just know she left before we did, and I have no idea where she
is. She might be halfway to the East Coast for all we know." I rub my
temples, trying to keep my rapidly approaching headache at bay.

"I want to know every single thing that happened while you were
there." She punches each syllable. "How she behaved, the weapons
she carried, what she wore, what she ate, and every word she spoke."
She sits back as if she's waiting for me to begin. Somehow, the Clark
family has managed to occupy the minds of my family to the point of
obsession.

I close my eyes and think of the way Dani looked that night in the
tavern. *I'm just trying to move on from being the woman I was* expected
*to be and start being the woman I* want *to be.*

When I open my eyes again, my mother is staring expectantly if
not curiously.

"Can we do this tomorrow? It's been a long few days, and I'd like
to get some sleep before the convoy departs tomorrow. I should at least
be there to see them off. I will account for everything."

She continues to stare until her expression shifts, and she smiles,
placing her glass on the table beside her chair. "Of course." She stands,
and I follow only to be pulled into her arms in an awkward embrace. I
pat at her shoulders. Two hugs in one day. This time I know for certain
that her overuse of affection is just for show. Perhaps she thinks she
can lure me into a false sense of security so I'll divulge everything she
wants to hear. She has no choice but to be patient and understanding as
my mother, not the general. It would feel endearing if I didn't know her
motives all too well.

She kisses my temple and pulls away with a smile. "Get some rest.
We will discuss this along with your new assignment as commander
tomorrow."

I do my best to smile, but it feels as though it's more of a grimace
as she watches me leave. I try not to let her see how it unnerves me.

Once I pull the door closed and walk past her security, Ryan rushes
to my side, concerned and curious. "I heard murmurings of a convoy
going to Omaha tomorrow morning."

"Yeah, and we aren't on it." Ryan looks confused, and I shake my head. "She wants us to rest, and she wants more information about Dani and our time in their town."

"I think that makes sense."

I say nothing as we leave the general's building and head in the direction of my quarters two streets over.

"You're awfully quiet. You okay?"

"I'm just tired." And I am, but I also have no desire to get into another deep discussion about politics or tragedy or an analysis of our time in the town that doesn't seem to exist.

"Are you sure that's it?"

"Well, I'm not very fond of the general giving away my assignment." I can't help sounding annoyed. I have officially run out of patience.

"She didn't give it away," Ryan says gently. "She wants you to rest, regroup, and make sure you're okay before she sends you back down. I mean, she thought you were dead. We were prisoners of war. Can you blame her?" I say nothing. "She's right, you know. With Danielle Clark back in the game and with William Russell lurking around, things have changed a little bit."

I shake my head. "We don't know that Dani is back in the war."

"Don't we?" He stops walking, getting in close and lowering his voice. "We don't know where she went. She could be in the next town over for all we know. You said it yourself, she's been keeping tabs on us. Not to mention she strapped bombs on us, Kate."

"You sound just like my mother," I snap. "Did you forget she also let us live and let us go and returned us here? We don't know what she's up to."

He looks taken aback, surprised this is even an argument. "Are we really going to sit here and fight about Danielle Clark?"

"No, we're not." I catch his surprised look and sigh. He's right. I know he is. Danielle Clark is the enemy, and here I am defending her. I'm not totally sure why that is exactly. Or maybe I am sure and just don't want to admit it. "I'm tired," I repeat, "and I need some time to process everything."

"Yeah, okay." He watches me for a second before shaking his head and turning away.

"Ryan?" He stops and turns. I want to tell him I'm sorry for snapping, that I just have so much going on inside my head and that being back isn't how I pictured it being and that I'm so irritated with Simon and my mother, and, again, that I'm tired and confused…

"Thank you. For being there." It's all I can muster. It seems to be enough for now because he smiles ever so slightly before walking away.

I nod at the guard patrolling my neighborhood, and he stops to salute before pressing on. I push the door open, looking forward to collapsing on my bed and sleeping for as long as I possibly can before seeing the soldiers off in the morning.

Stepping inside, I unbutton my uniform jacket and kick the door closed as I pull my arms from the sleeves. I'm just about to toss it on the armchair in the living area when I see flames roaring in the fireplace. I didn't start a fire, and I sure as hell wouldn't have left it burning when I left the house a couple of hours ago.

There is someone across the room. A soldier wearing fatigues removes a book from the bookshelf. Lower-ranked soldiers are prohibited from entering an officer's dwelling without explicit consent. Either this soldier is stupid or isn't one of ours. My gut tells me it's the latter.

Slowly, I place my jacket on the chair and reach for my pistol. I grab it with both hands, holding it steady and taking small, careful steps as I approach.

"Don't fucking move," I say, and the intruder freezes in place. "Put your hands on your head and slowly turn around." Instead of doing as I ask, the soldier closes the book and carefully places it back on the shelf. "I said, put your hands on your head and turn around."

It's a woman, her hair pulled back in a low bun. She turns but doesn't put her hands on her head. I rest my finger on the trigger, ready to fire, but she removes her hat with a conceited and familiar smirk on her face.

My nerves would've handled an intruder better. "Dani?" My stomach drops. I lower my gun and look around to see if she's alone.

"Miss me, sweetheart?" she asks in an equally pompous tone.

I aim at her again once the initial shock settles. "What the hell are you doing here?"

"I missed your smile."

There's no time for her games. Especially not when she could've been seen sneaking in here. I make a show of turning off the safety and cocking the gun.

"Plan on turning me in?" she asks.

I stare at her for a long time. We aren't in her territory anymore. We're in mine, and I have the backing of an entire base. All it takes is one single command, and Dani will be done for. What in the world is she thinking? The stupidity and the arrogance of her coming here is astounding. It both pisses me off and terrifies me.

Her brow arches slightly in challenge. She knows I'm not going to turn her in.

"You are a world class idiot, Clark," I whisper as I turn the safety on and slip my pistol back in its holster. "And where the hell did you get that uniform?"

"I was going for an officer, but I figured these will do." She glances at her attire. "Do you really want to know?"

Rushing to pull the curtains closed, I peer out the window to make sure no one is lurking around outside, then quickly lock the front door, too.

"Expecting someone?" she asks, amused.

"Are you alone?" I glance around once more. "Did anyone else come with you? How did you get on base? How did you even find me here?"

"Which one would you like me to answer first?"

I narrow my eyes. "You choose."

"I came alone, you have a predictable and boring guard rotation, and part of your perimeter on the north side is vulnerable." She takes a step closer. "As for finding you…" She shrugs. "I asked. Said I had an urgent message for you from the general. Your patrol gave excellent directions to your quarters and even let me in so I could wait. It was boring, really. I didn't even have to knock them out. I just held up this pretend note with a pretty awesome counterfeit officer's seal." She reaches in her pocket and holds a folded piece of paper between her index and middle finger. The red wax seal looks exactly like my mother's. She's taunting me.

"Have you lost your fucking mind?" I ask. Looking at her in that uniform pisses me off just as much as it excites me. I push those thoughts from my mind and close the distance, keeping my voice low just in case. "Do you know what would have happened if anyone recognized you?"

"I'd probably be shot," she says casually.

"Worse." I shake my head, my anger only growing the more I think about it. "Why are you here?"

"How long have you been stationed in Omaha?"

It's a strange question to ask, especially since she's been keeping track of our movements. "A couple months." I watch her face as her jaw tightens.

"And you were on your way to Pierre to seize the town when you were caught in the storm." It's not a question, but her tone tells me she's unsure of something.

"I thought you knew that." I'm confused. "Isn't that why you brought me back up here? Backtracking my movements? Reuniting me with my mother?" Dani closes her eyes for a moment and takes a seat in one of the large armchairs before it hits me. "You didn't know."

She says nothing.

"The entire time we were together, the questions and conversations, you thought I was on my way to Omaha?" That doesn't make any sense. "I thought William told you everything."

"Apparently not everything." Her expression hardens. "He left out the part about you marching into towns to take over."

"First of all, I was on my way to Pierre with a trailer of supplies. They approached us. When I go into these places, I do not 'seize.' I bring aid." She looks at me, really looks at me, as if this is the first time she's hearing of this. "Didn't you know that? That's my specialty. It's what I do. I help people who want to transition to NAF command, and I coordinate and see the transfer happens peacefully."

"What about Hot Springs?" Her gaze is burning. "Did *that* transition happen peacefully?"

I throw my hands up. That is the second time she's accused me of something I know nothing about. "I've never even been to Hot Springs. I didn't even know it had been destroyed until you accused me of it the first time."

Dani stands and takes a forceful step into my space. "Tell me the truth, Kate."

"That *is* the truth." I hold my ground. "I was on my way to Pierre with supplies. I know nothing about Hot Springs, and I definitely was not a part of the town being burned. I help people, Dani. I don't tear them down."

She stares at me for a long time, her eyes never leaving mine. For a moment, she looks lost, as though she's not privy to some inside joke. But then her walls are back, and she takes a step away.

"Why are you here?" I am desperate for something more from her. A touch, a feeling, anything other than accusations and sarcasm.

"Are you leaving with the convoy tomorrow?" Her voice softens. She looks almost defeated.

"How did you know about that?" She says nothing. I sigh. "No." My confession seems to appease her. "The general wants me to stay here for a few days and regroup. She wants to pry information out of me about you and your town."

"What will you tell her?"

I shake my head. I haven't thought that far ahead. "I don't know." I look at the flames dancing in the fireplace. "She knows your town isn't on our maps. She's going to go looking for it, and between her determination and Simon telling her everything he knows, she'll find it."

She nods. "I know."

I rub my burning eyes and debate making an offer. It'll be a long shot, but maybe I can help a little. "The best I can do is put in a request to meet with your town council about acquiescing. If the general approves and the council goes for the terms, perhaps she'll be more lenient. If you could get in touch with—"

Anything else I wanted to say is swallowed as Dani surges forward and presses her lips to mine. I freeze, unsure of what is happening. Of all the times I thought she would kiss me, this is not how I thought she would actually do it. She pulls back almost immediately.

It's so brief, it's almost as if it didn't happen. I release a shaky breath and search her wide eyes. As my body registers what just happened, I start to feel more alive with each breath we exchange. I want more.

Her initial expression appears to be shock but quickly settles into confidence. My gaze drops to her lips, and she licks them lightly before resting one hand on my waist and the other behind my neck, pulling me against her. She leans in close, waiting, and this time it's me who tips forward, pressing my lips to hers.

I grab the front of her shirt as her lips part, and she kisses me slowly and deeply. Leaning forward to kiss her back, I sink into this stolen moment. When we finally part, it's slow, tender, and makes me sigh. She presses her forehead against mine, and when I open my eyes, she's watching me curiously. Her gray eyes sparkle in the dim light, and her gaze is wide and wondrous. For a brief moment, all thoughts of the war and the convoy and the retaliation are forgotten.

"Finally," I whisper, scared of breaking whatever is happening in this moment.

She laughs softly. "Yeah. Finally."

I close my eyes again and hold on to her for a little longer, gripping her tightly and keeping her against me. My breath falls into sync with hers, and my body relaxes into our shared space.

Chatter outside my quarters breaks the spell, and I gently push away, stepping out of her embrace as I open my eyes and shake my head. "You are so stupid for coming here."

"I had to make sure you weren't on that convoy."

What a strange thing to say. "Why?"

She pulls the hat back on. "Just wouldn't want you to get ambushed." She pushes past me to the front door. "I need to get going. I'm expected back."

"Dani." I grab her arm, stopping her. "Is the convoy going to be attacked?" I ask, desperate to know what's going on.

She stops at the entryway to the living area and motions to the maps on the coffee table. "You might want to think about finding your soldiers a new route south to avoid Sioux Falls."

"Sioux Falls?"

She takes my face in her hands and kisses me gently. "Thank you, Kate. For trying to help."

I open my mouth to ask her to stay for just a moment longer. I'm not ready to let her go, but she backs away and is out of my house before I can speak a single word. I stick my head out the door and look both ways down the street, but Dani has already disappeared into the darkness.

I'm not sure what to think. It has been an absolute whirlwind knowing Danielle Clark. Just as intoxicating as it is frustrating.

I head to the table and look at the map. Staring at Sioux Falls, I know the route. It was the same one I took months ago the first time I left Grand Forks for Omaha. Sioux Falls was our last supply run before we closed out the trip in Offutt Air Force Base right outside of Omaha. Could the Resistance have tracked our movements and planned for another attack once we attempted a follow-up convoy?

We scouted several roads from Grand Forks to Omaha and went through the best possible options. We've stopped at Sioux City a dozen times and have had no problems. The city has always been accommodating to us. They are one of ours. I saw to the transition myself. Could the Resistance have taken over and are waiting within the walls? There's no way. We have people stationed there. They would've known. I would've known.

Were they waiting for us to become complacent? Why now?

I circle the area around Sioux Falls. There's nothing substantial on the map, nothing of substance to house a large ambush. But still, Dani came all this way, snuck in, and risked being found to tell me to avoid the area.

There's nothing on the map.

A thought suddenly nags at me. What if Dani's town really isn't on the map, and Simon was right? What if Dani's town was purposely *left off* our maps? That can only mean one thing.

A spy.

How could I have not seen this before? Why didn't I think of this sooner? My stomach lurches. It's taken me so long to realize, but there is no way my mother hasn't already thought of it.

Grabbing the map, I rush out of my house, forgetting my jacket and barely remembering to close the door behind me.

I go straight to his residence, fairly confident he's still awake. My mind is racing far faster than my legs could ever carry me.

Spy. Maps. Sioux Falls. Dani. She kissed me.

My chest flutters, but there's no time to dwell on it. People are going to die. On both sides, and Dani knows that. She came to help me. To help her people. She's not a villain, not in the way I always imagined. I round a corner and sprint the last few steps to his door and pound on it with all my might.

"Open up, Archie," I bellow through the wood.

"I'm coming. Give me a little time to get there," he yells back.

I don't have a little time. I pound again.

"I'm coming, dammit. What's the—" He throws the door open and swallows whatever snarky comment was about to escape his lips. "Major Turner." His back straightens, and his hand flies off the wheel of his chair to his brow.

"No need to salute, Archie, you're a civilian geospatial engineer," I remind him.

"I still like to show respect." He wheels backward, and I barge in past him. I take a quick inventory of everything in his living area, not sure exactly what I'm looking for. His house has been accommodated to his needs, with all the counters, tables, and surfaces lowered so he can reach anything from his chair. There are a few maps strewn about but nothing noticeably damning.

When I don't state my purpose, Archie wheels past and motions for me to sit. "I heard you were back. When we heard about the disappearance, we all feared the worst."

I ignore his offer to sit and his kind words and cross my arms, facing him. "How long have we known each other, Archie?"

"What?" He frowns and tosses his shaggy hair to the side with a flick of his head.

"How long have we known each other?" I repeat.

He sighs and looks off, counting in his head. When he settles on an answer, his eyes meet mine again. "Almost sixteen years. What is this about? Is everything okay?"

"And how long have you been working on our maps?" I finally take that seat as he shifts uncomfortably.

To his credit, he hasn't broken eye contact. Most people would be cowering under the questioning of an officer. He clears his throat. "Close to fourteen years."

I nod and continue just as casually as when I asked the previous questions. "And how long have you been feeding the NAF bad intel?" I tilt my head and narrow my eyes.

"I don't know what you're talking about," he replies evenly and straightens his shoulders.

"Don't lie to me."

"Why would I lie, Major?" For the first time since I entered his home, Archie's eyes drop to the map in my hand. I make a show of holding it up and waving it slightly before unfolding and spreading it out on his coffee table. He leans forward. "If something isn't correct on your map, I will gladly look into it."

I point to the map. "This is where we were held by Danielle Clark." He studies where my finger points and then sits back and looks at me with a blank stare. I point with more force. "Right here. In this area where your map shows *nothing*."

"Look." He holds up a hand. "Like I told the general and Corporal Alexander, I can have my people scout the area where you believe you were held captive and update the maps accordingly, but I—"

"What did you just say?"

His head tilts in confusion. "The general and Corporal Alexander were already here with the same issue and I—"

I shoot to my feet, nearly knocking the table over. He straightens as if surprised by my sudden outburst. "What did you tell them?" I all but yell in his face.

"The same thing I told you." His voice remains steady as I start to pace. "That I would look into it. I dug up an old map to compare before you came to my door. There used to be a town in that area called White River. We had information that it was destroyed so we removed it from the map several years ago."

White River. It's the first time I've heard the town's name, and it stabs through my chest. I stop pacing and pinch the bridge of my nose. "Archie. I need you to be very honest with me right now. Are you working with the Resistance?"

"Of course not." The rise of voice finally indicates some emotion. "How can you accuse me of something so heinous?" His tone is laced with offense.

"Archie," I implore, "what happened after you gave Corporal Alexander the old map?" My voice cracks with nervousness. Simon is the very last person who needs directions to White River.

His mouth opens and closes before he finally deflates. "He seemed intent on taking his own scouting party down there to confirm it was the town you were kept in."

I drop back onto the couch. He's going to find them. He's going to kill them. "It's not burned down." There are people there. Good people. I feel sick. I look to Archie with unshed tears in my eyes and clench my jaw. "You know it's still there. You purposely removed it," I accuse him with venom in my voice.

"With all due respect, Major Turner, what you are accusing me of—"

"Archie," I interrupt him again, "Danielle and Lucas built families there. They have a life there, away from this war. Their friends are there. It's their *home*."

"Danielle and Lucas Clark?" His voice goes higher. He looks away for the first time. "Why would I—"

"You knew the Clarks were there. You removed the town years ago to try to keep them safe." I feel absolutely betrayed. Not that he was unfaithful to the NAF, though that in itself is punishable by death, but that he's turning so easily against Dani and the others. "Archie, they aren't safe. That town is not safe. Simon wants revenge almost as badly as my mother, and you just led them straight to their home."

"Why would I care—"

"Stop lying." I come forward fast and slam my hands on the table.

He visibly shrinks and looks to his hands. "I heard Dani and Lucas got out," he murmurs. Calling her Dani has revealed all his cards, and he knows it. For a brief moment, I'm tempted to ask him exactly how deep into the Resistance his ties go. Did he work for Jonathan Clark? He clears his throat again. "Kate, please don't—"

"Dammit, Archie, listen to me." I stand in a rush, the pleading in his voice not going unnoticed. "Are you willing to let innocent people die just to keep your cover?"

"Innocent people die every single day. This is war."

As much as I hate it, he's not wrong, but I'll be damned if I don't at least try.

"I need to warn her," I say, softly. Then louder, "I need to get a message to Dani." I slowly meet Archie's eyes. "You're going to help me."

"I don't know where she is."

"We have to try," I bellow. He's visibly nervous as I continue. "Treason is punishable by death, Archie. The NAF hates traitors. It'll be long and painful. You'll most likely be tortured. If I figured it out, it's only a matter of time before the others catch on as well. They already found out about the missing town. And they will have no problem extracting other information from you. This is, as you said, war."

It must do the trick because Archie wheels to a side table and back. He hands me a piece of paper and a pen. "I'll do my best," he offers, and I believe him. He will try to get this to her. "I can't radio because I don't know which frequency to use. Too many outgoing messages is dangerous. The best I can do is deliver a handwritten message to one of the outposts. They can take it from there, but it might take a day or two."

We don't have two days. Not if I can't get my mom to let me take control of the town over Simon. I scribble a warning about Simon headed for White River before quickly folding the paper and handing it back. Disdain fills my body so deeply that I can feel it in my bones. Archie is a spy. Not only has he been lying to the NAF, to *me*, but he just put a whole hell of a lot of innocent people from his own "side" in harm's way with his good intentions.

"Make sure she gets this. No room for error, Archie. This has to get to her as quickly as possible. There isn't a lot of time."

He nods.

"One more thing," I say. He sits up straight. "Did you know about the ambush in Sioux Falls?"

He looks away and says nothing.

I tighten my fists. "I'll check back with you soon, but if you willingly allow any more of my soldiers to go through an ambush, I will turn you in myself." I realize my threat sounds a tad hypocritical since I am now also trying to help Dani and her friends, but at least I'm trying to save everyone, not get them all killed.

He nods. "Understood, Major."

I move past him to head out the door.

"What are you going to do?" He follows me, clearly nervous.

I don't stop to appease his worry. "I have to reroute the convoy you knew was going to be ambushed and try to convince my mother not to burn White River to the ground."

## CHAPTER FIFTEEN: THE PROMISE

### *Dani*

Before going back to my room, I refuel and return William's motorcycle. It's raining now, a cold and steady downpour, soaking me to the bone. I pull my jacket tighter around me as I dash across the deserted street. The doors to the tavern are unlocked, and I slip inside, ignoring the protests of the man behind the counter about dripping on his floor.

I dart up the steps, bypass my room, and head straight for Lucas's. I knock lightly, not looking to wake up anyone else staying on our floor. When the door opens, I'm only mildly surprised to see Darby standing on the other side.

"You look like a drowned rat," she says dryly. I push past her and strip off my jacket, tossing it on the back of a chair beside the door. "Here," she says, tossing me a towel as Lucas steps out of the bathroom.

"Thanks. When did you get in?" I towel my hair and glance at some of Darby's equipment spread across the table. She appears to be working on our radios.

"About an hour ago." She eyes me warily. "Do you want me to get you a change of clothes?"

"I'll manage. The others?"

"On their way back to town. They dropped me off at the gate like you told them to. It's bigger here than I thought it would be."

"Anything else?" I ask hopefully. Lucas and Darby share a look. "Nothing?"

"Jack said to tell you he knows the plan and will try to contact you later." She gives me a sympathetic look. "He'll get them all out of White River if he can."

I nod. Jack will do his best for the people, I know he will, but some of them seemed pretty hell-bent on staying no matter what. There's nothing else to be done except hope Kate can work some magic on her end.

"Status report?" Lucas asks.

"Better than expected." I toss the towel aside and put my gun on the table. I think about Kate and the way her kiss felt. It took every ounce of willpower to pull away from her. "She isn't headed to Omaha. She's also going to try to convince the general to allow White River to capitulate instead of burning it to the ground."

Darby and Lucas share a confused look. "Capitulate?" she asks.

I blow hot air into my hands and rub them together, trying to warm up. "Yeah, see if they'll surrender to the NAF. That is apparently what she does. She specializes in flipping towns peacefully to NAF rule. William seems to have conveniently left that portion about the Turner family out of his updates."

Lucas seems as surprised as I was. "Bad intel results in the most gruesome of circumstances."

"Oh, I know that one," Darby says. "Issue nine," she says proudly.

"*Twenty*-nine," I correct. Darby's pride shifts to dejection. "Yeah, William and I need to have a little chat." Lucas looks confused, and I fall into one of the chairs by the table and grab the virtually empty bottle of whiskey. "Speaking of good ol' Uncle Will, the general knows he's close. And it's only a matter of time before they realize White River isn't on their maps, so Archie could be in a whole helluva lot of trouble." I knock back the remaining whiskey in one large swig.

Lucas places a hand on my shoulder. "It's an impossible situation. One that no man must face alone." He's trying to be comforting, but it only makes me feel worse.

"Who's Archie?" Darby asks.

"Our guy on the inside." I put my head in my hands and rub my temples. "I tipped her off about the convoy." And I kissed her, but that's not something I plan on sharing, even if it is the only thought occupying my mind.

Darby shifts awkwardly. "You tipped off your girlfriend—"

"She's not my girlfriend."

"And compromised your inside guy and gave up the Resistance's one and only play?" She looks from Lucas to me. "That's your master plan?"

I take several deep breaths and let out a groan. I know how bad it sounds. If it doesn't work, then I made a very stupid call. "If we're lucky, Kate will buy us a day or two and halt the convoy. With no ambush, William will have men to spare, and maybe we can get some of his Resistance fighters down to White River to help. It's the best and only chance we've got."

Darby crosses her arms. "You're putting an awful lot of faith in someone who was your enemy just last week."

"Yes, I am." I tip the bottle and try to will more of it to appear. I'm almost always annoyed by Darby, but I'm particularly annoyed that she's trying to make me second guess Kate. "Did William notice I was gone?"

Lucas shakes his head. "It's nothing Maelstrom wasn't used to."

I smirk. William is used to me disappearing after I've had a blow-up. He always did leave me alone to cool off. "Good. I say we leave for Rapid City in the morning. I want to be closer to White River if we have to move in."

"That's it?" Darby asks, confused.

"That's it," I tell her and stand.

She seems positively annoyed. "You're not worried your girlfriend will sell you out? Or will have this Archie guy killed?"

"Quit calling her my girlfriend." Darby gives me a look, as if I'm missing something. "And no, I don't. If there's anything I learned about Kate in the time she was in White River, it's that she's not her mother. As for Archie, he's definitely compromised if the general figures out the maps. And she *will* figure it out. She's not stupid. We can only hope Kate figures it out first. She's probably his only chance of survival at this point." My grip on the bottle tightens.

"You're putting way too much stock in a girl who got all of her soldiers killed. And for what? Because she's pretty?"

I take a threatening stop closer, anger boiling up at the jab, but Lucas pulls me back.

"Please don't fight, comrades," he pleads.

I stare at Darby who, to her credit, doesn't back down. She does, however, put her hands up in surrender at Lucas's request. "Hey, what do I know? I'm just the tech geek."

"I'm going to get some sleep. I'll see you in the morning." I grab my jacket before shooting Darby one last look, and I leave the two of them alone.

She's not wrong. I did just sabotage the Resistance's chance at taking out a supply convoy. Something that is detrimental to us in this war. But what other choice did I have? I got White River into this mess. I need to get them out of it even if it does mean threatening the Resistance's game plan. On top of it all, I know Kate is safe, and somehow, that's just as important to me as saving White River.

❖

The following morning brings more bad weather. The skies are overcast and gloomy, setting an ominous feeling of foreboding within me. Did Kate manage to reroute or stop the convoy? Should I warn William that we've been made?

I glance at the sky and feel the cold drops of rain on my face. There's a certain buzz around this shithole of a town, one that comes whenever there's more than a single day of rain. No one here was around for the first big floods, but the rain still causes unease among many.

I toss the pile of bags in my Jeep, pull my hat farther down, and curse the constant drizzle that slowly soaks me to the bone. It puts me in a bad mood.

"So where are you headed?" Teddy asks as he approaches with a thermos. He hands it to me, and I inhale weak coffee.

"West," I tell him, taking a sip and wincing. I put the lid back on and place the thermos on the hood of the Jeep.

He chuckles. "That's rather vague. Any reason you're not going south with William?" He sticks his thumbs in his belt and rocks back and forth on his heels.

"No." I look over his shoulder at William headed this way, and I'm already over this conversation.

He gives me a look that screams annoyance and curiosity. "You're rather tight-lipped today."

I don't know what Teddy is fishing for, but I am not in the mood. "Aren't you needed at the gate?"

William puts his hand on Teddy's shoulder as I stare at his now fully annoyed expression. "You mind if I have a private word with Dani?"

Teddy stares for another beat and then offers William a smile. "Sure." He nods in my direction. "Good to see you again, Dani."

"I bet," I mutter as he walks away.

William puts his hands on his hips. "Look, Dani, about last night…"

I square my shoulders, already defensive despite his defeated tone. "It's not that I don't want to help. You know I do."

"But you can't spare your people. I got it." I toss another duffel in the Jeep. "And just like Pierre, another town will fall to the NAF." This is how the military spreads, the fall of small towns here and there until there's nothing left. And it's clear that William is fine sacrificing them. It pisses me off that he can't see that this will be the Resistance's downfall.

"We're doing the best we can. We've had to make sacrifices along the way. We've had to make a lot of tough decisions." He looks regretful. "We've lost a lot of good towns to stay on the road to the bigger picture."

I take a step closer, my hands clenched into fists to keep from reaching out. "Not my town. Not White River."

My advancement doesn't even make him flinch. "You've been out of this for a long time, Dani, and that's fine. If you can find peace, well, actually, I think that's great, but things have changed. We have a goal, and it's in sight. We just have to stay the course."

"What good is having a goal if there's no one left to see you achieve it?" I toss the rest of my bags in my Jeep. I can't get out of here fast enough.

"Are you sure I can't convince you to come with us?" William asks.

I'd laugh if I didn't know how serious he was. "My place is in White River. I have a life there. One I intend to protect even if I'm the only one doing so."

"That's where you're headed?"

I shake my head. "Not yet. First, Rapid City."

He nods. "If there's anyone who can help you, it's them."

"That's everything," Darby announces as she and Lucas appear out of thin air. She glances at William and then me. She squeezes Lucas's arm and slips into the back seat. Whether it's to give us privacy or to get out of the drizzle, I'm not sure.

"You have the radio frequency?" I ask nodding to the long-range radio strapped against William's belt.

"Yes, I do," he confirms with a soft smile. "I'll let you know when we've successfully stopped the NAF from reaching Omaha and can get you those men for White River."

"I'll rest only when you're safe," Lucas says seriously.

William shakes his head. "You know, one of these days, I'm going to know which one of those comics you're referencing. I'm glad to see you still love them." He pulls Lucas in for a long hug and makes him promise to stay safe. When he releases him, he turns to me and extends his hand.

We stand there awkwardly for a minute, a million thoughts flying through my head. The war, the ambush plan, warning Kate and then kissing her, seeing William again after almost seven years and realizing just how out of the loop I am.

I'm so angry with him. Angry for not telling me about Pierre. Angry that he won't help me when I need him. Angry that my home may very well be under siege if Kate can't work her magic. I'm just angry.

Regardless, I take his forearm. "Don't die."

William clasps my shoulder with his other hand. "See you in White River."

I watch him head over to the cars along with his two new cronies and take a deep breath. Not much else I can do about the current state of events. Lucas waves, and Hugo waves back. I grab his shoulders and turn him toward the Jeep. He shoots me an annoyed look as I head to the driver's side, ready to get the hell out of here.

"We have plenty of fuel?" I ask as I bring the Jeep to life.

"Lucas added an extra canister earlier," Darby answers.

"Any word from Jack?"

"He said he's working on it and to leave him alone."

Of course he did.

I hear another door close and turn to see Lucas settle in beside Darby in the back. "Are you serious?" He ignores me as he rummages through his bag. "You're both going to sit back there like I'm a freaking chauffeur?"

Lucas finds what he's looking for and hands it over excitedly. "I am the leader of this operation, and you will do as I command," he says casually.

"Oh, I know this one," Darby yells excitedly as she takes the comics from Lucas. "Sixty-two."

I roll my eyes, face forward, and turn up the music.

The sun never comes out from behind the clouds on the eight-hour ride to Rapid City. We pass a few raiders along the way, but the rain must make them too miserable to attack. Lucas and Darby read for a bit and each take a nap, leaving me alone with my thoughts and music.

The idea of going back to Rapid City after all these years leaves me a little unsettled. For more than just the obvious reason of running into Jess. It was my home away from home growing up. Dad and William would take us sometimes, and we were allowed to run around and see what we could trade while they tended to official Resistance duties.

I had my first beer there. Lost my virginity there. Stole from a vendor there. I fell in love there. Spent six years of my life there. This was where I knew, deep down, that I wanted to be something greater than just Resistance, more than just an explosives specialist, more than just the war. So much happened there that it churns my stomach to think about. It took every ounce of willpower to leave and not look back. And now here I am, headed straight for the city that both saved and destroyed me.

Returning to make demands and beg for help doesn't sit right.

I know we're getting close by the sight of the tent city that has popped up outside the gates for travelers and traders who have no desire to enter the walls. People wander around the buildings that surround the gated city, waiting for those who leave or enter the walls, looking for anyone to do business with. Guards patrol all along the walls, walking back and forth and looking down with their rifles close to their chests.

I slow the Jeep, and Lucas and Darby wake from their nap. Unlike trying to get into Fargo, Rapid City opens the gates before we can even come to a complete stop. I have a strong suspicion William radioed ahead, but one look at the nodding guard who comes out to meet us and I know we will be receiving a much different welcome here.

"Afternoon," he says as he peers into the Jeep, the gate still opening behind him. I keep the fact that it's well into the evening to myself. "Danielle Clark," he says with a smile. "Lucas. Ma'am," he continues as he looks into the back. "Will you be staying awhile?"

"Unsure." I keep my answer as vague as possible. "I request a meeting with the mayor."

"Understood. I will put in your request as soon as possible. In the meantime, you'll want to secure some lodgings. There's one in the center of town down Main and off Sixth and a smaller, more private one down near Second."

"No, no. The one near Main is fine," I say much too quickly. "I know where it is."

He motions us through the gate. I grip the steering wheel tightly. The rest of the way is quiet and awkward.

Nothing has changed. There are still people milling about, even in the rain. The streets are lined with shops and houses. They've kept the buildings up rather well; everything looks sturdy and touched up. Children jump in puddles, and tradesmen are busy working.

There's a buzz that excites me, makes me eager to be in the place that holds so many firsts for me. It counters the heavy feeling of total and utter dread that rests low in my belly at being back. It isn't long before we reach the center of town, and I take a deep breath.

I pull up to the side of the street and turn off the Jeep. "Okay," I say, breaking the silence. "We're here."

Lucas pats my shoulder. He gets out and begins to take the bags from the back. I stand beside the Jeep and look at the large, mostly preserved, Alex Johnson. One side of the building is missing, but it still manages to stand in pretty great condition, considering all it has seen.

Darby and I help Lucas with the bags, and between the three of us, we manage to bring all of the duffels, mainly filled with Darby's electrical crap, to the entrance.

Stepping through the front doors hits me hard in the chest. I hoist the bags higher on my shoulders and take a deep breath. It smells exactly the same: firewood and leather. The large open lobby hasn't changed at all since the last time I was here. There are a few people milling about, most sitting in large plush chairs around the fireplace on the far wall. The same old grand piano sits in the corner, silent and probably collecting dust. I look at the balconies that overlook the lobby from the second floor, where a young couple leans against the railing, engrossed in conversation.

A large chandelier hangs directly in the center of the room, lit and burning with electricity. I always thought it was a waste, but they love to roll around in the lavish here, and they love bragging that it's the best lodging this far west. I look up at the intricately carved Native American heads complete with the headdresses staring at us from high on the walls. My mom once said they were meant to be a tribute to the Native Americans and people of the Black Hills. I always thought of them as my ancestors looking down on me in judgment.

The counter is occupied by two young women happily chatting and sharing a drink. "This place is huge," Darby whispers.

"Come on," I tell them as we press forward to the counter. "Three rooms, please." I look to Darby, who rummages through her bag for some items to trade.

"Do I know you?" One of the girls asks as she squints at me. She doesn't look familiar, all blond hair and bright eyes, a slim figure with a kind smile. "Yeah, yeah, I do. You're Danielle Clark," she says after snapping her fingers.

Lucas shrugs when I look at him. The girl appears young, maybe mid-twenties, which would put her in her late teens by the time I left this place. I try desperately to place her.

"I remember seeing you around. You, too," she says, pointing to Lucas. "It's been a while, yeah? A few years. We all kinda thought you were dead."

"Nope. Not dead." I'm getting irritated that everyone seems to think I died so easily.

"This city loves the shit out of you," she continues and reaches behind the counter for three different keys. I sigh in relief, glad there was no other connection between us. "Top floor, you each get suites. No need to trade. You guys are legends."

The comment makes me uncomfortable, and I know we'll pay for the rooms somehow, but right now, I'm wet, tired, and cold. I just want to get into some dry clothes, drink some whiskey, and avoid every single person in this town for as long as I can. Especially one in particular.

"Thanks," I tell her as she shrugs, as though it's not a big deal in the slightest. "Do you think you could have something to eat brought up? And whatever drink you have brewed?"

"Food and beer," she notes. "You got it."

We don't wait for our bags to be taken, and we don't wait for any other questions. It won't take long before the entire city knows we're back, and I'd like to be ready when the mayor can see me.

I stay by the radio in case William checks in. Either he's in the middle of one hell of a fight or he's still waiting on the convoy that Kate managed to stop. I refuse to think of a third, deadly option.

While trying to distract myself, I've showered, napped, and eaten. I still haven't heard from Jack or about my meeting with the mayor and I contemplate going around protocol and knocking on doors, but I don't want to make a bad situation worse.

I wish I'd remembered to take the journals back so I could update the section on Kate. If William writes it, I can only imagine how inhuman he'll make her seem. Just another officer in the NAF, with none of the spirit she possesses. I guess it's best to keep those thoughts to myself.

Unable to sit still any longer, I glace out the window for the millionth time at the setting sun. Waiting on updates in this room is suffocating me, so I opt for some fresh air.

Grabbing the radio, I take to the roof. The rain has finally stopped, the night is chilly and the skies clear, revealing a blanket of stars. I sit in the corner, away from the handful of patrons enjoying the cool evening and ask for a whiskey neat from the barkeep with his pushcart.

The light of the moon and the lanterns outside of buildings brighten the streets enough that even from this height, I can see people bustling about. It's past the normal dinner hour, but that doesn't stop people from walking, no doubt glad that two days' worth of rain is over. Shivering as a cold breeze comes through, I close my eyes, enjoying the small moment of peace.

Before I can even take my first sip, Lucas plops down in the chair beside me. "Any news, soldier?"

"Not a damn thing." I roll my shoulders. "If the mayor doesn't get back to me soon, I might have to do something desperate."

"Desperation is a useful weapon in the right situation." Lucas reaches behind him and shakes out his hair. It catches the light from the lantern as he pushes it off his shoulders. "A damn battalion is coming through, and I don't know how to stop them?"

He phrases it as a question, and I shake my head. "No news of the convoy, either." It has me a little worried. There's been nothing regarding the convoy. I still have no idea if Kate managed to reroute or stop it from deploying. Either way, we should've heard something. "I hope they left White River," I say, barely above a whisper. "I told them I would try, and I have, but I don't have any answers. William turned me down in Fargo, I've heard nothing about the convoy leaving Grand Forks, and the mayor here hasn't gotten back to me. If I don't hear something tonight, I'm heading back to White River first thing in the morning."

I'm scared, and I'm certain Lucas can tell. He pats my shoulder reassuringly. "The bravest of them all keep trying even if all hope is lost."

It does little to actually reassure me since he's chosen a line about losing all hope, but I nod and change the topic anyway. "Where's Darby?"

"All this technology right at our fingertips," he says after a moment to think.

"So she's tinkering." Lucas laughs and nods. "She's not killing anything or destroying anyone's property, is she?" He laughs again and shakes his head. We both look at the city below, and I sigh. "It's strange. Being back."

"Those were the good old days."

I hum in acknowledgment, but I'm not so sure I agree they were good. We were different people then. Part of the war. Things were messy, dangerous, complicated. I was trying not to be reckless but wasn't sure how to stop. I was unable to let go of my past or my rage no matter how hard I tried. It was like a drug.

I wanted to be better. I needed to be better. And right when I thought I was on that path, I'd slip and fall right back into the same cycle. I was arrogant, stupid, and I hurt people.

"You see her? You see that lady over there?" Lucas asks, pulling me from my thoughts, probably guessing exactly what I was thinking about.

Knowing who he's referring to, I sigh. "No. I know I need to, but I'm not ready. I'm not sure I'll ever be ready. Besides, that's not why I'm here. This isn't really a social call."

He straightens and looks away. "Strap in, soldier, it's showtime."

I look at him, confused, and then follow his line of sight. My stomach plummets. There, standing in front of the entrance to the roof access, is a teenage girl. A very grown-up-looking teenage girl. Even though it's been seven years, and the childlike features have vanished, I still see the nine-year-old I remember.

Jess.

The one person I hoped to avoid is heading in my direction.

Lucas stands with a large grin, and all I can do is stare. She's grown into a beautiful young woman. Her wavy red hair falls over one shoulder, and she stands tall as she takes confident strides, barely relying on the walking stick she clutches in one hand. She's wearing a flowing, light blue dress under a cardigan, the color reminding me of her blue eyes. I want to look away, knowing I'm unworthy to gaze upon her, but the scars around her eyes draw me in, and in that moment, it takes everything in me to keep the contents of my stomach from coming back up. Not because her scars are grotesque, but because I'm the reason they're there in the first place.

"If you're here to celebrate my sixteenth birthday, you're both late by a few days," she says seriously but with the slight hint of a smile tugging at the corner of her lips.

"It was so beautiful that Maelstrom was unable to look away." Lucas beams as he swoops in to give Jess a large hug.

She laughs and wraps her arms around him, leaning on him for balance. "Lucas Clark," she says with a smile as he steps out of her embrace. "You are still the most charming man I know. Let me get a good look at you."

He stands still as she loops her stick over her wrist with the band attached at the end and runs her hands over his shoulders and up his neck. She traces his jaw and nose, feeling along his eyes, forehead, and ears and finally running her fingers through his long hair.

It's intimate, the way she examines his face, remembering, learning. She cups his cheeks, and tears well in her eyes. "You are even more handsome than I remember. Your hair is beautiful. You must let me braid it while you're here."

I take another sip of whiskey, not sure what else to do while I stare at their interaction. I think back to how Lucas would allow Jess to braid his hair from time to time. She was the only other person besides our mother he allowed to do so. As far as I know, not even Darby is allowed that privilege.

Lucas sighs happily. "Maelstrom finally felt happiness."

Jess beams, her hands still on his face. "Issue eighty-seven. My absolute favorite. How I've missed reading about Major Maelstrom with you."

I close my eyes and try to settle the emotions running through me. They're different from the feelings that used to course through my veins at the mere sight of Jess. It used to be elation and wonderment. A protectiveness I never felt before. She was a little sister to me, someone who reminded me that life was worth living. But now I'm being crushed with overwhelming guilt. The harsh reality that I will never be able to fix this, to fix us, makes my throat tighten to the point of pain.

"Danielle Clark," Jess says, releasing Lucas and turning in my direction. "I know you're here. I can smell the whiskey."

There are so many quips I could make, so many things I could say, but words fail me as I stand slowly and face her. Face the child, *woman*, I have been hiding from for so long. "I'm here," I finally manage to say.

Jess takes three steps closer until her walking stick hits my boot, and she closes the distance, propping it against the nearby table after a brief moment of fumbling. I allow her into my space and hold my breath. She's almost as tall as I am. Her eyes are focused somewhere near my neck, but mine are zeroed in on hers. Slowly, she does the same with me as with Lucas. She starts with my shoulders and trails her hands softly up the sides of my neck, making me shiver. She traces the curves of my ears and my jaw. She runs her fingers across my mouth and nose. Over my eyebrows and eyes. My hair is pulled back, and she takes her time, untying it and raking her fingers through, smoothing out the tangles.

She leans in close. "You should probably breathe," she teases gently.

I exhale, and it comes out in a wet burst, a choked sob, as tears fall from my eyes. Carefully, Jess wipes them away and offers a kind smile. The gesture pierces me. It's impossible to hold in the regret I feel any longer. "I'm sorry."

Jess shakes her head and wipes away another fresh batch of tears. "For what?"

"Everything!" I shake my head and try to look away, but Jess holds my face firmly in her hands. "For leaving you, for not letting you know I was okay, for…" I stare at her scarred and damaged eyes. "For hurting you. You were just a child. What kind of person does that to a child?"

"Oh, Dani," she says, tears falling from her eyes now. "I knew you were okay. I knew where you were." She must feel the change on my face as she chuckles lightly. "Do you really think my grandfather wouldn't tell me about you? I'm his only grandchild. Why do you think he stopped in so often? It's not like we needed batteries to exchange." She grins as my mouth opens in shock. "Don't be mad at George. He was only doing what I asked. Entertaining a child's curiosity."

"Why didn't you…if you knew where I was…I don't…" My words aren't forming as I stand utterly speechless and confused.

"You needed privacy, Dani. Time to heal. Believe me, the older I get, the more I understand that. You needed to get yourself together. You left for a reason. I respected what you needed."

"But…" I wrap my fingers around her hands and gently move them from my face. She squeezes my hands gently. My mouth opens and closes twice, but words escape me. She knew the whole time? And she never came after me. I'm not sure what I expected her to do or say if she had. I was careless with a bomb, and the shrapnel took her eyes. I tense at the memory. I hurt the little girl who wormed her way into my heart. I hurt the most innocent person I knew and who I swore to protect after the NAF took her mother. I was careless, and she was nothing but understanding. Even now. "Jess, I—"

"Shh." She covers my mouth playfully. Just like she used to do as a child when I would sing songs for her. "Now, come on and let's sit. We have a lot of catching up to do."

Lucas takes Jess's arm and helps her sit in his chair. I slowly reclaim my own, my eyes never leaving hers, and my mind still reeling. She knew where I was and kept tabs on me. She's more like me than I ever realized.

Jess settles in. "I suppose you're angry that I took the initiation."

I grind my teeth to keep from uttering the words I desperately want to say. To pledge your loyalty to the Resistance when you're sixteen is absolutely ludicrous. I thought I had to wait forever to take mine, but now that I'm an adult, having been initiated for more than half my life, I think the guidelines are stupid and reckless. Sixteen is too young. *Jess* is too young.

"I don't like the idea of you being involved," I say. "But I suppose I don't have much ground to stand on."

Jess smiles. "I value your opinions. Even when I don't agree."

"Aren't you cold?" I realize that Lucas and I are both dressed in layers for the cool weather, and her legs are bare below the knees.

She laughs. "Not really. I like the chilly weather. You know that."

I do know that. I used to know everything there was to know about her, and now I'm an outsider in her life by my own doing.

Lucas leans nearer to her. "Is there really another in your life?"

Jess laughs happily and stokes his hair. "Yes, I have a boyfriend."

I clear my throat, and even though I'm still surprised, I respond in a soft, happy tone. "Yeah, we heard. Who is he? Does he treat you well?"

She claps her hands happily and nods. "Wyatt Richardson," she proclaims proudly. "He's so sweet. Patient. Kind."

My nose wrinkles in disgust. "Wyatt Richardson? That little brat who used to pull your hair?"

"He's not a brat anymore," Jess continues with a laugh. "He's grown to be quite a gentleman. He's helping me run the lodgings now that I've taken over." There's a pause before her voice softens. "We aren't kids anymore."

Unsure of what to say, I nod as I continue to take her in. She's gone from a cute kid with freckles to a beautiful woman with fair skin and a full figure.

"Maelstrom inspected his new body—"

I kick Lucas's legs to keep him from continuing any further.

I pinch the bridge of my nose, embarrassed and mortified that he would mention anything about her body. "Seriously, Lucas." Jess chuckles, and I want to sink into the ground and hide. "Do you want something to eat?" I say, desperate to change the subject. I sit up and make a move to stand. "Or drink? I can go get—"

Jess places a hand on my forearm, stilling me, "I'm fine, Dani."

I sit back at her request, but I can't stop my legs from jumping or my fingers from fidgeting. Being in Jess's presence after so long has me on edge. I want to cry. I want to learn about everything I've missed. I want to apologize over and over. I want to…I don't know. Hug her, I suppose.

After a moment of awkward silence, she speaks first again. "I heard William is in Sioux Falls. Any word?"

I shake my head and then remember, like a punch to the gut, that she can't see me. "Not yet." My voice scratches in my throat.

She sighs and relaxes. She tilts her face to the sky. "He'll check in soon."

"Jess," I start, trying to voice all my emotions. "I know you want to help, but joining the Resistance, even if it's just the communications part, delivering messages, manning the radios, it's dangerous, and you could get hurt. Look what my involvement did to you."

"Dani, listen to me." I sit up a bit at her firm tone. She reaches for my hand again. "What happened with me and you, with the accident and losing my sight, I don't blame you. I've never blamed you. I snuck out. I followed you when you told me not to. If I had listened, I never would've been there. You need to stop feeling guilty and blaming yourself." She strokes the top of my hand. Leave it to Jess to go through hell as a child and come out on the other side so good, so kind, and stronger than before.

"It's not just that." I flip my hand and lace our fingers. "It's everything. I loved you so much. You were like my little sister, and I wanted to be better for you. You were one of the few people who loved me despite everything, and then I caused this." I lightly trace one of the scars. "Nine years old! And I couldn't even face you. I ran from you after everything, and I…Jess, I don't deserve to be around you."

She abruptly wraps her fingers tightly around both my wrists and forces my hands into my lap. "You are so fucking selfish, Danielle Clark."

Lucas sits straighter. "Maelstrom takes his leave," he sputters quickly as he moves to his feet.

"No, you stay right where you are, Lucas," she commands. Lucas, almost comically, drops to his butt. "Dani, not everything is about you." She pokes my chest, and I resist the urge to rub at the spot. "You don't get to decide what's best for others without consulting them. Losing my eyesight isn't what hurt me." Her voice cracks. She swallows hard and pokes me again. "You running away because you *thought* that's what I *wanted*…hurt me."

"I didn't know how to fix it," I whisper. "I was so scared of hurting you again. That I was a bad influence. I didn't want you to turn into me. I thought by leaving…" I shake my head at my own excuses. I'm talking in circles at this point. "It was stupid. And I'm sorry. I should have said it years ago."

Her face softens, and she smiles. I look to Lucas. He's mirroring her delicate smile. "Did you find it?" she asks simply. "The peace you were looking for?"

"Yeah." I breathe out as I think of White River. Rhi, Jack, Mike, Darby, Elise. They are our family now. I look to Lucas as his smile turns to me. "I mean, I thought I did…until recently."

Jess hums knowingly. "William sucked you back in."

I scoff and relax. "More like I screwed up. Again." I reach for my glass and down the remainder. "Been doing a lot of that lately." My decisions regarding Kate could've gotten my family killed. It's still a possibility. I'm sure my friends think it would've been best to let the raiders take care of Kate and her soldiers instead of intervening.

The mere idea of anything happening to Kate hurts worse than taking a knife. I would know, too, since I've been stabbed several times. Selfishly, I wanted her alive for answers about her mother. And now…now it's different.

"You have a good heart, Dani." Jess reaches and finds the side of Lucas's head and mindlessly runs her fingers through his long locks. He melts under her touch and rests his head on her shoulder. His eyes drift shut. As if she knows she's putting him to sleep, she whispers, "You need to stop blaming yourself for every bad thing that happens." After I don't respond, she changes the subject. "Grandfather said you seemed happy there."

"Yeah. I was." I lift my glass to take another drink and am greeted with nothingness. I groan. "I need another."

She ignores my last statement. "Fix it. With your town. Your new family. Whatever happened, fix it. You want to make amends for this?" She points to her eyes. "Then fix it. Be better."

"I'm not sure that's possible anymore," I reply as I pick at an invisible spot on my empty glass. "But I'm trying."

She nods.

"Are *you* happy?" I ask.

"I am," she singsongs.

"Good." I nod. "That's all I wanted." And it truly is. After everything. All I want is to know that Jess, the bouncing energetic child who opened my heart, is happy.

She lifts her free hand and strokes the side of my face once more. "You will always have a piece of my heart, Dani. You're the sister, and Lucas is the brother, that I never had."

"No matter how big you get or how much you grow, you'll always be that four-year-old who came running up to me with a skinned knee wanting me to fix it," I whisper as I lean forward and gently place my lips on the middle of her forehead. The gesture brings back so many memories. Holding her tightly when the boys wouldn't let her play, teaching her how to throw a punch, tucking her in at night when George was away. It all comes flooding back. My heart aches.

"Now. That wasn't so hard, was it? Facing big ol' scary me?" she teases.

I laugh and tick my fingers against the empty glass. "I guess not."

"Then we are allies once more," Lucas happily mumbles against Jess's shoulder as he looks up to smile at me.

"Okay, you two," she says. "No more snuggling. You are both way too old, and I am taken."

I groan at the idea of Jess thinking we're old and of little Wyatt Richardson courting my adopted little sister.

The radio placed near my empty glass crackles to life, interrupting the moment.

"Skull Splicer to Maelstrom, can you hear me? Come in, Maelstrom."

I give Lucas a look. "Seriously? You *know* I hate the name Skull Splicer." Lucas merely shrugs as the radio roars again.

"Repeat, this is Skull Splicer, do you read me, Maelstrom?"

I grab the radio. "Maelstrom here, we read you...Skull Splicer." It's hard to get the words out, not to mention how absolutely silly I feel saying them. I'm never letting Lucas designate call signs again.

"The convoy never arrived at rendezvous point one. New intel reports convoy never deployed. Repeat, the convoy never deployed."

The irritation in William's voice is clear. I feel a buzz of excitement. "Can you confirm, Skull Splicer?"

"Affirmative. Confirmation received."

"Holy shit, she did it," I whisper to Lucas. "Maelstrom to Skull Splicer, message received," I say into the radio. My heart races.

"Stay put, a more secure message coming through official channels. Skull Splicer out."

I place the radio on the table and stare at Lucas in disbelief. I can't believe she did it. My first reaction is relief. Now I have people to help with White River. But on the flip side, I've set back a large Resistance plan by disrupting their ambush. I might've just done more damage than good in the long run.

But Kate.

Beautiful, smart, Kate. She did it. I trusted my gut and knew I could count on her.

"Okay, what's going on?" Jess says, breaking the silence. "Why didn't the convoy deploy? And what is your involvement?"

It never ceases to amaze me how quickly she catches on. She's always been freaky observant. Before I can respond, the door flies open, and a young boy frantically looks around the roof. He spots me and rushes over, sweaty and out of breath.

"Excuse me for interrupting." He thrusts a sealed letter into my hands. "This is urgent and for your eyes only."

I break the seal and open the message. A seal I've never seen before. My heart pounds in my chest.

*Attempt at surrender failed. S is on the move, arriving in WR ASAP. K*

I give the note to Lucas and stand so fast that my chair falls backward. "Stay close to that radio in case William gets back in touch. I need to get the other one from Darby and try to get a hold of Jack. Burn that note." Once he's read it, Lucas holds it over the flame of the lantern.

"What's going on?" Jess asks worriedly. "What happened?"

"The NAF is on their way to White River," I explain as I lean in and kiss on her cheek. "I have to go." I look to Lucas, who stands with the radio in his hand. I know he wants to come with me. "Wait until you hear from me and stay here."

Lucas nods. "I am able to follow orders."

I grip his shoulder for a moment and then rush out, needing my weapons and the radio from Darby. I have no idea when Kate sent that note or how she even found me, but I have to make it back to White River before Simon. And there's absolutely no time to wait for reinforcements.

❖

I press the gas pedal the entire way. It takes me two hours. I've tried countless times to get ahold of Jack, but the only response is static. By the time I get close enough to cut my lights and drive by the light of the moon, I can see it. Smoke. Even in darkness it floats into the sky and disappears among the stars.

I park on the cliff that overlooks the back of the town and see the fire blazing orange and yellow. There are several military vehicles surrounding the town, some with soldiers watching, others dismantling the fence with sledgehammers. Bile rises in the back of my throat as I try to will it not to be true.

I get out and look down, my hands clenched into fists as I watch White River burn. I'm too late. I'm too late, and they didn't even have time to arm their defenses.

The smell of fire burns my nostrils and awakens a rage in me that I haven't felt in years. The tanks will roll in next, making sure nothing is left standing. All alone, there's nothing I can do.

A feral scream gets caught in my throat at the thought of my friends, my family, my neighbors caught in the firestorm Simon and

NAF have brought upon them. That *I* have brought upon them. The radio crackles from the passenger seat of the Jeep.

"Dani, it's Jack. Come in, Dani. Are you there?"

I stare at Rhiannon's tavern as the roof crumbles into blackened ash. My chest heaves, and I clench my fists tighter as I try to keep from shaking. My jaw tightens to the point that I may very well crack my teeth.

I do the only thing I can. I watch.

Something shifts inside me. Something dark. Something angry.

"Dani, it's Jack. Are you there?"

My head reels, and my heart pounds heavily. They thought I was dead. They thought I wasn't a factor. Out of this war.

But I'm not.

If war is what they want from Danielle Clark, then that's exactly what they'll get. I hurl the same promise into the universe that I made when my father died.

"I'll kill every last one of them."

# About the Authors

ALLISA BAHNEY grew up in a small town buried in the cornfields of Iowa. She works in education and has a Master of Science degree in education with minors in creative writing and film studies. Allisa spends her free time coaching eighth grade volleyball, binge-watching all the TV shows, writing, playing with her son, and entertaining her wife. She loves to travel and misses her dog literally every minute she's not with her.

KRISTIN KEPPLER was born and raised in the DC metro area. A lifelong sci-fi and film nerd with a degree in production technology, she owns a small media production company that endeavors to help other small businesses succeed. Kristin spends the majority of her free time helping her husband wrangle their two young sons and their dogs. Any additional free time is devoted to writing, gaming, and cheering on the Virginia Tech Hokies.

# Books Available From Bold Strokes Books

**A Turn of Fate** by Ronica Black. Will Nev and Kinsley finally face their painful past and relent to their powerful, forbidden attraction? Or will facing their past be too much to fight through? (978-1-63555-930-9)

**Desires After Dark** by MJ Williamz. When her human lover falls deathly ill, Alex, a vampire, must decide which is worse, letting her go or condemning her to everlasting life. (978-1-63555-940-8)

**Her Consigliere** by Carsen Taite. FBI agent Royal Scott swore an oath to uphold the law, and criminal defense attorney Siobhan Collins pledged her loyalty to the only family she's ever known, but will their love be stronger than the bonds they've vowed to others, or will their competing allegiances tear them apart? (978-1-63555-924-8)

**In Our Words: Queer Stories from Black, Indigenous, and People of Color Writers**. Stories Selected by Anne Shade and Edited by Victoria Villaseñor. Comprising both the renowned and emerging voices of Black, Indigenous, and People of Color authors, this thoughtfully curated collection of short stories explores the intersection of racial and queer identity. (978-1-63555-936-1)

**Measure of Devotion** by CF Frizzell. Disguised as her late twin brother, Catherine Samson enters the Civil War to defend the Constitution as a Union soldier, never expecting her life to be altered by a Gettysburg farmer's daughter. (978-1-63555-951-4)

**Not Guilty** by Brit Ryder. Claire Weaver and Emery Pearson's day jobs clash, even as their desire for each other burns, and a discreet sex-only arrangement is the only option. (978-1-63555-896-8)

**Opposites Attract: Butch/Femme Romances** by Meghan O'Brien, Aurora Rey & Angie Williams. Sometimes opposites really do attract. Fall in love with these butch/femme romance novellas. (978-1-63555-784-8)

**Swift Vengeance** by Jean Copeland, Jackie D & Erin Zak. A journalist becomes the subject of her own investigation when sudden strange, violent visions summon her to a summer retreat and into the arms of a killer's possible next victim. (978-1-63555-880-7)

**Under Her Influence** by Amanda Radley. On their path to #truelove, will Beth and Jemma discover that reality is even better than illusion? (978-1-63555-963-7)

**Wasteland** by Kristin Keppler & Allisa Bahney. Danielle Clark is fighting against the National Armed Forces and finds peace as a scavenger, until the NAF general's daughter, Katelyn Turner, shows up on her doorstep and brings the fight right back to her. (978-1-63555-935-4)

**When In Doubt** by VK Powell. Police officer Jeri Wylder thinks she committed a crime in the line of duty but can't remember, until details emerge pointing to a cover-up by those close to her. (978-1-63555-955-2)

**A Woman to Treasure** by Ali Vali. An ancient scroll isn't the only treasure Levi Montbard finds as she starts her hunt for the truth—all she has to do is prove to Yasmine Hassani that there's more to her than an adventurous soul. (978-1-63555-890-6)

**Before. After. Always.** by Morgan Lee Miller. Still reeling from her tragic past, Eliza Walsh has sworn off taking risks, until Blake Navarro turns her world right-side up, making her question if falling in love again is worth it. (978-1-63555-845-6)

**Bet the Farm** by Fiona Riley. Lauren Calloway's luxury real estate sale of the century comes to a screeching halt when dairy farm heiress, and one-night stand, Thea Boudreaux calls her bluff. (978-1-63555-731-2)

**Cowgirl** by Nance Sparks. The last thing Aren expects is to fall for Carol. Sharing her home is one thing, but sharing her heart means sharing the demons in her past and risking everything to keep Carol safe. (978-1-63555-877-7)

**Give In to Me** by Elle Spencer. Gabriela Talbot never expected to sleep with her favorite author—certainly not after the scathing review she'd given Whitney Ainsworth's latest book. (978-1-63555-910-1)

**Hidden Dreams** by Shelley Thrasher. A lethal virus and its resulting vision send Texan Barbara Allan and her lovely guide, Dara, on a journey up Cambodia's Mekong River in search of Barbara's mother's mystifying past. (978-1-63555-856-2)

**In the Spotlight** by Lesley Davis. For actresses Cole Calder and Eris Whyte, their chance at love runs out fast when a fan's adoration turns to obsession. (978-1-63555-926-2)

**Origins** by Jen Jensen. Jamis Bachman is pulled into a dangerous mystery that becomes personal when she learns the truth of her origins as a ghost hunter. (978-1-63555-837-1)

**Unrivaled** by Radclyffe. Zoey Cohen will never accept second place in matters of the heart, even when her rival is a career, and Declan Black has nothing left to give of herself or her heart. (978-1-63679-013-8)

**A Fae Tale** by Genevieve McCluer. Dovana comes to terms with her changing feelings for her lifelong best friend and fae, Roze. (978-1-63555-918-7)

**Accidental Desperados** by Lee Lynch. Life is clobbering Berry, Jaudon, and their long romance. The arrival of directionless baby dyke MJ doesn't help. Can they find their passion again—and keep it? (978-1-63555-482-3)

**Always Believe** by Aimée. Greyson Walsden is pursuing ordination as an Anglican priest. Angela Arlingham doesn't believe in God. Do they follow their vocation or their hearts? (978-1-63555-912-5)

**Courage** by Jesse J. Thoma. No matter how often Natasha Parsons and Tommy Finch clash on the job, an undeniable attraction simmers just beneath the surface. Can they find the courage to change so love has room to grow? (978-1-63555-802-9)

**I Am Chris** by R Kent. There's one saving grace to losing everything and moving away. Nobody knows her as Chrissy Taylor. Now Chris can live who he truly is. (978-1-63555-904-0)

**The Princess and the Odium** by Sam Ledel. Jastyn and Princess Aurelia return to Venostes and join their families in a battle against the dark force to take back their homeland for a chance at a better tomorrow. (978-1-63555-894-4)

**The Queen Has a Cold** by Jane Kolven. What happens when the heir to the throne isn't a prince or a princess? (978-1-63555-878-4)